Also available in Large Print by
Rosemary Rogers:

Lost Love, Last Love

Love Play

ROSEMARY ROGERS

Love Play

G.K.HALL &CO.
Boston, Massachusetts
1984

Besame mucho by Consuelo Velazquez. Copyright
1941, 1943 by Promotora Hispano Americana de
Musica. Copyright renewed by Peer International
Corporation. Used by permission.

Published in Large Print by arrangement with Avon
Books.

British Commonwealth rights courtesy of Sphere
Books Ltd.

Set in 16 pt Times Roman.

Library of Congress Cataloging in Publication Data

Rogers, Rosemary.
  Love play.

  Published in large print.
  1. Large type books. I. Title.
[PS3568.O4553L6 1984]   813'.54   84–6755
ISBN 0–8161–3674–2
ISBN 0–8161–3716–1 (pbk.)

DEDICATION

With love and thanks to all those people
without whose support and understanding I
might never have finished it — and particularly to my son Adam who guarded my long
nights, my friend Martha who made sure I got
enough sleep, and my own particular "Duca"
who taught me the Italian love words.

Chapter 1

The singer's voice, husky and accented, breathed through the headphones that Sara had stubbornly worn from the beginning of the flight. *Bésame, bésame mucho* . . .

With her eyes closed, she grimaced slightly. Love songs! All she needed. And especially in Spanish, reminding her too vividly of Eduardo, his mournful dark eyes fixed on her, pleading with her. "But, *tesoro*, I want to *marry* you! How can your father object to *that?* Also, you know that I have enough money, so that is no object, *sí?* We can live anywhere you want to live. . . ."

No, no Eduardo! *Poor* Eduardo! She should have been honest with him, instead of hiding behind excuses. Her father. Her education. But how to tell a man that she simply couldn't stand to have him touch her because his hands always felt so clammy?

The captain's voice cut through the music, reminding everyone that they would be landing at Kennedy Airport in fifteen minutes. And anyone who wished to listen to the pilots' communication with the traffic controllers could switch to channel —

Sara got rid of the headphones and smoothed her hair by running her fingers through it. Scanning her face in the small mirror she had produced from her purse, she grimaced again. Bad habit she'd have to stop.

"Darling child, you simply have *got* to stop making *faces!* You don't want to have lines and wrinkles later on, do you? Look at me . . . ."

Well, Mama was easy to look at anyhow! Especially if one judged by the millions of filmgoers all over the world who adored Mona Charles.

Everyone said that Sara took after her mother. But people never recognized her — or thought they did — in spite of the fact that she and Mona had the same coloring.

The tiny mirror gave back an uncompromising image of a face that was too pale except for spots of color on the cheekbones. Dark mahogany-colored hair swinging straight and smooth to her shoulders, lashes just as dark and just as long as Mona's, over the same emerald-green eyes. But nobody asked her if she was Mona Charles — and maybe it had to do with the slim, almost girlish figure and her height. Mama-Mona had *breasts,* and she wasn't over five three. She was still gorgeous- five children and four husbands later.

"And *I*," Sara told herself severely, snapping the compact shut, "will probably have all the lines and wrinkles Mona warned me about before I'm thirty."

Thanks to Daddy, she was the daughter that hardly anyone knew about. Mona had been married for a short time to Sir Eric Colville — one of her "settling down" periods when she had decided, publicly, to give everything up for love and an English title. When she'd left Sir Eric for a Shakespearean actor, their daughter Sara had been left behind too, along with Nanny Staggs and an Afghan called Goldie.

But that hadn't meant that Mona didn't *love* her daughter Sara. There were always The Visits — perfumed embraces and afternoons at the zoo. Expensive toys and introductions to new people. It was almost like being part of strangely parallel worlds until Daddy had insisted on the private schools and *no* publicity. But that was after Sara had been introduced to her half sister Delight, who was, as Mona always said on a sigh, a love child.

Delight was only eighteen months younger than Sara, and yet, after the few summers they had spent together, Sara always felt younger. Delight had been everywhere and knew everyone. And Delight had *done* practically everything. She was physical, where

Sara was cerebral. Above all, Delight was excitement, and a whole different world. A world Daddy didn't necessarily approve of, but Sara was over twenty-one now and could do as she pleased.

The runway lights winked below her, and she took a deep breath as she settled back for the landing. New York! And Delight would be there to meet her. A whole week in New York before she had to fly to Los Angeles to settle down to studying. But with her sharing a Brentwood apartment with Delight, post-graduate classes at UCLA could never be boring, to say the least!

"Darling! Sara, darling!"

She had not recognized her sister until she waved and burst through the clustering crowd that waited for disembarking passengers. Delight was wearing an Afro and enormous sunglasses that shaded her eyes and most of her face as well. The last time they had met, Delight's hair had been worn long and straight and almost down to her waist, and she had worn no makeup at all, but tonight she had on shiny red lip gloss and faint color along her cheekbones. She was slimmer and had acquired a glorious tan.

"Hey, Sis!" They hugged, both talking almost at once as they began to catch up on the past three years.

"I'd *never* have known you if you hadn't

4

called out!"

"You need to soak up lots and lots of sun — haven't you been playing any tennis recently?"

"Only indoors, I'm afraid! And you . . . ?"

"Wait till I *tell* you! Oh, wow! And I've got a part in a movie — only a small one *this* time but in a *straight* film, you know?"

Her sister's giggle reminded Sara of the time that Delight, to Mama's horror, had appeared in a couple of *very* sexually explicit X-rated movies. "What one might do in private is one thing, but for all the world to see . . . !" Poor Mona! It wasn't often that she came over "all proper," as Nanny Staggs would have put it.

"Do you have a lot of luggage? For God's sake, let's get out of this madhouse!"

People looked curiously at the two young women who were such a contrast — Sara Colville in her smart Givenchy suit and Delight Adams in tight-fitting Levi's tucked into boots — a tiny cotton tank top that clung almost too tightly to her firm young curves. They didn't even look like sisters now, with Delight's green eyes hidden; and yet when they had dressed alike and worn their hair the same way people used to take them for twins.

"Do you remember the confusion we used to cause? Poor Pietro — he was always *my* favorite of Mona's husbands because I felt he really *liked* kids."

"Oh, yes, I liked Pietro too, but I *hated* Virgil! All that hair on the back of his hands

5

and those smelly cigars — I used to wonder how she could let him near her!"

"He was a monster in bed! He used to make her do the most outrageous things — and love doing them!"

Delight giggled at the look on her sister's face. "I watched them! You never knew that, did you? I was afraid you'd tell on me, and besides it was *my* secret. I used to hide in the closet. It sure taught me a lot!"

"I'm sure it did!" Sara said dryly, but she was still horrified, although Delight would only laugh if she knew that. Delight would probably laugh even harder if she knew that Sara, who was older, had not yet slept with a man.

A bloody virgin at twenty-one! I ought to find a man — any man, and get it over with! She'd tell herself that over and over — and not do anything about it. Few of the men she had met had really turned her on, and of those, none of them had passed what she called to herself Test Number Two, which was meeting — and resisting — the still-gorgeous Mona.

An hour and fifteen minutes later as they sat on floor cushions in Delight's little studio apartment, Sara watched her sister's animated face and hands and wondered how it must feel to be Delight who'd done *everything* — or practically everything — before she was eighteen! Life never stood still for long enough to

6

become dull around Delight.

"More wine?" Without waiting for Sara's reply Delight was already pouring it. "You still need to loosen up a little, big Sis!" she said, only half kidding, and then, sitting back on her haunches she lifted her wineglass in a toast. "Here's to me and the one thing I haven't tried yet — marriage!"

"Marriage!" That *was* a shocker, and Sara sat up straight, her winged dark brows questioning. "Why didn't you tell me before? And who is he — or are you teasing again?"

Delight shook her head vigorously, her eyes shining with mischief and the big gold hoops she wore in her ears flying.

"Nope! I'm not teasing this time. But you know me — I always save the best news until the last. We've been living together, but he's had to go back to California to meet his big brother, who's flying in from Rome. He's Italian, and . . ." Delight paused long enough to take a deep breath before kissing her fingers in a very Italian gesture. "He's a fantastic lover, and he's — God, wait until you see him, he's beautiful! He's even old-fashioned enough to want kids — can you imagine that? We're going to honeymoon in India — I've always wanted to see the Taj Mahal by moonlight! So what do you think?"

"Well, I must say I'm *surprised!* The last time we met I remember your telling me you'd never get married! You said —"

7

Delight waved her hand impatiently, silver bangles jangling. "Oh, yes, I remember very well! I said I believed in variety, and that I wanted to try everything . . . and I have — or *almost* everything, you don't have to look so shocked! But — people change, you know that yourself, look at you! Who would have thought, three years ago, that you'd actually run away from home and come to UCLA instead of some stuffy old school like Oxford or Cambridge? I'll bet that's what your daddy wanted you to do, wasn't it?"

The slight flush that rose in Sara's pale English complexion gave Delight her answer, making her add quickly and contritely, "Darling, I didn't really mean to sound like a snot! All I meant was . . . was, well, you know what I mean! Three years ago I was a different girl, I really was. I was wild — well, I still am, a little bit — and I enjoyed every minute of living and experiencing life. And after Mama-Mona — wouldn't that turn *you* off marriage? Remember when we'd both swear that we'd never, ever get married? I didn't even believe in love, just *making* love, or . . . or screwing, as the case may have been, depending on the circumstances and who I was with. And then I met Carlo, and suddenly . . . I don't quite know how it happened or exactly when it happened, but I was in love! And the magical part of it was that he was too! Oh, Sara! Haven't you been

8

in love? Or had a crush on somebody?"

"Oh, lots of crushes, but I think I'd much rather avoid falling in love, thank you! Look how many times Mama-Mona's been in and out!" Sara's voice was light, and she hoped her eyes didn't show her slight uneasiness. Delight sounded happy, and Sara was happy for her, but her sister was such a volatile, changeable creature, it was hard to conceive of her actually settling down — if that was what she planned.

Tactfully, Sara said: "Do tell me more about this Carlo of yours, though. Is he kind to you? What does he do for a living? And what will you two do *after* the moonlight and the Taj Mahal?"

For the first time she saw Delight frown slightly before turning away with a muttered: "Do you mind if I light up a joint first? It's a long story, and you — well, if I didn't *explain* it all, give you the background, you really wouldn't understand. And I do want you to understand, Sara! You're the levelheaded one of us two, and you were always getting me out of scrapes, remember? Anyway . . ." She turned back, offering Sara a thick, expertly rolled joint; grinning when Sara shook her head. "Don't tell me you've never tried one yet? Oh, come on, *everyone* has in this day and age! Look, this is all you have to do. . . ." Sucking acrid-smelling smoke deeply into her lungs, she held it there with her eyes closed, seeming, under Sara's fascinated eyes, to swallow it deeper and deeper inside until there was no smoke left to be exhaled. The strange thing was that Delight seemed quite unaffected by it — Sara had almost expected her to keel over immediately!

"Come on, try it! Just one toke, it'll relax you, I guarantee it! And you might as well practice some under my expert supervision before you get to UCLA and try it there. And you will, Sis, you will. Don't look at me like that! Because if you don't they'll think you're some kind of weirdo!"

"I could say I'm allergic?" Sara said hopefully, wrinkling her nose at the bittersweet odor.

"Then they'd expect you to be into something else, like coke. Ever snorted?"

"No! And I don't intend to either!"

"Oh, Jesus Christ, Sara, you've got to stop being so . . . so damned straight! Why don't you learn to relax and have some fun for a change? I don't mean like *me*, I know my type of fun isn't yours, but you don't want to stay on the outside looking in forever, do you? You've got to try a few things, take a few risks, *live* a little, you know?"

Other words floated into Sara's mind as she returned her sister's teasing, slightly mocking gaze. "Such a good child, Miss Sara. Never a moment's trouble, she gives me. Always so well behaved . . ." Nanny Staggs, dear old Nanny!

And her father, after one of Delight's rare visits, saying approvingly, "I'm glad you're such an obedient, *quiet* child, Sara. Never let others influence you or change you."

But now, looking back, she saw with sudden clarity that what he'd really meant was that she mustn't deviate from the rules and regulations he'd hedged her about with. Not that Daddy hadn't *meant* well, but . . . damn it, she was an adult now, and she had to learn to coexist with other young adults. She didn't want to be an outsider, looking in, as Delight had pointed out.

"Here, watch me again — and try not to choke. It's easy, really — and it won't hurt you, I promise. This is good stuff, it'll just make you feel real mellow and kind of laid back, you know?"

She didn't know, Sara thought defiantly, but she intended to find out! After all, she'd read enough to know that marijuana, in small doses, wasn't harmful — not as bad for one as cigarettes or alcohol.

She coughed after the first drag and managed to hold the next one quite creditably. Nothing happened. Delight had refilled their wineglasses and Sara sipped the chilled Chablis, wondering if she was disappointed or relieved.

Braver now, she took another drag before

11

Delight, producing a silver roach clip shaped like a crocodile, finished it off.

"Feel a buzz yet? Oh, well, you will real soon. Let me turn the music up a little, it always sounds better after you've done grass."

There was a whole new vocabulary she'd have to learn, Sara thought, settling back more comfortably on the big cushion as Delight began, at last, to tell her all about Carlo, how they'd met, and how impossible his older brother was. The wine sparkled enchantingly in her crystal glass, and the music was wonderful — soothing, with an undertone of fierceness at the same time — a swelling and a diminishing of sound. Wagner had never sounded so beautiful before, nor had she, Sara, ever felt so relaxed.

"What's his name?" she demanded suddenly, wanting Delight to know she was really paying attention.

"Whose?"

"Big brother's . . . what did you say his name was?"

"Oh, *him!* The overbearing, arrogant — Giovanni. Big bad John!" Delight giggled. "Only don't ever let Carlo know I called him that. Carlo really looks up to him, I think he's even a little bit scared of him. It's Giovanni Marco Riccardo Marcantoni — can you imagine a name like that? Carlo has two other names too, I guess it's a custom or something, but no one ever calls him anything but Carlo, and it suits him. It's a beautiful name and he's a beautiful person, unlike his brother who lords it over everyone just because he happened to be the firstborn and a conte or a duke or something equally silly — I mean who gives a damn about titles anymore? And everyone knows that Italian titles are a dime a dozen, some stupid society woman is always marrying one and I mean . . . what was I saying?"

"You were saying that this . . . big bad Marco or whoever had to approve of you before he gives Carlo permission to . . ." Sara sat up straight, brushing her hair away from her eyes, which had begun to flash angrily. "Why does Carlo have to have his *brother's* permission for anything? How old is he anyway? Isn't he man enough to stand up for what he wants?"

"I was just telling you, they're *Italian,* and Giovanni Marco — they call him Marco within the family, how'd you guess? — as the head of the family runs the whole show. He's the one who made most of the money, you see, and he controls everything. He's into automobiles and shipping and . . . you name a pie and he has a finger in it! He's *rich,* and Carlo works for him. He's also quite ruthless. . . ." Delight gave an exaggerated shiver as she lowered her voice dramatically. "In fact, I wouldn't be at all surprised if he's even mixed up with the . . . you-know-who.

13

The mob."

"You mean the Mafia? Oh, *no,* Delight, surely not!"

"I'm not sure at all . . . and of course Carlo would *never* say anything, and it's the one thing I'd never dare ask him about. But I have my suspicions . . . and he *did* tell me once that his brother would stop at nothing to gain his ends. So you see what we're up against, and why you've just *got* to help? Sara, I'm afraid he's going to try and break us up, and I'd just kill myself if that happened, and so would Carlo!" Delight's huge emerald eyes that were so like Mona's filled with tears.

"But why would he want to break you up, even if he could?"

"Because . . . because he's a straitlaced *prig!*" Delight wailed. "They're strict Catholics, of course, the whole family, and Marco's the type who believes in work, work, work and no play, and when the time comes around — and that'll be when *he* says so, of course — then Carlo will be expected to marry some stupid cow of a girl his brother will choose for him from one of the *right* families, with money, of course, and without" — her voice quivered over an incipient sob — "without *my* lurid past! Everything I've done — all that stuff in those nasty rags and the gossip columns and the pictures . . . oh, *you* know what I mean, Sary, and *you* know I only did it all for kicks and for experience, but *he'd* never buy

14

that! Carlo understands and doesn't care, but his brother never would! So you see why I do need you so!"

"No, I don't, not really!" Sara objected reasonably, trying not to let Delight notice that the use of the old childhood name "Sary" had gotten to her. She had to blink her eyes in order to focus them on Delight, sitting cross-legged so easily without any sign of strain; two large tears trickling forlornly down her face. Poor, darling Delight! Of course she was reckless and a little bit wild and wayward, but that was part of her nature and part of her charm — she just *did* things without thinking of the consequences, but that didn't give any stuffy, arrogant outsider the right to look down on her either!

Wrapped up in her own thoughts, Sara hadn't been paying attention to what Delight was saying until her sister said urgently: ". . . so you see why Carlo and I have to run away and do it secretly, to throw *him* off the track! And if you'd just cover for me . . ."

I really feel quite strange! Sara thought dazedly. Not *bad* strange but funny strange. Kind of floaty . . .

Aloud she said stoutly, hoping she wasn't slurring her words, "Of course you *know* you can count on me, darling! *I'll* take care of Mr. High-and mighty Marco . . . yes, and I'll give him a bit of what-for too if he *dares* say anything against you!" And then she couldn't

15

help giggling, because "what-for" had been Nanny Staggs' favorite expression, especially when Delight came to visit: "You come down from off that tree, miss, or I'll give you what-for!"

"Oh, Sary, I *do* love you! I *told* Carlo you'd do it!"

Warm arms hugged her fiercely until Sara said weakly: "And now it's all decided, do you think you can show me the way to bed? I feel very sleepy, all of a sudden!"

Chapter 2

Discovering New York and rediscovering Delight was a continuous, kaleidoscopic play of light, color and activity that never seemed to stop. They went everywhere, saw everything, ate at obscure little restaurants in the Village and the most elegant dining rooms Manhattan had to offer. There was endless shopping to be done in the afternoons and the theater in the evenings; Broadway shows and off-Broadway shows — the Met and the Philharmonic. Delight made New York City come alive and become a *real* place for Sara, who could not have imagined its hectic, electric pulsebeat by herself.

Sara learned to stay up all night, snatching a few hours of sleep before she was ready to go again. And she learned to disco all night at elegant places like Regine's and popular fad places like Bond's Casino and Magique and Xenon and way-out places like the Mudd Club.

"Don't New Yorkers ever stop *going?*" Sara asked wonderingly and had her rather naive question answered by a giggle.

"Hardly ever, sweetie! There's always so much to do, you see! And I *never* get tired — it's my vitamins and health food that do the trick! How's your energy level? And how did you like Carlo's friend Giacomo? I could tell he dug *you!*"

"Don't matchmake, Delight!" Sara said severely, and her sister rolled her eyes upward in mock despair.

"For God's sake, who's matchmaking? I mean . . . he liked you, and you liked him, right? So you could have asked him up — I would've slept on the couch, you know!"

"I didn't like him *that* much, and anyway he had a wet kiss, like Eduardo. . . ."

"Aha! Eduardo, huh? So you *have* been around some. Thank God, I was beginning to wonder!"

Learning to talk like a native, Sara said, "Oh, cut it out, Delight!" adding quickly, "When do you expect to hear from your divine Carlo anyhow? Shouldn't he have called to give you a report?"

She was sorry she'd said that when Delight's vivacious face clouded for an instant.

"Big brother's probably keeping him busy — on purpose, of course! He only flew to Los Angeles because he'd heard the rumors, you know. And now he's probably giving my poor

Carlo a hard time. But Carlo's got a stubborn streak in him, just like I have, and *this* time he's not going to give in. I'll hear from him, you'll see!"

"Well, I was just thinking that it might be hard for him to reach you on the telephone since we've hardly been home!"

"He'll call me at about six some morning — that's the time he always calls when he has to be away."

Delight was sure of her Carlo, still steadfastly In Love and just as steadfast in her resolve to elope. Sara couldn't help sighing inwardly as she wondered, with her practical mind, whether such an elaborate plan as her sister had outlined was really necessary. Whether the Marcantoni family was old-fashioned or not, this was still the twentieth century, after all, and all Carlo had to do was to tell his brother to . . . to go to hell!

Since that first night they'd spent quietly talking in the apartment, the volatile Delight — taking Sara's participation in her plans for granted — hadn't said much more on the subject. Now, as they shared the same tiny bathroom, Delight applying her makeup while Sara soaked in a tub that was deliciously perfumed with Halston, Sara found herself hoping fervently that it would all be worked out quietly in the end. Delight, bless her heart, *did* tend to overdramatize things!

As if she'd been a mind reader Delight said

suddenly: "You think I'm kind of crazy to be going to such lengths to get away from big brother, don't you?" Turning around with a pot of lip gloss in her hand she gave Sara an unusually serious look. "Well, I'm not. I'm . . . I guess I'm really a little bit scared, you know? And it's only because *Carlo's* scared — and Carlo's not scared of anything or anyone but his brother Marco. That's what I meant the other evening when I said — " Then with a switch of mood that was typical, she suddenly turned back to the mirror. "I guess it doesn't really matter, because by the time anyone finds out we're both missing, Carlo and I will be married and safely tucked away in some remote corner of India! And once I have a baby, well . . . even Marco wouldn't dare do anything *then* because my baby will be a Marcantoni! And you can bet I wouldn't let anyone boss a kid of *mine* around!"

"Well, as long as you name me godmother . . ." Might as well give in gracefully Sara thought ruefully. And in a way, wasn't she quite looking forward to her confrontation with the overbearing Marco? Oh, she'd give him a piece of her mind, all right!

For the rest of the evening, while they were part of the crush at the rock concert in Madison Square Garden, both girls were able to forget everything but the fact that they were having fun. Sara even took a surreptitious drag off a joint that someone passed around and found that it *did* make her feel more — what was the term Delight used? — laid back, that was it!

With the rest of the crowd, all friends of Delight's from her modeling days, they went to a Greek nightclub that was noisy and lively and had great food. Sara got a little drunk on Demestica and had a wonderful time; dancing until her feet ached and she kicked off her shoes and danced some more, with Delight applauding.

"I *love* New York! I really do — and maybe I'll just decide to stay here and do something. . . ."

"You're going to California and bail me out *first*, my girl!" Delight uttered severely, doing an imitation of Nanny Staggs that had them both in gales of laughter, so much so that it took at least five minutes to find the right keys that would open all the locks on the door.

"God, is it actually getting to be *light* outside or am I seeing things?"

"It *is* light outside, and that reminds me of an old song — you know, the one about Broadway babies. . . . Whatever did I do with my shoes?"

Sara collapsed onto a pile of cushions, half asleep already and barely hearing Delight say: "You're still carrying them, you dummy!"

And then the phone rang and Delight ran to answer it in the bedroom and was *hours,* or so it seemed, so that Sara really did fall

21

asleep and stayed there until the sun woke her, streaming in through the venetian blinds. Her head ached, and the smell of perking coffee and burnt toast assaulted her nostrils. Why did Delight *always* burn the toast?

"Rise and shine, kiddo!"

A blanket was flung over her and Sara burrowed her head under it, making protesting noises.

"Baby, come *on!* We got things to do. Gotta pack and make reservations, and — don't you want to know what Carlo told me? Hah! I knew I was right about that bastard of a brother of his! Well, let *him* find out he's not quite as smart as he thinks he is! Hey . . . !" The blanket was tugged away revealing Sara's tousled dark hair and mascara-smudged face, and Delight said soothingly, "All you need is coffee and a couple of aspirins and you'll be just fine! I'll bring them to you, huh? And then you can listen — we need to talk, Sary. And . . . and *plan!* Nothing's going to go wrong, hear? Because I'd kill myself if it did!"

"What I don't understand," Sara said later, sitting hunched over the kitchen table with her head supported by palms pressed against her temples, "is whether this is plan A or plan B — and how I let myself get dragged into it!" Her attempt at humor had a hollow ring to it, even in her own ears.

"Well, you *did* promise and you can't back

out now," Delight stated unsympathetically. "And besides, if you'd taken those vitamins like *I* did, you wouldn't have a hangover. *Do* pay attention, sweetie, this is *important,* a matter of life and death — *my* death if it doesn't work out, and you wouldn't want that, would you?"

"No . . . ." Sara muttered obediently. And then, with a decided effort, "I really *am* trying to pay attention, but why don't we give my head a chance to stop pounding like a trip-hammer? It really *is* hard to hear you. . . ."

"The aspirins are going to work in a few minutes, I promise you! And while they're doing their thing, I'm going to run it past you again. Slowly, this time. Maybe it'll soak into your subconscious or something, hmm?"

Delight's plan really did sound simple and uncomplicated, except that — and Sara shuddered at the thought — for the next few weeks *she* was supposed to masquerade as her sister. All her weak objections were brushed aside as she was reminded that she couldn't — she *wouldn't* — back out now, surely? Not after she had *promised.* . . .

"It's only to throw Marco off the track, love! To give us time, so he won't be able to stop us. He's determined to break us up, and his sending Carlo off to the absolute *wilds* of Argentina, of all places — and at a moment's notice, really proves it! Why, he actually told Carlo that he would not allow — *allow,* can you beat that? — a member of his family to be associated with the likes of *me!*''

"He didn't!''

"He sure did! He's a prig — and a hypocrite as well! Why, Carlo told me that his brother keeps dozens of mistresses — all over the world, in fact. But just because Carlo is a few years younger and not yet in control of his share of their father's money he's forced to go along with whatever Marco dictates. He was *furious* when he learned that we'd been living together, and he made all kinds of threats. . . .''

"Honestly, Delight, surely the man wouldn't dare — and anyway, I hate to say this, but it has to be said — why doesn't Carlo just stand up to his brother and refuse to budge? He can't be exactly a *child,* after all, and if it's only his brother's money that makes him a lackey, why doesn't he get a job?''

"You don't understand!'' Delight burst out. She paced the confines of the small kitchen like an angry young panther. "Carlo doesn't care about the money — in a year or so he'll inherit plenty of his own. He's just worried. He *knows* his brother, you see, and how unscrupulous he is! He'd have — don't laugh, but he'd actually have Carlo abducted, if he had to. Or he'd . . . he'd have something drastic happen to *me.* And I'm not being dramatic this time, I swear it! The man's an absolute, fucking autocrat of the old kind —

24

he belongs in the Dark Ages! It's that violent Sardinian-Sicilian blood. Why, their father had his first wife killed because he thought she had a lover!''

"And you want *me* to face a man like that?"

"Who said anything about facing? Darling Sary, all you'd have to do is to be me for a couple of weeks. Go the places I usually go, do the things I usually do. So he'll think I'm still in town and stop worrying that I might run off to meet Carlo somewhere."

Sara said a trifle grimly: "And when he finds out you've done exactly that and I've duped him . . . will I meet with some unfortunate 'accident,' do you think?"

"Well, of course not! You're the respectable one of the family, he'd never do anything to *you*. And he doesn't *have* to know anything. You can just go back to being yourself, and no one will be the wiser."

"It's not as easy as that!" Sara tried to warn her sister; and indeed she had a peculiar feeling — nothing to do with her hangover — that something was bound to go wrong. Delight's scheme, while it sounded deceptively simple, all hinged upon *her* part in the masquerade — and how on earth could she possibly go on playing Delight for two whole weeks? Apart from the surface similarity they had both inherited from their mother, they were two very different women.

In the face of Delight's obdurate, closed

25

look, Sara tried again: "Darling, *do* think carefully! I mean, if this man is . . . is as clever as you say he is, and if he's had you investigated, surely he'd know about *me?* If he should find out that I'm in Los Angeles too; that we're sharing an apartment . . ."

"But he'll find out nothing of the kind!" Delight said triumphantly. "Sorry, darling, but we can't share my apartment. You're going to stay on campus, or in a hotel if you can't stand *that* thought. And we won't be seen out together. And as for the rest of your objection — why should he care if I had a half sister or not? He didn't need to have me investigated all that much — I've really never been really secretive about the life I've led, have I? No, we'll stay away from each other and go our separate ways. You'll live *very* quietly and unobtrusively and I'll make sure everyone sees me everywhere until it's time for us to switch, and then . . ."

Grasping at straws now Sara said weakly: "But . . . but the film! Remember, you told me you had a small part in a straight film — you were all excited about it! Surely you're not going to turn it down?"

Delight grinned wickedly. "Turn it down? Hell, no — that *would* be out of character for me! But if they don't start shooting soon enough — haven't you ever wondered, sister dear, if you've inherited any of Mama-Mona's talent?"

Chapter 3

Los Angeles in the fall was hotter than anything Sara could have imagined, even though she had been warned. Her coolest summer cottons were no match for the searing heat that seemed to soak through into her bones, depriving her of her usual brisk energy and even, so it seemed, of her will. Why else would she still be going along quite unresistingly with Delight's crazy plan? Because it *was* insane of course; the whole idea that between them they could hope to deceive a hardheaded, coldly arrogant Italian tycoon who had had the wits and the ruthlessness to amass an enormous fortune on his own. Sara had tried to tell her sister so on several occasions, but Delight had refused to listen.

"Of *course* our plan — *my* plan — is going to work, and don't you dare think negative, you hear? It's going to work because it *has* to, that's all. I'm going mad, not being able to see Carlo or talk to him on the telephone, while he's stuck in the absolute wilds of Argentina!"

"Darling, I can quite imagine what you must be going through, but — well, it *does* rather sound like something out of a novel, you know! If your Carlo is going to take off on his own in any case, then what's to prevent *you* from . . ."

Seeing the storm clouds gather on Delight's expressive face, Sara had sighed, ending rather lamely, "Well, I really don't see how this monster of a big brother could *do* anything to you! Or *what* he could do to you."

"You don't know him!" Delight said darkly. "I told you, he's capable of anything, even arranging for a convenient 'accident' to happen to me. You have to believe me, Sara — this is the only way."

It meant they couldn't really see each other and do things together as Sara had anticipated earlier when she had arranged to go to college in Los Angeles. And it also meant that, trepidations or not, she was committed to keep her word — take Delight's place in public at a moment's notice while her sister slipped away to join her lover. Her situation was hopelessly melodramatic; but she could at least cling to the thought that Mama-Mona, who was a romantic soul at heart, would have approved, just as definitely as Daddy would *not* approve, had he only known. Sara shuddered at the thought that he might find out.

More than ever she found herself wishing that she hadn't agreed to go along with her sister's crazy plan. The whole scheme was beginning to sound more and more like a plot of a cheaply made Hollywood spy drama, especially when the only way Sara and Delight could communicate was by telephone. And Delight always used a pay telephone when she called because, she said quite seriously, "I wouldn't put it past that Marco creep to have my apartment bugged, just to find out if Carlo and I are still in touch!"

Even their telephone conversations smacked of melodrama, with Delight constantly coaching or cuing Sara for the "role" she must soon play.

"You make this sound like 'Mission Impossible'!" Sara grumbled, adding, "I suppose I should feel grateful that you've stopped smoking those ghastly strong cigarettes — that's one habit I'd have absolutely *refused* to take up, even for you, sister dear!"

"Well, Carlo didn't like my smoking . . . *cigarettes*, that is!" Delight gave an irrepressible giggle before she continued patiently: "All right — now tell me the name of my hairdresser and how much I always tip him. . . ."

"Don't you think this is all kind of . . . ridiculous? Marco's never met you, and he probably doesn't know anything about your . . . your hairdresser or your favorite saleslady

29

at Fiorucci — or care either!" Sara's voice showed strain. *"Honestly,* Delight . . . !"

"You don't know anything about Carlo's big brother!" Delight retorted obdurately. Sara could just imagine her sister's purse-lipped frown. "He's the kind who wouldn't miss a trick. Are you kidding? He'd have had me investigated only too thoroughly. Sara," her voice quivering slightly, "you just *have* to mind what I tell you and not let your guard down for an *instant,* do you understand? The longer he continues to think that you are me, the longer we'll be safe, Carlo and I and . . . and our unborn baby!"

It was Delight's trump card, and just as she had no doubt anticipated, it put an end to all Sara's arguments — rallying all her sympathy and fierce protectiveness to the forefront immediately.

"Why didn't you tell me before? Oh, *darling,* what you must be going through! And I've been giving you such a hard time too . . . . ! You can stop worrying, I won't let you down, and I'll put that nasty, cold-blooded . . . *gangster* off for as long as I have to. And believe me, he'll get a piece of my mind too, before this is all over. My God . . . . !" Sara's voice suddenly registered delayed shock. "I can hardly believe I'm going to be an *aunt,* of all things!"

Privately, after she had hung up and Delight's abrupt revelation had had time to be absorbed, Sara still felt some misgivings about the role she had committed herself to play. Not quite the same as playing Ophelia in the drama society's staging of *Hamlet* — and she'd been scared sick before every performance. At least there'd been lines and stage directions to memorize then, but on this occasion she'd have nothing to guide her but her instincts and her knowledge of her half sister's mannerisms and lifestyle. And her own common sense, of course.

The very next day, she found herself suddenly *become* Delight, her mind cluttered with all the bits and pieces of information and trivia she was supposed to remember. She *had* to remember and carry it through.

Sara blinked her eyes and turned away from the open sliding doors that led onto a tiny terrace with a wrought-iron railing.

"You can *almost* see the ocean from here . . . ." Delight had boasted once. How she wished Delight was here with her! Or that she was back where she belonged, playing tennis or riding. Damn — she had forgotten to check whether Delight rode or not. Probably not, unless it was a Harley-Davidson!

The phone rang, making Sara jump. She felt nervous, edgy. And with good reason, she reminded herself stoutly as she snatched the receiver, hoping it would be Delight herself. Instead the voice she heard at the other end was masculine and sounded slurred.

"Heyyy . . . baby! Heard you were back in town. And you didn't call me. What's up? Got someone new on the scene?"

Sara swallowed hard. "I don't . . ." She hoped she sounded like Delight. Damn, what now? She could never fool any of Delight's really close friends or acquaintances, and who was this clown anyway?

"Hey, this is *Andy!* Good ol' Andy, your fuckin' stud. Remember the last time we made it . . . ?

Sara's face had flushed a bright red in spite of her resolve *not* to be shocked.

"That *was* the *last* time, Andy. Good-bye!" she said smartly, hanging up. He'd better not call again. To make sure, she unplugged the telephone. Better to be a coward than to have to put up with *that* kind of thing!

To keep from thinking too far ahead, Sara planned what she would say if anyone asked her why she hadn't answered her telephone: "I knew I'd have to be up early, and you *know* how badly I need my eight hours sleep! So . . ."

She bit her lip, stung by an unpleasant recollection. Damn — she *did* have to be up at an extraordinarily early hour tomorrow morning. Through some quirky twist of fate she, Sara, would be reporting as Delight for the first day's shooting on *Mohave,* the new Garon Hunt movie. Now Delight's almost prophetic words to her before they'd left New York were coming back to haunt her, over the sounds of jazz music on the radio she'd turned up in defiance of the street sounds outside. "Haven't you ever wondered, sister dear, whether you've inherited any of Mama-Mona's talent?"

Well — Sara turned slightly, facing her grave, rather uncertain expression in the mirror. Well, *had* she? The face that looked back at her didn't even look like herself. Involuntarily, Sara put her hand up to her hair. Amazing how different Delight's "natural" hairstyle made her look. Wiping away her scared-rabbit look, Sara practiced curving her mouth into Delight's impish smile that showed off a dimple. This was acting, wasn't it? Compared to playing the part of her tempestuous, volatile sister, doing her bit in front of the cameras was going to seem easy.

She felt like a zombie the next morning; dozing in the back of the limousine that someone had been thoughtful enough to send for her. The driver seemed to know her, and it was partly to avoid his sly grins and his almost *too*-knowing looks in the mirror that Sara decided it would be safer to keep her eyes closed until they had arrived at the studio — wherever it was located. She supposed they'd have to take one of the freeways to get there — one did, she had already discovered, just to get from one part of Los Angeles to another.

"Sure like that picture spread you did for *Fun and Games*. That publicity for this new pic you're in?"

Sara's face had grown as hot as her voice came out frostily. "No."

Maybe he'd take the hint. There was a long pause, during which she almost fell asleep, knowing she was escaping again.

"Tired, huh?"

"Hmmm."

She wished he'd shut up. What would *Delight* do?

Drawing her legs up and stretching them along the luxuriously padded length of the seat, Sara said in what she hoped sounded like a sleepy mumble: "Do be a sweetie and wake me up when we get there, hmm?"

She actually *did* fall asleep and didn't wake up until they stopped at the gate to be checked in by a uniformed security guard. The limo drew up with a flourish in front of a drab-looking building that was dwarfed by the huge hangarlike proportions of the shooting stage behind it.

"They said you was to be delivered to Makeup first. Good luck, huh?"

Feeling slightly guilty Sara flashed him a grin and a "thank you — I appreciate your letting me sleep!"

"Sure." He was a young man, and he looked

after her rather wistfully as she disappeared into the building. She sure didn't look much like her pictures! Hard to tell if she had that luscious body he'd lusted for or not, under that bulky sweat suit she'd worn against the morning chill. But he'd sure have liked to have found out! So that was Delight Adams. Funny how they all looked kind of disappointing when you saw them close up, especially early in the morning!

"Delight!"

The man who'd called her name and came hurrying toward her had a prematurely lined and lugubrious face — a British accent. Remembering who he was from pictures, Sara allowed him a smile. Lew Weisman was her mother's agent too, and he had recently stepped into the picture to "look after Delight" during the making of *Mohave* at Mona's insistence.

"He's always *nagging,* and he drives me up the wall sometimes, but I guess I do like Lew," Delight had confided during one of their "indoctrination sessions." "At least I'm sure he isn't trying to screw me — in more ways than one!" And she'd laughed at the outraged look on Sara's face.

"Hi, Lew!"

He didn't smile back, his face long, his eyes darting almost accusingly over her. " 'Hi, Lew,' she says. Just like that. Just like we

35

weren't supposed to have dinner together last night. And when I tried calling, you weren't home. So what's the story this time?"

As his eyes continued to search her face, Sara wondered for one ghastly moment whether he was tumbling to the fact that she *wasn't* Delight after all. She had to remind herself sharply that Delight and Lew hadn't actually met face to face since Mama-Mona had asked him to become her agent. So he didn't really *know* her.

"I unplugged the phone." When in doubt, tell the truth! Sara gazed at him limpidly before lowering her eyes. "I . . . I'd been getting some nuisance calls before, and I wanted to get some sleep."

"Hah!" She couldn't tell from his snort whether he believed her or not — but it didn't really matter, did it? Delight wouldn't let *anyone* browbeat her! "Maybe no one ever told you that an Agent's time is valuable. I've got other clients to nursemaid, kid, and don't you forget it!"

"Like Garon Hunt? Mmm — he's gorgeous! Are you going to introduce us?"

She was actually *becoming* Delight with remarkable ease, Sara thought distantly, applauding herself. She looked back at Lew, challenging him.

To her surprise, he was shaking his head. "Jesus Christ! That all you can think about? I must be crazy, taking you on — almost busting a gut to get you this role so you can change your image. Maybe you need a PR firm instead of an agent!"

She put her hand on his arm and it too, like her made-up face, looked different with its long red nails. "Come on, Lew, be nice, can't you? I'm sorry about last night, but I really *did* need the rest. I . . . I was a bundle of nerves!"

"Holy shit . . . the things I put up with! You're more like your mama than I'd have guessed, you know that? But don't ever pull that kind of crap on me again, you hear? I don't have the time to waste my time, Miss Adams!"

"I'm sorry, I truly am. And I really do mean to behave myself. I . . . I've decided to change. Sort of . . . be born again, you know?"

She might have been carrying things too far, Sara conceded, watching the changing expressions on Lew's face as he gazed at her measuringly.

"Never mind that," he said finally in a gruff voice. "You just prove to them I was right to push you for the part of Fran, hear? You'd better do even better than you did in your test, or I'm going to be a laughingstock."

She hadn't done anything but sit around yet. There was the possibility that although she had to report on time each morning to be costumed and made up, they wouldn't be shooting any of the scenes that *she* was to be in. But sitting quietly tucked away in a corner of a sound stage, watching the actors and the action, wasn't all new to Sara, who had watched her mother "playing make-believe" (as she'd called it as a child) on several occasions in the past. It was funny, but she'd even got herself past the feeling of stage fright that had dogged her all last night.

Sara found she could laugh — lightly, even — and she was suddenly optimistic: Maybe I'm more like Mama-Mona than even *you* could have guessed, Lew. I intend to be good in this part. So good they're all going to sit up and take notice.

Chapter 4

The short but crucial love scene between Garon Hunt, playing an undercover cop, and Delight Adams as Fran, a spoiled rich girl whose father heads a dope ring, was taking longer than anticipated.

"What the hell is wrong with the stupid little bitch? She's taken all her clothes off for the cameras before, and now she's fussing about baring her boobs. For Christ's sake, *you* talk to her, Lew!"

Dan Raymond, directing this scene, was about ready to tear his thinning hair out. So it was a last-minute switch in the script, but it was Garon's idea, and Garon was producing this one himself.

"Dan, you know damn well Delight wanted this part because it's a *straight* role — a change from that other stuff she's done. She wants to show the public she can *act,* not just strut around showing off her fine tits and ass. And it says in her contract —"

"Lew's right, Dan. And I'm sure Garon will let it go — it was just an idea, trying the scene out with a different twist. You know what a perfectionist he is!"

Lew Weisman's crooked smile acknowledged the unexpected support he'd just received from Sally Lockwood, Garon's co-star and wife of fifteen years. Theirs was one of Hollywood's more stable marriages, and Sally never displayed any jealousy, even if Garon *did* occasionally play around on the side. Insiders whispered that that was why she kept him.

"Thanks, Sal."

She smiled, watching Dan stomp off.

"That's all right. Garon's a breast man, you know. And he wanted to find out if hers were real or not. I rather think, though, that now he's more intrigued by the fact that she was so stubborn about taking her blouse off for that scene . . . oh, dear!"

"She won't go out with him. She's in love, she says. With a young man she plans to marry. She told me he's the reason for her . . . change of heart, shall we say?"

"That's nice. And she really does seem nice. I've always liked Mona, you know. Garon used to have quite a crush on her — when they were doing *Bianca,* do you remember? We were newlyweds at the time, and she turned him down. Delight *does* look a lot like her, don't you think?"

"Yes — and I've always had a crush on you, or have I told you that before?"

While they were adjusting the lights and the makeup man was patting at her face, Sara could see Sally and Lew laughing comfortably together. Lucky Sally, to be married to a man like Garon Hunt . . . and to be so sure of him. She must try not to remember the way she had blushed when Garon had said so matter-of-factly: "Why don't we try it one more time — this time without the shirt, huh, sweetie?"

Now he came sauntering up to her, one eyebrow cocked. Thank God he wasn't angry with her!

"So we get to do this one more time. And since you won't take the shirt off, how about unfastening a couple of buttons for me?" His eyes were an intense blue, and Sara found herself almost mesmerized by their clarity as he called over his shoulder, "Let's try it this way, Dan. I start on the buttons while I'm talking to her — don't worry, baby, we'll keep the nipples covered — and that'll ease us into the rest of the action."

Delight would *not* be embarrassed! Delight would probably have taken her shirt off quite nonchalantly, no matter who was watching. Sara bit her bottom lip, and the makeup man ran up to retouch her lip gloss, clucking at her crossly. She tried to meet Garon's amused blue gaze with insouciance.

"Okay — quiet please!"

This was take six and, please God, it would be the final one. She could act. Acting was only playing make-believe — charades and pantomimes and dressing up in grown-up clothes when she was a child. Thanks to Mona, it was in her blood. And as she'd promised Lew, she was going to prove it to them all — especially to Garon Hunt!

It was strange, how make-believe could almost turn into reality, especially if you were really trying hard to *believe.* Sara, who was actually quite shy and comparatively inexperienced, became lost somewhere behind the brighter, bolder image of Delight — who in turn was playing Fran, a mixed-up young woman who had grown up grabbing too much, too quickly. Delight could relate to Fran, would know exactly how Fran would react to this very exciting, tough man who seemed to see right through her insolently challenging facade.

Time seemed to rush by in undulating waves of light and color and heat. Sara wasn't conscious of herself as herself any longer, although she supposed afterward that she must have done everything she was supposed to do, even to responding to a kiss that was hardly make-believe as it forced her lips apart, bruising them against her teeth and stifling her instinctive, protesting murmur. When she blinked herself back to reality it was to face

42

Garon's quizzical look — those blue eyes of his seemed to see right through the thin silk of her shirt to discover her rapidly pounding heart.

With shaking fingers, Sara began to do up her buttons, hoping he wouldn't notice. God, he'd only left one button undone!

"Well!" he said half under his breath with his eyes still intent on her damp, flushed face. "Maybe we could replay *that* one later, with a few changes? I'll call you, baby."

"Sure!" she said too quickly, hoping she'd sounded light enough. Of course he didn't *mean* it — and anyway he didn't have her number. But she'd been well and truly kissed by Garon Hunt — no wonder women were crazy about him!

People were milling around now, and Garon had disappeared. Sara was relieved when Lew came up to lead her off with him.

"You were just great, kid! This part could be the start of a whole new career for you, if you wanted it that way."

"Mr. Hunt — Garon — made it easy for me. . . ."

Sara found herself responding mechanically, knowing she should sound more excited. But all she wanted to do was to hide away somewhere alone so that she could examine her feelings. Suppose Garon *did* manage to discover her number and call — what would she do then? She hadn't been kissed too many times before, and *this* kiss had certainly been different! She still felt weak in the knees. And — oh, darn, he thought she was Delight, of course. Did he think . . .

"Delight, I want you to meet Sally Lockwood. She's an old friend of Mona's."

Oh, God! Garon's *wife!* Sara hoped she hadn't blushed guiltily.

"You were very good, honey. I'm glad you didn't let Garon bully you!"

"Oh — thank you! I was hoping my bad case of nerves wouldn't show."

Sally Lockwood had a lovely smile; one that reached her eyes.

"We all have to cope with that, I guess! My hands always get ice cold just before I have to face the cameras, and I've been known to forget my lines."

"Not too damn often! Hi, Sally — Lew — and. . . ?"

"This is Delight Adams. Paul Drury, our executive producer. Paul darling, what brings *you* out here this early?"

The thickset, burly man with black curly hair looked like an ex-football player and probably was. He acknowledged Sara's presence with a nod and a curious, somehow sharp look before he bent over the back of Sally's chair to kiss her cheek.

"Money — what else? This picture is running over budget, and I thought I'd remind Garon of that — and reintroduce him to an

44

old friend who's willing to invest a couple of million more in *Mohave,* so we can afford to go on location for those chase scenes after all."

"That's *wonderful,* Paul! And it's going to put Garon in a good mood too — maybe I'll get my diamond earrings in the end!"

Feeling like an intruder, and with reaction already setting in, Sara signaled to Lew with a small wave of her hand as she started to move away.

"Hey! Not so fast, Miss Adams!"

She hadn't imagined that Paul Drury had really *noticed* her at all, from the casual nod of his head a few minutes earlier. But suddenly *his* eyes and the eyes of all the others were on her; and Sara felt the telltale color stain her cheeks.

"The friend I was talking about — he wants to meet you. Quite a fan!"

"Oh?" Tongue-tied. Now she really understood what it meant. "Well . . ."

Sara looked toward Lew, but he wasn't concerned with her; all his attention seemed concentrated on Sally Lockwood.

How would Delight have reacted? Having to be someone else made it easier somehow. Sara's head went back, and in a remembered gesture she ran impatient fingers through her hair, pushing it away from her face as she flashed an impudent, challenging smile.

"Well — why not? Who is he, this friend

of yours? I should be extra nice to him, shouldn't I, especially if he's going to invest money in our movie?"

Paul Drury's eyes flickered over her assessingly while Sara held the smile. A good thing he couldn't read her mind. And if his old friend was anything like *him* . . .

"He's *very* rich, Miss Adams. And he'd like to take you to dinner tonight — that is, if you're not already tied up."

She definitely *didn't* like Paul Drury, Sara decided. And she probably wouldn't like his rich friend either. But Delight would accept such an invitation and as long as she was playing Delight . . .

"As a matter of fact, all I'd planned on was washing my hair. But . . ."

"Garon was talking about expanding your part. You know — giving you more dialogue, more action. And I guess we can afford extra footage now that we have the financing. I'll talk to Lew about it, shall I? And about dinner — will eight o'clock suit you? My wife and I could pick you up."

It was all she could do not to raise her eyebrows. She was being invited to a *respectable* dinner? Maybe she had Paul Drury figured all wrong. And if she hadn't — it would still be a pleasure to prove to them all that Delight Adams wasn't everybody's one-night stand!

Sara smiled demurely. "That would be very

nice of you, Mr. Drury. My . . . my car's in the shop right now."

As she gave him her address she was thinking, almost panic stricken, that never, *never* would she be able to find her way about Los Angeles — let alone drive with careless confidence in the heavy rush hour traffic. Delight had left her little VW behind, but as far as Sara was concerned it could sit in the garage forever!

There was a different limousine with a different driver to take her home this time — an older man with graying hair who hardly said a word to her except to ask for her address. Sara settled back against the padded velour seat with a sigh, stretching her feet out ahead of her, feeling thankful for the footrest. Thank God for air conditioning and soft music! She found a classical station on FM and consciously willed herself to relax; wishing now that she hadn't agreed to go to dinner tonight. This morning had been enough of an ordeal — why had she willingly volunteered for more punishment?

But you can *act*, Sara! They all said you were good, didn't they? Even Garon Hunt . . .

The thought made her sit a little straighter, remembering the way he had kissed her as if he had really meant it — the way those bright-blue eyes of his had looked at her as if . . .

as if he'd wanted to kiss her again and not stop at that!

Ever since she had been a lonely little girl in a big house, missing her warm, frivolous, perfumed mother, Sara had been in the habit of carrying on a kind of dialogue with herself in her mind. Now she warned herself sternly: He's a married man, remember that, you imbecile! And you're not a teenager with a crush on him any longer, either. Kisses, even ones like *that*, don't mean anything anymore, and especially not to someone like Garon Hunt, who could have any woman in the world he really wanted. Better stop thinking along *those* lines if you know what's good for you!

The inside of the small apartment was hot and muggy, and Sara hastened to open the glass doors that led to her tiny terrace — but the air out there wasn't much cooler. Los Angeles was blanketed in a pinkish haze that made the distant mountains seem blurred and unreal. Traffic noises seemed magnified as they floated upward, and someone next door was playing one of the current disco numbers with the bass turned up so that it seemed to pound rhythmically against her temples.

Retreating indoors again, Sara turned up the air conditioner and took off her clothes, luxuriating in the feeling of freedom it gave her body as she stretched. How wonderful it would feel right now to walk around naked, feeling the rush of cold air against her skin! But she wasn't really Delight and not quite as uninhibited yet, so she compromised on a pair of *very* brief denim shorts and a bare-midriff halter top that actually belonged to her sister.

Paul Drury and his wife would be coming to pick her up at eight for a late dinner, which gave her a few hours in which to unwind and read the newspapers. Why didn't Delight have any *books?* There were only magazines, none of them current.

Pouring herself an ice-cold Perrier with a squeeze of lemon, Sara curled up on the couch and took stock of her surroundings and her circumstances while she tried to push away the rapidly growing feeling that she had bitten off much more than she could chew. There was no getting away from the fact that she and Delight were very different in their tastes and attitudes. How long would she be able to keep up this ridiculous masquerade?

Chapter 5

Sara had developed a slight headache and no answer to her dilemma by the time the electronic buzzer sounded. Damn that silly squawk box anyhow! She *still* hadn't quite figured out which button to press!

The voice that answered Sara's tentative "hello?" sounded harsh and unrecognizable, and she had to repeat herself before she could make any sense of what he was saying. It sounded like one of those ancient radios that kept cutting on and off amid crackling atmospherics.

"Miss Adams? Paul Drury . . . me to pick you up."

His chauffeur? Another studio limo?

"I'll be right down!" Sara shouted into the box, feeling herself bristle. Paul Drury had better have his wife with him!

She paused to glance at herself in the mirror one more time before she dimmed the lights. Lots of makeup of course, but not too garish.

A spaghetti-strap Calvin Klein dress in a flower-patterned silk that came to just below the knee. Huge Elsa Peretti hearts in her ears, and a matching one on a thin gold chain around her neck. Very high-heeled shoes — she'd be lucky if she didn't break her neck!

Delight hadn't said anything about clothes, and as she slung the thin strap of her small Louis Vuitton disco purse from her shoulder, Sara hoped she wasn't overdoing it. But Delight *did* wear nice clothes and jewelry, particularly in the evenings or when they went to places like Regine's in New York. Whatever Mr. Drury — or his wife — expected, she hoped they were going to be pleasantly surprised.

The lobby of the apartment building was small and unprepossessing, with its drooping potted plants and ugly chairs arranged stiltedly around a Formica-topped table. The tall man who stood there had been leafing through the pages of an old magazine, which he dropped carelessly as Sara emerged from the elevator.

Not someone's chauffeur, for certain! The rich friend of Paul Drury? Sara's thoughts became quite jumbled as she looked into a pair of coal-dark eyes that seemed to burn into hers. He certainly wasn't American — at least he wasn't like any American she had met so far. The suit he wore with casual elegance had obviously been tailored for him to fit in all the right places without being too tight. His hair was night-black and somewhat curly; neither too short nor too long. But taking away from his obvious good looks there was an unrelenting harshness about the planes of his darkly tanned face — the arrogant curve of his nostrils, and even the accented voice that said pointedly: "There is no doorman on duty here, Miss Adams? That is not safe in a city such as this, surely?"

Sara had been staring at him, unable to help herself, when his words jerked her back to reality — and her role.

"It's perfectly safe — why shouldn't it be? You couldn't have got as far as this if I hadn't unlocked the front door from upstairs. And you *did* mention that Paul Drury had sent you. . . ."

He was the kind of insufferably arrogant man who, of course, did not believe in compromise. She saw it in the lifted black eyebrow, even while she was noticing, helplessly, that he had a slight cleft in his chin.

"I suppose I am forgetting that you American women are all very self-sufficient. Pardon me, Miss Adams! And yes, I told Paul that I would come and drive you to the restaurant — his wife, Monique, is always late."

It was anger at herself, especially for having gawked at him like a love-struck teenager, that made Sara snap back: "I do hope that doesn't mean that Mr. and Mrs. Drury will not be there? After all Mr. —"

She was sorry after the words had slipped out; seeing the tightening of the muscles in that hard, implacable face. Something flamed out of his eyes at her that made her want to flinch away before they became as stonily opaque as chips of obsidian.

"So, Miss Adams, you are concerned that we have not been formally introduced?" The deceptive softness of his voice reminded Sara of the velvet paw-pat of a great cat before its claws sprang out for the kill. "But you see, since Paul told me you had agreed to meet me at dinner, I naturally took it for granted that you had no objections to meeting a stranger who happens to be an admirer . . . of your talents. However — please allow me to introduce myself — I am the Duca di Cavalieri."

His formal bow as he kissed Sara's nerveless hand was altogether correct, but his lips seemed to burn like fire against her cold skin, so that it was all she could do not to snatch it away from his gracelessly.

He had left her speechless, and as if he fully realized and relished her discomfiture he smiled — a mere pulling upward of his lips that could also have been a sneer. "You are obviously Miss Delight Adams, yes? And since this is America, where people are not as formal as they are in Europe, you may call me Riccardo — if I may be permitted to call you Delight? Such an unusual name — like a promise . . ."

"It . . . it was merely one of my mother's flights of fancy, I'm afraid!" Finding her voice at last, Sara strove for coolness while he watched her like a smiling predator who was only too sure of his prey. Well, she'd show him! And she'd ignore that last suggestively questioning statement! She must strive for her sister's air of cool impudence and face him down. Now she pouted slightly, putting her hand on his arm and feeling steel-corded muscles tense under her touch.

"Look, I'm sorry if I sounded rude just now, but a girl in this town learns to be cautious, if you know what I mean? It was nice of you to come pick me up . . . Riccardo. Can we start all over from there?"

A Duke, no less! Was he real? And Paul Drury had said "rich" — she had imagined that what was left of the Italian nobility were penniless, for the most part.

"We can start from anywhere you please, Delight." Another one of those double-edged remarks, Sara thought mutinously, feeling her temper rise. But she didn't protest when he gripped her elbow firmly and led her out to where his car was parked, guarded by an admiring teenager who accepted the unobtrusively passed bill Riccardo handed him without taking his eyes off the shiny Lamborghini.

"It was my pleasure, mister. That's some mean machine!"

"Yes — but hard to drive here in Los Angeles." Helping Sara in, his fingers brushed against her skin for an instant, and she was glad he could not feel the involuntary catch of her breath. "A machine like this is meant to be driven very fast, especially this one, for I have had the engine modified for racing."

"You ever raced her?"

"A few times. But not in this country. Not yet."

"Well — good luck!"

As they drove off Sara could not help murmuring, "A democratic Duke?"

Concentrating on the traffic, he did not look at her, although she could feel, rather than see his slight shrug. "We had something in common. The love of beautiful machinery and the taking of risks."

"Well, I'm glad you save that for the racing track. It's risky enough just driving around Los Angeles as it is — especially during rush hour!"

"It depends on the driver of course. Do you drive . . . Delight?" She thought he said her name almost reluctantly — perhaps it sounded too fancy and frivolous for his taste!

"Just a plain, ordinary Volkswagen, I'm afraid!" Sara said, shrugging. "I can't afford one of these — yet."

"Ah, but perhaps you hope to, someday?"

His voice was without inflection, but Sara could feel herself tense. She felt, for no real reason, as if he was playing some cat-and-mouse game with her. She forced herself to sound casual.

"Of course — doesn't everyone have dreams? But I think I'd settle for a Mercedes myself — a white SL convertible."

"And — if I may ask without appearing to pry — what of your other dreams? I am sure a beautiful young woman like yourself will have no difficulty in getting anything you desire."

"Well, I do try to think positively!" Sara affirmed lightly. Wishing he'd drop the subject, she added quickly, "Where are we going for dinner?"

This time she saw him glance briefly at her before he turned his attention back to the traffic.

"I am staying at L'Ermitage — you have heard of it? A European-style hotel, with an excellent restaurant that caters only to guests . . . and *their* guests, of course. Paul and Monique ought to be waiting for us in my suite by now, and after a drink we shall all go to dinner."

All Sara's suspicions surfaced again.

"We're going to . . . your hotel suite?"

She heard him sigh impatiently. "Miss Adams, I do not know what events have occurred to make you so . . . . shall we say wary? But I assure you I have no intention of luring you up to my suite in order to seduce you. Believe me, Paul and Monique Drury will be there — and if they are not, we can leave a message for them and go straight to the Café Russe, if that will make you feel . . . safer.''

Sara was glad he could not see the flush that made her whole face seem hot. He was an arrogant, impossible man, and she hated the way he kept making her appear ridiculous; ''putting her down'' as Delight would have said.

''I'm *quite* capable of looking after myself, thank you!'' she said frostily. ''And I'm sure, besides, that the average mass murderer or rapist does *not* drive his victims about in a Lamborghini!''

''Oh, but you are right to be cautious. I have heard that the famous Jack the Ripper was really none other than the heir to the throne of England!''

Sara gritted her teeth.

''What an interesting piece of gossip! But I'm sure none of *his* victims knew karate. I happen to have won my black belt.''

''That is indeed admirable. Perhaps we might practice together sometime? I also am a black belt. Fifth degree.''

So much for her bluff! ''Stay cool, Sara!''

''Thank you, but I'm really very busy most times, and my instructor —''

"Oh, but I am also a qualified instructor. And since Los Angeles seems to be quite a dangerous city for attractive young women on their own such as yourself, perhaps I could teach you a few useful little tricks to help you defend yourself against *other* karate experts?"

"I'd really rather not. I do it mostly for the exercise, anyway."

"I see. And what other kinds of exercise do you enjoy?" He had to have heard her furious gasp, but he carried on smoothly without so much as a look in her direction, "Every day through my window I see people jogging. Is that what you would call the 'in' thing these days?"

Remembering her role Sara said briefly: "I really don't like getting up early in the morning unless I'm working and have to. And jogging's far too strenuous for me."

They should have reached the hotel by now. Was he driving with deliberate slowness? Or taking her there the long way around so he could torment her with questions and sly double entendres?

"Jogging is also not the most glamorous form of exercise, I suppose. All that puffing and panting! But I would guess that you might enjoy dancing. Am I right? The disco, for instance?"

She almost slipped there. "I don't — that is, I just *adore* dancing, but I don't go too often. I can't afford late nights when I have to be up bright and early."

"You sound like a case of all work and no play! For shame, with a name like Delight."

She didn't choose to answer *that*, responding instead: "I'm glad you like my name. It *is* rather unusual, isn't it? Mona told me that she was quite high on champagne and orange juice when they asked her what she wanted to name me!"

"Mona?"

"My mother. Mona Charles. Not the sort of mother one calls mom or mother!"

"I see." For some reason his voice sounded grim; but at least he paused in the third degree, and with a small sigh of relief Sara caught sight of the hotel up ahead.

I'm almost sure I don't like him, Sara thought. But what a strangely complex man he was! All contrasts — one moment she could swear he was flirting with her as he dropped those suggestive comments, and the next he was quizzing her with what seemed to be a sneer underlying his voice. Why had he wanted to meet her? How could he have become a "fan" as Paul Drury had put it?

But then, with a strange wrench of feeling Sara realized that it wasn't *her* the Duca di Cavalieri had gone to such lengths to meet, but her sister. Delight, whose very name seemed to fascinate him. A name that held promise, hadn't he said soon after they had met?

"Well, here we are." Before one of the red-tunicked attendants had rushed forward to open her door he had leaned across her to unlock it himself. Sara felt the hardness of his arm against her breasts like a jolt of electricity, jarring her all the way to her ankles. She felt — even when the bright-faced young man had assisted her out and she stood there on the lighted sidewalk waiting for Riccardo to come around and lead her into the hotel — as if she had been naked and he had touched her with deliberation. She wanted to slap him, and she wanted to run — but she stood there, outwardly cool, until he put his hand on her elbow again, saying in his deep, rather grating voice: "Come."

And the only way her feet would take her was the way *he* was taking her, without a will of her own.

Chapter 6

Sara's first feeling of relief when she discovered that Paul Drury and his wife were waiting for them in the Duke's suite had soon dissolved into watchful caution. The Drurys would be no help at all, should she happen to need help. They were both obviously too impressed by the combination of a title and money! But at any rate they were *there,* and Sara was thankful when after the usual small talk Monique decided that she was ravenously hungry.

Monique Drury didn't look at all like a Monique, Sara thought irrationally. They had retired to the ladies room, and Monique — tall, skinny and slightly stoop-shouldered, was combing ineffectually through her straight, blunt-cut blonde hair.

"I really have to change hairdressers. Which one do *you* go to?"

Remembering what Delight had told her, Sara grinned. "A gay friend of mine does it

— in her spare time."

"Oh — really?"

In the mirror, Monique Drury's eyes looked startled. Childishly, Sara thought, Well, I don't care if I *do* shock her! She's so impossibly vulgar and pretentious! Making sure everyone knew from which side of the family the money had come.

It had been "Daddy used to say this" and "Daddy used to do that" all through the first part of what was turning out to be an interminable dinner; with Paul Drury sitting in grim silence and the Duke di Cavalieri leaning back in his chair with a smile of sarcastic appraisal on his saturnine face. Sara could almost *feel* him thinking: A typical American female! And it irked her so much that she had deliberately encouraged Monique to boast.

"I've got to use the loo." Shameless escape from Monique's narrowly questioning eyes. But what did she really care what Monique thought?

What Sara was trying not to think about was the Duca di Cavalieri and the mixture of emotions he had managed to evoke in her; very much in spite of herself. Telling herself she disliked him immensely did nothing to help. The fact remained that she was fascinated by him, like a bird by a snake; hardly able to force her eyes away from him. There was something feral and very primitive about him, barely veneered by the politeness that civilization demanded. And he was treating her like mesmerized prey he was already sure of; with offhand gallantry that was merely that and nothing else. Why had he wanted to meet her in the first place? Why had he pushed and maneuvered for this meeting with her, only to sit and observe her from across the table with those inscrutable black eyes?

The two women returned to their table in silence, and with formal politeness both men rose. Again Sara felt the brush of those strong, tanned fingers across her bared back, and could barely repress a shudder that mixed fear with apprehension.

"Would you like to go dancing after dinner? You have the figure of a good dancer and you walk lightly."

Sara forced her head back, her mouth tilting in a challenging smile. "Do you like disco? That's the only kind of dancing I enjoy. It's tremendous exercise, you know."

Monique gave an exaggerated shudder, her mouth puckering as if she'd tasted something acid. "I love to watch dancing. The ballet . . . Paul and I see every performance of the New York City Ballet, you know. Daddy was a patron."

Monique had her uses, after all! Sara let her smile become brilliant as she murmured challengingly, "I don't really care for *watching*. I like music with a beat that makes my body want to move."

What was she talking about? Actually, she loved ballet — adored the opera even more. But the man had wanted to meet Delight, and Delight he was going to get!

His eyes had narrowed slightly, the only reaction she was able to obtain.

"So you'd rather participate than watch? I was talking of dancing of course, Miss . . . Delight." From holding hers, his eyes moved casually away, as if her answer didn't really matter. "And how about the two of you? Paul . . . Monique . . . what do you say, shall we all go to a disco tonight? I leave it to you — or my delightful dinner partner — to name the place, since I am a comparative stranger here."

"I really don't feel up to a late night tonight, thank you all the same." Sara was remembering with panic that Delight was a really fabulous, uninhibited dancer, while *she* hadn't had enough practice to know if she could or not. And no doubt *he* was a fantastic dancer too — the light-footed way he moved and the way he held his body reminded her of a fencer or a fighter. He was a karate black belt, fifth degree, he'd said. No doubt he danced very well, too. Well, he wasn't going to show her up!

"You're the one who's always complaining about having to get up early in the morning. . . ." Paul and Monique were engaged in a low-voiced argument, ignoring her. Riccardo leaned close to her with a quiz-zical lift of one black eyebrow. "I have read everything about you in the press, but if I didn't know better I would think you were . . . afraid, for some reason. I do not bite, signorina, nor do I believe in . . . forcing a woman who is not willing."

Sara could feel the warmth of his body, far too close to hers. And the warmth of the tell-tale blood that rushed into her face. To hide it, she bent her head, pretending to rummage in her purse as she said lightly: "Oh, good! Then I can trust you to take me home without the usual hassle, can't I?" Looking up at last she met his angry eyes with what she hoped was an air of insouciance. "It's not that I haven't enjoyed the dinner, but I *am* a working girl, and six o'clock comes awfully early!"

"You are very good at evasions, are you not? For all that on the surface you appear to be a typical example of an extremely liberated young American woman, I think you are a little bit afraid of a man who does not fit into the mold you are used to."

"Aren't you flattering yourself, Duke?"

Her deliberate vulgarity was rewarded by the tightening of his jaw muscles as his eyes flicked over her like whips.

She would not — could not back down now, but Sara was miserably conscious that Paul and Monique had declared a mutual truce while they watched and listened with barely concealed curiosity.

"Perhaps I am — but I do not think so. From the moment we met, I have sensed your hostility — or is it a game you play? Is this attitude of yours meant to lead a man on?"

"Ohh!" Sara sucked in her breath, fingers tightening over the napkin in her lap. She would have dearly loved to have thrown something at him, if she wasn't being stared at.

"Have I made you angry? Is this possible?" The note of false concern in his voice taunted her before he leaned back in his chair to drawl sarcastically, "I am sorry if my plain speaking offends you, Signorina Delight. But I am long past the stage of playing silly games. There is no reason why there should not be frankness between a man and a woman, without either one being diminished in some way. But perhaps you do not agree?"

"I think . . . I think . . . ." From the corner of her eye Sara became aware of Monique Drury's fascinated, watchful gaze, and sanity came back to her along with the resolve that she was not going to let this monster of a man get the best of her. Deep breathing, Sara! her other voice admonished her, and she in her turn paused to take a sip of wine, touch her lips lightly with her napkin before she leaned back, crossing slim legs.

She was rewarded by a flicker of those

hawklike eyes; bolstering the smile she awarded him.

"But of course I agree with you. Game-playing. Such a silly waste of time. True. And I don't, usually — play games or waste time, that is. Only — my mother *did* din into me that I should be *polite,* especially to my elders. But we're not playing charades or 'Who's Afraid of Virginia Woolf' are we? So I'm getting tired of all the innuendos and your rudeness, Signor Duca!"

His face had become impassive, like a mask carved from mahogany, but his eyes remained alive; like coals pinning her in place when she had planned to push her chair back and leave.

He said stiffly, as if the words had been forced out of him: "To be rude was not my intention, signorina. But if I seemed so I accept your rebuke. As . . . one of your *elders,* and a foreigner at that, I did not realize that you misunderstood me and the words I used."

"Oh, but this is all so silly!" Monique interrupted suddenly, her voice querulous. "Honestly, Paul, I can't think why *you* haven't said something yet. What on earth are we all getting so uptight about? I mean, we're all here because Riccardo wanted to meet Delight, and now he has and they keep saying these *pointed* things to each other. Does that mean you two like each other or not? It really doesn't matter to me, of course, but it *is* getting late, and the waiter keeps *hovering* around, far too nervous to beard us with the check. And I'd also like to know who's going home with whom. Paul and I live in Malibu and it's a long drive out there."

"Shut up, Monique!" Paul said without heat, but his eyes were questioning as they went from one stony face to another. He added with forced humor: "Now that you two have finally met — and clashed — what is it to be? I have a feeling they'd like to close this place up, but of course you can always come out to *our* place (this last with a quelling look at Monique who had opened her mouth and closed it sulkily) for bed and breakfast!"

At this point the last thing Sara wanted was more Monique — or more Paul for that matter. And she didn't care if they cut her out of the picture or not, why should she? The thought made her brave.

"I can get a taxi . . ." she said at about the same time her dinner partner uttered between clenched jaws:

"*I* will settle the check with the waiter and *I* will take the signorina Delight home, since I brought her here." He didn't quite snap his fingers, but a gesture brought the waiter almost running to his side.

While he signed the check, Sara sat stiffly on the edge of her chair, debating whether she should just get up and march out — or whether that would seem too much like a retreat to *him*. Above all she didn't want him to think she was afraid of him — what a ridiculous thought!

Afterward Sara couldn't quite remember how they all found themselves outside the hotel again. That second bottle of Puligny-Montrachet with dinner perhaps? She took several breaths of the warm night air, and the next thing she knew Paul and Monique Drury had disappeared and she was being helped into the Lamborghini once more.

She leaned her head back against the soft upholstery, closing her eyes for an instant. No more fencing, she wished silently. Let him be quiet, or let him . . .

Her mind jerked sharply back from her own half-finished thought, and she straightened up abruptly, not willing to have him recognize any signs of weakness in her. No doubt he was used to women who would swoon all over him, encouraging him to think himself irresistible. There were some women who actually *liked* arrogant, forceful men, but *she* wasn't one of them!

Sara suddenly became aware that he had said something, addressed some question to her. Now he repeated it in an exaggeratedly patient voice.

"I was asking you, signorina, whether you still wanted to visit a discotheque. . . . But of course it's obvious that you are too sleepy

— or too bored!"

"Bored? Of *course* I haven't been bored at all! Honestly, it's been *such* a fun evening, and I just love Paul and Monique, but you must understand, signor (is that correct?) that I didn't get too much sleep last night, and I had to report to the studio by six this morning. Normally I'm quite a party girl, but tonight . . ."

The way the car took off, Sara thought her neck might snap as she was slammed backward in the seat. She heard herself gasp, and almost immediately his arm was banded across her body, robbing her of breath.

She heard him swear under his breath before he said in comparatively civilized tones: "I am sorry. Normally I am a very fast driver, and when I am here I find myself forgetting that there are speed limits. You are all right?"

"You don't have to . . . hold me! I'm fine. . . . I just wasn't expecting . . ."

"No?" The words sounded grated out between his teeth. "I wonder what it is that you were expecting from this evening, party girl? You love to dance at discos, but when I ask you, you are too tired — from last night, I am correct? And when I try to prevent your being hurt you object to my arm against your body. What are you afraid of? Yourself? Or the fact that you have met a man who is a man and not one of your easily manipulated puppets?"

70

"You're really conceited, aren't you?"
Sara's voice was breathless from anger.
"Honestly — you belong in the Dark Ages!
I accept a dinner invitation, and you act as if
that means I'm your property for the evening!
Well, I'm not. *Capisce?* I belong to me, and
nobody else; and I *pick* my . . . my lovers!
And if you don't like hearing that, you can
drop me right off here and I'll find my way
back home."

"How? Hitchhiking? That would be an invitation to rape — unless, like some women,
that is your secret fantasy."

Sara gasped again. "You . . . you're really
sick, you know that? I'm sure you read both
Playboy and *Penthouse* — probably *Hustler*
in your spare time. You certainly have a lot
to learn about women — women, that is, who
aren't after money, or whatever it is you
promise them. I'm an actress, not a call girl,
Signor Duca! Don't look to me for having
your fantasies fulfilled!"

"What a temper! Your accent becomes very
English when you get angry, did you know
that? Is that your mother's influence?" He
was laughing at her!

Almost blind with rage, Sara reached for
the door handle, but with the speed of a
striking puma he reached across her, trapping
her fingers painfully.

"No, no! That would be stupid! And you
do not seem like the suicidal type. Sit quietly,

for I do not believe in rape, only seduction. You will be delivered to your door quite safely, believe me."

Just when she thought her fingers might break under the pressure of his, he released them — almost contemptuously.

"Please lean back and try to relax. It will not be more than a few more minutes. Quite frankly, melodramatic scenes do not appeal to me."

Tears of sheer rage filled Sara's eyes and she was glad of the darkness that prevented him from noticing. Why, oh why, did she always bawl when she was furious? But she wasn't going to — no, she'd rather die under torture than give him the satisfaction of knowing how he affected her.

Speechless now and stiff as a board, she leaned back in her seat; trying to pretend to herself that he did not exist. Deep breathing, Sara! she told herself. It was what she did before a tennis match, when she knew she was up against a formidable opponent, and it helped now.

From the corner of her eye Sara caught his sideways glance at her, while she stubbornly continued her silent disregard of his presence. He was not only insufferably arrogant, this Duca di Cavalieri, but in spite of his title and his wealth he was also the rudest and most obnoxious man it had ever been her bad fortune to meet! Why had he been so anxious to meet her when he so obviously thought her cheap and easy? And now that she had let him know she *wasn't,* would he give up?

"Are you warm enough?" he said abruptly, cutting into her thoughts as if he had been able to read them; and Sara realized that she had given an involuntary shudder as a slight *frisson* of apprehension had coursed down her spine.

"I'm quite comfortable, thank you," she said stiffly, wishing that he would hurry. Surely they were taking an unconscionable time to get back to her apartment?

"Good." He pushed a couple of buttons and soft music from superb speakers filled the silence between them. Beethoven's *Pastorale,* with every note as clear as a bell. Spellbinding music, mood music. But dangerous in conjunction with the dark, dangerous masculinity of this man beside her. Sara shifted uncomfortably on the heels of that thought, and catching her slight movement he said rather sardonically: "This music does not appeal to you? Would you care to hear something else?"

Her lips parting to contradict him, Sara remembered again that she was supposed to be Delight, and she forced an indifferent shrug.

"It doesn't matter. We're almost there, aren't we?"

He was persistent, his voice grating against

her ears. "Tell me, Delight, what kind of music do you like?"

This time she forced herself to look at him, catching the arrogant planes of his face and the slight twist of his lips in the light from a passing car.

"Well — anything with a beat to it. You know, some jazz."

"I see. And your other likes and dislikes?"

She was beginning to feel trapped. Why was he practically interrogating her suddenly?

"Why would you want to know? I mean it's been quite obvious from the beginning of the evening that you don't exactly approve of me, hasn't it? Sorry if I've been a disappointment — but a blind date is a blind date, even in Hollywood!'

He stopped the car so abruptly that Sara gave a little cry as she was flung forward, only to be held back by the steely strength of his arm. When she would have pushed it away he continued to hold her pinned in place — a terrifying sensation, especially when his dark, angry face was far too close to hers.

"Tell me then, Signorina Delight, why you go out on these . . . blind dates, as you call them? You are an attractive young woman, but you don't have a husband or a lover. Why? Is it because you prefer variety?"

Fighting back panic and the impulse to tear at him with her nails until he set her free, Sara forced herself to be still, staring back at him defiantly.

"You have no right to question me — or to expect answers! And you are not only *rude,* you . . . you're the most . . ."

"Ah — but whatever you say and whatever I am, there is still an attraction between us, is there not?" He gave a short laugh that sent ripples of fear along Sara's nerves.

"You're crazy! I don't know what kind of game you think you're playing with me, but I'm not playing along, do you understand? Why, I . . . I don't even *like* you, do you understand that you . . . you arrogant bas—"

"Swearing does not become a woman," he interrupted her; and now, to her horror, he had turned his body so that she was well and truly trapped; his fingers closed over one bare shoulder, forcing a gasp of sheer terror from her before he said slowly and with deceptive softness: "And what has liking got to do with *this?*"

This was nothing like the kiss that Garon Hunt had given her. The kiss of this dark stranger did not give, it took — and took — and took. Sara could feel her mind spinning — swirling spirals that took her away from herself while her body seemed to melt and was incapable of resistance.

Fingers warmly caressed the back of her neck and moved alongside her face to tilt it up to his. And all the while he held her mouth captive; first harshly ravaging, like a barbarian conqueror, forcing her lips to part for him; and then, as if he had sensed her surrender he took time to be almost tender, kissing the corner of her trembling mouth, going back to cover her lips possessively with his.

It was only when his hands moved down to touch her breasts — seeming to burn through the thin silk of her dress — that Sara recovered some semblance of sanity.

She felt as if she had been drugged, as if even her voice didn't belong to herself any longer.

"No — don't! Please don't!"

"Delight . . . *cara*. You see how much we want each other? Let's go upstairs quickly — you're right, this is too public a place for making love."

His words shocked her back to reality; her eyes, half closed and unfocused blinked into sharp awareness that they were parked in front of her apartment house. And that he had called her "Delight"!

"*Cara* . . . come."

She was shaking all over — she had dropped her purse and had to grope for it, thankful that that small action hid her turmoil from him.

"No! And please don't . . . touch me again." She had to keep talking, to keep him at bay, and her words stumbled and jostled against one another while she fought for control. "So you proved whatever it was you wanted to prove — that . . . there's a certain physical chemistry between us. But honestly — one kiss and you expect me to take you to bed? I'm just not . . . that free and easy. And I don't go for one-night stands."

She didn't know, not knowing him, what she could expect. Rage? Bitter, caustic words? She didn't, at this point, really care — needing only to get away from him and his over-powering closeness. Her lips still burned from the force of his kisses and her nipples felt hard and swollen from the caress of his fingers.

While Sara held her breath with terrified anticipation she tried to read some expression on his shadowed face. Why didn't he *say* something?

Surprisingly — annoyingly — his voice sounded quite calm; politely regretful, nothing else. "That's so? Well — then I'm sorry. Although I must admit that now . . . there is still the anticipation of what might yet be between us — yes?"

Without giving her a chance to respond he had already opened the door on his side and was walking around to let her out with long, impatient strides that made Sara feel, with a sudden jab of irritation, that his try at seduction had been merely perfunctory and now he was bored and anxious to be rid of her.

"Good night."

He saw her into the lobby and as far as the

elevators. She imagined that his eyes dwelt, for an instant, on her mouth, but the next instant they were hooded and unreadable.

"Good night!" she said brightly. "Thank you for dinner."

"You made it a very interesting evening."

Sara was left alone to ponder on those words when the elevator doors slid shut. Riccardo had already turned away.

Chapter 7

By the time Sara was able to fall asleep she had noticed the almost imperceptible lightening of the night sky that always presaged dawn. She had done everything she could think of to compose herself for sleep — made herself a cup of steaming hot tea, creamed and massaged her face, brushed her teeth, brushed her hair. She had even tried reading a couple of scripts that had arrived for Delight with Lew Weisman's office address on them. The trouble was that whenever she tried to visualize herself as the female lead, the leading man in her mind movie seemed to look too much like the Duca di Cavalieri.

How dare he invade even the privacy of her imagination? Squeezing her eyes shut Sara began to think of all the things she should have said, should have done to put him in his place. Once and for all . . .

When did she slide into sleep and when did dreaming take the place of conscious thought?

He had kissed her — she had slapped his face with all the scorn and hate she could muster; was running away from him with the sound of her heels echoing hollowly on the stairs. Why on earth hadn't she thought to take the elevator? She was getting tired, slowing down to almost a crawl when she heard him behind her. No — no! There was something relentless about the way he was pursuing her like a wolf loping after a wounded deer.

Sara wanted to scream, but there was no breath left in her body. Helplessly, numbly, she lay sprawled across the steps with her fingers clinging to the railing.

"Did you think you would escape from me so easily?"

She managed a last, despairing cry as he swooped down on her, lifting her easily in his arms as he bounded up the stairs, kicking open her door far too easily — striding in to fling her down across the bed.

"No! Oh, please! What do you want with me anyway?"

"Little fool! What do you think?" His meaning was unmistakable — and when she would have tried to evade him, to beat at him, she was trapped by the covers that held her like ropes; by the weight of his body and the force of his kisses that drained everything from her. . . .

"No!"

Drenched with sweat Sara bolted upright in

80

bed — the sound of her own voice and the malevolent buzzing of the electric alarm in her ears. Her heart was pounding, her head ached. And she had kicked the bedcovers off so that they were all tangled about her legs, imprisoning her.

Had she really been dreaming? *Had* she? There was no one else in the room. She was alone and the small night lamp was still on, the script she had been reading had fallen open on the rug beside the bed, along with one of her pillows.

"Oh, *damn!*" Sara said aloud, rubbing childishly at her eyes. How many hours of sleep had she had — two, three? And then to have a nightmare like the one she'd had . . . her body still felt strangely weak from it.

Face flushing, Sara forced herself to briskness. Enough of that! She wasn't going to waste any more thought on either her ugly nightmare or its cause! And she had — glancing at her clock — barely an hour and a half in which to put herself together for the studio.

Lew wasn't there this time, but Sara found her way to Makeup, her sister's identity firmly donned to mask her own weakness.

"You probably won't be needed today — Garon's doing some of his scenes with Lockwood." Mike, the slim young makeup man clucked disapprovingly at the dark smudges under Sara's eyes. "You certainly do look like hell this morning, darling! *Late* morning? I hope it was worth it!"

He started patting white stuff under her eyes, and Sara managed what she hoped was an insouciant shrug.

"Just a dream!"

"Lucky guy! Hi, everyone — Mike, how about some hot coffee before we get started?"

Too late, Sara saw Garon Hunt himself come up behind her in the mirror. His eyes grinned into her startled clown-face, grin widening when her cheeks began to burn with spots of color.

Sara longed to cover her face like an embarrassed child as he lowered himself onto the stool beside her.

"Hi!"

"Hello." Her response was diffident.

Garon Hunt! And he had to see her looking like *this* — a mess! If she had dared, Sara would have grimaced nastily at her own reflection.

"Heyyy . . . ! Can't you think of anything more to say than just 'hello'?"

Garon's voice was teasing; he put a finger under Sara's elevated chin and turned it gently toward him. Sara's eyes darted about the narrow, brightly lit room with the beginnings of apprehension, and found that they were alone. She and Garon Hunt. Quite alone!

What would Delight have done? The

thought rescued her.

"Well . . . I could say 'good morning, Garon Hunt'. . . ."

"Good morning, Delight Adams." He was smiling his famous, slightly crooked smile at *her!* "What comes after that?"

Her mind raced desperately: I hope he doesn't try to kiss me! At this angle, if I turned I'd fall off this stool! And so would he, probably.

Sara's smile had a desperate brilliance to it that came across as being provocative.

"Isn't it *your* turn now, Garon?"

"How about dinner tonight?"

Unprepared (even Delight would have been taken aback surely?) Sara's voice deserted her — she could only stare at Garon, wondering if she had heard right.

She had. Obviously taking her silence for acquiescence Garon squeezed her nerveless hand and gave it a light kiss.

"Look — before Mike comes back in here — Sally's going off early this afternoon and we'll probably stop shooting around four. You start walking toward the gate at five sharp and I'll be coming out of my bungalow at the same time, right? I'll offer you a ride." He smiled at her again, more deeply this time, with those bright blue eyes almost mesmerizing her. "I'm going to be looking forward to this evening, baby. And to learning about you."

"Well!" Mike said on an expelled breath when Garon Hunt had walked out. "And what was *that* all about — or can't you tell?" He had a pointed, pixy beard that positively quivered with curiosity.

"What *are* you talking about?" Sara said evasively as she leaned forward pretending to admire her makeup.

"As if you didn't know! Think *I* don't know that when he comes in early and asks someone to go get coffee, that that someone isn't supposed to come back in for at least five minutes? Ha! I've been around long enough!"

"Well . . ." Sara conceded reluctantly, turning back to face his indignant expression.

"He asked you out, didn't he? That'll mean another late night, I guess. Come in extra early and I'll do an extra-special job on you — while you tell me all the details!"

"I'm sure you already *know* all the details!" Sara muttered equivocally as she left.

Garon Hunt! Sara's mind was in such a whirl that she couldn't be bothered by Mike and his sly insinuations. Garon had asked her out, was going to pick her up precisely at five this afternoon. . . .

Of course I'm going! Sara answered her own question. She felt both scared and elated. Delight would *never* turn down Garon Hunt!

The long, slow morning in which she was called upon to do nothing gave Sara time enough in which to think, and even to doze off as it became hotter and hotter on the huge sound stage.

She had been lying on the small couch that took up most of the space in the "dressing room" she shared with two others. It felt good to feel herself float off into nothingness. . . .

With annoyance, Sara at first tried to pull away from the rough hand on her shoulder. And then she remembered that she was supposed to be on call and sat up with a dismayed murmur.

"Well, I see that at least you are alive. I am sorry if I was rough and startled you, signorina, but I knocked first, and came in when you did not answer." Of course he wasn't sorry at all! Sara thought inconsequentially as she heard that harsh, rather grating voice and met obsidian eyes. Catching her look he continued in a rather mocking tone, "You looked pale enough to be actually dead! Did you not sleep well last night?"

It was he. It was actually *he*, the *bête noire* of her nightmares! Sara pushed hair back from her eyes, blinking them to glare at him.

"What are you doing here? This is supposed to be a closed set!"

"Ah, but you see I happen to *own* a part of this picture. So I am a privileged person — I'm afraid." He added the last softly, like a challenge, his hard eyes flickering over her rather disheveled state.

"*Not* privileged enough to be able to walk

in here without knocking!" Sara responded heatedly, choosing to forget what he had told her earlier. "This is *my* dressing room, and . . ."

"Of course I knew it was your dressing room!" he said smoothly, one black eyebrow tilting with mocking amusement at her sputtering fury. "Why else would I be here, after all? I thought I would take you to lunch, since everyone else has gone to the cafeteria. Or are you fasting as a form of penance for some sin?"

"*Sin?* Why . . . now just you listen to me . . . !"

"It is too bad that American schools do not teach that sentences should never be allowed to trail away into nothing! If you begin to say something, then you should finish what you have begun, yes? But no matter — there is still time for lunch if you hurry. Come."

He had uttered that curt command to her before, taking it for granted that she would follow her leader. But *this* time . . .

"No!" Sara said loudly, hoping *she* had sounded curt and positive enough. He ought to understand that one word, surely!

But no — he already had hold of her wrist, pulling her with him, seemingly without any effort at all. Her wrist felt paralyzed and her feet seemed to move of their own volition. Sara could have cried with rage and frustration. Why had he come back to torment her, the dark demon of her dream? Why wasn't she fighting with more determination his arrogance, his calm presumptions?

"It is very obvious that you are the kind of woman who subconsciously desires having her mind made up for her. I am sure you did not take the time for breakfast this morning, and you do not look as if you can afford to miss another meal!" His black eyes raked over her slim body with scathing impatience, as if she had been a stupid child who needed to be reprimanded.

"It . . . it's really none of your business if I miss a meal or not!"

Sara's words came between gasps. If he hadn't been dragging her along quite so fast she would really have enjoyed giving him a piece of her mind! Bully! Her mind hesitated over the word before she thought it defiantly. Bastard!

He chose to ignore her feeble rebellion, hurrying her along with only perfunctory words of caution before she (inevitably) tripped over trailing wires, having to be recovered by him with the same careless ease that he might retrieve a long pass in football.

"Here we are." His voice sounded brisk and businesslike. The black-lettered sign over the door read: Paul Drury.

Not another meal with Paul and Monique! Unable to speak by now, Sara shook her head vigorously, hanging back against his grip in a last, rebellious spurt of energy.

This time it took his arm around her waist to take her inside. He was frowning at her. "You are acting very strangely, Delight. Have you been drinking — or is it those pills that everyone here seems to take?"

She wouldn't deign to answer his sneering question even if she could! Sara turned her shoulder on him after he had released her; leaving her to sink down ungraciously into a chair.

"Paul is kind enough to let me use his office when I need it. Unfortunately, he will not be here this afternoon. But the lunch is all ready as I ordered it, and I am sure you will find it a little better than your cafeteria food!"

A chilled glass of white wine appeared before her; tiny globules of water misting its crystal surface. The hand that set it down was strong and tanned — a few black, curling hairs growing around the wrist and forearm. He wore a strange signet ring of gold with a raised, encrusted seal in diamonds.

Pulling her eyes away hastily, Sara gulped in a deep breath of air.

"You would not be out of breath, Signorina Delight, if you had enough fresh air and exercise of the right kind — and fewer late nights." His deep voice was without inflection, but his words were enough to goad Sara into lifting her chin and meeting his taunting eyes head-on.

"Oh? And what right do you have to offer me advice? Or to *drag* me down here without offering me a choice. . . ."

"You knew very well when we parted last night that I would come for you today — did you not? Come, Delight, let us not carry our little mating dance to extremes! We have each made our moves and now it is *your* turn to come forward a little, hmm?"

He put his long fingers on the nape of her neck, sliding them up into her curls to keep her head from turning away from his frowning face.

Sara's eyes widened, feeling his eyes burn into her; dark coals, as they had in her dream last night. She would never, never understand what held her there silent and unmoving. Through her body crept the same languorous weakness she had felt on waking this morning. Why couldn't she take her eyes away from his face with its harsh, almost Arabic planes to it? There was something cruel and merciless about his face that made her want to shiver with helpless fascination. *Could* he be cruel? Why was he pursuing her with the softly lethal efficiency of a hunting leopard? *What did he want with her?*

Sara began to shake her head as a shiver of pure terror trickled down her spine, and his fingers tightened slightly — but enough to hurt when she tried to move her head again.

"Delight . . ." She saw how his eyes dwelt

on her mouth and shivered again while his voice turned slightly husky. "You were named for your mouth that promises just that. Why do we waste time with the games we play?"

He bent over and let his lips brush against hers with deceptive softness while all the while she could feel what was almost the vibration of the leashed tension of passion inside him.

It frightened her enough to push her hands against his shoulders with a strength born of desperation.

"Stop it! Stop it at once! I'm not playing games at all! And I . . . I like to be *asked* first, if you please!" Belatedly remembering that she was supposed to be Delight, and her sister would definitely have sworn under like circumstances, Sara added strongly, "And I'd thank you to get the hell away from me — and stay away!"

He had released her, but the cowardly, cowering side of Sara had noticed that he had merely stepped back to stand with his back against the door. Strangely enough, except for his threatening stance he did not appear to be perturbed by her rude rejection — merely quizzical. "Why do you say things you do not mean?"

She shrank back as if she expected him to touch her again, but he merely crossed his hands over his chest, continuing to watch her in a somewhat detached sort of way.

"And why are you afraid to answer me?"

His nostrils flared slightly in a way that was somehow menacing, before he added in a softer tone, "I think you feel the same thing that I do, but because you are a *liberated* American woman you fight against your own basic instincts. I had expected a more open, more courageous young woman, Signorina Delight Adams! A woman more like your mother who, with all her faults, is at least a real woman!"

If his sarcastic words had been meant to sting like whips they stung hard enough to rouse Sara's temper — which was almost never aroused.

She erupted off the chair to take a stand right before him, hands planted on her hips. On the mirrored wall of Paul Drury's office Sara caught a glimpse of herself slim to the point of skinniness, but a good figure for jeans. Hers were tight and faded, with a short-sleeved red silk shirt (only three buttons to *this* one!) tucked in. Pale in the face except for the blusher that exaggerated the hollows beneath her cheekbones. Eyes made bigger by makeup. With her hair tied back she looked more like an adolescent boy than a . . . hadn't he said "real woman"?

Chapter 8

Afterward Sara was to wonder what might have happened if he hadn't interrupted her raging tirade — couched in language she was ashamed of and Delight would have no doubt applauded. "Now just you *listen* for a change, you conceited, arrogant, despicable . . . ."

He began by hearing her out with his arms still crossed — an unsufferably bored and tolerant expression on his face. But by the time Sara had told him a few Home Truths (oh, Nancy Staggs would have been proud of her!) his expression had changed to one of towering rage. He reminded her very much of a wild animal ready to pounce in order to rend and tear at its prey. But Sara was too far gone to care any longer. She heard her voice become almost strident and saw how his eyes looked, narrowed almost to slits as he squinted them dangerously at her. Thin white lines of tension had appeared on either side of that harshly cruel mouth of his, and even his nostrils seemed pinched with fury.

When she paused for breath he said with steely softness: "Is that all you have against me for the moment?" prodding Sara into answering rage.

"No, it isn't, as a matter of fact!" She drained off a glass of wine to moisten her throat. "As a matter of fact . . . ."

This time he interrupted her, his fingers sinking painfully into the softness of her skin through the thin red shirt.

"As a matter of fact, you are drunk, and incapable of making sense! Did you not notice that I opened the second bottle of wine during your tirade? Perhaps you did not want to — you seem overly fond of wine, and unable to handle the quantities you choose to swallow! Stop it, now!" He shook her roughly, with enough real force to frighten her. "Stop behaving like a cheap, abusive bitch I might have picked up off the tinsel streets of Hollywood!"

Sara was horrified — both at herself (had she *really* drunk all that wine?) and the storm of the rage she had provoked in him. All the same, she couldn't seem to still her runaway tongue.

"I should call Security and have you thrown off the set for . . . for molesting me! You drag me here by force, insulting me all the way, and then you . . . oh!"

He shook her again until she thought her

neck would break.

"Will you be quiet? Molest you indeed — if it's rape I have in mind I don't go to all this trouble. If that was what I desired I would have had you on the floor of that stark little lobby the first time I ever set eyes on you! Do you understand that? Do you understand seduction or do you prefer — a more direct approach?"

"Stop. . . ." Her voice came out slightly above a whisper that he crushed ruthlessly into silence.

"Stop —" He echoed her mockingly with his lips hovering over hers predatorily. "There is only one way to stop your mouth, isn't there? And we both know it. . . ."

To the remembered cruelty of his bruising kisses there was added the humiliation of having her body held forcibly against the hard, hurting length of his, feeling . . . feeling everything he meant her to feel, no doubt! The primitive terror, the wonder and the threat of the growing thrust and hardness pressing against the inside of her thigh as she stood closely pressed against him with his arms holding her at the waist and shoulder like iron bands.

There were some moments of pure, unreasoning terror when Sara felt as if she was being consumed, burned up by the flame of his passion and his fury. She beat against his chest and shoulders ineffectually, trying to reach his skin through his immaculately tailored sports jacket. And then, after the terror came a strange kind of calm — almost of resignation or surrender.

Give in! *Delight* would have! Diabolical, cynical whisper from the dark corners of her mind. What would it feel like to hold a man against her, pulling his arrogant head down to hers? How would his hair feel under her fingers?

With a sigh, Sara let her arms, now strangely weak like the rest of her — will and all — slide upward to lock about his neck. After all, the way he kissed her robbed her of all reason . . . she didn't *want* to reason, only to feel what she was feeling now. Heat and cold — fire and ice and fire again as now her untried body molded itself against his of its own volition.

Ohh . . . Sara! Maybe this is going to be *it!* Even the familiar voice in her mind sounded ecstatic and not at all *sensible*.

And what might have happened if the door had not opened? There was a comfortable sofa against one wall of the large, comfortable-looking office that might have been a living room. No desk — Paul Drury didn't believe in them.

Sara found herself filled with annoyingly contradictory emotions when she tried, later, to analyze what had happened and how.

"My goodness! Oh, I *am* sorry! But I

95

thought Paul would be expecting me and there was no one out here. . . ."

The sharp-featured redhead who stood there gaping at them through gold-rimmed spectacles had an all-too-familiar face, even to Sara, who seldom watched television. Brenda Rowan — the home screen's answer to Louella Parsons and Hedda Hopper in their heyday. She had her own television show and a syndicated column; and here she stood in person, making no move to leave, while her round, brandy-colored eyes kept darting between them.

The Duke was more composed than Sara ever possibly could have been. He kept a firm grasp on her arm, which was probably all that kept her standing there to face Brenda Rowan's piercingly curious eyes. Sara could, with a sinking feeling of despair, see those eyes going beyond her to the couch — cutting to the table where an elegant lunch was laid out, uneaten — cutting to the *second* open bottle of wine; empty glasses. Oh, *God,* what now?

"Are you a friend of Paul's? And this is Delight Adams, of course. . . ." Sara found herself skimmed over cursorily as Brenda's eyes fastened on Riccardo's saturnine face. "Don't I know you from somewhere?"

"Perhaps!" He was all smooth politeness as he maneuvered Sara toward the door he had kept her from earlier. "But I am certainly not my friend Paul Drury. Would you care to wait for him? I was about to take Miss Adams back to the set."

Brenda Rowan smiled suddenly, her mouth surprisingly wide in a pinched-looking face. "Oh — of course! And now I *do* recognize you. Is this a new romance? Is it a secret?"

"It . . . ." Sara started to say when *he* cut her off without seeming to, his manner perfectly charming as he smiled at Brenda.

"It's a secret, of course. Both Delight and I need time — to sort out our feelings."

That got them past good old Brenda, and Sara forced herself to keep silent until they were out of earshot.

"What did you mean by that . . . that . . . !"

He was back to cool sarcasm.

"You are not going to call what I told that nasty little woman a lie? Of course we are sorting our . . . feelings out. And you, especially, *carissima,* should not let yourself be caught out too often in lies yourself, or I might not believe anything you tell me!"

"I don't care if you do or not! And now will you please let me *go?*" Sara's voice shook, and she was beyond caring whether he noticed or not.

"A few minutes ago you were clinging to me! Why do you fight against yourself?"

Goaded beyond endurance, Sara looked for words that would stop him — keep him away from her. Delight. *She was supposed to be Delight;* she mustn't forget that.

The words tumbled out as she twisted out of his grasp, staring him in the eye. "I . . . I happen to be in love with someone — although perhaps you're not capable of understanding what that means. I'm engaged to the man I love, and I don't need any substitute lover!"

"Are you sure of that? You missed your lunch — so why don't we talk about it over dinner? You seem to be a very confused young woman!"

"I won't have dinner with you — you must be insane! I'm having dinner with someone else tonight."

"Oh? With whom?"

He was insufferable! "It's none of your . . ." Sara had begun when she saw Garon Hunt, saying good-bye to his wife. Sara watched fascinated in spite of herself. Were they friends or lovers? Or both, as rumor had it? He bent his head to give Sally a light kiss on the tip of her nose — patted her on the bottom as she went through the door with a laughing comment over her shoulder.

"With *him?*" Riccardo's voice was disbelieving.

Sara flushed against her will, hoping he hadn't noticed as she said with distant stiffness: "I really can't see how it could possibly concern you. And now if you *don't* mind . . ."

When he stood back without another word to let her pass, Sara didn't dare look back — far too relieved at having been set free to question his sudden acceptance. She didn't care *what* he thought! And after all, Garon had only asked her out to *dinner* — it probably didn't mean anything except gratitude toward Mona for giving him his first big break when she picked him to co-star with her in *Bianca*.

For once, Sara was glad to see that the other two occupants of "her" dressing room were there when she returned. Ignoring their curious, rather sullen looks she curled up in the one available chair and closed her eyes, willing herself not to think. At least, not until it was five o'clock and she had a decision to make.

Sara was drifting in the nebulous never-never land between sleeping and waking when she was made aware that they had all been dismissed for the day.

"See you tomorrow?" Voices calling to each other, lights being dimmed. She couldn't possibly *stay* here in hiding!

She had been half-afraid, but when she emerged, still wearing her makeup for protection, the Duca di Cavalieri was nowhere to be seen. Thank God! Sara sighed. Maybe now that he thought she was taken he would leave her alone. Italian men and their pride!

Consciously pushing the thought out of her mind, Sara hurried toward the parking lot where the limousines waited. She had no idea what time it was, but Garon would surely have left by now! She had deliberately dragged her feet, guiltily remembering how nice Sally had been to her. She must have been crazy, letting Garon think that she . . .

"Hi. Need a ride?" He must have waited, unless he was running late. Sara could feel the eyes of the security guard at the gate and some of the other members of the crew lingering on her curiously. No doubt they all knew exactly what was going on and that this casual-seeming meeting had been contrived.

"Well . . ." Sara hesitated. "I don't know if the limousine . . ."

Garon's blue eyes pinned her in place. He leaned sideways to unlock the door of his latest pet Maserati, this one a convertible done in shades of gold and black.

"Get in." His voice didn't leave her a choice, and feeling like a tiny leaf bobbing on the crest of a tidal wave, Sara obeyed meekly, without any further argument. This was Garon Hunt. She must remind herself of that. She had had a lot of secret fantasies about this same man less than two years ago, when she would save every magazine article, every newspaper clipping or picture that had anything to do with him. This was her dream man . . . and one of the most secret of her fantasies had been that *he* would be the one to take her virginity, the one man *she* chose to set her free into the world of sophisticated, liberated women. And as long as the choice was hers she didn't have to feel like the prey of some stalking predator!

"Close the door, huh?" Garon's voice was perfunctory; he was acting in front of all those people as if this had been a casual impulse and he was just being kind. And maybe he *was* — why should she flatter herself?

All over again, Sara was jolted back to the reality of her position. She *wasn't* herself. She was her bright, volatile, outgoing sister who didn't let *anything* faze her. And she didn't really look enough like Delight to pass, unless she acted enough like Delight so that no one who knew her would bother to look further than her laughingly flippant and bold manner. She had almost slipped with Riccardo, Duca di Cavalieri. She mustn't with Garon!

Garon Hunt drove one-handed with careless competence once they had left the studio gates. His other hand he had placed firmly over Sara's hand, pressing it down against her thigh occasionally as if to remind her that he was aware of her.

Lean back — relax! Isn't this what you've fantasized about for years? Sara *did* lean back, trying to act as if she was quite relaxed and in control of herself. Garon drove very fast, she noticed, trying not to. Maybe she ought to fasten her seat belt? Only she couldn't find it, without pulling her hand free of his, and she couldn't do that without appearing gauche.

"Turn some music on, huh, babe? Anything you feel like hearing." Sara flinched as he passed a slow-moving truck and swung in front of it with inches to spare.

She found a station that was playing Pink Floyd and left it on, remembering that Delight had all of the Pink Floyd albums. What now?

Garon gave her one of his crinkling, lopsided smiles that made women all over the world sigh with longing.

"Still tired? I thought we'd drive down to Malibu — visit a friend of mine who's a great cook. I have a standing invitation to dinner. You'll like Ted. I've known him a long time."

"It sounds great!" Sara said brightly.

Maybe — just maybe Garon was just being nice to her, and his friend the cook would stick around. And if not, Sara thought fatalistically, closing her eyes for a moment, wasn't Garon Hunt exactly what she needed to set her free? An attractive, sexy, *uncomplicated* married man. What reluctant virgin could ask for more? Remembering the tenderly passionate love scene from *Deal in Death* when he had first made love to his frightened Indian child-bride, Sara felt reassured. If it happened, it would be like that. Didn't everyone say that Garon Hunt didn't *have* to be an actor because he always played himself?

Chapter 9

What had she expected? Sara couldn't be quite certain afterward. A small and cozy beach cottage, perhaps? But she didn't really do too much thinking all the time Garon made his way in and out of the traffic at a high rate of speed that reminded Sara of the articles she had read about his racing cars as a hobby. At least he *concentrated* while he drove, and that made her feel a little easier — a little less like her death was imminent.

She was relieved when, at last, Garon slowed down; slightly confused when he stopped before massive iron gates that were almost concealed by shrubbery and flowering trees.

"Just give me a minute. . . ."

Sara watched, fascinated, while Garon went through what Delight would have called "the whole bit." What a security system! He said something into some kind of hidden voice box and came back to the car, glancing sideways at Sara with a grin and the air of a conjuror about to produce a rabbit. And sure enough, under her fascinated eyes, the gates swung open soundlessly.

Looking back over her shoulder, Sara noticed that the gates had already closed again behind them, and she quickly pushed away the slight feeling of unease that threatened to spoil her excitement and anticipation.

"Reminds me a little of Ali Baba's cave!" she said flippantly out loud, and Garon chuckled.

"That's what *I* thought the first time Ted showed it to me! Takes getting used to, I guess." He gave her that appealing little-boy-found grin and Sara could feel her heart beginning to beat faster. "What happens is that the computer — Ted calls her Big Mother — recognizes my voice and opens the gates. But there are also guards, with their dogs, even if you don't always see them."

They were driving down a long avenue edged with cypress trees — very Greek or Italian. *Brooding,* Sara thought with a little shiver.

"How far is the house, for goodness' sake?"

This time Garon patted her thigh — almost absentmindedly.

"Right around the . . . next bend! See up there? Sits right on the ocean, and there's a stretch of private beach too." He glanced at her appraisingly now. "I'd like to bring you out here during the day sometime, you'd love it. Maybe after the picture's in the can, huh?''

Sara hardly heard him as her eyes widened over the house. "First Ali Baba and now *Gone with the Wind!*" She hadn't realized that she had said her thought aloud until Garon chuckled.

"I like your sense of humor, kid! But don't get *too* bowled over by the house. In spite of all his dough, Ted's a real down-to-earth, regular guy. And a football fan like you — didn't I read that somewhere?''

Garon was helping her out of the car while Sara tried to hide her dismay. *Football?* And of course he didn't mean soccer. Oh, God, how was she going to bluff her way out of *this* one?

"Oh . . . yeah. But tennis is my game *this* year! I'm bored with football now.''

"Tennis, huh? My game too. Maybe we can have a game sometime?''

Moving ahead with the easy assurance of a man who knew he had plenty of time and not much effort to make, Garon slid a casual arm around Sara's waist as he dropped a light kiss on her temple.

"Mmm!" She couldn't think of anything else to say! What was she supposed to do next? Say next? Thank God there was someone at the front door — now she didn't have to do or say anything except "hello" and "thank you" to their host.

Sara had her first unpleasant shock of the evening when she recognized the voice that hailed them. Theodore Kohler — one of the richest men in the world, it was whispered; who also happened to have been a close friend of both her mother *and* her father. *Uncle* Theo of her childhood, who, of course, had always been "going back to America."

"Hey, Ted!" Sara hung back, giving her nerves time to stop quivering. She reminded herself that she hadn't met Uncle Theo for at least five years, and she'd changed a lot since then — and so had Delight. But now Garon was performing swift, casual introductions. "Ted — Delight. Delight — Ted! And now I could sure use a drink!"

"It's waiting for you." The tall, slightly stooped man still looked the same, except for the fact that his hair had gone almost entirely silver.

Sara had no more time to hang back as Garon propelled her forward with a slightly quizzical glance.

"What's the matter? You've met Ted before, haven't you?"

"Ted's met the whole family! What's the matter, young lady, you forgotten your Uncle Theo?"

Wafting forward on Delight's favorite perfume, Sara reached up to kiss a bearded cheek. "Of *course,* I remember! But I didn't know if you had. . . . I was just a little kid, wasn't I?"

"You two know each other — great! And now a drink, please, Ted?"

"Told you it was waiting — and you know where! Well, come along, Delight. Did you know I tried to persuade your mother not to call you that? Naturally, she wouldn't listen. And what are you doing with Garon?"

"He asked me to dinner, that's all!"

"That's *all,* huh? I don't know about you kids these days — and I don't *want* to know either! Do your thing . . . if you're sure you know what's good for you!"

Garon turned around to study them both with interest, a question in his eyes. "You two know each other awful damned well! How?"

"Hell, it's a long story. I used to be in love with Mona and ended up in the role of 'best friend'!" Theo/Ted Kohler shrugged expressively.

"Yeah, I guess I can understand how. Mona's quite a woman." Garon grinned irrepressibly, clamping an arm around Sara's waist to pull her closer against him. "As a matter of fact, don't you think little Delight here looks a whole lot like her mom?"

Ted Kohler snorted. "Hell, *I* don't know! Ask your shrink! But I'll tell you one thing, *all* of Mona's children take after her."

Sara forced herself to smile brightly and a trifle impudently back at him under his suddenly frowning perusal, relief flooding her when he finally allowed in an annoyed tone of voice that he could have sworn for a few minutes that she had reminded him more of her sister.

Skating on thin ice, Sara said pertly: *"Half* sister, Uncle Theo! *I'm* the make-it-on-her-own kid! And I am, aren't I, Garon?"

I'm a better actress than Delight! Or any of them! Sara's mind soared, as she threw herself into her role for the evening. Garon was already intrigued — much more so than he had been in the beginning. His fingers brushed very lightly against her breast, and he was really *looking* at her, bright blue eyes probing.

"Your half sister was much more sensible than *you* were, and I'm sure she probably still is!" Seeing that they had hardly heard him, Ted Kohler gave a mental shrug. He was no daddy to Mona's kids anyhow, and *this* one, from all accounts, was quite street-wise.

"I'm afraid I have a few people here," he said, turning back to Garon, who shrugged.

"Anyone I know?"

"No one I wouldn't trust. So feel at ease, old buddy!"

"Come on — we'll check them out and then I'll show you the tennis courts by moonlight!" Garon grinned down at Sara.

"How romantic!" Sara kept it light, already beginning to feel insecure. How long would she be able to keep Garon at bay? And it was only when she *thought* that that the realization came. She really didn't *want* to be made love to by Garon! Even if Delight would have. If she was going to lose her damned virginity someday, it had bloody well be very special! No married man with one eye on the clock, even if he *was* Garon Hunt. But how was she able to break it to Garon without . . . without blowing her cover?

It was hard on the heels of that thought that Sara received her second shock for the evening.

"My house guest, the Duca di Cavalieri. . . ." And if Garon hadn't been *holding* her —!

"Oh, yes. We have met." His voice was completely indifferent, his eyes hard and disinterested — like twin black pebbles striking hers. Sara noticed, belatedly, that he had on his arm the most gorgeous female she had ever seen — a honey blonde with exquisite porcelain features and expensive jewelry.

Well — *good!* she thought indignantly. Let him pursue someone else for a change! What a relief! She floated by him with a vague smile, as if she was trying to remember him.

And maybe she *would* let Garon seduce her after all. Someone had to be first! Sara began to set the scenario on her mind. They would leave soon — there would be flowers and champagne and soft music. Wagner, perhaps. She hoped Garon liked Wagner.

A waiter came out with a tray, and Sara

reached out automatically. She had better get slightly tipsy, it might help. She had to relax — learn to relax. A second drink might help even more, because the first one had been just orange juice in a tall glass.

"Not many people can drink a second Harvey Wallbanger in two swallows and remain standing. My . . . friend and I have a bet going on you, Signorina Delight." Riccardo's voice made Sara grit her teeth, even as the woman with him smiled sweetly and a trifle condescendingly. She spoke with a French accent. "Of course I have my money on you. Two drinks . . . *phoo!* They are nothing, in spite of what they call them, *oui?*"

"Of course! And *your* money is safe, I assure you."

She didn't care if he *did* raise one deliberately sarcastic eyebrow at her. She was here with Garon Hunt, and Garon was going to look after her tonight — in more ways than one, probably!

The Duca di Cavalieri moved on with his companion and Sara resisted sternly the temptation to stick out her tongue at his retreating back. Part of her mind was appalled at herself. She had never, ever, done anything as impossibly *vulgar* as that in her life before! Maybe she *was* tipsy enough already.

"Feel like exploring?"

Thank God Garon had seen fit to rescue her. Sara's smile burst out at him brilliantly.

"I'd *love* to. Especially the tennis courts."

"You got it!"

Sara was to wonder, afterward, what might have happened if all of the others hadn't come traipsing after them.

"What's the bet, anyway?" someone said vaguely, and she shrugged.

"How would I know?" But she had begun to have a suspicion. *More* than a suspicion, especially when Uncle Theo came up to her, still frowning.

"I put my money on *you,* darn it, in spite of the fact that your sister Sara's the tennis champ! Maybe she's taught you a few pointers."

"Oh, but she's taught me everything she knows!" Sara was hefting the racquet she had chosen from the five Ted had handed her. She hoped she felt as cocky as those words sounded. "Who am I playing against?" *Now* she was on familiar ground!

And she should have known who would answer her! What was Riccardo doing without his clinging lady? Sara swung around, looking him in the eye.

"But against your *innamorata,* of course! The challenge was between you two — although frankly, signorina, I cannot imagine why you would challenge a man for a game of tennis! Because either way, you will be the loser."

"*I* challenged? Challenged who?"

He didn't need to answer, and maybe that was just as well. On the other side of the net, Garon Hunt waved at her.

"Okay, baby! Let's go. And remember you promised not to be mad at me if I get too rough on you. Tennis is like driving a car to me — once I get into it, I forget about everything but winning!"

"So do I."

This was going to be very quick. She was going to let Garon beat her — putting up enough opposition not to make her look silly. And as for His Grace, the Duca di Cavalieri, Sara hoped fervently he had bet a lot of money on her!

Then, when the first game started, Sara forgot everything else but her concentration, pushing away the memories.

You could be a professional! And in fact you would be wasting your talent if you didn't at least try out as an amateur!

Shades of Pat, who had taught her tennis. Sara had worn her hair in pigtails at that time. She remembered the weight of each braid against her shoulders as she shook her head vigorously.

"You know Daddy wouldn't hear of it! He'd stop my taking lessons or even playing for fun if he thought I might want to do it *seriously*. And it's too much *fun* for me, Pat!"

"Your serve, baby!"

What she remembered most of that first game was Garon's surprised face when she slammed the ball across the court, right in the corner. She saw the bright blue excitement leap into his eyes. From his eyes to hers.

"So you're good! I kinda thought so from the beginning. . . ."

He let the double entendre sink in, smiling at her. *His* serve was by no means patronizing, making her run for the ball. Sara felt elation rise in her. *He* was good! Would she be able to remember that she must lose this contest?

Chapter 10

"Fantastic game!" "Jesus Christ, the girl can sure play tennis!" Better to remember the accolades after the almost even game than her thirst. More Harvey Wallbangers. She never wanted to taste orange juice again!

Sara fought back a moan of sheer agony as she shifted her head on the pillow. Her insides felt sore and her throat ached too. Into her mind came a hazy recollection of herself, trying to fight back nausea and not quite succeeding. An even hazier picture of Garon's face bending over hers as he began to undress her. . . .

In a cold sweat, Sara jerked upright. Even her *eyes* ached when she moved them. But she had already seen what she had been looking for. On the other side of the king-size bed she had obviously slept in was a deep indentation where a head had lain on the pillow next to hers.

And she didn't even remember! Lying back

again, Sara pressed her fingers against her temples, trying to think. She didn't feel different. She didn't feel anything! Maybe she'd passed out *before* and he hadn't done anything.

Cautiously, Sara opened her eyes again. No blood — no nothing. Garon had been a gentleman, after all — not that it mattered, because he probably would never want to see her again.

"Oh, good! Mr. Kohler was real worried about you. Had me come in here to watch over you after your gentleman left." The maid spoke from the doorway.

Sara could have groaned out loud. Now she had to face Uncle Theo. And Garon must be disgusted with her. She shuddered at the recollection of herself, getting sick. No more Harvey Wallbangers, ever again!

Efficient fingers felt her forehead, touched her pulse. "You'll be fine. Just a slight hangover, maybe, and I'm going to bring you something to fix that right away!"

"Well . . . ! I feel as if I've had to kidnap you in order to have you spend some time with me! I'm surprised your mother didn't have you get in touch!"

Uncle Theo's voice sounded gruffly annoyed, before he brightened up briefly. "At least you play a damn good game of tennis . . . Sara, is it? And don't think I didn't notice

115

that you let Garon win that last game!"

She *had* to try to keep her voice from shaking. "No, Uncle Theo, it isn't Sara. It's *Delight,* remember? The black sheep."

His eyes, still alert and intelligent, swept over her before he shrugged impatiently. "Well — Delight or Sara — it doesn't really matter. Both Mona's daughters, aren't you? And both take after your mother, I guess!"

"When did Garon leave?" It was a deliberate non sequitur, but Sara was beyond the point of worrying about it.

Uncle Theo merely grunted. "Right after you fell asleep, I reckon! He had a call from Sally — something to do with one of the kids. But he *did* ask me to tell you that he'd like to see you again."

"Oh . . ." Sara said bleakly. What an idiot she'd made of herself! And poor Garon, having to be *kind.*

"I think . . ." Sara massaged her temples exploratively, "I think I was supposed to report to the set today. Oh, God. Lew will be furious!"

"What the hell use you think all my money is? Nobody's going to miss you. You've got a week off while they're shooting the chase scenes."

Belatedly, Sara remembered that Uncle Theo "dabbled" in almost everything. Just like her father (she winced at *that* thought).

"Great. I think I'm going to go into

hibernation."

"Well, if you really feel that way, you're welcome to stay here! I tend to get lonely sometimes."

"I just don't believe that!" she teased him gently, knowing better. Uncle Theo had always surrounded himself with people. "And besides, you have a houseguest."

"I like Riccardo . . . but he doesn't stay around much."

"You wouldn't like it if he did, would you?"

He gave an explosive chuckle. "Damned if you don't sound more like Sara! She always did lock horns with me — contradict me. Well, I'll give you the same license! But come along now — I've fixed you one of my special omelettes!"

Afterward Sara would wonder why she hadn't stayed longer to enjoy the comfortable familiarity, the security, that Uncle Theo offered. She could rest, be herself, gather herself up. . . . The thought might have been too tempting not to accept if Uncle Theo had not had a houseguest. To stay under the same roof as the detestable Riccardo, Duca di Cavalieri, was more than she could cope with at this point in her life — especially since she had to think very seriously about Garon, and how she was going to deal with him.

Sara spent the rest of the afternoon sunbathing under Uncle Theo's benevolent aegis.

To anybody watching she might have appeared to be sleeping in the golden warmth of the summer sun — but her mind was far too busy with questions and imagination. Deliberately centered around Garon. . . . Was she going to have a properly casual affair with him or not? Under the unraveling heat of the sun, Sara's mind-pictures were ambivalent, and she wavered between being herself and being Delight — reminding herself firmly that as far as Garon was concerned she was Delight the outgoing; not Sara the introvert. And did this fact allow Sara the inhibited to let down all her barriers while she playacted at being Delight, who lived up to her name in every way?

Oh, yes, she could have stayed there forever under the sun, forgetting about decisions and answers and limitations — not having to deal with anything more serious than the effort of turning over from her stomach onto her back. Could have and *would* have perhaps, if not for the *feeling* of a shadow across her relaxed body, and a harshly grating voice that seemed to rasp across her nerves:

"You look as if you were giving yourself up as an offering to the sun! And unfortunately I am no Apollo — being a more comfortabe citizen of hell than of heaven! Are you awake?"

"I'm awake — now. And you're Pluto, not Apollo. What do you want?"

"Obviously, you were not taught any manners!"

"That's right! I was never in one place long enough to get taught much of anything. So — I just evolved. My own way."

She was Delight. This was what Delight felt, only she never said it, barricaded by her stubborn, fragile pride. Everything Delight had had as a child had been borrowed from someone else, never altogether her own. No settled-in home, no comfortable Nanny Staggs to take the place of a beautiful-butterfly mother. Not even a father who cared enough to acknowledge her.

How dared this man, or anyone else, criticize her?

Rejecting him and his dark, impersonal arrogance, Sara turned back onto her stomach, pillowing her head in her arms. Maybe he'd go away if she ignored him.

"I'm sure your many analysts have helped this — *evolving* as you call it. And perhaps your many experiences? Or do you prefer to call them experiments?"

"Go away!" She was proud of the evenness of her voice. "I'm not any of your business. In fact — since we're being honest with each other — I don't even *like* you."

"Is that supposed to be an incentive for me? Is it a challenge or a goad?"

"What an ego!" She stirred angrily — then held her breath as she sensed that he had lowered himself down beside her. For some reason, he wanted to do battle with her. He was pushing for war, and the realization made Sara cautious. For a supposed "fan" he was turning out to be more of a cynical critic. An irritant, in fact!

"Why can't you leave me alone? I was hoping for some peace — some space. . . ."

"And, poor little girl, here you are subjected to the harsh demands of an ogre. Or — do you compare me to a ravening wolf, in your imagination?"

"I try not to think about you at all . . . !" Sara said frostily, turning her head away from his annoying voice. "And I usually succeed. Where is Uncle Theo? I think I should go home."

"As a matter of fact, that is why I ventured to disturb your . . . 'space,' as you call it. Our host has been called away on urgent business, which will take him several hours — perhaps as much as a day. He asked me to tell you that you are welcome to stay on here; or, if you want to go home, that there will be transportation arranged at any time." His voice lowered to a deceptively silken purr. "I'm afraid that I have already dispatched Albert, Ted's reserve chauffeur, to drive my friend home. It will be a long drive — she lives in San Diego. But I will gladly drive you anywhere you wish to go . . . *if* you wish to go, that is."

120

So much for relaxation and letting go! Sara tensed for battle, willing herself not to stir. While her mind was searching for a suitably scathing response, she was silent — and obviously he mistook her silence for surrender, for his hand touched her shoulder in a way that was almost possessive; stroking lightly from there down her back to the curve of her hip and up again — fingers lingering as they traced the canyon of her spine from her coccyx to her neck.

"Why don't you stop fighting me — and yourself? Garon Hunt is very much married — all he wants on the side is a little piece of . . . . you Americans have a crude expression for it that I will not repeat; I think you know what I mean! Why don't you forget about him?" Warm, strong fingers massaged her shoulders and the back of her neck. Oh, God, it would be all too easy to give way. To *let* him, and go along with the tide that was building up inside her. Let herself crest like a slowly gathering wave . . . not thinking, only feeling. Letting it happen while the warm trickle of feeling became a dangerous current that alarmed her into belated awareness.

Somehow, his hand had moved downward from her shoulder to insinuate itself between the brief protection of her borrowed bikini-top and her skin. And if she let it be, if she continued to let feeling take her, then maybe she would discover what it was all about.

Maybe . . .

But the sudden rush of emotions she wasn't used to jerked her upright, tugging minuscule straps back into place.

"Cut it out! And I'm nobody's piece of you-know-what — better get that clear."

In a thin madras cotton shirt and tight-fitting denim pants, he was hunkered down far too close to her, like a sleek-muscled animal so sure of his prey that he would allow her to run — as far as *he* chose before he caught her; enjoying her futile struggles before he . . .

Sara looked furiously into his eyes, challenging their coal-dark depths. "I really don't understand where you're coming from — and I don't care either. I'd just be . . . much more comfortable if you left me alone — *capisce?* I'm your typical obnoxious American liberated female, remember? And you, Signor Duca, can, I'm sure, have your pick of panting, submissive, docile women who'd be *happy* to lie down and roll over for you. Why don't you take what's *freely* offered?"

To her renewed fury he laughed shortly; letting his eyes travel over her body in an obvious way that was meant to be insulting. "Why? But I'm sure you know. You are deliberately making of yourself a challenge . . . or is it a victim? Would it be worth my while to find out?"

He was really going too far! Sara felt the anger she had been fighting to hold back heat her face until it seemed to be burning. And yet she tried to choose her words carefully — flinging each one at him with calculated coldness that was meant to negate the downpouring, enervating heat of the sun.

"I've always found that the best way to find out about anything is to ask! But in order to save you the expending of any unnecessary energy, I might as well tell you right now that I am *not* trying to lure you on — even if you might like to think so. I don't know and I don't care what you might think of me, but let me tell you one thing, I'm a one-man woman. I happen to be in love with someone who wants to marry me, and . . . I'm not looking for anything else, thank you!"

"Ah, so you are marriage-minded, are you? And in California, so I've heard, everything is community property — fifty-fifty, even if the woman has done nothing to help earn the money to which the courts say she is entitled. No wonder marriage is so desirable here — for a woman, especially!"

With deliberately faked sweetness, Sara widened her eyes at him — mainly to hide the simmering of her temper, just below the surface.

"But how old-fashioned you are! Haven't you heard of *palimony?* If I want to be married, it means giving up my freedom — it probably means having children. It would mean commitment . . . but you wouldn't understand that, would you? I'm sure your head is still in the Dark Ages where women had their place — several paces to the rear!"

His voice was dangerously soft: "And what a pity we are not now in what you choose to call 'the Dark Ages.' You would have been married by the time you were fifteen — with two or three children to keep you busy, by now. And you would be more of a woman because of that!"

By now it was no longer just a duel, but open war. Refusing to flinch from his derisive look and his subtly threatening closeness, Sara hoped that the scorn in her eyes showed itself as obviously as she felt it.

"I suppose I should be thankful that I live in a more advanced and *civilized* culture where I really don't have to prove I'm a woman by being a mother at sixteen! And at least when I do have a child it will be because I *want* to, instead of being a circumstance forced upon me."

The hard-edged line of his jaw warned her of a fury in him that held her back from any further taunts. In fact, Sara turned away from him deliberately — lying back on her sun-warmed pad with her head turned away from him.

She said in as light a voice as she could manage: "Oh, please *do* go away! There's no reason for you to feel responsible for me — or for us to quarrel. We're strangers to each other, after all, and I think it's really better that we stay that way!"

"But are you really sure that is what you would *prefer?*" His voice rasped across her nerve ends with a subtle reminder of her earlier confusion, and for all her studied ease, Sara could not help the ripple of apprehension that made her shiver in spite of the heat. Strange how the same voice could be gratingly harsh at one moment and as smooth as silk the next. He was a monster, this man.

"Delight . . . I have no wish to argue with you, even though you constantly provoke me to anger. *Dio mio!* I only came out here to deliver a message to you, and to offer you transportation back to your apartment if you wished to go. Or would you like better to stay here with me? It is very private. . . ."

Sara refused to meet his eyes, willing herself to lie still in the studiedly relaxed position she had taken up. "Yes, it is, isn't it? And that's why I'm here. Thanks for the offer of a ride, but I'm sure I can find my way back later — if I don't decide to take Uncle Theo up on his offer, that is."

One up for *her,* Sara thought, although the silence that followed her impudent speech left her slightly unnerved. What if he . . . what was she afraid of? He was a despicable, detestable man, but he *was* Uncle Theo's houseguest, and the proud Duca di Cavalieri for all his arrogance would hardly attempt to take her by force; not here, out in the open!

"Very well." His voice was hard-edged with an anger that belied the overt politeness of his words. "I will not, in that case, waste my time waiting for you to make up your mind. You will find your . . . transportation waiting for you outside, should you decide to leave. Just inform one of the servants. Have a pleasant afternoon with the sun, Miss Delight Adams."

Chapter 11

"Have a pleasant afternoon with the sun. . . ." Oh, indeed! And the *way* in which he'd said it, as if he'd have been glad to consign her to the devil instead.

He probably wishes I'd fall asleep out here and get burned to a crisp, Sara thought hatefully; picturing those harsh, saturnine features gazing contemptuously down at her mortal remains. It was *that* vision which spurred her into life from lethargy soon afterward — once a surreptitious glance in either direction had assured her that *he* was no longer to be seen.

She wandered back to her room, longing to be able to throw herself down on the freshly made bed and *sleep* — with no more nightmares to bother her, thank you! But Uncle Theo wasn't back yet, and the thought of being locked up in the same house with Riccardo made a coward of her. Better to leave while she was still safe . . . and without stopping to ponder *that* strange thought, Sara showered and dressed briskly before she summoned one of the smiling Korean houseboys.

"Ah, yes!" he informed her with his smile widening. Any time she wished to leave there was to be a car waiting for her. It would only take a moment. . . .

Outside the colonnaded "front porch" *it* waited for her. Shiny white and brand-new, with a removable hard-top that had already been removed for her. The Mercedes-Benz SL 450 sport coupe of Sara's dreams.

Uncle Theo . . . a surprise . . . but how would he have known what kind of car she'd always craved? And why would he —

"It is a gift. For you."

Delight would have leapt down the white marble steps with a squeal of joy. Sara frowned and questioned.

"From whom? From Uncle . . . from Mr. Kohler?"

The man shook his head. "Oh, no, miss. From the other gentleman. He said to tell you the keys are inside."

Sara cast one long, wistful look at the shiny new car before she turned her back on it, hoping her voice sounded even enough not to give her feelings away.

"But of course I can't accept gifts like that. You must tell the gentleman so — with my thanks, of course, for the kind thought. Could you call me a taxi please, Kim?"

The man's eyes widened in puzzlement,

even while he shook his head.

"Sorry, miss. Taxis not allowed here."

Belatedly remembering the gates and the elaborate security arrangements, Sara frowned with vexation. No taxis — of course *he'd* have known that! And now he thought he had her backed into an untenable position. Suddenly, her frown turned into a smile that warmed the worried look off Kim's face. "Of course I should have remembered. Well, that doesn't leave me with much choice, does it?" This with a brightening of her smile. "I'll just have to accept the transportation offered me — but as a *loan* of course, and not as a gift. You *must* be sure and tell the Duke that."

She hoped he would be furious. Especially when she had the car delivered back to him with her casual note that would say something like "thanks for the great ride. . . ." Damn him anyway, for thinking she could be bought!

Anger alone carried Sara safely through the usual traffic. The Mercedes, of course, drove like a dream — but she wasn't going to let *that* affect her better judgment. For reasons of his own, the Duca di Cavalieri was stalking her — alternately provoking, insulting, and yes, enticing her. Obviously, he had remembered her casual statement about the kind of car she'd always wanted. Just as obviously, money meant nothing to him except as a means to an end.

"Quarry." Unbidden, the word sprang into Sara's mind, bringing with it a strange *frisson* of apprehension that made her fists clench around the wheel. What had made him decide that he wanted her? And why was she running from him? Attack was the best form of defense, she had heard — and surely her sister, who was used to dealing with all kinds of men, would have stayed to face him down! Approaching the apartment, Sara started to drive more slowly, her forehead puckered in a frown that was partially hidden by Delight's huge sunglasses. Now, belatedly, she was annoyed at herself for leaving Uncle Theo's in such a hurry. She should have stayed, to show *him* how little his presence meant to her. She shouldn't have let herself be driven away, especially in view of his sly insinuations that she was deliberately playing hard to get. Now, as conceited as he was, he might actually imagine that she had run away so that he could pursue her all the harder. Oh, *damn!*

If she had had any doubts, the hot stuffiness of the cramped little apartment decided Sara on her next move. Here, surrounded by Delight's scattered possessions, she was more able to put herself into her sister's personality — to be the daring, impudent Delight Adams who wasn't scared of anyone or anything, and would dare anything at all for experience or for "fun." No, Delight definitely would *not* have fled in horror from the advances of a decadent Italian Duke!

Come to think of it, that was a nicely turned sentence! Sara applauded herself as she started to throw a few essential things into her overnight case. "Decadent Duke" . . . very well done, Sara! Her old habit of holding mental conversations with herself kept nervousness at bay as she took a deep breath, letting the door to the apartment slam shut behind her. Well, here we go. And this time, so help me, I really *am* going to be Delight. I'm going to tell him off the way *she* would.

She had, with bravado, parked the white Mercedes in the loading zone outside the building. Perhaps they had towed it away! But if it was still there, then she would return it to him — with a flourish and a few words of hypocritical thanks, which *he,* of course, would immediately see through. There was actually a feeling of anticipation growing in her, Sara realized with a sense of wonderment as she pushed through the revolving doors.

She must have been holding her breath . . . and now she released it with a sigh. There it was, still parked where she had left it, after all. A middle-aged man with a camera slung around his neck was circling the sleek white car with interest. Sara's high heels clicked on the sidewalk, and he turned with a grin that was at once sly and ingratiating. "Hi! This little beauty yours? I was admiring her. Brand-spanking-new, ain't she?"

Thank goodness there was still a lot of traffic, and even a few pedestrians, which was unusual for Los Angeles where *everyone* drove. Sara resisted her impulse to give him an icy brush-off, because she was still trying to be her sister — seeing everything from a different perspective; reacting that way. "Hello. It is a pretty car, isn't it?"

She thought she had handled it pretty neatly! Giving him a vague smile from beneath enormous sunglasses, Sara began to rummage through her cluttered purse for the car keys. They had to be in here somewhere. She remembered . . . .

"You're Delight Adams, ain't you? Saw Brenda Rowan's story on you on TV this morning. You mind if I take a picture of you with the new automobile? A present from a certain Italian Duke, maybe?"

Sara looked up with a gasp — and he was already taking the pictures. He moved very fast, like a professional photographer, she recognized with dismay.

"You're not to —"

He didn't give her a chance to finish, putting his hand up placatingly before he handed her a card. "Hey — thanks for the pictures. I'm Gordo Rapp. And you're a real cute girl. The publicity ain't going to hurt you, huh?"

All she — or Delight — needed was the

paparazzi! How on earth had the man happened to be hanging around, and what had he meant . . .

The raucous squeal of brakes just behind her and the explosion of a car door slamming made Sara's indignant protests catch in her throat as she jumped. Just like Gordo Rapp, who had hastily moved several steps back.

"Are you bothering the lady?"

Oh, *no!* Not Riccardo, not *now!*

With what she hoped was magnificent disregard, Sara said coldly: "I was looking for the keys . . ."

At about the same time she felt the warmth of his fingers, contrasting with the cold of the keys he pressed into her hand, wrapping his fingers around it with a strength that held her fast when she tried to resist him.

"I brought you the extra set of keys. Were you coming to look for me, or did you guess that I would come for you?" His blackly inscrutable eyes flicked from her angry face to a point beyond her as he added, in a deceptively soft voice: "As for you — I would move on if I were you."

"Sure — anything you say, Duke! But lemme take just one more picture first, huh? I'll be sure and send you proofs — okay, okay!"

As the man made off around the corner, clutching his camera protectively, Sara turned indignantly on her tormentor.

133

"Do you realize that that man . . . that our picture is probably going to be in all the nasty little gossip *rags* all over the world? And you let him think that you . . . that I . . ."

How *dared* he still continue to hold her hand? Although if he had not, she might have attempted to throw his keys in his dark devil's face!

"Ah! Do you think I should have attempted to go after him? To smash his camera, perhaps? But then — think of the publicity you would miss." His voice held drawling sarcasm that made Sara suck in a breath of pure rage. "I didn't really think you would want me to do anything violent to your . . . friend. After all, you seemed happy enough to pose for him as I was driving up!"

Almost incoherent with rage, Sara attempted to tug herself free of his grip, while her other hand fisted tightly, itching to strike out at him. Only the long training of discipline and self-control held her back.

"You're — how *dare* you follow me here? How dare you insinuate that I — why the last thing I need is to get a rumor started that *you* . . . that you and I — let me go!"

He acted as if they were the only people in the world, with a careless disregard of the curious looks they were getting from some of Delight's fellow tenants going in and out of the building.

Speaking with exaggerated patience, as if

to a child, he said: "If you will desist from making a public scene that might draw your photographer friend back to take more pictures, I will release you by all means. And no pretended hysteria please! After all, little tease, weren't you coming back to me?"

She had to control herself — she had to! The man was obviously a monstrous egomaniac.

"I was about to return your car to you," Sara said carefully, biting each word off between her teeth. "And I *did* intend to spend some time visiting with Uncle Theo — in private!" she added pointedly, relishing the narrowing of his eyes at her barb. "And now . . ." She looked down at her hand, still imprisoned by his, and hoped that he could not feel the jumping of her nerves.

"And now if I let you go, in which direction will you run? Are you sure that you want to run?" His voice was tinged with taunting mockery. As if he had been a familiar friend or lover, he suddenly reached for her other hand, swinging both between them once and then drawing her toward him.

"*Stop* it!"

"What are you afraid of? Or are you playing a game of intrigue?"

"I tried to tell you before — I . . . I'm engaged! And I happen to love him — very much. And as for you, Signor Duca, I'm not running away from you, I've just been trying to *avoid* you, that's all!" She forced herself to throw her head back, meeting eyes like black ice; keeping her voice light. "Don't take it too much to heart, though — if I hadn't met Carlo and fallen for him I just might have gone for you!"

And now his voice was as cold as his eyes as he released her so suddenly she almost stumbled. "Carlo, eh? An Italian name — and I warn you, sweet Delight, that if he happens to be from the old country, he would be jealous — and no doubt expect purity of his bride . . . you did say you planned to be married?"

"Of course we're going to be married. Very soon, as a matter of fact. As soon as . . . as I've finished with my part in the movie, I'm going to join him."

The key to the Mercedes seemed to burn into her palm, impressed there by the pressure of his fingers. Clumsily, Sara tried to hand it back to him.

"Please!" What a man of surprises he was! Now it was as if the barely checked anger she had sensed in him just seconds ago had never been, and instead he held one hand up, shrugging as he looked at her with indifferent coolness.

"Since you are going to visit your 'uncle' in any case, you might as well drive the car back. I cannot drive two cars at the same time."

He could change as quickly as a chameleon!

Sara glared at him suspiciously, but while she stood hesitating on the sidewalk he already had the door of the Lamborghini open, easing long legs in.

"Do you remember the way, or shall I go slowly in order that you may follow me?"

What she *really* ached to do was to throw the keys at him and storm back inside, leaving *him* to figure out what to do with the Mercedes. But would Delight back off from a battle? Never!

"Thank you, I'll follow you if I may," Sara flung over her shoulder in her breeziest Delight-voice. Inside, she was still shaking with a mixture of emotions she didn't want to analyze just yet — but at least he couldn't know that; and this time, by God, she wasn't running away!

Chapter 12

The next day the newspapers were full of gossip — even the "trades," as everybody called them. Uncle Theo's houseboy brought them to her stacked neatly on a brass tray, his face expressionless even when he informed her that she had been mentioned on Brenda Rowan's morning gossip show again — and that there was a telephone call for her to return as soon as she woke up. Mr. Hunt.

Garon? Sara's face flushed hotly, remembering. Oh, God, what must he think of her! And now all these ridiculous stories . . .

"Well! Should I say congratulations?" Garon's voice was dry, and she had difficulty guessing what he might be thinking. "I'm just calling to let you know that you can have a few more days off — at least through the weekend. We're having weather problems on location."

Sara got through the rest of the conversation with difficulty. She couldn't very well burst out *denying* all the gossip, when Garon hadn't questioned her about it at all. And she couldn't very well hint around to show him that she'd like to see him again, because she wasn't sure if she really did or not. And how could *he* want to date her again when she'd passed out on him? In any case, and somewhat to her chagrin, Garon was casually friendly — and businesslike.

"Tell our friend Riccardo that I'll probably catch him later, huh? And you have fun, kid."

Sara stared frustratedly at the phone for a few seconds before she put it down and reached for the newspapers, shuddering as she encountered a simply ghastly photograph of herself, rummaging in her purse and looking like a female bank robber in those sunglasses. And another, worse picture in which she seemed to be looking up adoringly into Riccardo's profiled face while he held her hand. . . .

Oh — insufferable! Maybe Uncle Theo would know what to do. Maybe she could sue them — and especially that sneaky Gordo Rapp. A written item caught Sara's eye and she could almost have cried aloud with vexation as she skimmed down the column.

Were Paul and Monique Drury playing Cupid when they introduced the multimillionaire Duca di Cavalieri to aspiring model-actress Delight Adams? It must have been love at first sight, with dinner at the exclusive Café Russe and a *very* private lunch on the set — in Paul Drury's office, no less. And now a delighted Delight is driving around in a brand-new Mercedes SL 450 — a gift, from an admirer. Dare we guess who?

The phone at her bedside rang and Sara snatched at it almost thankfully; only to grimace, her nose wrinkling, when she recognized the drawlingly sarcastic voice that grated in her ear. "You have seen the newspapers?" And then, coldly, "I suppose this is what you would call here 'good publicity'? However I find the liberties your press takes offensive!"

Surely he didn't think . . . he *couldn't* think . . . Sara could feel herself getting hot all over and couldn't prevent it — any more than she could stop her voice from rising. "This is all *your* fault! You're the one who insisted on meeting me, and you're the one who — *I* certainly don't need any of *this* kind of publicity, let me tell you!" Remembering her role, as she paused to draw breath Sara fought to make her voice sound even as she went on more calmly: "I have a very jealous fiancé who would . . . would kill both of us if he thought all this nasty gossip was true!"

"Oh, yes — this Carlo you were speaking of? I will, of course, be glad 'to set him straight' as you say here — should he approach

140

me. Perhaps I should also advise him that if he has a fiancée as . . . attractive as you are he should not leave her alone so much?"

Even when he softened his voice, it had rough edges to it, rubbing her up the wrong way like a cat's tongue against her flesh, so that she shuddered first and then bristled instinctively.

"Carlo is none of your business. And if you don't like the newspaper stories then you ought to deny them, don't you think? I'm sure you're some kind of international playboy, but I wish you'd realize that I'm not interested in the kind of games you're playing!"

Silence stretched tautly between them. Had she gone too far? Sara heard her rings tap edgily against the telephone receiver. Wasn't he going to say anything?

To her amazement, she heard him laugh softly — even his laughter sounded more like the growl of a big cat, making her jump nervously.

"Why — because you have not set the rules? You should take chances sometimes . . . Delight!"

"I take chances all the time!" Anger made her voice sound brittle to the point of breaking. "But in this case I really don't choose to get involved. And I don't like to see lies printed about me."

"No?" And then, curtly, as if he'd grown tired of the entertainment she must have provided, "I am no longer enjoying the hospitality of Mr. Kohler — I am back at my hotel. But I was calling to suggest we meet again — privately this time — to discuss how we should put an end to these rumors. If you will call and leave a message as to a time that will be convenient to you?"

Why hadn't she refused him? Afterward Sara could not decide why she had allowed herself to be so weak in the face of his "request" that had been phrased more like an order. She never wanted to meet him again and rediscover in herself that frighteningly helpless weakness his darkly arrogant presence seemed to evoke. Delight wouldn't have been threatened by him, but Sara was. Threatened — and also drawn, as much as she might want to deny it.

Moths were drawn to candle flame — and inevitably ended up with their wings singed. And for all that she might *pretend* to be Delight, this adventure actually belonged to Sara, and Sara had better be very careful if she didn't want to end up burned!

The drive back to Uncle Theo's house gave Sara time to deliberate on what she might be getting herself into, but the way the security guards greeted her made her feel welcome and *safe,* even if Uncle Theo seemed to have misunderstood completely her relationship with his erstwhile houseguest — with whom she was supposed to have dinner tonight!

"You can meet here, it's more private. And I'm sure you know what you're doing by now — you've spent enough time in this town. You should have got in touch with me before, you know!" Uncle Theo was gruff but helpful, and Sara hugged him impulsively.

"I *know*, I'm sorry — but I wanted to do it all by myself. And I didn't even know you still lived around here."

"Well, now you know! No more excuses for not coming to visit, eh?"

Uncle Theo was a love, but how should she describe Riccardo, Duca di Cavalieri? While she was thinking it over, Sara was getting herself ready, wondering why she was taking the trouble. A trace of eye makeup, a touch of blusher. And red lip gloss to outline her lips.

Really, Sara, you ought to be ashamed! she scolded her image in the mirror, but without much conviction. Sara, standing in between roles, was actually *enjoying* all this! Even if he thought she was Delight, the woman who was intriguing him was Sara, was *her;* and instead of being ashamed, she relished the thought. Slipping into a silk Missoni dress that clung to her like a second skin — so soft, bodice crossed over in front and dipping low enough to show the cleft between her breasts — Sara turned in front of mirrors that reflected her from all angles. These were *her* clothes, not her sister's, and she was glad now of the European shopping trip she had indulged in before she had flown to New York. Slipping her feet into high-heeled shoes with thin straps of soft leather crossed over her instep and a real gold chain encircling each slim ankle, she turned again, skirt barely covering her knees. She looked more like her mother than she ever had before. She looked less like Delight, with some of the tight curl in her hair beginning to loosen; slipping down against her neck and brushing her temples and cheeks. Looked not at all like Sara, who was proper and self-controlled and a real, twenty-four-carat virgin to boot!

Be careful! With her last caution to herself still echoing in her mind Sara left her room, walking quickly down a pillared gallery that was hung with flowered vines; round a bend and through a small patio that led into the larger one that surrounded the huge pool. This was where they were to have dinner, because of the balmy weather and Uncle Theo's romantic nature.

There was a table, covered by a spotless white linen cloth. Candles in crystal holders and a crystal vase filled with perfumed red roses. The candles were lit, and real silver flatware gleamed beside fine china and matching crystal wineglasses. Two white-jacketed waiters hovering unobtrusively in the background, and a strolling guitar player as well.

Sara had to fight back the rising bubble of hysterical laughter in her throat. What on earth was Uncle Theo up to? It looked like a set from an old Audrey Hepburn movie — but was she capable of playing the lead?

Of course, she had deliberately made herself late — and Riccardo was already here, betraying no sign of impatience or anger as he rose to acknowledge her arrival. One black eyebrow raised, he lifted his glass to her.

"To — Delight. You look charming."

"Thank you." Of course she must ignore the way his glance raked over her insolently as if he was stripping her bare. She must remind herself that she was in control. She had accepted his invitation tonight only in order to show him that he didn't intimidate her in the least.

One of the waiters seated her and she asked for Perrier alongside her wine. The guitar player started singing softly — some old, sentimental Italian song. Oh, no! Uncle Theo was surely going a little too far; or maybe the only movies he *watched* anymore were the old ones.

Her antagonist was leaning back in his chair, eyes hooded. "You like this corny music? I seem to remember reading somewhere that your favorite music is rock and roll — *punk* rock?"

"You shouldn't believe everything you

145

read, should you?" Brightly, Sara lifted her glass to him and tasted her wine, which was very good — dry and chilled just enough. Emboldened by his speculative silence she continued, "I thought we were meeting to discuss how to squelch the gossip. Perhaps you could threaten to sue? I'm sure you could afford it better than I can."

She saw him shrug, shoulders lifting under his closely fitting linen jacket. "To sue would only create more gossip — and more publicity." His voice was deliberately uninflected, but his eyes taunted her, flushing her face more brightly than her carefully applied blusher.

Putting her glass down carefully, Sara said, controlling her voice: "And since neither of us desires more publicity . . . what would *you* suggest?"

"You really want to know?" His voice was as rough-edged as the way his eyes traveled over her, taking in everything from her nervous flush to her plunging neckline. "Then I will tell you. Why pay any regard to gossip? To deny merely gives credence. And after all, both you and I know how much is true and how much is not . . . don't we? If your fiancé *trusts* you, I am sure there is no problem at all. He *does* trust you, I presume?"

"Of *course* he does!" Sara affirmed hotly. "We love each other. . . ."

"Ah yes. Love. You love each other — he

trusts you. But where is this Carlo of yours? Why isn't he here with you to protect you from just such gossip?"

"He's had to go away! On . . . on business. But he'll be joining me soon, of course — or I'll join him. And then we're going to be married."

"Yes — I believe you said so before."

Plates had been set before them, and Sara attacked her salad, skewering tiny shrimp on her chilled fork. She wasn't going to let him get the best of her! He was here, after all, for the same reason *she* was. Because she represented challenge; because he was the type of arrogant, chauvinistic male who couldn't believe there was a female impervious to his sex appeal. Hah!

"I beg your pardon?"

Surely she hadn't said it out loud?

Sara opened her eyes innocently at him, continuing to collect shrimp on her fork. "Oh — I didn't say anything. Isn't this salad great?"

"You have not tasted it yet. Only your wine."

"How observant of you. But I wish you'd stop staring."

"At you or at your salad?"

"Both." She proceeded to nibble at her shrimp, eating them one by one. Hah! she thought again. This time *she* had the upper hand. The trick was to ignore him. Then maybe he'd go away and leave her in peace!

Unfortunately the guitar player chose that moment to come up close, singing what was obviously a love song, to judge from the way his voice sobbed and his eyes closed when he hit the high notes. Politely, Sara pretended to listen with rapt concentration, noticing from the corners of her eyes that Riccardo was *not* entertained — in fact there was a tightness to his face and a tenseness in the long brown fingers that toyed with surface casualness with a silver napkin ring. Once again Sara noticed the signet ring he wore — heavy yellow gold with a heraldic design in diamonds and rubies. It was the only ring he wore, but on one wrist he sported a linked gold bracelet that only served to emphasize the masculinity of its wearer.

For an instant she let her eyes flick upward and caught him watching her. Quickly dropping her glance away Sara thought she heard him swear under his breath. He said something to the guitar player, who seemed to melt backward into the shadows. I don't know what's happening to me. . . . Sara thought lucidly before lucidity seemed to leave her.

"I think we are both wasting time. . . ." he said quietly from across the table, and his hand reached out to seize hers, drawing her to her feet without any effort at all. The guitar was still playing, only very softly now — just music, no singing. And across the pool, on the other side of the Spanish tiled courtyard, a fire flickered; each tongue of flame sending red-hot pincers to tear at her nerve endings.

Speechless, Sara let it happen. Where had everyone gone? The white-jacketed waiters were nowhere in evidence, and all that remained of the guitar player was his music. She was where she wanted to be — within the circle of hard arms that held her closely against the different hardness of his body. Fingers caught impatiently in the thick masses of her hair, pulling her head back to meet the assault of his mouth over hers — capturing and plundering; not giving her a chance to say no, even if she had wanted to.

This was like shooting a rapids — being swept over the edge, no longer in control. Without her willing them, her arms had gone upward to hold him — perhaps to keep herself from falling. His kisses were both harsh and gentle, while his hands, once they were sure of her willing captivity, roamed from her shoulders down the length of her spine; tracing the curves of her hips and buttocks before he pulled her roughly against himself.

She had never felt this way before; never felt herself melting, being absorbed, being concentrated; all feeling and no thought. Even when his fingers burned through the thin silk of her dress, teasingly caressing her breasts — impatiently pushing aside the silk so that now she felt the slight roughness of his fingers against the untried softness and sensitivity of her skin — even then she could not speak the protests that formed in her mind.

"Come." One word. *What about dinner?* What did dinner matter, or anything else, compared to this degree of feeling? She stumbled on her unaccustomed high heels, and with a muttered imprecation — just like a scene from a movie! — he lifted her off her feet to carry her against his chest.

Somehow, they had arrived at her room, and he shouldered the door open. Only the light beside the bed was on, and it was to the bed that he went directly, lowering her onto it.

Now what? Now that he was no longer holding her, Sara began to feel silly, lying sprawled there. Unconsciously, she tugged down her skirt, drawing her knees together. What was she supposed to do next? He had closed the door, and now, standing at the foot of the bed, he had started to loosen his tie, shrugging off his jacket. Dark, impenetrable eyes traveled over her, and his voice was as casual as his kisses earlier had *not* been.

"Why don't you undress and slip under the covers? I'll join you soon."

To Sara, his matter-of-fact approach was like a glass of cold water thrown in her face. He was taking for granted that she was his. He was treating her in the same, almost pragmatic manner that he probably treated all the women he went to bed with. No doubt his every move tonight had been carefully calculated; carefully timed. And now that he was sure of her, how cool he was!

Disbelievingly, Sara watched him begin to unbutton his shirt. From being swept away by the flights of fantasy, she was beginning to come back down to earth.

"Delight . . . such a promising name. Are you waiting for me to undress you? Or do you like to be taken with your clothes on?"

Standing there like a jungle animal, muscles rippling under darkly tanned skin, he made her breath come shortly. He would be the kind of man who took what he wanted without any regard for the feelings of anyone else. *And if she tried to back off now he would take her by force* . . . sheer instinct told her that, as she stared back, half-mesmerized, at his implacable eyes.

Think of something, Sara! her inner voice urged her — and quickly! He isn't a patient man. . . .

He had come closer to her, his shirt discarded now, and in the dim light Sara saw his mouth twisted in a sarcastic smile that wasn't a real smile at all.

His hands were at his belt now and she hastily averted her eyes, fixing them on his face instead.

"I . . . I don't think we'd better . . ."

"What's the matter now, are you still

thinking of your Carlo? I'm sure he'd understand. After all, you're a special kind of woman. Does he know of those very sexy movies you've made?"

"Of course. Carlo knows everything about me! And I'm glad you reminded me about Carlo, because I . . . I've changed my mind about this. I'm sorry — I didn't mean to lead you on, but you've . . . quite managed to turn me off with the things you say. Please . . ."

He stood poised, looking at her; reminding her frighteningly of a black panther crouched and ready to spring. Scrambling to her knees, Sara backed away as far as the width of the bed permitted. Dear God. Would he *rape* her now? Was he capable of such an act of violence?

Words spilled from her, spurred by the need to stave him off.

"Do you understand? I've changed my mind. I can't . . . with anyone else when I'm so in love with Carlo. I'm sorry — I suppose I was really testing myself, to be *sure;* and now I am."

Still standing looking down at her he gave a burst of raucous laughter that made her cringe in spite of all her strong resolutions.

"*Testing?* How American. But are you sure an Italian man would understand? Will you tell Carlo of this little incident? Shall I?"

"What do you mean — shall you. . . . Are

you threatening me? Trying to blackmail me?"

He said reflectively, as if he hadn't heard her at all: "If I followed my instincts and *yours* — yes, no matter how fiercely you deny them! — I would take you right now, and it would not be rape. I think you are too easily seduced, my Delight — also the Delight of so many other men before me and before Carlo! But like yours, my appetites, too, are jaded, and I enjoy challenge. So I say to you that I will never take you by force, because if I or anyone else should choose to exert enough effort you will willingly yield that which it suits you now to hold back. Why?" He flung the word at her, voice rasping like a saw blade. "Didn't I offer you enough? Should it have been a Rolls Corniche instead of a Mercedes? Would you enjoy a charge account at Charles Galay? I have noticed that you wear expensive clothes and Elsa Peretti earrings. Have I taken you too cheaply? Offered you too little?"

His words pricked at her like so many thrown daggers, each meant deliberately to pierce and hurt. They forced a reaction from her that was sheer self-defense, negating those *other* darker emotions that had almost drowned her.

"Have I taken you too cheaply?" he had said. "Offered you too little?"

Sara drew a deep breath, thankful for the dim light that shadowed her face, hiding her expression from him.

"Both," she said shortly, "but not in the way *you* mean. And now, if you don't mind . . ."

Long after he had gone, closing the door with controlled softness behind him, Sara found that she could not move. The rigidity she had forced on herself held her stiffly, still staring at the door as if she expected him to come back through it to attack her again — her body as well as her too-treacherous senses. But he didn't come and sanity flowed back into her eventually and with it the release of a storm of weeping that was quite unusual for her. Just rage, Sara told herself. And frustration, because it was *Delight* he wanted and not *you,* her mind answered her, making her sob all the harder; hating both herself and him.

Chapter 13

Some women could cry themselves to sleep and wake up fresh and unscathed the next morning. Obviously, *she* wasn't one of them. After she'd grimaced crossly at her red-eyed morning reflection in the bathroom mirror, Sara grimly set about bathing her eyes with cold water. One of Nanny Staggs' old tried-and-true remedies — guaranteed to get rid of puffy eyelids. And like most of Nanny's remedies it did work in the end.

"Is there anybody home?" Sara asked the houseboy who brought her late brunch out to the secluded terrace where she'd been sun-bathing. She hoped her question sounded as ingenuous as she'd meant it to be.

Her eyes disguised by Delight's oversized sunglasses, Sara lay bikinied and oiled on a chaise lounge; her hair tied back from her face with a yellow bandanna.

"Only the Master. The other gentleman he go away last night already."

He'd gone! And of course that pang that shot through her body was one of profound relief. Naturally, he'd never want to see her again, and that was just as well. He was the kind of man that no woman could, or should, ever trust! The kind of man to stay far away from — the kind of man that she, *Sara,* would never ordinarily encounter. And it was high time she was able to go back to being herself again, Sara thought almost desperately. How long had she promised Delight? Two weeks — a month?

You don't have to think about it right now, Sara commanded herself, turning from her stomach onto her back, feeling the heat of the afternoon sun assault her flesh. Better to suspend all thought and lie in the middle world between dream and waking.

"Well, well! You asleep or not? Falling asleep in the sun can be dangerous, my dear."

"Uncle Theo!"

"Who else? You're my only houseguest right now, and I thought this might be as good a time as any for us to get reacquainted — if you feel up to it, that is."

Why was her heart pounding so damn hard? Of course she was glad that it was Uncle Theo who had caught her sunbathing with her arms and legs spread wide as if to receive the sun god of the ancient Greeks. Anyone else might have . . .

Sara caught herself up, checking the unfinished thought. She'd had almost too much sun for one day — it was a good thing that she had the kind of skin that tanned easily and seldom burned, thanks to an Italian great-grandmother.

Sitting up, Sara said brightly: "Offer me some *very* cold Perrier with lime and I'll follow you anywhere!" It was the kind of thing Delight would have said. But while they were talking, why did Uncle Theo keep forgetting and call her Sara instead of Delight?

They talked while Uncle Theo took her on an impromptu tour of his private gallery of paintings. "No good locking all this beauty up in a vault! I want to be able to *look* at them whenever I want to."

For all her finger-popping waywardness, Delight must surely love *these!* Sara didn't want to hide her excitement, and couldn't. She could tell Uncle Theo was pleased.

"I've always loved beautiful things," he told her. Perhaps that was why he had adored Mona so. "And then — there's that Gains-borough that your father has tucked away; such a waste with no one to admire it. You couldn't persuade him to sell it to me, could you?"

"Of course I wouldn't — and especially since I persuaded him to give her to *me*. She's hanging up in my bedroom right now!" Sara responded heatedly, and then could have bitten out her tongue. But Uncle Theo, bless his heart, merely gave vent to a meaningful "Hah!" and said no more than that.

He took her out to the poolside patio at one of the tables in the shade, and chilled wine flanked by crystal glasses seemed to appear as if by magic.

"Well — have some wine. You've been a good audience — made me realize I actually tend to get lonely sometimes! What do you think of that?" And then, without giving her a chance to say anything at all, he said without further preamble: "Speaking of that — why don't you think about spending some time *here?* You could have your own separate wing — come and go as you please. You don't have to say anything now, just think about it."

He had taken her by surprise, and her words stumbled over one another as she said: "That . . . that would have been so wonderful . . . you're a *love* to suggest such a thing, but . . . I'm going to be working again on Monday you know . . . the movie . . . Garon's movie. . . ."

His voice was matter-of-fact. "Oh — I'd meant to tell you before. Had a call from Garon this morning, and they're not going to be needing you again." He held his hand up as if to ward off her protests, although Sara could not have spoken a word right then. "Of course you'll be paid according to your contract, and it's nothing to do with you — Garon asked me to tell you that you're a great little actress and he'd like to use you again in his next film. But they're having to do a lot of editing because the chase sequences are running longer than anticipated. So one of the writers came up with the idea that the one scene between you and Garon was all that was needed. Cut to your 'suicide' — and the fall from the roof is going to be done by a professional stuntwoman."

He looked at her quizzically, gauging her stunned lack of response. "You're not imagining you're in love with Garon are you? Didn't think so — you'd be too sensible for that! And as for . . . well, never mind! I've promised myself I'm not going to meddle. And I'll give you that promise too, my dear, if you decide to keep a lonely old man company." He added craftily, "You could dust the pictures in my gallery if you *insist* on keeping busy, you know. And you must remind me to show you my collection of snuffboxes. Not to mention —"

By this time Sara had recovered herself sufficiently to interrupt. "That's also known as bribery. And moreover — lonely old man indeed!"

He chuckled delightedly. "Aha! That's the Nanny Staggs coming out in you now, isn't it? Did you think you really had me fooled?"

"I . . . couldn't be sure. But you won't give me away, will you? Not to *anybody,* please!"

He snorted explosively. "And why in hell should I do that and spoil the show? Believe me, my girl, I'm having more fun watching the little game you've been playing than I've had for years. You're not doing too badly, either! Got everyone else fooled that you're really your half sister, haven't you? Well, good for you — whatever crazy scheme you two females have cooked up between you. Mostly Delight's pushing, I can guess. . . . But as I said before, I'm not going to meddle!"

Thank goodness for Uncle Theo! What would she have done if they hadn't rediscovered each other? Sara returned to her room thoughtfully; part of herself tempted to stay and be a lotus-eater for a while — the other half not wanting to drop a challenge. And besides, she had *promised* Delight. What did it matter what she did with the time she had left? Delight should be safely in India by now, and if Carlo was as resolute as her sister believed, *he* should be on his way to join her there. All Sara had to do was buy them as much time as she could — for as long as she could continue her masquerade.

She had almost made up her mind to surrender and be coddled in luxury when a telephone call disrupted her brittle sense of serenity.

"This is di Cavalieri."

Her heart had started thudding unpleasantly, and her fingers curled and tightened around the phone. Please — let her voice sound calm!

"Oh . . . hello! I hadn't expected to hear from you. . . ."

His voice was as harshly uncompromising as she remembered. "No doubt. However, there is something that we must discuss. All these articles in the newspapers, for instance."

"I —"

He swept on arrogantly, as if he hadn't heard her.

"I am not blaming you. I am sure you're used to whatever you do being 'news' . . . I am not used to such publicity. But there is an article that is to appear tomorrow, in one of the weekly scandal sheets, I understand." She could almost see his thin nostrils curling with disdain, even while she looked down at her strain-whitened knuckles, clutching the receiver. She wished she couldn't picture him at all, chauvinist brute that he was! But why on earth had he bothered to call her? Something about an article in a scandal sheet. . . .

". . . And so I think it is important that we meet to discuss certain matters. You will understand when I explain. And please — you need not worry that there will be a repetition of last night. You may pick as public a place as you wish."

"If there's anything you think I ought to know about that article you *say* is going to appear tomorrow — and how do you know about it ahead of time, by the way? — then you could just as well tell me over the telephone."

His voice deepened to what sounded like an angry growl. "There are some things that should not be discussed over telephones! Unless, for some reason, you are afraid to meet me face to face . . . ?"

It was both a challenge and a slap across the face with a velvet glove. Oh, but he was a bastard! Knowing exactly what buttons to press. *Afraid* to meet him — that was ridiculous! Afraid of what? Certainly not of herself. . . .

"I'm not afraid at all!" Sara hated herself for sounding almost defensive. "It's just that I . . . I might be tied up this evening."

"Think of Carlo. Your fiancé. Is it fair to him, this date that may tie you up all evening? At least, with me in a public place you could tell him truthfully that it was all merely business. So — where would you like to go? The Polo Lounge? El Padrino? Both places are usually quite crowded all night. You will feel safe."

Of course, she shouldn't go. She shouldn't subject herself to the anger and the turmoil he aroused in her. And yet, Sara knew with a feeling of fatalistic despair that she *would* go. Hear whatever it was he had to tell her so urgently. Watch his dark, dangerous face across a table in perfect safety, knowing he

162

couldn't very well sweep her into his arms and carry her away *this* time. Maybe seeing him again was exactly what she needed to rid her of her stupid fixation. She'd look at him, and listen to him tell her that he really couldn't afford any more gossip. He was probably *married*, why hadn't she thought of that? All the better — she would be haughty and aloof. *Listen* to him, sipping her Perrier-and-lime with a bored air. And then she would leave, to be driven back in Uncle Theo's chauffered Rolls. *Finis*.

Hanging up, Sara stared blindly at the telephone. Hopefully, she'd sounded casual enough — even slightly distracted and impatient. Hopefully, she'd be able to act that way when she was faced with him — Il Duca di Cavalieri — custom-tailored clothes masking the feline ripple of muscles underneath. Somehow, she could more easily imagine him in the past, as a pirate or a mercenary with a dagger at his belt, rather than in the role of a modern-day Italian aristocrat, moving in polite circles.

Stop it, Sara! You're becoming quite silly, my girl. Better straighten yourself out! The mental admonishment helped. What Nanny Staggs would have recommended was a bracing cold shower, "to clear the mind." Determinedly, Sara jumped off the bed and headed for the bathroom. She had two whole hours in which to make herself presentable enough for the Polo Lounge.

She was fifteen minutes late, in the end, but her makeup was understated and flawless; and *he* would never know how many dresses lay discarded across her bed, and at least, thanks to the smoothly effortless efficiency that surrounded Uncle Theo, she now had her entire wardrobe here to choose from.

She was shown to a table by the windows, and Sara hoped that her smile was as brilliant as the bright red lip gloss she had used tonight. He stood up, the lean, dark length of him dwarfing her — his perfunctory kiss not even a lip-brush across the back of her extended hand.

"It was good of you to come." Even his words were politely formal, pushing her into exclaiming:

"Oh, that's all right! But I really do have to rush, you know. I've promised some friends of mine to go roller-skating tonight. *'Flippers'* — you know where it is?"

"I've heard of such a place." His voice dismissed it and her attempt at coolness.

Sara's eyes were drawn to his hands — strong fingers unadorned except for the one ring she had noticed before. It was all she could do not to shiver, giving herself away. "Well, it's really a young people's place, I suppose."

This time she was rewarded by a flicker of

flame beneath the surface of those night-black eyes. But instead of retorting sarcastically he inclined his head. "I suppose that is true. Certainly it is not the kind of place I would choose if I felt like going out to dance! But what does Carlo think of your going out without him?"

Sara couldn't help the angry flush that heated her cheeks. "That's really none of your business, is it?" She really did detest him after all!

He had already ordered a bottle of white wine, and his fingers had been toying with the stem of his glass as he studied her. Now, without asking, he poured her a glass.

"On the contrary," he said slowly, his words without inflection, "it is very much my business. Carlo happens to be my younger brother."

"Your . . . ." Sara thought for one horrible moment that she was going to choke on her wine. His flat, unembellished statement kept repeating itself in her mind. Repeating, while she stared at him over the rim of her glass. Until the meaning of what he'd just said sank into her consciousness.

He made the mistake of pressing home his advantage, his voice coldly sarcastic. "You knew, surely, that Carlo had a family? And did he neglect to tell you that he works for me and has no money of his own yet?"

The wine she was finally able to swallow

went to Sara's head with a rush, reminding her that she hadn't eaten since brunch in the early afternoon. But it helped her look him in the eye.

"Carlo has told me *everything!*" she exclaimed with dignity. And then, not able to resist it: "So *you're* big bad John! I'm sorry — it's really Giovanni, isn't it? How do *you* prefer to be called, though? Riccardo — or is that just your alias? — Marco. . . ."

"That's enough!" His voice cut across hers like a whiplash, and if she hadn't been so angry she might have flinched.

"Oh, is it? I don't really think so. *You* started this, remember? You asked me to join you here for a drink because you had to tell me something. What made you decide to drop your cute little masquerade — Riccardo?"

He reached his hand across the table to take hers, and though it might have looked like a gesture of affection to anyone who might have been watching, Sara had to bite back a cry of pain at the hard pressure of his fingers over hers. And yet, in spite of the violence she sensed in the studied cruelty of his grip, his voice remained coldly warning. "Please try to keep your voice down. A public scene here would certainly do nothing to help your . . . career." The pause before he pronounced the last word was deliberately insolent, making her want to scratch at his black, mocking eyes.

She fought for control, trying to remember

that he, at least, still believed she was who she said she was. He still thought she was Delight!

"Please let go of my hand. You're hurting me. You don't have to try and prove what a big strong man you are!"

"I'm sorry." He withdrew his hand, and Sara rubbed at her fingers. It gave her an excuse not to have to look at him.

"Well? What else did you have to say to me? And what was all that about an article that's supposed to appear tomorrow? Another phony story?"

"Unfortunately not." She had the feeling that he was speaking from between gritted teeth. "The story *is* appearing, and it says something to the effect that you must like to keep it in the family. First the younger brother, and then — when he's gone — the elder. I thought it best that you hear the truth from me before you heard the version of the press."

Sara was still rubbing at her fingers. "How very considerate of you!" she uttered coldly. "And was that all? The car's waiting for me — and as I said, I have a busy night ahead of me. Want to come along to make sure I don't misbehave?"

She stared at him challengingly, observing almost impersonally the muscles that bunched along his jaw, giving him an even more dangerous look than usual.

"No — that was not all. Why don't we stop playing games? Now we are unmasked. You know who I am, and I know . . . what you are. Carlo may be infatuated by you but he will never marry you — did he tell you that he was engaged already?"

"You sound like something out of feudal times!" Sara snapped at him, her temper rising again. "Carlo and I have been completely honest with each other from the beginning, and I happen to know that he's not engaged — except to me! You'd like to push him into some loveless marriage that *you* think is suitable, wouldn't you? Well, it's not going to happen that way. Carlo and I are going to be married, and we *don't* need your blessing. I can support Carlo until he . . . he finds himself."

"Or until he comes into his inheritance? No doubt he told you that, too. Very well, Miss Delight. Let us both come to the point. How much will it take for you to promise to leave Carlo alone? I promise you that I could make it much more worth your while than whatever you might earn for performing or posing in the nude."

It was her moment, and she took it. If she had stayed she *would* have created a scene. With commendable self-discipline Sara set down her glass and rose, her body slim and enticing in a Chloé dress that bared one gold-tanned shoulder.

"I really don't care to sit here and trade insults with you. And get this straight — I'm *not* for sale. *Capisce?* I'm going to marry Carlo — and what's more, I'm going to issue a press release to that effect. I might also mention how impossibly medieval *you're* being. . . . And all the world loves a lover, isn't that so? We're going to have a lot of sympathy on our side, Carlo and I!"

To her surprise, he displayed none of the anger or chagrin she had expected. He came to his feet in an easy, fluid motion that took her by surprise, his hand going out to halt her. A somewhat unwilling smile twisted his lips. "Hold on! Perhaps I was . . . testing the strength of your love for my brother. At all events, we're better off friends than enemies, don't you think? Carlo would prefer it that way — he is rather spoiled and used to a certain style of living. Haven't you noticed?"

Nonplussed, Sara stared at him suspiciously. He could change moods and directions as quickly as the wind and, like the wind, he was completely unpredictable.

"Delight . . ." he said almost coaxingly, his deep, rather grating voice making a rough caress of the name. "Shall we learn to be friends instead of enemies? Wait here with me a minute until I have found our waiter, and I will take you home — or to this favorite roller discotheque of yours, whichever you prefer. Is it a bargain? I think we have a lot to talk about — and you have a lot to learn about my family. Perhaps you might hesitate in joining it after I have produced all of the skeletons out of the closets!"

That fast, he had managed to pierce her armor of self-righteous indignation, leaving Sara bewildered and uncertain of her next move. What *should* she do? All her own instincts urged her to run, cowardly or not — but if she was supposed to be Delight, and she could help Delight and Carlo by winning Carlo's big brother over. . . . Rationalization certainly helped!

"Well . . ." she said uncertainly, and he seized on her hesitation. A waiter materialized out of nowhere; and perhaps he didn't realize that he was still holding her hand. After he'd made overtures of peace it might seem rude to pull away.

She ought to feel relieved, Sara thought dully as she walked out beside him, still all too conscious of the firm pressure of his fingers over hers. No more conflict, no more tension. Delight and Carlo would be happy, and she — well she could settle down to studying, which was why she was here in the first place — and she could just hope fervently that he would never, ever find out about the part she'd played in this masquerade. She'd never see him again, and that thought should have made her glad. Why, then, did she feel so empty inside? Why did she allow him to continue holding her hand, even after they were waiting outside, with several pairs of curious eyes staring?

Chapter 14

"Request you fasten seat belts. . . ." Fuzzily, the words penetrated through the fog in Sara's brain. Surely she had already done so?

"Please fasten your seat belt," Riccardo had said before he had turned the key in the ignition of the sleek Lamborghini, making her thankful a moment later that she had obeyed him. And then, from somewhere, he had produced a bottle of champagne. The best, naturally. Nothing else would do to toast her forthcoming wedding to his only brother and heir-apparent.

"Here's to an understanding brother-in-law!" Had she really said that, or was that a part of the dream? How many glasses of champagne later had he finally taken her back home?

Home — where was home, where was she? Why did her eyelids feel as if lead weights had been attached to them? Very faintly, echoing emptily in her ears, Sara heard a small moan she recognized as being her voice. She wanted to wake up — and she didn't.

"Sleep, *cara*. You need sleep. I'll wake you up when we arrive."

Dear God, even in her sleep she recognized that sand-under-silk voice. Why was he calling her *cara?* She wasn't his love, she was supposed to be his brother's fiancée.

Oh, well — it probably didn't matter. Didn't everyone know that all Italian men were inordinately promiscuous? They all had wives as well as mistresses — and what would *she* be? Wife, mistress, or a combination of both? Good old multiple choice! Thinking became too much effort and Sara snuggled back against her comfortable seat again, letting herself drift.

When she did wake up, Sara found herself shocked into groggy awareness. Someone had taken her by the shoulder and was shaking her.

"Come — we have landed. We have an hour until they have refueled and checked everything mechanical."

She *could* open her eyelids after all! Sara stared up into a dark, saturnine face that wore a caustic expression, and blinked her eyes again to make sure she wasn't seeing things.

"Riccardo?" Her voice sounded like a croak. What on earth was wrong with her? Had she passed out? Had he brought her home and then stayed? She should say "where am I?" but that would have sounded too corny. Where *was* she?

He leaned over impatiently to unfasten her seat belt (she *was* wearing a seat belt!), pulling her to her feet in almost the same motion. His arm went around her, steadying her when she swayed uncertainly.

"Come — you probably need something to drink. Perhaps some repairs to your makeup. There's not much time, so we had better hurry."

"I . . . I really don't understand! What am I doing here? What are *you* doing here? And where is here?"

"So you don't remember anything, eh? I suspected as much. If you want to remember things, you should not drink so much champagne." He was leading her down the aisle of a comfortably furnished plane. Sara tried to hang back and he propelled her forward, his arm about her waist becoming as hard and inexorable as a steel band.

"But . . ." There was a little door that said Toilet and Sara pointed toward it desperately. "Stop! I have to . . . you had better let me go in there, or you'll be sorry!" she ended darkly.

For a long, unpleasant moment she thought he might continue to drag her onward, but after a long, considering look he released her, pushing the door open for her with an offhand gallantry that almost smacked of contempt.

"Very well, then. But I will only allow you five minutes. I have a key to that door — you might remember that."

Resentfully, she slammed the door shut behind her, clicking the bolt into the locked position. How *dare* he? Who did he think he was? And worst thought of all, what was she doing with him, alone on an airplane?

She had no answers to her questions. Sara exited with as much dignity as she could muster, wishing she could sweep past him without acknowledging his presence. He gave her a sarcastic inclination of his head.

"You are refreshed? Good. I am glad to find that you are a woman who does not waste time in unnecessary primping. Come — you might also wish to stretch your legs. We have a long flight ahead of us."

She managed, at last, to catch her breath, pulling against him indignantly.

"Stop *dragging* me along! And would you mind telling me what I'm doing here? What you're doing here? Where are we going?"

"Very good —" He ushered her down two steps and into a plushly furnished office whose occupant, a young brown-skinned woman, disappeared soon after they had entered. "You are obviously feeling better — well enough to ask questions. Although I'm surprised that you do not remember."

"Remember *what,* for heaven's sake?"

"Why . . ." He had led her to a couch, almost forcing her to sit, and now he looked down at her with his mouth twisted in a travesty of a smile. "Why — we're going home, of course. Last night you expressed a desire to visit Carlo's ancestral home, which happens to be mine as well. You are going to wait for him there — surely you remember *something*?"

She had the feeling that he was mocking her, taunting her, but her head had started to pound, hurting her so badly that nothing mattered but the alleviation of the pain.

"I don't remember anything at all!" Sara whispered, not wanting to remember now. Oh, no — she wouldn't have. She *couldn't* have! She pressed suddenly clammy fingers against her temples, willing the pain to go away, willing this all to be nothing more than another bad dream.

"Perhaps you should cut down on your drinking!" he said harshly and without sympathy. "Does Carlo know, or have you hidden this side of your character from him?"

Now was surely the time to tell him he'd made a mistake, that he had the wrong girl. And *then* she would have the last laugh . . . wouldn't she?

Sara opened her mouth, and closed it again, sullenly deciding to ignore him instead. She didn't dare. He was capable of *anything;* she believed Delight now. He was capable even of killing her to save his own pride.

"Oh — I do wish you'd stop nagging!" she murmured, still massaging her throbbing temples. "Can't you find me some aspirin? And some iced water, please, that might help."

He wasn't used to waiting on anyone — she could sense that. But perhaps in order to keep her acquiescent he brought her what she had asked for before he seated himself behind a desk with a phone on it, immediately becoming engaged in a low-voice conversation that Sara strained her ears to undersatnd and could not. She could speak Italian, but the dialect he used was beyond her. She closed her eyes and leaned against the back of the couch, trying to muster her wits — and her courage. What had she got herself into *now?*

The aspirins had helped her headache, but she still felt unaccountably drowsy. Sara let herself be helped back into the sleek Lear jet without a battle, too tired even to wonder where they had stopped to refuel.

Her seat reclined backward into a bed — how marvelous. Once they were airborne and the Fasten Seat Belts sign had been turned off, a young man appeared to bring her a blanket and made her comfortable, disappearing again soon afterward. Riccardo, she noticed from under her lashes, was reading from a thick folder, his slanting black brows drawn together in a frown of concentration.

He seemed to have forgotten her presence until, without looking up, he said in his grating voice: "There is a curtain that you can draw for privacy if you wish it. You have only to pull the cord — or press the buzzer that will summon Damon again. Try to be comfortable — it will be about eight hours until we are there."

Without a word, Sara yanked the curtains closed. Eight hours! He was actually taking her to Italy — to "the ancestral home" — wasn't that how he'd put it? And he still thought she was Delight. Now she could shiver without being afraid of giving herself away. What did he really plan to do with her?

When she had been a child — even as a teenager — she had always secretly dreamed of embarking on an Adventure. In her fantasies Sara had always been a Princess — or at the very least the daughter of a Duke. Kidnapped by a gentleman-pirate or carried off by a highwayman who was a Duke himself, all her fantasies had had happy endings. In all of them she had been almost ravished — but never quite violated. The innocent maiden always overcame the rakehell hero-villain and had him worshiping at her pedestal in the end. A passionate embrace — and fadeout. What happened after the fadeout? Sara shifted uncomfortably, trying to still her overdramatic imagination. All she had to do was to keep her head, remembering that she was buying Delight and Carlo more time. And by now she was fervently on their side. What an impossibly arrogant, overbearing man! How she would enjoy seeing his face when he learned the truth — that he had gone to all this trouble to carry off the wrong girl!

She must have slept — as improbable as it would have seemed. And slept heavily, her sleep laced through with dark dreams.

"Please fasten your seat belts. . . ." Wasn't that how this particular dream had begun? Still drowsy, Sara appreciated the help of the young man who now made sure that her seat was back in position, her seat belt securely fastened. With the concealing curtain drawn back again, she could not help noticing the man she still thought of as "Riccardo."

The thick folder he had been studying so intently had been set aside, and he was studying *her* instead, his eyes heavy-lidded and enigmatic. She looked away immediately, pretending to peer out the small window. In a short while they would be landing in Italy. If not for the circumstances she would have been thrilled.

Dante and Beatrice. Romeo and Juliet! Fountains and light, a timeless place. She had *always* wanted to visit Italy, but Daddy wouldn't hear of it. Whenever she'd tackled him about it he'd always blame the communists, although his prejudice was probably based on Pietro, one of her mother's ex-husbands. Pietro had been the one to follow Daddy. Almost guiltily, Sara had always liked Pietro, who had been warm and affectionate and had carried her hoisted up on his shoulders, pretending to be a fierce stallion. Delight had liked Pietro too.

"We shall be landing in a few minutes. And then we will have to take a helicopter. I hope you are not the nervous type."

He *would* have to intrude, forcing her back to unpleasant reality. Sara shot him what she hoped was a quelling look.

"I'm not nervous at all. But all this flying is tiring, you know! I do hope we won't be too much longer."

"Once we are in the helicopter — about thirty minutes, perhaps. Has Carlo described our home to you? It is not very accessible, and the roads are rather primitive. We do have other amenities, however."

"And indoor plumbing, I *hope!*" Sara retorted flippantly; deriving a fleeting satisfaction from the tightening of the muscles in his face.

"We are not exactly backward, even in Sardinia. I am sure you will be comfortable. If you like to swim, we have two pools. There are also four tennis courts, if you would like to improve your game while you are waiting for Carlo. You play quite a good game of tennis, I have noticed.

How dared he sound so condescending? She played "quite a good game of tennis" indeed!

Sara smiled with obvious sweetness that was meant to get under his skin. "Tennis — oh good! It's the greatest exercise in the world, don't you think? I hope you'll give me a game sometime." And then, playing her role to the hilt, she sighed deeply. "How I wish Carlo would *hurry!* It was really mean of you to send him so far away." Now was the time to pout, if she knew how. Fearlessly, Sara returned a black-browed scowl with a widening of her artificial smile. "But I suppose you were testing us both. The strength of our feelings for each other. But you mustn't worry, really. Carlo and I love each other — and I have always longed to have a big brother!"

Perhaps she had gone too far. Thank goodness for the seat belt that prevented him from assailing her physically. Watching him with interested fascination, Sara observed the tiny white lines that formed beside his mouth — the tensing of his jaw. His eyes, black as tar and just as opaque, swept over her; a long, measuring look that was accompanied by the contemptuous curl of his lips.

"You are looking for a brother?" She didn't know if there was a tinge of sarcasm underlying the question or not.

"I have two brothers, by Mama's first husband. But they are archeologists — or something equally dull — they're twins, you know. And I've never really known them or been around them, so this is a whole new experience. Carlo never did tell me how . . . *protective* and considerate you are. It was *so* thoughtful of you to have one of Uncle Theo's maids pack all my stuff for me. . . ."

Judging from his expression, she had gone far enough. Sara subsided with a last insincere smile in his direction; turning her head to pretend concentration on the view as the jet circled and then swooped down for a landing.

Chapter 15

"How did people come and go from here before they had helicopters?"

"Very slowly!" There was a certain grim humor in his voice. "There is a road, of course, but a very bad one. Not good for the kind of low-slung automobiles they make these days."

"But . . ."

"In these days there are also the terrorists. Murders and kidnapping." He shrugged. "There are also bandits in the mountains — angry, hungry men. A helicopter is the safest way to get here. Why take unnecessary chances, after all?"

"Why indeed," Sara murmured. In order to avoid his eyes she looked over the low stone balustrade that ran the length of the terrace where they were being served drinks.

The palazzo (it was at *least* a palace!) had been built very high and the view was breathtaking, including, as it did, the ocean very far below. It had also been built very securely — perhaps, in past centuries, to ward off Moorish raiders and mercenary armies who roamed about looking for plunder and women. At any rate, the ancestral home of the Duca di Cavalieri was surrounded by high walls that in turn were topped by electrified barbed wire. A medieval fortress, in fact; but with all the comforts and luxuries of the twentieth century here behind the forbidding stone walls. There were tennis courts — even a miniature golf course. The housekeeper had shown Sara to a suite that overlooked a formal garden; perfume from the flowers that grew there rising in the warm air as she had stood there, leaning over a low stone wall. There was even a magnificent indoor swimming pool with azure tiling — cunningly concealed underwater lighting making it seem like an enchanted grotto. Two marble staircases led down to the enormous ballroom that had the blue pool as its center.

Her tour had been very short, merely skimming the surface. Through it all Sara had tried to maintain a wide-eyed, ingenuous image. It might be wisest to keep her claws sheathed — at least, until she understood why he had brought her here. It was hard, though. . . .

Sara brought her eyes back deliberately to that dark, implacable face — the caustic twist to his mouth already becoming familiar to her as his eyes, in turn, flickered over her measuringly. She was being overly imaginative, of course, but she could almost feel them burn into her flesh through the thin cotton of the dress she'd changed into. The way in which he looked at her made her feel very much alone — very vulnerable, although she would have submitted to torture rather than let him discover any weakness in her facade.

Sipping her lemon-flavored mineral water, Sara made herself smile.

"It's really beautiful here . . . how kind of you to bring me! And now that I've seen what a *fortress* you have here I feel so safe! When do you think Carlo will come?"

"Who knows?" His shoulders lifted in a far too casual way. "In recent times my little brother has become quite unpredictable. Although I'm sure that when he learns his *fiancée* is here waiting for him impatiently, I'm sure he will be just as impatient to come home."

Perhaps she needed to show a little bit of backbone! Dropping her eyes so that she wouldn't have to meet his, Sara pretended to pout.

"But in the meantime — where is the nearest town to here? What's the action like? I really do love to dance, and of course I love people. Carlo won't grudge me a little entertainment, I'm sure."

The twist to his hard mouth seemed more pronounced for an instant, before he masked his expression. *"Entertainment?* Ah, yes. I suppose you are used to television, for instance, and we do not have it here. And as for dancing . . . I am sorry, but there *are* no discotheques in the nearest village, which happens, I'm afraid, to be a hundred miles away. We are quite isolated here, and the only way — the only *safe* way to go anywhere from here is by helicopter. But is anything not to your satisfaction?"

"Well . . . but what is there to *do* here?"

"If you wish amusement or entertainment I am sure you will find it here. There are two swimming pools — and the tennis courts, of course. I would be glad to give you a game — and perhaps a little more competition than your idol Garon Hunt. He was being very polite the other night, but I should warn you that *I* am not soft enough to sacrifice victory for gallantry!"

His mocking words were meant to be barbs that would embed themselves under the skin. But *oh!* This time he had mistaken his victim!

"Gallantry? Well, of course I don't expect gallantry — and especially from you. Thanks for the offer of a tennis game, though — and don't expect *me* to be polite either. I happen to enjoy winning myself."

Sara met his eyes defiantly, not realizing in her anger at him that the setting sun had brought out fiery lights in her dark-mahogany-colored hair and seemed reflected in her green eyes, reminding him of a young, spitting mountain cat. It both annoyed and intrigued him to find that this young woman he had been prepared to despise from the beginning had managed to make herself a challenge to him. Damn her! The investigations he'd had carried out into her past had presented a three-dimensional portrait of a typical "liberated" young female with hardly any morals to speak of — and no false modesty either. She had taken her clothes off for the inquisitive cameras as easily as she had for a dozen or more men. What did she think to prove by playing hard to get with him? Was that how she had entrapped his susceptible young step-brother?

His dark brows had drawn together as he studied her with a brooding scowl that made Sara shudder involuntarily. Hanging unspoken in the air between them was the *real* reason for his having brought her here. What did he mean to do with her? How long could they both continue to cling to the pretense that he had brought her here to wait for his brother? "Brought her" indeed! Sara corrected herself indignantly. "Abducted" her was more like it! Only, she must never let him discover that she was afraid, or the dark, dangerous animal she could sense beneath the light veneer of civilized politeness might make a sport of her destruction.

"Can you possibly be cold? Or were you

perhaps thinking of — victory and defeat?"

Never let him see her weakness! Sara shrugged with pretended indifference, letting her eyes wander to the vine-hung balustrade of rough stone that plunged steeply down to the wrinkled-looking ocean below.

"Oh, but I never think of defeat!" Deliberately, she turned aside the pointed provocativeness of his questioning with an air of studied naiveté. "Actually, what I *was* trying to imagine was this . . . this castle as it must have been hundreds of years ago. It's built like a fortress, isn't it? Whom did your ancestors have to fight off?"

Now he leaned back in his chair, watching her through slightly narrowed dark eyes as if to gauge the effect his words might have upon her.

"My ancestors built this place to fight off the Moorish pirates who marauded the coasts, carrying off the most beautiful of our young women as slaves — sometimes as their wives. In fact, legend has it that the man who founded our line was part Moor himself, like Shakespear's Othello. In any case, he built this impregnable fortress to protect himself, his family and the peasants who farmed his lands from other mercenaries like himself. Hasn't Carlo told you anything of our family history?"

"No . . . but it's easy to imagine. Except for the tennis courts and the swimming pools and of course the electricity, it would be all too easy to imagine that we're still trapped in the past and not in the twentieth century at all!"

"And you will find, I'm afraid, that in a lot of ways this is still so." He had discarded his dark jacket and his tie, and his ivory silk shirt was open at the throat. Against the black, crisply curling hair of his chest a heavy gold medallion caught Sara's unwilling glance — a raised, intricately carved design of a crouching wolf with emerald chips for eyes — mouth open in a snarl. How well it suited him!

Now, as if he had somehow been able to sense the sudden agitation of her thoughts, Marco touched the medal lightly, his eyes never leaving hers. "This interests you? It's very old — the story has it that it belonged to that Moorish pirate ancestor I was telling about just now, who was a wolf of the sea and carried off as his captive bride a fifteen-year-old maiden who persuaded him to come back to live here in these savagely beautiful surroundings that matched the temperaments of them both! The eyes remind me of yours. . . ."

He was playing with her, of course, and she mustn't let him. Sara reached for her glass with a light laugh that dispelled all shades of the past.

"And I, of course, owe my eyes to my mother! I would like her here when Carlo and

I are married — *shall* we be married here, by the way? I would really prefer Los Angeles, where most of my friends are; unless it's some kind of a family tradition that all Marcantoni brides are married here. It *is* rather remote, isn't it?"

She had changed into a pale-green cotton dress that was lined with flesh-colored chiffon — the scooped neckline demure enough to reveal just the slight curve of her breasts. His black, enigmatic eyes had been studying her in much the same fashion as his ancestor might have studied the maiden he meant to ravish, but now her flippantly worded speech made his mouth tighten before he said cuttingly: "I should think these are matters you should discuss with my brother, and not with me. And perhaps . . . after you have spent a few weeks here in this . . . *remote* place in the mountains of Sardinia, you might change your mind. We live very simply here."

Pretending not to notice that he meant to quell her, Sara said brightly, "But you *do* travel quite a lot, don't you? With a private helicopter it can't be *too* isolated here! And I've heard there's always a lot going on on the Costa Smeralda. Do you have a yacht, by the way?"

"I have usually no time to waste on pleasure cruising. I do not believe in leaving my affairs to be run by lawyers and accountants, and there is always much to be seen to. When

190

Carlo is ready, then he too will be kept busy. I hope you won't find yourself too bored!"

Sara shrugged, still keeping her smile, even if it *had* turned a trifle brittle around the edges. "I'm sure I won't let myself be — I've no intention of playing the conventional wife, you know! I intend to travel *everywhere* with my husband, and interest myself in everything he's interested in."

Hopefully, he wouldn't throw her over the stone walls to be smashed to pieces against the jagged rocks below — all traces of her being sucked away by the hungry waves. He *could,* and no one would ever know.

Black eyes, as jaggedly cutting as the rocks Sara could picture all too clearly, seemed to slice right through her hastily erected defenses before he hooded them.

"Is that so?" the Duca di Cavalieri drawled. "One would hope, of course that your intended husband knows of your . . . um . . . ambitions. Italian men, and especially those of us from the south have not learned to be tame and easily manipulated as your average American male!"

The little bitch! he thought consideringly. Was it possible that she was deliberately trying to bait him? And if so, for what reasons of her own? He was having an unusually difficult time keeping his temper under check — all the more so because he had the annoying feeling that so far the advantage in their

191

contest of wills and words was hers.

If he hadn't been a man whose appetites had been jaded by too much being available to him too easily for most of his life, he would have been tempted to put her too easily professed devotion to Carlo to the test by forcing her to yield to him . . . he let his eyes dwell with open insolence on her mouth — rewarded in part by her slight flush. But no, he thought, that would be too easy. What he really wanted was for her to give up without coercion; yielding to the demands of her own promiscuously passionate nature. No — when it was all over and he had proved his point she would not be able to tell Carlo that his older brother had raped her. He wanted to be able to show Carlo how easily vanquished this woman who had been named "Delight" really was. And it should not take too long . . . there was a small pulse that throbbed in the hollow of her slender throat that showed the agitation she was trying to mask. Good! Give her a few days of boredom — romantic, star-filled nights without a man to satisfy her sexual nature . . . and she would be easy.

The setting sun cast a light that was as red as the stain of blood against ancient, weathered stone. Sara remembered the story Delight had told her of the unfortunate first wife of the last Duca di Cavalieri — murdered like Desdemona, because she had, perhaps, looked too long at another man. And before her now, lounging in his chair while his eyes assessed her insolently, was the son of that same dark-natured Sardinian — his proudly proclaimed Moorish ancestry showing all too clearly in the darkness of his skin, the blackness of his hair, the lips that were both sensual and cruel under slightly flaring nostrils.

"I . . . don't care for manipulation of any kind!" Sara said abruptly, wanting only to break the strange tension that had begun to stretch between them. How quickly the sun seemed to swoop down — how long and cold the shadows that followed its descent! "Please — I'm beginning to feel rather tired. Perhaps I'd better go inside and try to find my room."

Surprisingly, as if he'd grown tired himself of the sport she provided, he rose to his feet, helping her politely from her chair.

"Of course — forgive me. And if you don't feel up to a formal dinner, I'm sure Serafina will see that one of the maids brings you a tray."

Chapter 16

Sara had flung back the shutters that opened onto large, grilled windows sometime last night when the closed room had become too oppressive for her. Now, in the morning, she was awakened by the sunlight that streamed in to force her eyes open.

In between sleeping and waking there was a strange sense of disorientation while she wondered, fuzzily, where she was. Had she been dreaming — was she still dreaming? Everything was unfamiliar, from the enormous four-postered bed in which she lay, to the brilliance of the sun and the harsh screeching of the birds outside. Harsh — stark. Oh, God! She was actually in Sardinia, of all places, in a ducal palazzo that was really a medieval castle-fortress; the unwilling captive of an Italian duke who was a throwback to the Dark Ages himself.

"There, there! Things will always seem better in the morning!" Another of Nanny

Staggs' favorite sayings; but hardly apropos *this* morning! Sara bolted upright, discovering to her relief that she was alone. Memory came flooding back, heightening the sense of unreality she had felt upon first waking. She blinked fiercely and took a deep breath of clean-smelling air that smelled partly of the ocean and partly of the mountains and hoof-crushed herbs.

Take a hold of yourself! she commanded herself, letting her eyes wander around the room in order to familiarize herself with it.

The style was Regency, a period she had always loved. The walls were paneled with brocade — a richly woven pattern in which gold gleamed against pale green and ivory with touches of crimson for contrast. Her bed had a canopy of ivory and gold and matched the draperies hanging heavily on each side of the windows. Each item of furniture was exquisite and would have fetched a fortune at Sotheby's. Eastern rugs were scattered carelessly over polished floors.

From the bedroom an arched doorway led into a private sitting room that was dominated by a Directoire couch; hanging above it a painting of a lovely dark-haired woman who reclined on the same couch, her chin propped up by one ringed hand while the slender white fingers of the other played with a heavy gold pendant that lay in the hollow between her breasts. Last night, everything had been dimly lit and Sara had been tired, hardly having the energy to study everything around her. But today the sun fell directly on the portrait, and fascinated, she climbed out of bed to walk barefoot through the Moorish arch of the doorway — standing before the picture of a woman who must have been long dead, and yet seemed alive; her slanting, light brown eyes holding a promise of laughter and gaiety. And the pendant — surely it was the twin to the medallion that the Duke had worn? Who was she? The gown she wore fell in heavy, artful folds that only served to emphasize the rich curve of hip and breasts — suggest the outline of long legs. Her hair was long and slightly curling; one heavy ringlet falling across a white breast. Disappointingly, the portrait was unsigned.

"Did you wish breakfast, signorina?"

Sara had not heard anyone come in and she spun around on her bare feet, despising the way her heart had begun to jump. She seemed to remember locking her door — was she to be allowed no privacy, like a woman in a harem? She would have snapped out a reply, except for the fact that the brown-skinned maid was hardly more than a child, and obviously nervous.

"I . . ." Sara gave an impatient sigh. "Yes, please, I'd love some juice. Orange juice, if you have it — or coffee, if you don't. Or do I have a choice?" Noticing the girl's puzzled look she switched to Italian —although the girl probably spoke a dialect — and managed to make herself understood with the help of gestures.

"By the way — who is she? The lady in the picture, she's very beautiful."

Poised at the door, the girl looked frightened, as if she would have preferred not to give her stammered answer.

"She is . . . the first wife to Il Duca's father, signorina. The mother of Il Duca."

His *mother* — the murdered first wife of the last Duke di Cavalieri? Sara found herself staring at the hastily closed door with too many unanswered questions swirling around in her brain before she turned at last to study the portrait with new interest. Was it possible that this pale-skinned woman with the enigmatic half-smile was the saturnine Marco's mother? What had really happened to her — and why? In the portrait she seemed very sure of herself and her beauty, with her slender fingers toying carelessly with the image of a gold wolf with emeralds for eyes. Had she been too careless, perhaps, and too sure of her charms — until the wolf that she thought tamed had turned on her savagely, stilling her laughter, destroying her beauty? How had she died?

The silent maid came to draw her a bath, and with a shiver, Sara turned away from the portrait whose eyes seemed to follow her as if to warn her. Oh, God — she must guard against becoming morbid! After all, *she* wasn't married to a dark-skinned Sardinian who carried in his veins the fiercely unrelenting blood of his Saracen ancestors! She wasn't even married to his brother, she was merely playing a game of make-believe for Delight's sake, and she could escape any time she wished, merely by telling him. . . .

By telling him how you've made a fool of him? her mind jeered at her, and the thought of how *he* might react made her flinch in spite of herself. Well, Sara, you've certainly landed yourself in a pretty mess *this* time!

Railing at herself wouldn't help at all. Here she was, and she had best rely on her wits to get her out of an impossible situation. Kidnapped by a Duke — who would believe it? Soaking in perfumed water that jetted from gold faucets, her sunken marble tub large enough to accommodate an orgy, Sara tried to consider her situation rationally — but the answers she came up with only served to depress her. By pursuing her publicly enough to make them An Item in Hollywood, he'd craftily set the stage for their disappearance together. He'd even got her out of the movie with Garon; and her jetting off with a rich Italian nobleman would be considered just the kind of madly impulsive action Delight Adams was known for.

Scrubbing her back, Sara looked consideringly at the blurred, steamy reflection of herself in the mirrors that paneled the walls of her private bathroom. Well, here she was in what might have been a Hollywood set — in the middle of what she would have much *preferred* to have been a typical Hollywood soap opera. Just a few months ago she had been thinking how dull and sterile her life was, with everything mapped out for her, including a future "suitable" marriage. Poor Daddy, how hard he had tried to make sure she didn't emulate her mother — or her half sister. How carefully he'd tried to guard her from publicity and what he considered were "bad influences." He had meant well, and he loved her in his reserved way, but she *must* have more of her mother in her than either of them could have guessed.

Sara had pinned her hair at the back of her head in a makeshift knot, but short tendrils had escaped to cling damply against the nape of her neck and her heat-flushed cheeks and temples. Her hair was beginning to straighten out again and she felt more like herself, better able to deal with anything. All she had to remember was *not* to slip, and not to think — she shuddered — too far ahead!

It was more a sudden strange *feeling*, rather than any sound she had heard, that made Sara realize with a sudden, unpleasant shock that she was no longer alone. Instinctively, she lowered her body under the water as far as she could without drowning, her green eyes flashing with indignation.

"So — where are you hiding? You're late for our tennis match!"

"Go away! I'm taking a bath. Or aren't I to be allowed any privacy?"

"Certainly! But you must forgive me if I'm surprised at your sudden show of modesty! After all, as you expressed yourself in one interview that I read, you have a beautiful body — why should you be ashamed of showing it?"

He stood in the doorway (another arched Moorish doorway with no door, unfortunately!) wearing closely fitting tan linen pants, with polished high boots that gave her the impression he'd been out riding. His black eyebrows were raised; his mouth twisted in a sarcastic grimace that didn't quite rate as a smile. He was absolutely hateful!

"Never mind my body! It's nothing to do with you. Or had you forgotten that I'm your *brother's* fiancée?"

Perhaps Delight would not have stayed submerged in water up to her neck — Delight would *not* have been ashamed of her body — in fact she would probably have flaunted it in his face while she challenged him with the fact that she belonged to Carlo. But she wasn't Delight. . . .

"Naturally, I had forgotten nothing!" he drawled. And then, with a grating laugh: "Did you think I meant to ravish my *brother's* fiancée? Believe me, I have never had to resort to rape to get what I have wanted from a woman. Why should one attempt to take by force that which is freely offered? At least, in *this* day and age!"

How *dared* he sound so patronizing, so . . . so damned arrogant? And the way he stood there with his booted feet astride, looking *down* at her. . . .

Sara felt sheer rage flood her, blinding her, for some moments, to both reason and restraint. If she had had a gun, she would have shot him; if she had been in the habit of carrying a little dagger to guard her virtue like some Sardinian peasant woman, she would have flung it at him, aiming straight for his black, cruel heart. But as it was, without thinking, she acted instinctively — scooping up water in her cupped hands to fling it at him just as an angry child might have done.

Dark water stains spread on those immaculate linen pants; raised drops of water stood out on his polished boots. And what did she care what he thought of her? Why should *she* be the only one to act polite and civilized? "Well, *I'm* certainly not offering you anything — and I never have . . . so you have no excuse for wandering in here while I'm taking a bath! I do wish you'd just go away!"

There were a few taut seconds in which Sara thought that he might actually leap into the

tub in which she sat crouched defiantly —
joining her in order to punish her insolence.
His face had darkened, and the words that
emerged harshly from between his clenched
jaw were fortunately couched in Italian;
certainly *not* the kind of words she had learned
in any of the schools she had attended.

"I'm the one who should be swearing at
you!" she reminded him indignantly. "Aren't
there any laws of hospitality in this part of
the world? I thought I was supposed to be
your *guest. . . !"*

He would have loved to have wrung her
neck, of course; and the smoldering look in
his eyes told her so before he accorded her a
stiff inclination of his head — all expression
left his face; it looked like a mask carved out
of hardwood. "My apologies. I suppose it is
because I have been privileged enough to
have seen all of the motion pictures you have
made that I felt a sense of . . . familiarity
with you. Wasn't there a bathing scene in
Love's Essence when you were not nearly as
modest as you appearto be now?"

Love's Essence! What a simply ghastly title!
Sara wanted to wince — but not in front of
him. Still keeping as far under water as she
could without drowning she glared moistly at
him, deciding to ignore his sly innuendos.

"Well, I'm not on screen now, am I? And
I'd really appreciate it if you left, so I can get
out and get dressed. I'm sure Carlo wouldn't

like the idea of my traipsing around naked in front of you — he has *such* respect for you!"

Advantage Sara. At least this time around. Sitting later in the mirrored dressing room while she tried to decide if she should use any makeup or not, Sara tried to compose herself for the match of wills and wits that would surely follow their earlier encounter and *his* none-too-willing retreat.

Staring back at her triple-mirrored reflection she was struck all over again by the unreality of the predicament she found herself in. *Love's Essence* indeed! How long could she go on playing Delight? And — worst thought of all — what would he do with her when the masquerade was ended?

Be like Scarlett and think about it tomorrow! Sara told herself; deciding that she was far too pale and needed some color in her face. *He* wouldn't like it — the thought prodded her into applying a touch of blusher to her cheekbones and Lancôme's Glace D'Or lip gloss that made her mouth look full and inviting.

Her hair fell as far as her shoulders in heavy waves, and Sara ran impatient fingers through it. So much for the "natural" permanent she'd had to get in order to be Delight. She hoped Delight and Carlo had had their happy reunion and were safely married by now. And what would Delight think if she *knew* what had happened?

She'd probably laugh hysterically, Sara reminded herself wryly. She tied her hair back from her face with a silk scarf and stood up, twirling around once in front of the mirrors in her pale-green tennis dress; smiling at herself because she knew she looked good. Beyond that, she preferred not to think.

"Excuse me, signorina. . . ."

Flushing, Sara whirled around to face the impassive-looking housekeeper.

"If you're ready, I have been instructed to take you outside. It is difficult to find the way unless you have been here some time."

"Thank you. . . ."

What did the thin, stone-faced woman really think? How long had she been here, serving the family of Il Duca di Cavalieri? On an impulse, Sara added: "Do you know Carlo? My . . . fiancé?"

There was still no expression in the woman's voice as she said, "Since he was a little boy. If you will please follow me, signorina?"

"Goodness, it *is* difficult to find one's way around, isn't it? How kind of you to come and show me."

"I was instructed. . . ." the woman repeated stiffly, although the rigid set of her shoulders seemed to relax slightly.

"By Marco? Have you known him since he was a boy too? What was he like?"

Sara didn't quite know why she persisted in her questioning as she hurried in the wake of the black-clad housekeeper; only this time she was rewarded by a sideways look that seemed to reassess her.

"I have been with the family since just before the coming of the second Duchessa. . . . Duca was then a boy of about seven. Please be careful of the steps, signorina. . . ."

She would probably *never* be able to find her way about this rabbit warren of a palazzo on her own! There were rooms leading into passageways that led into more rooms — and then suddenly they emerged into a gallery that was hung with portraits, most of them very old. Twin marble staircases led downward to an enormous, vaulted hall in the center of which was a swimming pool that looked more like a Roman bath, with steps leading down to the shallowest part and a ledge running all along three sides. The pool itself was blue-tiled, giving the water in it the illusion of a miniature sea.

"How lovely!"

There was an artfully contrived waterfall at the deep end of the pool; the water seeming to gush out of the wall, falling over polished stones.

"The water comes from a stream high in the mountains. It is caught first in a cistern on the roof, where the sun warms it. In case the signorina wishes to swim, the water is always warm enough."

"It's solar heated — marvelous!"

"This way, please. . . ."

The sunlight was almost blinding after the cool darkness of the house. Sara shaded her eyes, squinting them against the glare.

To one side of the twin tennis courts there was a comparatively shady area where trees had been planted, and huge umbrellas shaded tables and chairs.

Marco, Duca di Cavalieri, rose to his feet with exaggerated politeness.

"How good of you to join me! And I see you are dressed for tennis — good. *Grazie,* Serafina."

The woman bobbed her head and disappeared into the comparative coolness of the house, and Sara sat unwillingly in the chair that he had pulled out for her. Were they supposed to forget about their *earlier* meeting today? Perhaps it was just as well! She noticed, irrelevantly, that he had changed into a pair of brief white denim shorts that fitted him almost too closely. His pale-blue cotton shirt was open almost to the waist. With his high-boned corsair's face and those brooding black eyes that narrowed as they rested on her face he looked devastatingly handsome, Sara thought and then caught back her own thought with a feeling of annoyance. She mustn't forget that he was the Enemy! Nor that they had an unspoken bet going. . . .

"You slept well?" Sara had to tear her eyes

away from the wolf medallion that winked in the sun, almost blinding her to reason.

"Yes, thank you. I was very tired." She made her voice cool, but her fingers played nervously with the short hem of her finely pleated skirt.

"And now? Your bath refreshed you I trust?" In the grating roughness of his voice was the memory of the way he had seen her this morning soaking in a marble tub with strands of hair escaping from a careless knot to cling to the curve of her neck and shoulders — outline of firm young breasts only partially concealed by the steamy water. In the darkness of his eyes, as they swept deliberately over her, lingering on her bare arms and legs, Sara could sense the crouched animal that waited, only half-hidden; sure enough of his prey to give her room to run free for a while longer.

Would she be able to escape?

Chapter 17

"I'm surprised that you don't have a moat and a drawbridge to keep yourself *really* cut off from the rest of the world!" Skewering an ice-cold melon ball on her fork, Sara popped it into her mouth; looking across the length of the candle-lit table with a trace of sarcasm in her voice. "How can you be sure that your walls are high enough and your stone gatehouse strong enough to hold off . . . whoever it is you are hiding from? Are there really bandits in this part of the world?"

Her face was slightly flushed, both from the searing heat of the Sardinian sun and from her victory over him in their last tennis match this evening. Oh, but he had been furious, looking at her through those obsidian eyes of his as if he would have burned holes into her too-pale skin, if he could. But now, as he played casually with the stem of his wineglass, his face might have been a dark mask, giving nothing away as he answered her with lazy tolerance: "Bandits? A few fugitives from the law, perhaps — some men who make a livelihood from stealing what others work for. But my stone gatehouse and my guards with their guns are to ward off terrorists, who are not as romantic sounding as bandits and much more dangerous. Why do you ask all these questions? Has something happened to make you nervous?"

"Of course, I'm not nervous! Just curious, that's all," Sara retorted flippantly. "I've been reading a little about Sardinia's history, that's all. You have some nice books. . . ." And then, remembering her role she added hastily, "Those with pictures in them, anyway!"

"I see!" How she hated the caustic tilt of his thick black brows. "You read Italian then?"

"One of my mother's husbands — Pietro Ferrero — was Italian, and he stayed around long enough so that I picked up a few words here and there."

"How useful. But if you are actually interested in the history of *Sardegna,* perhaps I can help you. For instance . . ."

"Oh — I guess the history really doesn't matter!" Sara smiled brightly, knowing from the almost imperceptible tightening of his face that she had succeeded in annoying him again. "What *I'm* really interested in is the Costa Smeralda, which I've heard is a *very* swinging place! Can't we go there?" She pouted. "It's been ages since I've danced, and I'm sure Carlo wouldn't mind — if I was with *you!* Besides . . . I've already been here for what seems like *ages* instead of just days!''

She must go on being her sister, acting as her sister would. And she must continue to keep him at arm's length with her flippant tongue and her independent attitude. This morning, rising early, she had wandered out onto the small terrace her room opened onto, determined to let the sun lend some color to her pale skin and *he* had found her lying out there in her briefest bikini. Again, she had almost forgotten her part; not expecting to see him so early and halfway between waking and dozing Sara had left the powerful transistor radio he'd allowed her on a classical station that played opera. Of course he'd had to make some sarcastic comment, which she had brushed away with the explanation that the station must have changed while she was asleep. And then, as if he had had to find something to attack her about, he'd begun to lecture her about falling asleep in the sun, and the consequences it could have.

All the time he'd been speaking, Sara had been acutely, angrily aware of the way his eyes seemed to range over her with deliberately insolent slowness, lingering on the cleft between her breasts, the shadow between her thighs; and since she did not have a wrap or a towel to cover herself with, it had been too annoying! Especially when her heart had begun to thud unaccountably and her breath caught in her throat, holding back the angry words she had been about to fling at him.

"You had better put some more of that suntan oil on yourself if you mean to stay out longer!" he had said finally, "and keep the radio turned up louder, on a station that plays music that will keep you awake in our hot sun!"

Rock music blasted out to assault her ears under the contemptuous flick of his fingers before he had reached, surprising her, for the brown plastic bottle of tanning oil, warmed by the sun.

"I don't need . . ." she had begun rebelliously — but she might have known he would ignore her protests!

"Turn over." If she had obeyed rather sullenly he would probably have taken her by the shoulder and forced her around. "You cannot manage to apply the oil to your back by yourself. Lie still and I will oblige you."

The pressure of his fingers had been strong and sure, massaging in oil until it felt like silk against her burning skin. She wanted to pull away from the man, run away from his maddening arrogance and subtle cruelty to the safety of her room — but was there anyplace in this palace-fortress of his where she would be safe from him? The crouching wolf, waiting to spring. . . .

He'd noticed the shudder of strange apprehension her thought had produced and had given one of his harsh, grating laughs. "Were you afraid I'd beat you for being a wicked little girl? Not *this* time at any rate . . . unless you relax those tense muscles of yours! Don't you enjoy being massaged?" His voice like sand under silk. His hands hard, and yet almost gentle as he massaged the back of her neck, slid down the canyon of her spine to where she'd knotted the two tiny red strings holding her minuscule top. "Why do you think you need to wear this ridiculous excuse for a bra? I am surprised at the hypocrisy of women, especially those who preach liberation and equality! Didn't you give an interview once in which you stated that you always sunbathe in the nude or not at all, because you like your body to be the same color all over? I will see to it, if you wish, that you have complete privacy up here for as long as you wish to sunbathe each day." His hands slid down from her bra until they cupped and lightly kneaded her tensed buttocks. He ignored Sara's indignant *"Stop it!"* — and moved his hands down the back of her thighs, and then slid insidiously up the softness of their inner sides, while he murmured softly: "I can feel the vibration under your skin! What are you afraid of? That having encouraged you to strip off your clothes and offer your fair body to the sun I will play Apollo myself and rape you? When you came to lie out here this morning, knowing that I would be the only man who would find you, did you think that *this* would have stopped me if I'd been of a mind to exercise my *droit du seigneur?*"

Feeling the light brush of his fingers against her sensitivity had acted like an electric shock, stunning her into awareness. "No!" she had flung out sharply, jerking away from his touch and bolting upright to glare at him indignantly behind tumbled hair.

He had been hunkered down next to her and now his dark, inscrutable face was far too close to her. "No . . . what?" His voice taunted her deliberately, and his eyes dwelt for a moment on the small, agitated pulse that leapt just above her collarbone, before moving to her mouth.

If he touched her she would scream . . . in spite of the fact that there was probably no one who would hear her, or care if they did. But he hadn't touched her, after all — leaving her with an abruptness that startled her.

Now, that same evening, Sara discovered on his face the same strangely tense expression he had worn just before he left her with her frightened mouth and both pieces of her bikini untouched. It was there for one moment only — and then it had disappeared to leave his face expressionless.

"So you miss your discotheques? What would you do if I had to transfer Carlo to

213

some remote part of the world? There are places he might have to go to that do not even have electricity!"

So he was testing her again?

"Isn't *that* the kind of place that you've sent him *this* time? Argentina . . . ugh! But I guess I'll survive — as I'm surviving here!"

"I am glad to hear that — and since you are bored with nothing more than taking the sun and an occasional game of tennis I will certainly try to make arrangements to provide some kind of . . . suitable entertainment for you."

"*Thank* you!" He rewarded that effort with an outright scowl and, encouraged, Sara proceeded just as blithely, "I was beginning to feel as if . . . like I'd been locked up in Bluebeard's castle — something like that — no offense, of course!"

"*Bluebeard . . . !*"

"Yes!" Sara said helpfully. "You'll remember he was the man who used to kill his wives when he got tired of them and then keep their *mutilated* bodies in this little room he used to keep locked up, and —"

"Please! Enough!" He rapped out the words, the dark scowl he directed at her even more pronounced. "Yes. I happen to have heard of this famous Bluebeard as a matter of fact, but I must say that I fail to see the comparison between Bluebeard's last wife and you! I have no secret room where I hide the bodies of all my past *innamorate* for *you* to discover, and moreover'' — his voice becoming slightly menacing — ''should I ever wish to get rid of *you,* there could always be an accidental fall from the high turret, all the way down to the black rocks and the hungry waves below. . . .''

''Are you . . . are you *threatening* me?'' Sara hoped there hadn't been a quaver in her voice. She stared at him wide-eyed across the table, trying to control the agitated thumping of her heart. In his veins, after all, ran the cruel vengeful blood of both Moor and Spaniard. Had he brought her here thinking that she was Delight, thinking to take her out of his brother's life forever?

There was a depth to the greenness of her eyes in which lay a fine shower of gold, barely escaping from making her eyes appear hazel. Sun-flushed cheekbones high enough to shadow her face, especially in the leaping orange and gold candle flame. And a mouth . . . *Dio!* he swore at himself in his mind. Why must he always look at her mouth and want to capture it and crush it with his again — and then remember how many other men had used those same red lips and been used by them.

She had been needling him for days, her tiny, sweetened barbs getting under his skin until it had been hard not to seize her slim shoulders between his hands and shake her violently.

She had actually had the final temerity to beat him at tennis — *his* game — playing like an amazon and returning his most vicious slams. He had snarled at her unpleasantly then: "I must confess myself surprised at your game — but I suppose I should have remembered that tennis is the 'in' game these days!"

She had been too elated then to acknowledge his ill-disposed comment, but now he had managed to make her afraid — and he had a good mind to let her stay in that frame of mind. The little bitch certainly deserved it! Not only had she all but enticed him into bringing her here, but in spite of the way in which she'd responded to his kisses and his touch she continued to voice her devotion to his brother! Scenting his inheritance, no doubt — the girl had hardly any money of her own and a famous father who had never bothered to acknowledge her. Well, he had brought her here to teach her a lesson and to force Carlo to see at last what kind of woman he'd actually wanted to *marry*.

Marco had been studying her broodingly, almost *consideringly*, not troubling to answer her blurted-out accusation that he threatened her. Let her start to cower! Let the same look of fear spring into those great green eyes that he had seen in the eyes of animals who knew they were about to die. Let her be afraid of him, for a change — it might alter her dispo-

216

sition and make her more eager to please him!

"*Oh!*" Hating both his ominous silence and the way in which his eyes seemed to pierce her coldly, Sara sprang to her feet, snapping the building tension between them with her impatient cry.

"Ohh . . . *you!* If you think you can *frighten* me, then you're quite wrong! And if I started to tell you exactly what I think of you, why I . . . I . . . I'd probably take all night! And I *don't* think I want any more dinner, thank you. In . . . in fact I'd like to leave — *very* early tomorrow, please!"

In her eagerness to leave the room and Marco's detestable presence, Sara almost knocked over her chair, ignoring the impassive footman who sprang forward to retrieve it. Damn him for a devil who was even worse than the one Delight had described to her. Now she *had* to escape him.

"Your manners are atrocious! Come back here." If his steel-edged voice was meant to bar her half-running, half-stumbling progress across the impossibly large formal dining room it would not succeed.

"Go to *hell!*" Sara flung over her shoulder without pausing. Let him just *try* to throw her over that broad stone wall, so innocuously hung with flowering, perfumed vines that smelled of the tropics. The least she'd do was take him with her, locked closely together on that long, last fall to the sea.

Rage propelled her forward over the last few steps to the ornately carved doors, hardly hearing the command his voice snapped out in the harsh Spanish-Italian dialect his servants used. She stopped before the doors, wondering why the two servants who would normally open them before she reached them had instead stationed themselves *before* the doors, barring her passage — and then the meaning of his order became apparent, even before he spoke again, his voice harsh.

"You will only embarrass yourself even more if you attempt to continue in this mad flight of yours! Come back here and sit down."

Sara stood staring at the doors with their winking gold handles that were always to be touched with gloved hands. She didn't want to turn around to face him — he couldn't make her!

"And . . . and if I don't want to? If I refuse, will you have your *feudal* servants carry me bodily back to my chair? I tell you, I want to leave here. This place — and your presence! How dare you treat me like . . . like an inmate of a Moorish harem who is not allowed the privilege of freedom?"

"If you had truly been a harem woman, my dear Delight, I think you would not want to leave, for you would be too busy trying to make yourself your master's favorite plaything! But if you were stubborn . . . then you would have been either whipped or drowned.

Be thankful that I don't intend to do either — unless you push me too far! And now — please come back here and take your seat again. Why humiliate yourself?"

There was no help — not so much as a flicker of feeling — in the faces of the two men who faced her with their eyes fixed on some spot far above her head. No help anywhere. For a split second Sara weighed choices, and then with a bitterness that seemed to stick in her throat she took the obvious one.

"Very well. You haven't left me with an alternative, have you?"

Squaring her shoulders like a young soldier on parade Sara swung around, with the silken skirt of her short, bare-shouldered dinner dress brushing her knees. Her chair was pulled back for her smartly, and she accepted the attention with a curt nod before she sat down once more, holding her back rigid, her face stony. Damn him! What did he think to achieve by this piece of high-handedness? What else did he think he could force her into doing?

Chapter 18

"Do you usually have to *force* women into keeping you company at the dinner table? Or . . . or abduct them for your amusement? Why am I really here?"

From the other end of the table those night-black eyes, whose scrutiny Sara had already begun to fear as well as hate, seemed to eat through her poorly erected defenses.

"Why?" his caustic voice drawled at her as his long fingers cut a slice of cheese and balanced it on the edge of his knife. "Why do you think, Delight? Perhaps I could not help wondering whether you would live up to your name . . . Perhaps I wanted to find out how much you *really* love my brother. Do both my answers agitate you? I can see the breath fluttering in your throat!" And now his voice took on an edge that was almost as sharp as the knife he played with. "Come, let's be honest with each other, *carissima!* After all, I did not exactly *abduct* you. *I* recall clearly, even if *you* claim not to, that you came along with me quite willingly. . . . Didn't you say that my invitation 'sounded like great fun'? And you even left a message on your Uncle Theo's tape . . . surely you remember *that?* I had to remind you that if you did not stop giggling so hard he would not be able to understand one word you said when he played it back later. So why are you suddenly ready to run away from me so soon? Or was this temper tantrum of yours a typically feminine way of reminding me that I should devote more time to you?"

Sara dragged a deep, ragged breath into her lungs, her chin tilting defiantly. No, she wouldn't allow him to play cat-and-mouse with her. She'd face him down no matter what he tried to do with her, the brute.

"You are saying things to me now that are meant to hurt and humiliate, aren't you? And I wonder why. Are you angry because I beat you at a match of tennis? Or because I so obviously prefer your brother's lovemaking to yours?"

Soon after the words had escaped her, Sara found herself wondering whether she had gone too far. He had eyes as black as the coals of hell that would have consumed her if she had let them. All the way across the table she heard the hiss of his indrawn breath, and to stop herself from flinching she challenged his fury instead.

"Of course I'm only a helpless female and no match for you physically — and you do have your servants who obey you blindly, too, don't you? Now that you've reminded me that I'm completely at your mercy, might I ask you what exactly you mean to do with me? Murder me? Rape me?"

"Enough!" With a voice that sounded more like a growl of thunder he plunged the blade of his knife into the board before him. "Enough of your questions, your accusations, your insinuations and the challenge of your much-vaunted sexuality, which you constantly throw in my face. Let me tell you this. . . ." Yanking the knife free of wood he pointed it at her in a way that made Sara quake inside, wondering if he meant to throw it at her heart. "Let me remind you that I have already told you I had no intention of raping you — as much as you might try to incite me to such an act. And let me tell you too that I will have you in the end, brother or no brother, hate or not; and when I do it will be as much *your* doing and your wanting as mine."

Unable to prevent it, Sara could feel a heated flush rise in her face as the *meaning* of what he'd just said registered belatedly. She found herself staring at him silently with her lips parted and her breathing unpleasantly quickened — just like a terrified rabbit mesmerized by a snake, she was to think later, with a rush of self-disgust.

He gave a short, ugly laugh. *"Maledizione!* Have I actually startled your sharp tongue into silence? You are looking at me as if you are waiting for me to leap out of this chair in which I sit and pounce on you . . . like this crouching wolf I wear about my neck! Are you afraid . . . or fascinated, my fickle Delight?"

"Your . . . *your* . . . don't you dare call me yours! I'm *not* your anything — I never will be yours, not if you were the last man left on earth — never of my own volition, never!"

"Is that a challenge or merely another piece of hypocrisy? For a young woman of *your* experience who has 'been around,' as your expression goes, you are certainly acting prudishly — unless you thought to impress me?"

He was absolutely the most despicable, most *conceited* man she had ever encountered! The way he twisted all her words around . . .

"I would *very* much like to throw something at you!" Sara said in a smothered voice. "Preferably something very heavy or very wet. . . ." Her eyes went with longing to the heavy silver urn in the center of the table that was filled with a beautifully arranged assortment of exotic orchids, and she sighed before she looked steadily back at him with spots of angry color staining her cheekbones. "But my — I've been taught to try to act like a lady at all times, even when I'm *not* in the presence of a gentleman!" Fingers gripping tightly over the arms of her chair, Sara willed herself not to drop her eyes away.

"You speak your lines well, like the clever actress I'm sure you are!" Savoring his second cup of espresso, he raised it to her in a sarcastic acknowledgment. "And you are right about me, Delight. . . . I am not a *gentle* man. This land does not breed gentleness, nor does it tolerate weakness. Here we have only extremes of nature, with nothing in the middle — and this is true of the Sardinians themselves too. You might do well to remember that."

There were times when her eyes became like sharp chips of green glass that longed to gouge and cut. Marco leaned back in his chair, studying her deliberately as he tried to gauge her readiness. In the end, he had no doubt that she would give in, but in the meantime she had certainly managed to surprise him with her stubbornness and her temper.

She had now chosen to erect a wall of icy, injured silence between them, turning away from him with an exaggerated shrug of one bare, silky sheened shoulder to play with a silver spoon. Damn her! She was nothing more than a slut of a girl — an amoral creature with a good body, which she obviously knew how to use in bed in order to gain her own ends. How dared she disrupt his life — prove so stubborn that he'd had to resort to the extreme measure of bringing her here? She was playing some kind of game with him, of course, alternately leading him forward with her pretended shyness and coquettishness and then fending him off with an exhibition of her temper or her infernal manner of self-containment.

What he wanted was her unconditional surrender. To have her admit to the strange, unwanted chemistry that existed between them, making the very air crackle with tension sometimes. And then — then he could show her up to herself; proving how weak was her fiercely professed fidelity to his brother Carlo whom she insisted upon calling her fiancé.

What he longed to do with her at this very moment was to crush her slim, promiscuous body against his, forcing her lips to part willingly under his, while he buried his hands in thick masses of her polished-mahogany hair. That was what he *should* do — ending once and for all this pointless farce she was trying to prolong. And then, once he had had her and put her in the right perspective, he could return to his business and to Francine, his mistress, who waited for him in Paris.

"You have been sitting there just *staring* at me for the past five minutes at least! Wouldn't you rather look at a picture that can't talk back? Honestly, I really *am* rather tired, and if you don't mind, I'd really like to go to . . . upstairs."

He had noticed the way she'd caught back

the word "bed" and substituted "upstairs" instead. Really, her persistent enactment of a shy-little-virgin role was a little ludicrous!

Sara had not realized that she'd been holding her breath until she saw him stand up with an exaggerated bow in her direction that was belied by the almost contemptuous look in his eyes.

"Of course. You must find the quiet life here rather boring, eh?"

Was it to prove that it could be otherwise that he had insisted on escorting her upstairs? Sara was all too much aware of the dark masculinity of him beside her — the pressure of his fingers over her elbow that seemed to warn her of the sheer futility of trying to run away. Was *he* aware, in his turn, of her almost primitive fear of the very nearness of him — that she might lose control over herself; lose a part of herself and all of the impossibly romantic girlish dreams she'd grown up with? If he took her as he threatened, this arrogant Sardinian Duke, it would be with no love and no regard. He would want to use his body as an instrument with which to use her and punish her; and if he whispered a name to her as he did, it would not even be her own name!

Sara fought against the strange feeling of fatalism that suddenly swept over her. No! She mustn't give in — *would* not give in, no matter how her own uncalled-for emotions might threaten to overwhelm her.

"It was kind of you to make sure I found my way, but I can manage perfectly well now, thank you. There's a light on in my room, and —"

"Wouldn't you like to step out onto the terrace and look at the stars for a while? They always seem exceptionally bright from up here."

So now he was trying to be charming, was he?

"No, thank you," Sara said firmly, adding for emphasis: "With Your Grace's permission, of course, your *guest* would really prefer to retire for the night."

Would he let her go? Sara wondered fearfully.

Should he end this stupid game they played right now or decide to prolong it for a while longer? Marco's eyes narrowed slightly on her defiantly shuttered face while he considered, and then he gave a mental shrug. What was the hurry? She was here, and whether she knew it or not she wasn't going anywhere unless he was ready to allow it. To win any contest too easily always ended in boredom.

"So . . . maybe tomorrow . . . ?"

He said the words aloud, deliberately letting her choose her own interpretation of his meaning. "And does my delightful guest have everything she needs for tonight?"

"Your housekeeper is very efficient. Thank you. . . ." Sara said with deliberate blankness, wishing desperately he would tire of fencing with words and leave her.

"Well, good night then . . . Delight."

With a light, teasing finger he skimmed the outline of her jaw and then her mouth, smiling rather mockingly when she jerked her head back as if he had burned her.

"If you should change your mind — about watching the stars, that is — I shall be working until late in my study downstairs. All you have to do is to lift up the telephone by your bed and dial the number seven. Good night again, then. Sleep safely!" And with that last rather taunting admonition he had actually left her!

Not caring what he thought, Sara almost fled into her room, leaning against the door that she could not lock and feeling her knees tremble with the weakness of reaction. And of course that was all it was, she reminded herself sternly. If she kept her head, and what Delight would call her "cool," then she would inevitably discover a way to extricate herself from this ridiculously *gothic* situation. After all, it could only be a matter of time before her wicked Duke (she couldn't help the wry smile that touched her lips) discovered that his precious half brother Carlo was no longer living alone in Argentina and that he had, in fact, carried off the wrong sister! And then the uninvited thought came: Oh dear — and then he'd probably kill me anyway, so that no one will find out how completely he was fooled!

Half-afraid that he might change his mind, Sara completed her ablutions as hurriedly as she could, slipping into a sheer white lawn nightdress that reached down to her ankles and had been patterned after a nineteenth-century chemise with its camisole top and white lace and blue ribbon trimmings.

Watch the stars with him indeed! Sara almost snorted aloud as she began to brush her hair, counting strokes. *That* would have been an invitation to disaster. There was nothing romantic or considerate about Giovanni Marco Riccardo Marcantoni, Duca di Cavalieri, for all that his titular name implied. Hadn't he jeered at the trait of gentleness tonight? No, he wasn't gentle — he was crude and demanding and cruel and ruthless, a man obviously used to taking what he wanted without a qualm as to the means he used. If he had taken her onto her small terrace with the tiled floor that would still be warm from the heat of the sun under her bare feet he would have . . .

She must be mad to let her thoughts follow such a dangerous direction! Springing to her feet Sara flung down her brush. Rather think of how she would contrive to avoid him tomorrow, she cautioned herself grimly as she turned off the small, dim light. And she could star-watch by herself if she wanted to — much safer!

Rationalization took her to bed and impulse took her out of bed again to fling aside the heavy curtains that shut out the sunlight streaming in from the terrace during the day; hesitating here on the threshold of a warm black night dense with the perfume of night-blooming flowers. Yes, the floor here was warm under her feet; and yes indeed the stars formed an almost blindingly bright pattern of pinpointed lights against the blackness of the sky. A wave of longing shook her for *something;* she didn't quite know what — yet. Maybe she was better off not knowing. Or . . . was it not really a yearning she had felt, but rather a sense of *déjà vu?* A sudden, strange feeling that this had happened before, her standing here hesitating, torn between going forward and holding back. She *wanted* to step outside, to lean her back against the warm stone wall and look up at the stars, imagining what it must be like to float among them. And if anyone whistled or called softly from below she would not turn her head, of course. She would stay where she was, gazing upward at the stars like drops of quicksilver she could never trap, never have, and must never dare yearn for.

It was almost as if Sara's feet carried her forward of their own accord. The feeling of strangeness kept deepening in her, as if every step she took, every move she made had already happened. There was a slight trace of moistness in the warm air — a faint smell of the sea mingling with all the other odors of the night. Leaning there against ancient stone with her face turned up to the stars, Sara found herself *waiting*. For the signal. (Why had her mind thought that?) For something — or for someone.

Chapter 19

The whistle that first startled her might have belonged to a night bird. Sara ignored it, although goose bumps had started to erupt along her arms and legs. She had begun to have a very uneasy feeling about the odd compulsion that had drawn her out here. The low, trilling whistle came again and the palms of her hands became clammy. It *had* to be a bird! And in any case she was going back in to bed!

"Pssssst!"

That was no bird and the sound snapped her head around, even if her feet had become anchored in place.

"No screaming, huh? All I'm after is talk — believe me!"

Sara had to close her eyes tightly and blink them open again before she could convince herself that she wasn't imagining things. From out of the blackness of a Sardinian night — a Brooklyn, New York, accent of all things?

That wretched Marco had probably ordered her wine drugged, and now she was high on acid or something equally dangerous. . . .

Did the voice belong to anyone or had that been the Cheshire Cat? And then, out of the corner of her eye, Sara saw a dark shape detach itself from the darker shape of the roof, to land lightly at her feet.

"Hi!" The voice said softly and with incongruous cheer. "Sure was nice of you not to scream. And I guess you're wondering who I am and what I'm doing here!"

At least he continued to keep his distance and hadn't made any moves to attack her. The thought emboldened Sara enough so that she was able to mumble shakily: "Well, I suppose that would help — as a beginning! You . . . you gave me quite a scare, you know! I thought this ducal castle was impregnable!"

"*You* gave me quite a scare too, let me tell you! For a moment there I thought you was *her* ghost! But, hey . . . ! You're certainly no ghost and you're the one I come to see. Just to talk to, of course! I promise you I'd never try nothing else — I'm not that kind of guy who takes — you know — advantage. Okay?"

"If you don't tell me —"

"Sure, sure — I was coming to that, Miss Adams. It *is* Miss Delight Adams, ain't it? One of Miss Mona Charles' little girls? Well — I'm related to the Duke!" Sara thought she could hear his soft, almost soundless laugh before he added, "The name's Angelo, although there are some folks who'd say that the name don't hardly suit me! And in case you're wondering how I learned to speak American so good, it's because they sent me to school over there. Had an uncle in New York, and then — Pop and I decided to try it too. Like I said — the family paid our way there. My *mother's* family, that is. They had the connections. Lived in New York more than fifteen years before I decided to come back home. And now they wouldn't let me leave anyway — hah!" Sara glimpsed a flash of white teeth and decided she didn't understand *anything*.

"Well . . . er . . . Angelo . . ." Sara tried to choose her words carefully because she didn't want to offend him, whoever he was. "What I don't really get is — who is *they* and why won't *they* let you leave here if you wanted to?"

"Ah — I suppose it's because I'm considered to be one of these bandits they are always writing up in the newspapers." He added quickly as if to reassure her, "That's why it's better that you don't get too close a look at my face, you understand? But everyone says I look like Marco — the Duke, that is. He's my half brother, you know."

"No . . . I really didn't know. Does *he* know?" Sara wondered if she sounded as hysterical as she felt.

"Marco? Sure he knows! But it's something he don't like to admit — or even think about, I guess . . . considering the circumstances of my birth!" Again that soft, almost silent chuckle. "Not that I really blame him — it must be embarrassing to be reminded that one of your parents wasn't satisfied with the other and went looking. You know what I mean?"

"Yes, at least I think so. But why —"

In addition to being an acrobat, able to leap parapets and scale roofs and unscalable walls, this Angelo must also be a mind reader.

"You're wondering why I wanted to talk to you? Because I'm a number-one fan of Mona Charles, that's why! Always have been — still am. I even got real close to her once — close enough to smell her perfume, that famous one they say she always wears, even to bed. She wrote me a letter too, a real nice one, and I still got that, and the picture she signed personal to me. And you're her daughter — look a bit like her too, don't you? I've seen a bunch of pictures of you too. Not too many of your sister though — the English one."

Dear God! Mama-Mona's fans tended to pop up in the strangest places, but *this* was stretching the imagination a bit. And he knew the whole family history too. Great! Sara thought grimly. What if he recognized her as Mona's *other* daughter?

Thank God for the darkness of the night

235

that hid her face from him as effectively as it hid his from her.

"You're one of Mama's fans? Wonderful — I'll be sure and tell her, the next time we run into each other. And . . . I don't suppose you have an address — I mean, because of *them* of course — but if you had I could probably ask her to write to you again and send you a more recent picture. . . . You know, she'd probably enjoy meeting you!"

"She is going to be making her new picture *here!* I thought you surely must know — but you don't? Well" — he cleared his throat before going on — "they will be shooting scenes in Cagliari — that's our capital — and also in Sassari, that's not too far from here. Now, I was thinking that if you planned to see your mother while she's here — which I'm sure you'll want to do now that you know about it — and if you needed an escort or a bodyguard because of these dangerous times, well, *nobody* dares mess with me, and that's a fact that even my half brother the Duke can't deny. Why do you think he turns a blind eye to my existence and to my comings and goings on his property? At least he retains a sense of family ties and family obligations, to give the devil his due! Yes — I can get in here any time I care to, as long as I keep up a show of sneaking in, if you know what I mean. Not that I'm not good at that too, because I used to be what they call a second-story man in

New York, and most of the time no one knows when I get in or when I leave."

"I . . . see!" Sara said weakly. She had already forgotten what they had been talking about to begin with while she tried to *follow,* and her mind was whirling with bits and pieces of trivia. A bandit . . . a second-story man . . . actually the Duke's half brother! And what would Marco think if he knew that she was out here sharing the stars with . . . with this very eccentric man? A shudder ran through her. He would probably kill her, since he had begun to treat her like an odalisque in his harem!

"Well, anyway, as I was saying, I hope you'll let me know when you decide to visit your mama. I would sure give a lot to be able to meet her and actually talk to her. If you could see me, I think you'd say I wasn't a bad-looking man at all — and I keep myself fit, as you might have noticed. I'd be available any time at all — business is rather slow these days, like it is everywhere else, I guess!"

Sara had to fight down the urge to burst into hysterical giggles that would probably make her his mortal enemy. *Don't* wonder about his business and concentrate on the advantages of this chance meeting. Why, dear Angelo could live up to his name and *rescue* her if she ever needed rescuing. The thought made her feel much more sure of herself.

"How can I let you know if — when I decide

I should pop in on Mama-Mona? And" — she hesitated, but finished saying it anyway — "what if . . . if Marco doesn't want me to leave? You might not want to make him angry with you. . . ."

Her strategy worked and he was immediately a strutting rooster, puffing his feathers. "Marco — hah! You don't have to worry about a thing there, kid. I don't know what's between you and Marco, and it ain't none of my business, but your wanting to see your mama, who happens to be the one pure love of my life" — he crossed himself quickly — "well, I make that my business, see? And to show I trust Mona Charles' daughter with my life I'll tell you how to send a message to me. . . . Just send it, and I will come right away."

Sometime during the night Sara managed to fall asleep, when her mind had become tired out with plans and speculations. Even her sleep was restless, and she woke up tired, not wanting to leave her bed; in no mood this heat-hazed morning for another confrontation with her tormentor. But hadn't she been promised that she might go riding with him?

"You said in one of your interviews that you are afraid of horses, so what is the meaning of this new whim of yours? I have no time to give riding lessons to timid Hollywood starlets!"

"But . . . but I truly want to get over my fear! It's probably just a stupid phobia that I could get over by just trying it. . . . With *you* to give me a few pointers, naturally. Please let me try! I do pick up things quickly, honestly I do!"

Oh, she'd really had to plead before he'd given in! But she'd been eyeing his horses, all blooded stock, and the urge to be on horse-back again had proved too strong to resist. The hardest thing she'd have to do was to convince Marco that she had never ridden a horse before — and was a natural-born rider by some fluke of fate.

Sara sighed deeply and closed her eyes against dustily intrusive arrows of sunlight that seeped into the room through cracks in the shutters and blinds. Fate was a funny thing, even if she had never quite believed that everything was preordained. It was also a useful word to help explain why she happened to be here; and why she had encountered the talented and talkative Angelo last night. What she could *not* explain was why she had been practically *drawn* out onto the terrace last night, and why she had almost *known* before-hand what would happen next. She frowned. Not quite. Angelo she had not expected!

"I beg your pardon, signorina. But I have been asked to convey Il Duca's apologies for not being able to take you riding today. He has been called away for a few hours on business. Do you wish to sleep a few hours longer?"

Sara had not heard the housekeeper come in, and her eyes flew open with a startled jerk.

"Oh . . ." she uttered blankly wondering why she felt so disappointed when just a few seconds ago she had debated sending *her* excuses down to *him!*

"If there is anything else you wish to do, signorina?" During the past few days Serafina had unbent quite a bit, especially when she had realized that Il Duca was not visiting the bed of his latest female guest. She had even shown Sara some pictures of Carlo as a young boy, over which Sara had had to exclaim fondly. There had even been a stiffly posed picture taken with his older brother. Marco's scowl that drew his black brows together in a dangerous fashion had certainly not changed with the years that had passed since then!

Now, not wanting to spoil her morning by thinking of her quarrels with the high-handed Duca di Cavalieri, Sara stretched languidly as she gave the older woman a sleepily apologetic smile. "I'm so sorry, Serafina, but I'm not quite awake yet, I'm afraid! I . . . I found I could not fall asleep too easily, and" — she laughed a bit nervously as she remembered her strange fancies last night — "and, well it almost seemed impossible to resist taking a look at the stars! In the end I —"

Sara broke off when the housekeeper said

with a sharpness that was unusual for her: "You . . . you didn't go out, signorina?" She seemed to have a peculiar look on her seamed brown face as she waited for Sara to answer, eyes fixed on Sara's face.

Why? Or was Serafina also aware of Angelo's nocturnal comings and goings? Was that why she suddenly seemed so nervous?

Sara tried to choose her words carefully, not wanting to betray Angelo, who had actually offered to *help* her. "Well . . . yes. But please don't look so worried, I only went out onto the terrace to enjoy the night by myself for a little while, and after a while I came back inside and went to bed, that's all."

Serafina continued to regard her intently. "That was *all?*" she repeated with a strange emphasis on the question. Then as if she had suddenly remembered herself the woman's eyes dropped away for a moment, and she said almost brusquely, "You might have caught a chill in that thin nightgown, signorina! The nights can turn cold when a wind comes up from the sea, and at night . . . everything is different. You might have lost your footing. . . ."

"But there's nothing there I could trip over," Sara objected reasonably. What on earth had upset the normally inscrutable Serafina? Angelo? Something else? Pacifically, she gave a little laugh and offered: "Actually I didn't even intend to go out,

I just opened the curtains for air and I felt —"

"You felt what, signorina?"

"Oh — I'm sure it had something to do with the beauty of the kind of night I'm not used to! There was the perfume of the flowers and the salt smell of the sea and the warmth of the stones . . . you must probably think I'm quite crazy, but I felt . . . as if I couldn't help myself — or was going through a set of motions I had gone through before. . . ." Sara had begun frowning as she tried to recall exactly what she *had* felt last night before Angelo had dropped in on her so unceremoniously. "As if I was *waiting* for something, almost. Silly, isn't it?"

"No, no — not silly! *Madre di Dio,* that *you* should feel it too, and you not yet in the family. . . ." Serafina's agitation showed openly now as she fingered her rosary beads.

"Not in — feel *what* too? Please — I can see that you're upset, and I'd like to know why."

Serafina's mouth pursed stubbornly and she shook her head. "The Signor Duca would say that I'm a silly, superstitious old woman and would send me away."

"I wouldn't tell him anything, I promise! But you *can't* not tell me now, can you? I'd die of curiosity — and probably imagine the *worst.* . . . Did someone fling themselves from the terrace wall? Is that why —" Sara had wrapped her arms about her knees almost apprehensively.

"No, *no!* What an idea!" Serafina said crossly. It was plain to see she was already sorry for having said too much. "It was nothing like *that,*" she said in a more subdued voice, and then gave a sigh. "The little terrace was more a setting for . . . *foolishness* than an act of violence, signorina. Since you are to marry the Signor Carlo, I suppose you would hear the story in any case. There is always gossip. . . ."

"What story?" Sara asked, with all the patience she could muster. "Please, what was this foolishness, and what does an old story have to do with what *I* felt — or thought I felt?"

Serafina's back straightened, and she gave a resigned nod of her head.

"Very well — I see I will have to speak. But first, if you don't mind, I will make sure that there are no maids working in the *galleria* outside who might listen."

Chapter 20

"She was Spanish, you see, and very beautiful, very young. Also of a good family — Il Duca would not have married her otherwise. You noticed her picture in this room and asked me who she was, did you not? These were her rooms, which she used when Il Duca was away — and he was away for much of the time. I myself was young at the time — I was one of the maids who cleaned her room, and sometimes she would talk to me, from loneliness." Serafina's mouth had seemed to soften for an instant, but now it turned down at the corners. "The Duchessa did not like to be alone. She had had a child in the first year of her marriage — a son — knowing it was her duty. But with the child being taken care of by his nurses, and her husband away, the young Duchessa had too much time to spend alone. She took to spending much time out on the terrace during the long, warm nights — sending away her personal maid and locking her door for privacy. Too much time, perhaps. She too loved the stars and the scents of the night."

Serafina's voice had suddenly turned dry, and she paused significantly. And suddenly, Sara understood. Of course. A lover. The young, lonely Duchess had taken a lover who used to meet her at night, when her husband was away. She might have been a sensual, passionate woman who longed for love — and made the mistake of looking for it in the wrong place, poor thing!

Defiantly, Sara said it aloud. "Poor thing! Think of how many nights she must have waited out there alone — and frightened, probably. Waiting for a signal that her lover had arrived. It's like an *opera!*"

The old woman's face wore a funny look, and she seemed to clutch her rosary tighter. "So you felt that too, did you? Yes, signorina, she used to wait for him to give a whistle that was like a bird call. She would go down by a stairway that is blocked off now to meet him. Or *he* would come up to her. After a while, it had to happen that they were found out. By the servants first. And later . . ."

Sara didn't want to hear the rest — the inevitable *un*happy ending to a beautifully romantic love affair. She interrupted quickly: "But who was the man — her lover? After all, the Duke himself couldn't have been much of a saint, could he? He probably had mistresses everywhere, while he expected *her* to do her duty and go on producing his children — *when* he deigned to help in the matter, that is! Oh — *honestly!* — I'm sorry, signora, you probably don't agree, but after all . . . all this took place about thirty or forty years ago, didn't it? And divorce wasn't too unheard of. . . ."

"In Sardinia divorce is *still* unheard of! The scandal would be a very bad thing even now, but in *those* days . . . coming from America you would not understand, signorina. For a married woman to be unfaithful to her husband is bad enough, but when the woman is a Duchessa and her love a peasant from the mountains who was formerly her groom — you understand the consequences?"

Sara had to swallow before she said in a strained voice: "She . . . *died*, didn't she? And he killed her, making it look like an accident . . . and they let him get away with it, didn't he? Because he was a *man* and it didn't matter if *he* had his village by-blows like Angelo, but for *her* —"

Suddenly realizing what she had said, she could have bitten out her tongue, but fortunately Serafina — who had looked shocked when Sara made her accusation — merely looked resigned at the mention of Angelo.

"Ah, that Angelo — I should have guessed that he would have found a way to see you! But you mustn't say that about Il Duca, signorina. Only God knows what he must have felt to come back home and find his Duchessa had run off to the hills with a peasant. And worse, to have everyone know."

"She ran *away* with her lover?"

"Yes." Serafina inclined her head stiffly. "And that was not the worst of the scandal. Much worse when she had the child, up in a small stone hut in the mountains where the bad men hide out. Her lover's child, who by law bore her husband's noble name."

This was even *better* than an opera, Sara thought, listening entranced. And maybe Delight had been misinformed and the story did have a happy ending after all.

"What happened to the child?" she prompted. "And to *her,* the lovely young Duchessa who gave up everything for love?"

"The poor Duchessa took ill and died — she wasn't used to the cold up in the mountains or to sleeping on the ground in a stone hut." The old woman's voice sounded harshly prosaic. "And as for what happened to child, signorina, why . . . you met him! Or you must have, to know his name."

"*Angelo?* You mean Angelo is *her* child and not . . . and not *his?*" Sara heard her voice rising and stopped to take a deep breath. "But what about the Duke? I thought he was —"

"Once she had left him, the foolish young Duchessa, the Duca had nothing more to do with her. How could he? No one *here* blamed him when she died — and she, poor weak thing, should have had more pride than to send word to him, begging for a doctor, begging to come back with her child. Ah — it was a bad thing, and better forgotten."

Better forgotten by her too, Sara reminded herself firmly after Serafina had left her alone to sort things out. Secure in the knowledge that her *bête noire* was not around to stride upstairs to torment her, Sara let herself relax in her sunken marble tub, enjoying the silken feel of the scented water against her skin.

Poor neglected Duchessa, dying of neglect of a different kind in the end; a sadly ironic way to end her short, unhappy life. And what a difference in the lives of the two sons of the Duchessa — the *first* Duchessa di Cavalieri!

"They" had taken care of poor Angelo by exiling him to New York and trying to forget about him. Sweep the dirty scandal under the rug and hope no one finds it. Or hope that Angelo, in the tenement jungle of New York, might not survive. But Angelo had fooled them all, hadn't he? Good for him. And as for Marco — he was probably the shadow of his father. Brought up to hate his mother and despise all women, except for one.

"What a fierce, unhappy little boy he was, to be sure!" Serafina had remembered. "But after the second Duchessa came — the signor Carlo's mother — things became different. Better for everyone. The Duchessa

Margharita is from northern Italy, and her son is blond like her, though of course you know that, signorina! Ah, but the new Duchessa changed everything here. And she became a true mother to the present Duca — he worships her like the Virgin and would do anything for her."

Typically Freudian of course! All her anger came back whenever she thought of *him!* Sara toweled herself vigorously. And of course she wasn't wasting any pity on him either! No matter what he'd been as a boy, she detested the man he had grown up to be. So damn sure of himself, so confident of manipulating everyone and everything in his path in order to suit himself! Except for *her.* Sara squared her chin belligerently at her steamy reflection. At this point of the game, knowing as much as she did about him, while he knew nothing about *Sara,* the advantage certainly lay with her.

The smug feeling of self-assurance carried Sara downstairs later, feeling poised and newly confident. And since she had spent quite a long time in front of her mirror, she was reasonably certain she looked that way too. She was confident enough to be able to ignore the curt rudeness of the note that had *informed,* instead of asking her, of an engagement he had made for them both this evening. He had returned from his mysterious trip of "a few hours" and now planned to take her to the Costa Smeralda for an evening of entertainment, as she had requested. It had been enough of a concession to raise her eyebrows, and keep her wondering.

"Good — I am glad that you're almost on time!" Marco glanced impatiently at his watch. "The helicopter has already been refueled and is waiting."

For the first time since he had taken her hand at the bottom of the staircase, raising it perfunctorily to his lips in a casually polite European gesture, Sara saw him *look* at her.

She'd taken a long time choosing a dress to wear, and even longer with her makeup, trying to remember the carefully detailed instructions she'd read in the book she'd found in Delight's apartment. Now, meeting his narrowing, unreadable black eyes, Sara clung to her feeling of self-confidence and performed a slow, coquettish pirouette for him; smiling her newly practiced *teasing* smile.

"Well? Do I pass? I mean, is this dress okay for a disco over here?"

The dress was a Halston — layers of sheer flame-colored tissue that bared one shoulder and most of her left thigh. It was really Delight's dress, but then Sara had already decided that this was to be Delight's night; and the trophy, when she won it, would belong to her sister.

His dry voice seemed especially designed to

grate along her nerve-ends. "It seems to suit your personality. Do you have a wrap or a shawl?"

It was much cooler once they had taken to the air and Sara was secretly glad that he had forced her to bring along her opulent Spanish shawl with the long tassels. They were both silent — she because she didn't quite *trust* a helicopter, and he . . . why would she know or care what his moods were as long as he kept the distance between them?

Rather than be forced to look at *him,* Sara looked down at blackness broken by a few pinpoints of light that seemed to flicker feebly — peasant huts or the piled-stone *nuraghi* that had been built by prehistoric inhabitants of Sardinia and were still occasionally inhabited by the poor who could afford no other shelter. But why should the aristocratic Duke bother about the poverty that existed side by side with the wealth contained in his palazzo, his estates and his bank accounts? He had been brought up by his implacable father who had refused the last, desperate pleas of his Spanish child-wife; begging for the medical care that would have granted her life. Yes, *this* Duke was molded after his father and had none of the weakness and the humanness of his mother. He had grown up idolizing his virtuous stepmother and intolerant of all others. Inside himself, he was probably as harsh and arid as the desert his ancestors had come from to conquer half the world they knew of.

"You seem fascinated by the jagged teeth of the mountains below us. Are you afraid they will chew you up?" His voice was as caustic as it usually was when he addressed her; but *this* time, Sara thought, she would not allow herself an argument with him.

Deliberately continuing to keep her eyes fixed on some imaginary point on the ground, Sara lifted one shoulder carelessly. "Why should I be afraid? *You're* here too, aren't you? And I'm sure your pilot is as efficient as everyone else you have around you."

For some reason, her polite, innocuous-sounding answer infuriated him. But *this* time, Marco thought as he gritted his teeth, he would keep a cooler head and a tighter rein on his temper. Soon enough she would betray herself for what she was . . . a promiscuous, *easy* little tart who would fall into bed with almost any man who offered himself; *except,* he had to remind himself grimly, when she had her eyes firmly fixed on the main chance — in this case, Carlo and marriage into a wealthy family. For her to hold out against *him* for as long as she had, Carlo must have been stupid enough to tell her about his inheritance.

Marco fought his impulse to lose his temper and tell her exactly what he thought of her.

But no — the teasing little bitch in her flame-colored designer dress, which must have been bought for her by a rich lover, would surely fall from her shaky pedestal tonight! He had arranged for everything — his cleverly calculated idea born during the sleepless night he had spent *last* night, while *she* no doubt had closed her eyes almost at once to fall into the slumber of the hypocritically righteous. Tonight, he was cynically sure, she would probably not care to fall asleep at all. He had made sure that she would be too busy.

Without knowing it, he smiled — more an ugly grimace that was a travesty of a smile. He had already wasted far too much time on her, and it was time for the moment of truth. And it was this particularly unpleasant expression, which seemed to turn his dark face into a devil-mask that threatened her with destruction, that Sara happened to surprise on his face by accident.

She should have carried a rosary like Serafina, so that she could finger the beads surreptitiously. But scowl or not, Sara was determined that this time he would not coerce her. She would make sure of that!

Chapter 21

The lights of the yachts moored at Porto Cervo — the plush hotels, the deceptively simple villas of the very rich — they seemed to get bigger and brighter as the 'copter circled in preparation for landing.

Sara pretended a naive excitement she was far from feeling. "Oh — lovely! Civilization at last, and I actually get to dance. How sweet of you to be so considerate!"

"We are going to the villa of a friend of mine who is giving a party," he said with harsh abruptness. "But don't worry, it'll be more than lively enough for you, I'm sure, and he has his own disco — the whole setup, including the flashing lights. It's a hobby."

"Ooh! What a great hobby! He sounds like a character."

And *she* was going to stick firmly to her role tonight. Careful what she had to drink *or* eat. She really didn't trust Marco's mood tonight, or his caustic insistence that she was about to have a Night to Remember. *Last night* had been strange enough, thank you, Sara told herself, brushing away as she had all day the questions that last night had left in her mind. There would be time later to rationalize, but for the moment she must stay on guard.

Her host's name was Vince something and he had a *very* recognizable face. As had most of the beautiful people clustered on his terraces and beside his enormous pool with scented, heavy-petaled flowers floating on its surface.

"Ah — Delight! So lovely!" Vince had murmured as he floated her around, introducing her to everyone. Never very good at names, Sara couldn't remember half of them, and if the names were famous enough to be popular, she couldn't fit the right faces to them. Nursing her Perrier-and-lime she managed (she thought) to give a creditable imitation of an ingenue having a good time. In Delight's sexy red dress she was soon surrounded — without wanting to be — by men who offered to replenish her drink while they sized her up, with special emphasis on the legs and the breasts; and men who didn't offer her another drink but *did* offer her almost everything else.

Sara allowed herself to become fascinated in a rather *sick* way by this new game she was learning to play — all the better *not* to wonder where her black-browed "escort" had disappeared to. Forget him — she was going to play Delight to the hilt! And, of course, this was the best chance she'd ever have to prove to everyone that Delight Adams just liked to *flirt,* and that was all.

"Listen — why don't you let me take you on a tour of the place? Vince won't mind." A pair of hot, piercingly blue eyes that reminded her too vividly of Garon lingered significantly somewhere just below Sara's navel, and she *almost* looked down to make sure she hadn't developed a run in her ultra-sheer panty hose.

"Thanks, but I'm enjoying it out here right now." The brilliance of Sara's emerald green eyes met and matched his. "Maybe later . . . ?" The smiling half-promise was enough to keep him at her side along with the others.

And was this what it felt like to be a *femme fatale,* a woman absolutely sure of her fascination and power over men? Sara felt a sudden, heady rush of sheer exhilaration that the more pragmatic part of her mind couldn't fight off any longer. Couldn't — and didn't want to! Oh, but this was *fun!* She felt witty, amusing, brilliant — and of course, irresistible. Womanpower!

"No, thank you. I really don't need another drink. See how much I have left?" Still sparkling, diamond-bright, Sara held her glass up for inspection.

"So here you are!" *His* casual air of owner-ship irritated her almost as much as the arm he had slipped around her waist, his fingers brushing the curve of her breast. "What are you drinking, *cara?*" As he must have known it would, his casual term of endearment irri-tated her even more than his possessive attitude.

"Vodka, of course!" Sara said brightly. With what she hoped seemed an insouciant movement she turned to face him, her clinging fingers over his managing to detach his hand from her. "Marco, sweetie, would you mind *very* much bringing me a refill? *Very* chilled, please!"

"I thought you were drinking nothing but Perrier!" one of her swains grumbled sulkily.

"Just in between the *real* thing, darling! How else is a girl to stay straight with all you fascinating guys around?"

"Hell — *nobody* stays straight at one of Vince's parties!" That was blue-eyes, with another burning look that seemed to strip away what little she had on. "Didn't Marco tell you? Listen, you can *relax* here, baby. No need to worry about getting busted or anything like that. Everything's real cool."

She had placed him now; he was a boy-wonder television newsman who specialized in taking risks that usually paid off, making him one of the highest paid in his field.

"Would you really like another drink?"

Marco's harshly grating voice had lowered to a panther's purr, coming from deep in his throat. "Or would you prefer something else that would do more for you than vodka? My friend Glynn is right — you can do whatever you wish here, without worrying about raised eyebrows or officious public officials. Yes, why don't you relax?"

"Here — have a toot!" A muscular, solidly built man with reddish brown hair held out a little bottle that was filled with white powder. "Go on — it's okay," he urged, mistaking her hesitation. "It's really great stuff — I get it pure and cut it down myself. No speed."

"Go ahead — you're among friends. And I'm here to make sure that you will be all right."

The Devil in Velvet, Sara thought irrelevantly, feeling a trap closing about her. Title of a book she had read very long ago — and how it fit him, this fierce dark Sardinian Duke who wore the emblem of a crouching, slavering wolf! By all means, she must never let him see through her deception of him until *she* was good and ready.

She improvised, feeling too many eyes on her. "*You* go first! And in any case I'm high enough already — I had an early start on the rest of you."

With a shrug, the redhead twisted the cap of the little bottle he carried before he closed one nostril — inhaling deeply with the other.

"Je — sus! This is good stuff!" He repeated his action, while Sara watched closely, all too much aware now that Marco had irritatingly decided to massage the back of her neck with dangerously insidious gentleness; his long fingers moving from her neck to her shoulders with a casually familiar air.

"Here — it's your turn now." The small bottle was held out to her, leaving her no more options.

Sara shook it with a professional air as she had seen *him* do. Inside her slender-strapped high-heeled shoes, *she* was shaking too.

"Well, for heaven's sake! What are you all staring at?"

"She's a Southern belle!" Blue-eyes bent over in a paroxysm of almost hysterical mirth; taking their eyes off *her* for a moment. Proud of her own resourcefulness, Sara pretended to twist the cap of the little vial around, breathing solemnly with a finger against each nostril in turn.

"Oh, boy — that *is* strong stuff. Much stronger than *I* can usually afford. Thanks, baby."

"Are you sure you have had enough? You don't feel relaxed yet." Why couldn't Marco leave her alone? Sara turned her head, trying to escape his deceptively gentle fingers.

"I'm just *fine,* thanks! You really don't have to *hover* over me to make sure I'm having a good time. I am."

"Someone neglected to teach you manners!"

Fortunately, Sara thought, she was saved by a feminine voice that was followed by the vision of a decidedly feminine body — about five foot six and amply curved in all the right places.

"Marco — *mon amour* — where have you been hiding yourself? We were supposed to meet last week in Marbella, surely you cannot have forgotten?"

Apparently he could be nonchalant enough when it suited him. Hatefully, Sara watched the close embrace, the embarrassingly passionate kiss that seemed to deny the existence of anyone else within their magic circle.

"Darling!" the woman sighed at last. "Should I be jealous? Why weren't you *there?* Everyone was asking about you."

What a disgustingly *public* scene! And if this over-dressed blonde was one of his mistresses, then it was obvious that — title or not — the man simply had no class!

Turning away from them, Sara put her hand on the redhead's wrist. His name was Cyrus, she remembered, and he looked, safely, as if he had retreated into a different world.

"Hi there again, you with the magic bottle. Shall we go and boogie for a while until we need some more magic?"

Grinning rather vacuously he followed her; easily persuaded by his own ego as well as her feminine blandishments. His name was Cyrus Richards and he specialized in owning things. Anything he damn well pleased to own. Oil wells, real estate, a gold mine and women. Maybe he might want to own this one. It all depended on whether she'd start to bore him or not.

Wild music with a pulsating drumbeat underlying the manufactured sounds of a synthesizer became louder as they approached one of the polished dance floors — this one outdoors by the pool. The floor seemed to pulsate in time to the beat.

"All *right!* Let's get loose, baby. Show me some of that stuff!" His sudden laugh didn't make sense to Sara until her dilating eyes, traveling over his shoulder, happened to see the larger-than-lifesize screen that held a few of Vince's less energetic guests enthralled.

No *wonder* she'd received all those whistles when she came onto the floor! Delight Adams in the flesh; disco-ing in her sexy red Halston dress, while there on the giant screen her pictured image flashed, unclothed and uninhibited; performing a sexual, sensual ballet that left nothing to the imagination. Dear God, how *could* she have? And she, her sister's surrogate, what did they expect of her?

"Hell, baby! Let's get *down!*" The redhead had started to gyrate his body, using his hips suggestively. "Let's *go!*" Eyes half-closed.

What would happen if she started to run?

Sara tore her eyes away from the screen, feeling, as if a switch had been turned on inside her, her body begin to move in time to the music. If she didn't think about it too hard she could dance with as much abandon as anyone else on the crowded floor. And no — she was *not* going to run away, she was going to show *them,* and *him* — in the end — that she wasn't the same girl on the screen, doing all those things.

Him . . . of course, shouldn't she have guessed he would plan some kind of nasty surprise for her? Delight Adams — good-time girl on- and off-screen. That's what *he* thought, and by bringing her here to this kind of party where she'd be thrown together with members of the fast international set he had sought to underline his contempt for her. A wave of pure fury shot through Sara's body, making her hot first and then cold — icy cold with resolve. Why, that smug, self-righteous, hypocritical *bastard!* If it was the last thing she ever did, she was going to teach him a lesson — oh, yes, she'd find a way to exact her own personal revenge and make him look foolish in the eyes of his friends and acquaintances as well.

Sara suddenly became aware that her partner had emerged from his glazed-eyed preoccupation with his own dancing and had asked her a question.

"I'm sorry, I didn't hear. . . ."

"That's okay. I'll come closer."

The tempo of the music had changed, becoming slower and less frenetic. Cyrus put both his arms around her, pulling her, slightly off-balance, against his body. "Hmm! Much better. Been wanting to feel you up close all evening, pretty baby."

And this close was far too close! Sara thought indignantly as he ground her hips up against him with one surprisingly strong hand at the small of her back and the other molding her bottom. Mistaking the angry jerk of her hips for a deliberately enticing wriggle, the red-headed man gave her a wink. "I sure do like what I feel! Tell me, like I was asking you earlier, do you really enjoy getting laid *that* much?" The jerk of his head encompassed the screen, now almost filled with a closeup of Delight's provocative, nude derriere, and Sara herself; and before she could utter a word he went on in the same casual manner, "because if you do I'm willing — *and* equipped — to please you. Maybe we could teach each other some new variations, what do you think?"

All that prevented Sara from telling him what she really thought was the sight of the Duca di Cavalieri's sardonic face as he looked directly at her from less than a foot away, giving her a sarcastic lift of one eyebrow over his partner's blonde head. How long had he been there behind her — *eavesdropping?*

She'd like to give *him* an earful too!

Switching her eyes away from that dark, sarcastic face, Sara stopped pushing against her partner's chest and slid her palms up teasingly to his shoulders. She hoped Marco, with his blonde floozie clinging to him like a second skin, would take note!

"Well?" Cyrus repeated impatiently. Sara could *tell,* from the juxtaposition of their bodies, exactly how impatient he was getting.

"Well . . . *I* think we ought to go somewhere and talk about it over something long and very cold. It's too hot and too crowded out here."

"Sweetheart, good old Vince has a wet bar in every bedroom! Yeah, why don't we go get that drink?"

She could get rid of Cyrus once they had gone back indoors, even if she had to lock herself up in the loo. But let Marco see her walk off the floor hand in hand with him, and let him think — as he surely would — the very worst! Sara could positively *feel* those coal-dark eyes boring into her back. Somehow, without having to turn her head, she *knew* he was watching her. Good!

With a deliberately sensuous gesture Sara shook the hair back from her face before she smiled at Cyrus. She wanted Marco to see — she wanted him to know that she would choose any other man, even a casual acquaintance, over *him.* She hoped he'd eat his heart out.

Because she knew he wanted her. Despised her — and yet couldn't stop himself from desiring her. The conscious thought flashed into her mind quite suddenly, but the secret, intuitive knowledge had been stored in her subconscious all along, perhaps. And now she wasn't playing a game against him for Delight, who had had enough time to be safe by now, but for herself and the salvation of her pride.

Chapter 22

How Sara hated the rough, stuttering sound of the helicopter blades that seemed to tear brashly and intrusively into the stillness of the night-blue sky. It must be very near dawn. With a restless movement she snuggled back into her seat; eyes deliberately avoiding looking toward her companion, although she was almost too much aware of his dark presence there in the small cabin that enclosed them both.

Like a wolf, he must have sensed her small stirring, for his grating voice came out of the darkness to her, pitched low. "We should begin our descent in less than five minutes now. Is your belt still fastened?"

"Mm-hmm." The sullen sound of assent would have to content him because she didn't feel like talking to him, with her ears still burning from the shred of conversation she had overheard earlier. Damn him, damn him, damn him! Sara felt her nails digging into her palms and wished she could sink them into his brown flesh instead. How she hated him! What a triumph it would be to humiliate *him* for a change. To prove to him that he couldn't ruthlessly use and manipulate *every*one who crossed his path.

With an effort, Sara forced her mind back to the party they had just left, retracing everything that had happened since she had left the dance floor with Cyrus. Cyrus someone-or-other — what did his last name matter, when she'd probably never have to see him again? It hadn't been too difficult to get rid of Cyrus, fortunately. The age-old "Oh, I'd better find the loo, my head's starting to spin," still worked. When she emerged, looking and feeling fresh a half hour later, Cyrus had disappeared — probably into one of the wet bars with his next dancing partner!

After that, Sara had circulated — but with more caution; discovering in time that the partying had extended to the grounds as well as every room in the rambling two-story villa. She smiled a lot and flirted a lot but kept moving to another group, another room, when things began getting heavy. Upstairs there had been a huge projection room that was actually a minitheater with plush-covered seats arranged in tiers, each seat a recliner — for added convenience, she supposed cynically! A young man called Barry who told her he was a singer took her in there. "Vince gets all of the newest skin flicks," he told her. He had seemed almost relieved that she didn't recognize who he was, and *she* had been equally relieved to learn that Delight Adams didn't ring a bell with him either, although he *did* tell her casually that it was a pretty name.

Well — since she had to pass the time *and* keep Marco thinking that she had spent it all in bed, why not? Watching a dirty movie might prove educational, and one glance had told her that *this* movie, at least, was not one that starred her sister.

Sara had sat through at least the first half hour of *Sinners,* proud of herself for not fidgeting too much. At first she had been fascinated — were there *really* that many ways to do the same thing? And then as the acts became repetitious — the "dialogue" mostly moans and groans — she discovered that she was bored. Barry continued to watch the screen, but with a rather detached air. There were other, softer moans and groans from some of the other plush recliners. Sara had begun to calculate in her mind just how far away she was from the exit when Barry, who had appeared to ignore her presence up to then, took her hand and put it on himself. Good God! Sara thought disbelievingly, he could probably tie in a competition with what's-his-face on the screen! And then, without any preamble, he'd asked offhand-edly: "Want to give me some head?"

She had taken her hand away firmly. "Not really. And I've got to be going." Well, she hoped she wouldn't see Barry again either! Or any of the other people at the party, especially not those three men who had been shooting pool with Marco when she'd passed by.

Sara found herself going rigid all over again with a mixture of hate and rage. Remembering unwillingly the words that had halted her there outside, coming over the click of a ball before it shot into a pocket.

"Delight Adams — didn't I read somewhere that she was supposed to be Carlo's girl?"

The only light in the room was placed directly over the green baize surface of the pool table where all their attention was concentrated — four swarthy-skinned men in tailored suits who looked as if they had been cut from the same mold. Rich, arrogant Italian tycoons, making idle conversation. And then *his* voice, rough-textured, and yet as cutting as a lash as he made *her* position clear to his friends.

"You must have been mistaken, my friend. Not Carlo's girl — my whore. I'm keeping her . . . for the moment."

She hadn't wanted to hear what else they said — not after he'd said . . . *that*. His whore — with all the ugly, old-fashioned connotations of the word and the way he'd used it sitting like a cold stone in her stomach. So *that* was what he wanted them all to think. That's what he thought she was. He'd taken her to that party to show her off as his latest plaything, his . . . *whore*. Her certainty that they all looked at her, especially the men, and thought that about her made her feel sick inside until she had willed herself to feel nothing but anger instead. Let them all think whatever they wanted to about her — for the moment!

"Well — did you have fun?" he had asked her on their short ride from Vince's house to his private helipad.

"Oh, absolutely! I met some of the most gorgeous men. Didn't you think Cyrus was cute? But of course Barry was even better — oops! Freudian slip!" She had giggled, enjoying the look on his face before he shuttered it, his lips curling in an unpleasant grin. And if he thought to make her quail with the way his eyes raked over her, she was going to show him how mistaken he was!

"I suppose one could say, to look at you, that you have probably been quite busy," he drawled, his eyes taking in her carefully mussed-up hair and rather smudged makeup (ten minutes in the loo had managed *that*).

"Well, isn't that why you took me to the party? To have fun?"

"Of course!" But she thought he'd said it from between his teeth.

There had been no more conversation between them until just now; and after making his rather curt announcement, Marco too had relapsed into brooding silence. What was *he* thinking? Probably of new ways in which to hurt and humiliate her. But this time she intended to turn the tables on him. His whore indeed! And what about his blonde? He was the type of man who probably kept several mistresses — and belonged in the nineteenth century!

Her righteous anger carried Sara through their descent and into the house; walking beside him straight-backed and stiff as she tried to pretend that he wasn't there. But once the doors had been closed behind them and she made a move toward the stairway, he halted her with a hand on her arm, forcing her to turn her head to him.

"I would suggest that you try to fall asleep before the heat of the sun makes sleeping difficult. But in case you need anything there will be a maid awake and ready to tend you." In spite of the lack of inflection in his voice his black devil-eyes held a gleam of mockery as he had sensed the sudden tension of her arm under his fingers that halted and held her.

"Thank you. But how very . . . medieval!" Sara didn't care if she sounded rude. He had told her often enough that she needed to be taught manners, hadn't he? "I feel sorry for the poor girl who's forced to stay awake all night, just in case someone should need waiting on!" She made an attempt to tug herself free and felt his grip tighten.

"You certainly don't strike me as the softhearted type!" he drawled, with his narrowed eyes enjoying her discomfiture.

"And I'm not interested in hearing what 'type' you think I am, if that was coming next!" Sara snapped, her eyes shooting sparks of emerald fire at him. "If you'll kindly let me go, I could follow your advice and take myself off to sleep like a good little girl!"

Under the chandelier that lit the entrance hall her disordered hair had rich glints of flame in its thickness. Almost dispassionately, for all that he acted purely on instinct, Marco put out his free hand and felt the weight of it as he lifted it off the back of her slender neck. Damn the promiscuous, greedy little bitch, she had no right to be so seductive, even after she'd played musical beds with as many men as she could find to satisfy her. And yet she continued to play games with *him*. Why in hell didn't he do what he wanted to do and take her — cutting short the game-playing? It was probably what she expected, anyway. He knew her kind very well — a pity that Carlo hadn't learned yet.

"*Stop* that! I can't stand for you to touch me!" Like a nervous filly, Sara tried to jerk her head away from his intrusive hand, her voice rising. She didn't like the way in which

272

he had begun to look at her, almost consideringly.

"Can't you?" he answered her tauntingly, a smile that was not really a smile twisting his lips for a moment. "I think you are a liar — Delight of many men! You've responded to me before — I think you respond very easily to anyone who uses the right stimulation."

"You . . . you're all wrong! Damn you, let me go!" Goaded, Sara put up a hand to claw at his face, but he caught it easily; laughing shortly as he twisted both hands behind her back to hold her an unwilling captive against his hard-muscled body.

"Shall we find out which one of us is the liar?" he taunted, keeping her there while he studied her flushed, furious face.

"You . . . make me sick!" Sara gasped, hating her own impotent weakness as she struggled against him and felt the strength and the hardness of him. "Don't you have any pride? Doesn't it make any difference to you that I don't want you? Or can't you find any women who do? I hate you, despise you. . . ."

"Shut up!" In his voice was the growl of the barely leashed animal that he was; mounting to the surface like the evidence of his desire for her, lying hard against her thigh.

"Shut up!" he repeated again, more roughly this time as he saw her lips parting, ready to form an angry protest. "What I want to prove

273

to you will not take long — little liar, with your jade-green eyes and your seductive body you take such pleasure in flaunting so obviously! There was a certain look on your face on the screen last night that revealed that the intrusive presence of camera and crew had ceased to matter for you. You are the kind of woman who is ruled by her senses alone, aren't you?"

"Stop it, stop it!" Sara tried to strain away from him, panting with fury. "You don't know *anything* about me, because you can't see further than your —"

"At this moment, as you mean me to, I can see no further than your tempting lips!"

In spite of the mockery in his voice he wasn't about to let her off lightly this time — Sara could sense that, with a feeling of desperation, before his mouth came down to hers with deliberate, calculated slowness, finally cutting off her last frenzied protest. He kissed her until she thought her neck would snap from the force of his kisses, until her knees became weak and her mouth opened blindly under his and her head whirled with myriad sensations that seemed to make rational thinking impossible. With only one hand holding her wrists pinioned together now, his other hand began to move with tantalizing slowness up her spine to the nape of her neck, long fingers caressing her with false tenderness before brushing over her shoulders and down to the curve of her breasts — easily finding the silkiness of her warm skin under the bare-shouldered Halston gown that revealed more than it covered. Finding, cupping and finally teasing lightly while her nipples rose against his touch, sending strange feelings that were like electric shocks jolting through every nerve in her body.

How could a man she hated so *do* this to her? Filled with revulsion at herself, Sara's body arched away from him, trying to avoid his touch. Her head fell back and she heard herself moan as his bruising lips left her mouth to move with agonizing slowness to the breast his impatiently seeking fingers had laid bare.

How could she actually enjoy the feel of his lips and tongue against the tautly sensitive peak he'd already roused to awareness? How could she begin to want what he was doing, even the slow exploration of his hand down across her belly, trapped between their bodies now as he touched her intimately, his fingers seeming to burn her through all the folds of red chiffon that lay between them. Her face had begun to burn too, and her body burned — like heat from a fire flooding through her, filling her with dangerous feeling of languor that accepted everything he was doing to her and waited for more.

And then, all too abruptly, she was free — almost falling until his hands caught her to hold her upright.

"You see?" His voice came harshly to her over the distance that had suddenly separated them once more. "You don't have the strength to fight against your own sensual nature, in spite of all your resolves and all your hate. I think you would probably lie with the devil himself, if he kissed you hard enough." She hated the sound of his laugh, driving splinters under the skin his calculated caresses had rendered all too sensitive. His eyes were hard and opaque, giving away nothing as they rested for an instant on her flushed face. 'You don't have to look at me like that — don't you think we've both had enough activity for one evening? Go upstairs to bed, my little liar, and I will see you later, perhaps."

Even after she had escaped from him, whirling about to run from his darkly satanic presence without a word, forgetting pride, burning with shame, Sara thought she could hear his words repeating themselves in her head. "Go upstairs to bed, my little liar, and I will see you later, perhaps."

Perhaps, he'd said. Last, mocking twist of the cruel knife he'd already pierced her with.

Sara fled upstairs as if the devil himself had been after her, leaning, gasping for breath against the thick wooden door that had no lock on the inside — symbolic of her position here and a reminder of another age where women had been *owned* like property, and used according to the dictates of the men who possessed them.

Chapter 23

Once she had managed to compose herself enough for sleep, Sara slept as if she never wanted to wake up. In her dreams she was pursued by a great beast of a wolf with slavering jaws and eyes that glowed redly in the night. And in spite of the fact that she knew he could overtake her with a single bound, he preferred to stay just behind her, toying with her, letting her exert herself until her heart was bursting; waiting until it was his whim to close his jaws about her throat, taking her to oblivion — taking her at last. . . .

"No!" She must have said the word out loud, startling herself into wakefulness. Her room was hot and she lay on top of the rumpled sheets in a bath of sweat.

Thank God she was awake! Gradually the pounding of her heart slowed and her quickened breathing came back to normal. The room was dark with all the curtains drawn. What time was it? And then with a hurtful breath that sounded too much like a sob catching in her throat, she reminded herself that time, in this prison, was of no consequence. What did it matter how long she slept or how late? She was *here,* like a small moth trapped in amber, or like any untried concubine in a Moorish sultan's harem who waited with mingled trepidation and curiosity on her master's volatile whim.

Sara pressed cold fingers against her temples. There had been other dreams as well — nightmares that she didn't want to think about or analyze just yet; nor did she want to remember what had triggered them all — by all means don't think of *that* and the way he'd shamed her and broken down her pride along with her defense.

Stop it! Today was another day and yesterday she had been tired and sleepy; her mind filled with too many sights and sounds and images that must have affected her thinking subliminally in spite of her *conscious* rejection. Today, if he sought her out, he wouldn't find her easy. He wouldn't be able to —

Pushing her shameful, half-formed thought away Sara forced herself out of bed, her eyes going with unwilling apprehension to the door. Would he come looking for her, intent on making his conquest of her a physical actuality? Or was he waiting, preening his masculine ego, for her to come to *him?*

Almost viciously, Sara stabbed her finger against the button that would summon either Serafina or one of the maids. Today, while she recovered herself enough to plan, she would play the part of a pampered odalisque, surrounded by servants. If he sent for her, she would plead illness and refuse to go downstairs. Let him think what he pleased!

Thankfully, it was the housekeeper herself who came in answer to the electric buzzer. It was, she informed Sara with a carefully guarded face, at least a quarter after seven at night — but she had been instructed not to wake her.

"Oh? How kind of my host!"

The woman ignored her sarcastic comment, reminding her, belatedly, that after all Serafina owed all her loyalty to the di Cavalieris and had served the family for two generations. Why should she care about the fate of a foolish moth who had chosen to fly too close to flame?

"Shall I prepare your bath, signorina? I have ordered you a tray with coffee and orange juice and a sweet roll, in case you were hungry. And if you will tell me what you wish to wear for dinner . . ."

"I . . . I really don't feel very well!" Sara said, speaking quickly to hide her nervousness. "I'd love a nice hot bath to soak in, but after that — do you think it would be all right if I just stayed up here in my robe? I really don't feel up to getting dressed and going downstairs to dinner — could I just have a tray up here? Something very light — just soup and salad would be nice."

"Nothing else? The signorina needs to eat. . . ." Serafina's eyes traveled disapprovingly over Sara's slim body and fine-boned face, resting for just an instant on the dark smudges beneath her eyes.

"I'm not hungry at all, but there *is* something else." She was babbling like a fool now, Sara thought despairingly, but she couldn't help it! "Do you think . . . do you think I could have someone to stay with me for a while? I know you have too much to do, but — one of the maids perhaps. I — that strange experience I had the other night frightens me a little. I don't want to feel tempted to go outside again to experience the strange headiness of a Sardinian night!"

She had said just the right thing, for Serafina crossed herself and nodded without questioning her. "I'll send Teresa. She speaks better than the others, and even has some English. I am sure she will be full of questions about America, but she is a good girl and very conscientious."

So for tonight, at least, she would be protected. . . .

Immersed in the deep marble tub with her hair floating in thick wet strands about her neck and shoulders and even later when she gave in to the sheer luxury of being pampered and let Teresa brush it, Sara tried to avoid the thought that floated threateningly just below the surface of her mind: Protected from what?

Teresa stayed with her, questioning her avidly, once the initial shyness had worn off, about America — just as Serafina had warned her, Sara thought wryly. She had eaten her light dinner and had paced about her room a few times, and now, catching the girl holding back a yawn, Sara took pity on her and dismissed her. It was late, she knew, and the house was silent. And by now she should be ready to sleep again, waking fresh and ready to withstand . . . anything at all! She'd had time to arm herself, and she was ready. He would dicover no more shrinking weakness in her, no matter how hard he tried to break through the freshly mortared barricades she'd erected against him. *Strategy*, Sara admonished herself sternly, was the name of *this* game.

Strategy — advantage — weapons. . . . Thoughts tumble-tossed in her mind as she continued to pace about the room like an angry young feline until, impatient at herself, Sara stopped in front of the long, gold-framed mirror, seeing her reflection frown back at herself. *Weapons!* The green of her eyes seemed to deepen as they narrowed slightly.

Delight, of course, would have known how to fight him by instinct. Just as Mama-Mona would have known. But I'm learning! Sara thought fiercely. I'm learning. Stepping back, she studied herself measuringly and a trifle critically.

Her eyes and hair were, of course, by courtesy of Mona, who had made hair of that particular shade popular. *Hers* was natural, like her mother's and was growing quite long — long enough to brush her shoulders and her breasts. . . . Staring at herself as if she had been a stranger Sara flushed, remembering what had driven her here into her room seeking sleep and seclusion. Just like a frightened rabbit! With a deep breath Sara continued her mental catalogue of plus and minus. The breasts were okay, but not nearly as . . . *opulent* as Delight's. Supposedly, men felt that the bigger the better. But the rest of her, too thin or not — impulsively her fingers undid the knotted silk bow of her silk robe, letting it slip to the ground. Small waist — thank God for that and a flat belly. And if her hips, like her breasts, lacked a certain lush curvaceousness, at least she had long firm legs and her bottom *didn't* droop!

Not too bad, Sara. Not a bad arsenal for an amateur.

Beyond her shoulder as she looked in the mirror, the eyes of the enigmatically smiling lady in the portrait seemed to watch her, making Sara whirl around, snatching up her robe as she did. The minute she had done so she was annoyed at herself. Honestly! She was getting almost as bad as Serafina. She remembered her strange words, "I do not know what it is, signorina, or why some feel certain things and some don't. But it's said that the stones here are very old and have absorbed many *feelings* along with the heat of the sun."

At the time, preoccupied with other things, Sara had merely shrugged noncommittally. Well, with all the research being done into parapsychology these days she supposed almost anything was possible. Strong emotions — leaving their imprint on the very air; their vibrations echoing in wood and stone. Or perhaps I'm a little bit psychic! she had thought then, without any feelings of fear, before she dismissed the whole thing from her mind.

But now . . . good heavens — giving herself a mental shake — this was only a portrait, after all! And the poor silly woman who was its subject had died in poverty and misery — and all for love! Walking deliberately closer Sara gazed up at the portrait. Had she, at the very last, regretted all that she had given up, the poor young Duchess? When she ran away, had she actually been running to her lover or just away from her despot of a husband who left her alone so much and had forced her to wear his wolf medallion to remind her that she was his property? The woman in the portrait kept her smile and her enigma. She was Marco's mother, and he had been just a few years old when she had left him, the ducal palazzo and this very room where she must have cried herself to sleep many nights as she wondered what to do. How men had enjoyed keeping women dependent and subservient. They still would, no doubt, if women hadn't decided to throw off the yoke. And there were *some* men who still continued to act as if they lived in the Dark Ages! Sara's face darkened. Had Marco's attitude toward women anything to do with his mother? No doubt he was just like his father, who had brought him up to treat women as domestic pets or casual play-things; easily bought and discarded. A man who probably sneered at the word "love" and when he married would do so for all the "right" reasons except *the* one. He had expected the same of Carlo and had shown no scruples in trying to ensure that *his* wishes would be carried out.

"Only," Sara whispered aloud, "I stopped him there, even if he doesn't know it yet!"

Strategy — she had been thinking earlier. There was one kind of strategy for love and one for war, and since between her and Marco there was certainly no *love* . . . Sara began to smile wickedly. Research was one of her strong points; and was she *ever* going to do some research. On Marco, to find out what made him tick. *Everything* about him, like what were his weakest points (if he *had* any that was!), his likes and dislikes and his taste in women . . . grimacing as she remembered the blonde. He might be an animal, but at least he was a human one with dents in his armor. Which she would find. And use; with no more scruples than *he* had shown yesterday.

The incongruously businesslike telephone on the stand beside her bed shrilled suddenly, making Sara jump. Who . . . ? And then, remembering that there were no outside lines and this was an internal phone only, she scowled at it. Was it . . . ? Should she or shouldn't she? But if it was him and she didn't answer he would be just as likely to come bursting in on her without announcement.

Sara snatched up the phone, pausing a minute to make her voice sound sufficiently sleepy.

"He — hello?" Not bad at all, Sara, she thought smugly.

"Don't try to pretend that you're asleep. I know what time Teresa left and I've seen your light from the tiled courtyard."

How she hated that harsh, mocking voice! Sara's fingers clutched tightly at the receiver. "Had you thought that I might like to sleep with a . . . a night light on?"

His studied pause was designed, of course, to point to the irrationality of her statement.

Then he said curtly: "I was about to go for a swim in the indoor pool and thought you might wish to join me."

Very carefully Sara managed to sound arch. *"Alone?"*

"Does the prospect scare you so much?" She could almost see the sarcastic lift of a black eyebrow before his voice continued smoothly, "but I'm afraid that the servants have all gone to bed — and since their quarters are on the other side of the main courtyard we are the only two people in this whole section of my palazzo." Sara caught her breath in his infinitesimal pause, and he said: "I merely wished, of course, to reassure you that there should be no embarrassment for either of us when we go swimming."

Now he had lost her. "What on *earth* are you talking about? What's so embarrassing about going swimming together?"

"I suppose I should have realized that swimming in the nude — or 'skinny-dipping' as I've heard it called in America — would hardly embarrass you, no matter who was around! But here in Sardinia we tend to be rather old-fashioned, as I'm sure you've discovered."

"No!" She had uttered it explosively and instinctively. The . . . the . . . there was a word she'd heard used that perfectly described a man like him, although she wasn't about to use it out loud.

"And what do you mean by that? I can't recall having asked you a question."

The heat of her anger overcame the coldness of his voice.

"You asked if I'd want to swim with you and the answer, *again,* is no!" Sara said clearly. And then, to make it even more clear: "I'm not a little puppet bound to you by strings you'd like to pull. And I don't trust you — nor your so-called word of honor!"

The harsh steel in his voice could have killed her had it been a tangible thing. "And . . . what was this promise I made to you that you do not trust me to keep?"

Ha! she thought elatedly, game and set! Aloud she said with false candor: "Why . . . why that you'd never . . . *rape* me or . . . or do anything by force. Or do you choose not to remember?"

"I happen to remember very well indeed." His voice was a snarl before he smoothed it out. "Why did you think I sent you on your chaste way to bed? And what did you imagine from the fact that I happened to kiss you on a wager?"

"A . . . a *wager. . . !*"

"Yes — a wager that I made and you accepted, little liar!" His taunting growl of a chuckle made Sara clench her jaws with silent fury. "I didn't rape you, did I? And believe me, I've no intention of exerting myself to such extremes — why should I? Perhaps it is yourself that you're afraid of, dear Delight! Don't you trust your own emotions if you were swimming naked, with a naked man? Might you find yourself wishing, longing for . . . the act you choose now to call 'rape'?" He made a sound of contemptuous disbelief from deep in his throat before he added briefly: "But all this is a waste of time! I'm going for my swim — and you are welcome to join me or not, as you wish!"

Chapter 24

Both fireplaces at either end of the huge marble chamber had been lit. Unnecessarily, surely, but the leaping, flickering flames provided an effectively flattering light that lent even Sara's fair skin a tawny, golden glow. As she walked barefoot down the marble stairs with their wide, curving balustrades, Sara became more and more aware with every step she took that she was doing something she had never done before; taking risks she had never dared run before in the safely prosaic life that had been hers until just a few months ago. And yet she refused to let her steps falter, even when the sounds of splashing in the pool stopped and she knew he was watching her.

There was nothing to be afraid of! There was nothing wrong or objectionable about the unclad human body — and nakedness was much less prurient or . . . or *enticing* than a scantily clad body that kept some mystery about it. Be brave, Sara. Think about the

Cause for which you're baring your virgin body — which really isn't a bad body at all!

"Well? Now that you're here, have you perhaps remembered that you cannot swim? Are you going to run back upstairs to your room to hide from the big bad wolf?"

He looked different with his thick black hair plastered closely about his head; but the rasping voice and the sardonic darkness of his face were the same as she remembered. To hell with him!

"And who's afraid of the big bad wolf?" Sara paraphrased smartly as she tossed aside her brief Japanese robe and dove in.

Oh, but this felt *good*, and she certainly needed the exercise. Both mental and physical exercise, she reminded herself as she swam half the length of the pool under water and came up blinded for an instant by heavy strands of her dripping, clinging hair.

"Please allow me. . . ." Long brown fingers brushed her hair aside and Sara looked up, treading water, to realize that she had almost cannoned into him.

"Thank you!" Taking a deep breath she practiced her crawl — in the opposite direction. Unfortunately, she found him there already as she clung to the side.

"So you can swim almost as well as you play tennis! You make me wonder what other sports you excell at!"

How much of her could he see under the

water? Oh, hell! Now she was beginning to think like a mid-Victorian herself! With a deliberately flirtatious gesture Sara pushed her hair back from her face. Now *that* crack deserved two barrels!

She said coyly: "But that's for you to wonder and me to *know,* isn't it?" And was rewarded by the tightening of the muscles in his face as he looked at her as if he'd like to drown her.

Without waiting to find out if he'd really try, she took off again, much more smoothly this time as habit and training took over. She could play tennis, she could swim, and she could ride. All very well. She could even play the piano in a mediocre fashion, strum an accompaniment on the guitar if she had to. Daddy had insisted that she have all the accomplishments of what *he* considered "a lady." And what would poor Daddy think now, if he knew what she was up to? Surfacing at the other end, the very thought made Sara shudder.

"Surely you can't be cold?" This time his biting voice came from a safer distance away. "But if you are, I could put more wood on the fire."

That would mean his getting out of the pool, and he obviously wasn't wearing swimming trunks!

"I'm just *fine,* thank you!" she said cheerfully.

"Bene."

Obviously, he had now decided to ignore her. Doing leg exercises with her hands clinging to the rail that ran around the inside of the pool, Sara could hear him go back and forth in cutting, vicious swath, feeling the ripples and vibrations of his passing against her body.

"Well — I've had enough!" When Sara turned her head he was sitting on the side of the pool with his legs crossed as nonchalantly as if he'd been wearing a pair of one of those impeccably cut pants he owned.

Quickly, she turned her head away, saying in a slightly muffled voice: "Does that mean that *I* have to come out too? That isn't fair, because I've only just got here!"

"Then of course you must do as you will. And since I too forgot a towel I will lie here in front of the fire to dry myself off. I wouldn't want to leave you alone, looking so little and defenseless in this great marble bathtub. It would be too easy to slip on the wet floor or to develop a cramp. I'll wait for you."

Calm announcement of fact — and of course he *would*. Courage, Sara! She swam three lengths of the pool before she was ready to face him nonchalantly.

"That was — wonderful!"

Sara raised herself out of the water and sat for a while with her back to him, wondering whether he had actually fallen asleep or was

— watching. A small shiver ran through her like a tremor under her skin. Could she really carry this off?

The fire at her back flamed up suddenly, sending misshapen shadows leaping and prancing against the wall. She recognized *his* shadow, his lean height exaggerated so that he might have been looming over her. Was he?

She felt relief when his voice came to her from a safe enough distance away.

"You are obviously cold and I have put more wood on the fire. Unless you intend to sit there staring into space while you catch a chill, I suggest that you do as I did and dry yourself by the fire's heat. Even the floor is warm over there, and" — his voice became caustic — "of course, you have my word that I will not . . . coerce you in any way!"

Preferring to ignore the other implications of his statement Sara said brightly: "That fire *does* look good!"

There was a *waiting* silence behind her while she gathered up her courage on a deep breath. Nude statues and paintings were everywhere! So were free beaches, topless-bottomless dancers and centerfolds. The centerfolds decided her. After all, *she* was supposed to be leading *him* on; only to reject him when the moment of truth arrived. "Would you mind passing me my robe, please?"

It must have just slipped out! The snort of

disbelief she heard behind her acted as a goad that sent Sara to her feet, holding herself straight as she turned around to face him, with his night-black eyes pinpointed with the red reflection of fireglow. Pride held her posed for an instant longer than necessary. Well, since he wanted to look, let him *look* — damn his hide — and eat his heart out for something he would never have!

With a deceptively guileless motion, Sara lifted her arms to lift up strands of dripping hair off her shoulders. "I'm afraid I'm *never* going to get my hair dry unless you're gallant enough to go and bring me a towel!"

"And what makes you think that I am *galant?*" His voice grated on her nerves, almost sending her back to being unsure of herself. But somehow, Sara managed a light, rueful laugh.

"Just trying, that's all. I suppose I should have known, shouldn't I?"

"Yes, I'm sure you should." The timbre of his voice had changed subtly, transforming it into a deep, lazy drawl. "But why don't you come to the fire now? I think I just saw you shiver again, and I would not like to feel responsible for having you catch cold!"

He, of course, lay to one side of the fire with his arms crossed under his head and one leg bent at the knee. Sara tried not to stare at the muscular, fine-planed length of his body as he lay there watching her with a total lack of modesty or embarrassment as she made herself walk casually forward. It was a relief all the same to be able to drop to her knees and lie on her stomach with her head turned away from him as if she preferred to study the fire.

In the silence that seemed to deepen between them Sara became suddenly aware of the music. Soft, subtle; winding like sensuous threads of silk around her. *Tristan und Isolde* — the love theme. The music only; without what had always seemed to her the intrusion of voices. Surely the most sensual music in all the world. Music to lose one's senses by.

"I suppose you would have preferred rock and roll, but this music happens to suit my mood tonight."

"You're always *supposing,* and you really know nothing about me. Nothing!"

"In that case — am I going to be allowed to find out?"

"I doubt that there's any need for you to bother!" Sara sniffed. Why did he keep sniping at her?

"But why not? Especially since you have managed to keep your . . . mystery. I am intrigued, and I admit it."

"Huh!" Sara had learned to love that particular expression, with its enormous range of nuances.

"You don't believe me? But there is a great

deal I would like to find out about you, Delight. For instance — do you enjoy being massaged? Your back looks very rigid and tense, even from here, and that's not good. Here, since I was not *galant* enough to fetch you a towel for your wet hair, let me make up for it by helping you to relax all those tense muscles."

"I don't really . . ."

He cut her off ruthlessly.

"Lie still. This is only oil that you feel and it contains Vitamin E, which is supposed to be very good for keeping the skin supple and young." Without waiting for a response he had already begun to massage her shoulders and neck with a lightness that surprised her. "Don't worry," he said mockingly from somewhere above her, "I am not trying to arouse you. Only to make you feel warmer and more relaxed."

Oh, sure! her mind jeered. But after carefully weighing her choices, Sara had decided that discretion was the better part . . . and she was surely safer lying on her stomach than if she had startled to scramble up onto her feet. In any case, she could not say that the pressure of his fingers was anything more than impersonal, moving from the damp nape of her neck to her shoulders and farther down, where he seemed to find all the tense spots and relieve them. As long as he stayed above the base of her spine . . .

"Am I hurting you or does it feel good?" She hadn't known till now that the wolf could purr. Did he think to get her guard down? "Now you're stiffening up again — haven't you ever learned how to relax?"

"I suppose I'd find it a lot easier if your sudden show of *niceness* didn't make me suspicious."

"What a cynic you are! Turn around and I'll prove to you that I *can* be nice, if that means in your vocabulary that I should remain completely impersonal. Shall I pretend that you are . . . a favorite niece perhaps? The pure daughter of a friend?"

"God help your nieces if you have any! And I tend to doubt that you have many friends left with pure young daughters!"

She cried out when his hands tightened over her shoulders as if he had been suddenly tempted to slam her head against the marble floor.

"Your tongue's too sharp, Delight, and it could very well get you in trouble sometime. Feel fortunate that you extracted a promise from me!" His voice was threatening enough to quiet her for the moment as she lay newly tensed under his hands that were strong enough to break her apart if he chose.

Abruptly, his attentions moved to her feet, startling her. First the soles of her feet, one by one, and then, with the oil making her skin feel as supple as silk, her calves — lingering over them long enough to give her a faint feeling of confidence. It was only when she felt the insinuating warmth and strength of his touch move slowly upward to her thighs that Sara protested sharply.

"Please stop! That's enough. I'm all relaxed now and I think I'd like to go back to my room."

"I didn't think you were a coward as well."

As well as what? Her mind snapped out the question she refused to ask.

"I don't really care what you think," she said instead, coldly.

"Good. Then perhaps I was mistaken in thinking that you were afraid of me for some reason. Come, you may turn over in perfect safety from *me,* I assure you. Since you can hardly be *shy* I presume that fear is the reason for your coyness?"

"You shouldn't assume anything! Why should I be afraid of you?"

"Well, in that case . . ." With surprising ease and swiftness Sara found herself held, lifted, and turned over onto her back as if she had been a limp rag doll.

"Why, you . . . !" She closed her eyes against the blaze that erupted in his for a fleeting instant, to hear herself cut off by his voice.

"It's not becoming for a *lady* to curse and swear — and you have been trying to convince me for these past few weeks that you are, in fact, a lady. So lie still and be quiet, unless my hands take any intimate liberties that you object to."

"Have I told you lately that I *don't* like you?" Sara said stonily into his darkly mocking face, and caught his twisted smile with a spurt of rage.

"Is that so? How ungrateful you are, when I am only trying to do something *nice* for you. Why don't you — how does the saying go? — yes, just lie back and enjoy?"

It seemed easier to close her eyes again, as if she could shut him off that way. Close her eyes and keep herself stiff; resisting the slyly insidious touch of his hands against her fire-warm skin with the oil sinking into it, making it shine like shimmering satin in the reddish-gold firelight.

He took her by the shoulders, massaging with deceptive gentleness there and along her collarbone until he could feel the almost imperceptible softening of her muscles. And then from there his hands moved lower, feeling her tense all over again and deliberately avoiding any contact with her nipples. Very gentle here, a lightly stroked curve as light as a brushstroke until he reached her firm, flat belly and moved upward again, still very lightly. In spite of her studied pretense of bored indifference he thought he felt a slight tremor run under the silken smoothness of her skin, betraying her.

Damn her for an experienced little tease who chose to fight her own instincts rather than give in too easily! And she must have surely realized by now that there was no longer any question of being allowed to marry Carlo? What did she think to gain by this virtuous act of hers? And for how long did she intend to keep it up?

Chapter 25

How incredible and how unbelievable this would have seemed less than two days ago! That she would be lying naked and on her back on a warm marble floor with a fire to heat her tingling flesh while the one man that she most hated and despised was seeing her as no other man had ever seen her; touching her as no other man had ever touched her before.

Why was she letting him? If his touch had turned harsh and abrasive again, or if he had in some sly way tried to skirt the strange pact they had entered into, *then* she would have stopped him — and left him. But he wasn't . . . wasn't doing anything she could protest against derisively; just massaging her as impersonally as he had promised. Or *was* he being quite that impersonal? She was sure she hadn't imagined the feather-light brush of his fingers against her inner thighs a moment ago. And, damn it all, *she* was supposed to be the

one to do the leading on, arousing him until
just the right moment, when she would reject
him. He and his teasingly sensual hands that
roamed far too familiarly with her body . . .
and God knew how many women he must
have played this particular game with.
"Massage," indeed!

Sanity and a sense of grim purpose returning
almost belatedly, Sara sat up, blinking her
eyes as if she had been on the verge of falling
asleep. "Mmm-hmm! That did feel good! But
turnabout's fair play, you know, and now it's
my turn. I'm really quite good at giving a
massage myself, you know."

Well, at least she *had* read a book on the
subject and her retention was excellent. With
a teasing smile, Sara reached for the open vial
of oil, steadfastly keeping her eyes on *his*
surprised face.

"And now it's your turn to let yourself relax,
so lie down do!"

"How . . . reciprocal of you! I'm flattered." But Sara noticed that even after he
had stretched himself out on his belly as *she*
had done in the beginning, he squinted up at
her suspiciously.

Pleased with herself she gave him an
upcurving cat-smile. "Oh, but I'm sure you
have lots and lots of eager female volunteers.
I'll try to do the best I can, though."

"Thank you," he growled dryly. "And I'll
give you your rating *after* you have done. I

have no desire to feel your sharp claws sink into my flesh!"

"Oh, but I might surprise you and rate a perfect ten — you never can tell, can you?"

"Go ahead!" He made a shrugging movement of wide shoulders and casually pillowed his face in his hands as if resigned to a not-too-pleasant experience.

Poised on her knees above him it was all Sara could do to resist pulling a face at the back of his arrogant head. He was right, she *would* like to sink her nails in him, but she was out to prove a point. And so, with fingers that he found surprisingly strong, she began to massage the back of his neck, just as he had done with her.

The oil, sliding like thick honey between her palms and his brown flesh, gave her the strangest feeling — almost of wonder at herself for doing what she was doing and actually *enjoying* in an unexplainable fashion, the unfamiliar texture of his skin and the hard contours of his back. She could feel the ripple of animal muscles under her fingers as if he was tensing and untensing, still not too sure of what she was up to. She slid her knuckles down the length of his spine and back up again; kneading his shoulders and trailing teasingly the next minute down to his waist — passing daringly over tightly held muscles to rest almost consideringly on his thigh.

"That's a *massage?*" There was a snarl in

his voice that only made her smile this time. She could sense from his restless stirring that he tried to control the disturbance that her touch had aroused in him.

"That's a *complaint?*" Her voice was deliberately provocative while her hands semaphored messages up and down the hard, harsh length of his body; learning new things all the time, and gradually beginning to feel a heady sense of power when she started to sense with her fingertips his unwilling reaction.

"You are . . . making me want you. Be careful!"

Her oiled hands continued to move with more and more assurance against his warm skin while she responded lightly: "But why? You swore to me that I could trust in your given word. Do you want me to stop?"

She was teasing, taunting, tempting — and a bitch of the first order, Marco thought grimly. Of course, she was out to get even with him, and his typically male reactions put him at a disadvantage. *Dio!* How he'd like to have her squirming, long-limbed body under his while he made her admit to what she was — nothing more than a cheaply available slut who was ruled by her senses; giving herself far too easily to any stud she fancied. It had been his intention to let Carlo discover that for himself. . . . He caught himself up sharply, angry at the slip. Had been? *Was!*

She might be spirited enough, but she was also a woman, and weak like the rest of her sex — including his own mother. His mouth twisted in a harsh grimace that was hidden from her by his arms. Putting Delight in that particular room had been a bitter private jest that only he could know the irony of. His mother, running off with her peasant lover, had been a slut too. Kindred spirits. And there was only one, obvious way to exorcise them both.

Gloating in her victory and yet fascinated in spite of herself, Sara could not repress a startled gasp when she suddenly found her wrist caught and held in a hurtful, implacable grasp.

"Enough!" Why was everything he said to her a command or a threat?

"What's wrong with you *now?* Let me go, you're hurting, and you promised . . ."

"I know only too well what I promised," he grated. "But you are, I think, trying to incite me into crossing the lines that *you* insisted on drawing between us. I am not a foolishly naive young man like Carlo, and *usually* . . ." He let the word drag out mockingly as he came up onto his knees in one easy, fluid motion; still holding her trapped there before him. "Usually," he continued in a harsh drawl that warned her to silence, "I do not deny myself any fleeting pleasures such as you might provide. So be careful, or I might choose to take your teasing for an invitation!"

His eyes traveled with slow deliberation over her nudity, lingering on her breasts and the shadowed vee of her thighs — a wash of telltale color rising in the wake of that insolent, somehow *consuming* look.

"Ohh!" Her breath coming shortly, Sara tried to tug herself free from him. "I should have *known* that you'd be a bad loser. First at tennis, and now . . ."

"But which of us the loser, and which the victor?" His voice was abrasive, like the feel of his thumb stroking against the sensitive pulse that beat erratically on the underside of her wrist. "Don't you want to find out?"

"I think" — she had to control the tremor in her voice with an effort — "I think that perhaps we ought to call it quits for tonight and . . . and just go to bed. Stop twisting — I said you were hurting me!"

"So you did. . . ." he said reflectively while his black, impenetrable eyes seemed to enjoy her futile struggle to be free. "Was that another promise you tricked me into making to you? That I would not hurt you? I don't seem to recall."

"Let *go!*" Sara hissed angrily into his dark, unsmiling face. "I'm not . . . not into S and M, if that happens to be *your* bag!"

"And if it were, do you think your feeble protests would have any effect?" he taunted her. "I think you know as well as I do that in

307

a very short time I could make you want anything I chose to do to you — to that slim, fire-flushed body you choose to flaunt so blatantly!"

There was a flicker of light in the depths of his eyes like a smoldering flame that hid beneath banked coals. A dangerous message that even she, with all her lack of experience, could read only too well.

"No!" She threw the word, sharp as a knife's edge, at his face; wishing bitterly that she could scar him, hurt him. If she had actually had a dagger handy she would have had no compunction at all about plunging it into that hard masculine body that could only too easily overpower her. "No — whatever you did you could never make me want *you!*" Her eyes glared moistly into his, bright with an utter desperation that could pass all too well for hate. Sara could not recognize the brittle, harsh laugh she gave as her own. "Because — you know what? Even if you did take me, even if you did manage to excite my body I would have to close my eyes while I fantasized about someone *else* — anyone else! Do you understand? I like to choose my own lovers, Signor Duca! And you just don't happen to be my type. Have I made myself *clear?*"

In the sudden, taut silence that followed her frantic outburst everything seemed to be suspended, even her breathing. Sara found that she literally could not tear her eyes away from his, watching them turn as hard as obsidian. No other change in his face that she could discern. Why didn't he *say* something? Or *do* something? She could feel, with shame, her heart start to pound madly until she was afraid that *he* would hear and discover how terrified she really was of him.

"Didn't you hear what I said?" Her voice sounded far too high and brittle, even in her own ears.

"Why, yes. As close as we are to each other, how could I fail to hear?" His voice sounded pleasant. *Too* pleasant, making Sara want to shy away. "And you can certainly be quite articulate and . . . forthright when you choose to be, can't you? You are also quite the little bitch — the kind who is known in your country as a prick-teaser, I believe. Hot one moment and cold the next. A born whore, in fact."

It seemed incredible and even slightly unreal that he could actually be saying all these ugly, degrading things to her in the same casually pleasant tone of voice in which he had begun.

Sara's face burned like the rest of her. Fight him, her mind told her. Fight him with any weapon you can find, or he's going to defeat and degrade you — that's what he's trying to do, saying those things, watching for your reactions with that cold, cruel smile that merely twists one corner of his mouth and isn't really a smile at all. . . . He had called her a whore! Again.

"If I really was . . . what you called me, you can be sure, signor, that there could be *no* price you could pay that would buy me! And you can be equally sure that I'd *give* it away to any man I really dug, even if he happened to be the garbage collector!"

"I am beginning to discover that in spite of that pretty body that has brought you so much notoriety, you also happen to combine all the worst traits of a female! Shall I detail them?"

"I don't want to hear any more from you. Let me go, I tell you!"

He went on implacably, as if he had not heard her protests: "You possess a too-hot temper and a vicious tongue, both of which you would do well to curb if you ever want to keep one of your many lovers for longer than a night or two. You are also, obviously, a coldly calculating, hypocritical little —"

"And *you* are nothing but a . . . a pompous *ass!* Studying me through a dirty microscope with that insufferably judgmental look, while all the time . . ." Sara cut herself short just in time, horrified by the implications of what she had almost said.

"All the time . . . what? You should also learn to finish your sentences." Jagged edges underlay the deceptive smoothness of his voice.

"When you are through with holding me here by force to listen to your insulting allegations, I'd really like to leave, you know. It's getting *very* uncomfortable kneeling here on this cold, hard floor — unless you were thinking of forcing me to do penance for my rumored sins?"

This time Marco did not try to smother the ugly oath that was jerked out of him as he hauled her roughly and unceremoniously to her feet. He half-expected her to be off balance and fall against him; but damn her, like a cat she kept her balance easily, looking at him out of those eyes like splintered green glass, glittering gold-edged in the firelight. Who could see through eyes like hers — or look beyond them? Eyes of a natural coquette, a born harlot. And a body to match, as he had not been able to help noticing — or reacting to. Calculating? Damn right she was calculating. And completely amoral, among a lot of other things. Bitch goddess! And — *penance* she had said?

"Penance is only for the truly repentant, I'm afraid! But had this been as little as a hundred years ago I would truly have exacted much more than a formal *penance* from you, believe me!"

She didn't like the way his voice had lowered into a deep growl at the last, nor the dangerously brooding look in his eyes when he watched her. But at least he had finally dropped her aching wrist, and Sara tried to act nonchalant as she massaged it — backing off slightly at the same time.

"You really don't have to go into *details,* thank you! I imagine you'd have me hauled off to a dungeon or something equally medieval; and tortured me gruesomely until I'd admitted to all the imaginary sins you'd accuse me of." She gave an exaggerated shudder, adding, "All I can say is thank God for progress! I've come a long way, baby!"

And that was her perfect line for an exit. Both graceful *and* dignified — if she could only find her wrap.

"I'm glad to hear it!" he said dryly, adding with false politeness: "You are looking for something? This?"

"This" happened to be the missing wrapper, wadded up inconsiderately and tossed at her so carelessly that Sara was forced to take several steps backward in order to catch it. Precisely as he'd intended, of course!

With the splash she'd made still echoing in her ears Sara went under, came up gasping to hear his harsh laugh and went under again. This time she didn't come up. Underwater swimming had taught her how to hold her breath for quite a long time, and there were no pool lights on to illuminate the water. If he thought she had hit her head on the edge and was stunned, would he come in after her or let her drown?

She had almost reached the limit of her endurance when she felt him dive in — and immediately she shot to the surface, keeping close to the side and pulling herself out of the water in almost one motion.

The pompous, arrogant bastard! Sara hoped he'd stay under a long time, looking for her. Long enough to feel apprehension at the prospect of a murder investigation — or to drown himself.

She was on her feet and running lightly for the stairwell, not daring to look back when his angry voice jarred her.

"You're wise to run from me, you tricky little bitch! If I had you here you would not need to pretend drowning!"

Sara kept moving, leaving him with the last word this time. It was all she could do not to glance apprehensively over her shoulder as she sped up the marble stairs, cool under her bare feet. In her sudden blind panic, she slipped and almost fell twice before she gained the doubtful shelter of her room to lean backward, panting, against the door. She remembered only then that she could not lock it.

Chapter 26

Afterward, Sara could not recall how much time she spent just *staring* at the heavy wooden door through which he might come at any moment — to exact his revenge. What if he did? The first thing she had done as she recovered her breath had been to snatch up her discarded nightgown and pull it over her head. She looked balefully toward the door again. So much for *la dolce vita!* Skinny-dipping in a marbled swimming pool with an Italian Duke who believed in bending all the rules to suit himself was *definitely* not her cup of tea. In fact, if she had any sense at all she would *never* have let herself be talked into this whole mess!

A pair of heavy silver-and-ebony candlesticks stood on either side of one of the ornamental mirrors in the room, and Sara picked one up. If he dared to push that door open she would brain him without hesitation and gladly face the consequences. A kidnapped virgin defending her honor to the death!

At last an unwilling smile quirked her mouth, and she started to feel slightly silly, standing here poised for battle. Nanny Staggs had always warned her about her overly dramatic imagination, and who knew her better?

"*That* way, Miss Sara, you're just like your mother, I'm afraid. Now, why would you think that poor Mr. Meeks is one of them mass-murderers! Honestly!"

The memory of Nanny's snort helped to bring everything back in perspective at last. If he had been coming after her, he certainly would have burst through the door long before this. Maybe he too had belatedly been overtaken by sanity.

She could feel herself sag with the sudden tiredness that followed relief of tension. Tomorrow she would take steps to extricate herself from her present untenable situation; and if *he* wouldn't let her go, then there was always the ubiquitous Angelo who had offered eagerly to take her to her mother. She had a feeling that in spite of his slightly slapdash manner, Angelo was really quite efficient at whatever he did. He struck her as being a survivor.

Tomorrow she really must ask Serafina to draw her some kind of map of this rabbit-warren palazzo of the Duke di Cavalieri.

Tomorrow — it was probably that already — and oh, but she was tired! Exhausted enough to feel as if her bones were melting inside her, leaving her incapable of keeping erect for much longer.

With the lights turned out, Sara almost collapsed into bed. Earlier she had left the folding shutters that led out onto the terrace open — a faintly stirring breath of air reminded her, but she was already half-asleep.

Sleep was welcome blackness — a place of no-thought — comfortable nothingness. And then came the unwelcome intrusion of dreams that made her move uneasily in her wide bed, wondering in her dreams why she felt as if someone was trying to ask her something she couldn't hear, repeating the same question over and over with silently moving lips. How annoying! Did they think she was deaf and a lip-reader? And why did they have to shake her so violently to make her understand?

"Oh, stop!" The protesting mumble of her own voice brought an almost-awareness.

"Maledizione! Why in hell do you wear this stupid garment? If you don't help me take it off, I swear I'll rip it off your body, my double-damned Delight!"

Oh, God — she *knew* that voice! Oh no! She gave a sleepy, protesting cry as an arm went under her shoulders to drag her up into a semi-reclining position, while at the same time her nightgown was jerked off roughly. And *then* he let her drop back onto the bed, jolting her back to fuzzy wakefulness.

"What — what do you think you're doing? How dare you . . . !"

"I think I told you before, it's called *droit du seigneur*. We have a similar expression in the local dialect, if you should care to —"

"Get out of here! You . . . you *promised*, remember?"

"You sound like a little child! What would make you think that I keep my promises?" His body lay partially over hers, Sara realized with a mounting feeling of dread. And his face was far too close to hers — close enough for her to feel the warmth of his breath and smell the tang of alcohol. She shivered.

"You're *drunk*, aren't you? You had to get yourself good and drunk so you could get up the courage to come up here and *rape* me! *Droit du seigneur* indeed — there's nothing gentlemanly or . . . or *civilized* about you! You're just a throwback to those pirate ancestors of yours who came here to sack and rape and make slaves of the women they carried off! You —"

"I never promised, *bella mia,* that I would not try to seduce you!" He put his lips against her neck for an instant and she almost cried out. "And yes . . . of course, I am slightly drunk. Why not? I thought the wine would bring me sleep, but instead — it brought me images of you, witch-woman. You make me want you even though I despise you and know you for what you are. Even though I often come near to hating you."

He spoke to her in Italian and there was a note in his voice that made Sara try to struggle against him. He had come here determined to take her! And now he talked to her in that rough steel-and-velvet voice that seemed to rub abrasively against her very nerves. As abrasive as the encroaching feel of his body over hers with its different textures of hair and skin and male roughness that frightened her instinctively.

"Go away; I want you to . . . just stop and go away!"

She despised herself for being driven to begging with that note of desperation in her voice, but could not help herself for reacting with traditional virginal terror when his hand began to caress her deliberately and intimately.

"I thought you liked being massaged. Stop wriggling so wildly, *carissima*, unless you want me to believe that you are already aroused."

She started to beat at him in retaliation, sobbing with a combination of terror and fury.

"*Basta!* What's wrong now? Stop it — I don't enjoy nail marks as a sign of passion." His voice snarled at her as he caught both her wrists in midair. "One would almost think that you were a frightened virgin from your struggles, instead of a seductive *cortigiana* who enjoys what she does."

He was so damned strong! She didn't have a chance against his determination and his strength unless she told him the truth — that she was not Delight but Delight's older sister. She'd rather face his anger than what he planned to do with her.

"I'm not . . . I don't . . . oh, damn you, *stop!* You don't under —"

His mouth silenced her effectively, dwelling over hers in what seemed an endless variety of kisses that blended into each other and went from savagely impatient and hurtful to become a slow and deliberate exploration of the shape and texture of her lips, her tongue, her mouth. He was harsh, then gentle, then harsh again while his strong brown fingers continued to do what they pleased with her. Deliberately inciting — almost teasingly slow, he began to play with the sensitive peaks of her nipples until she was gasping for breath under his predatory mouth. She felt almost mindless, torn helplessly between wanting and not wanting — between letting go to feeling and primitive fear.

Now there was no sound between them except their breathing and the moans that caught in her throat. Oh, God! Sara thought dazedly, I can't believe this is happening to me and I'm actually starting to *want* it to happen. . . . What she didn't want was to

319

think about anything at all, while she let her senses take over for the first time in her life; it was like falling very slowly from a great height, spinning in gigantic slow-motion circles, or being sucked into the center of a whirlpool that took her and took her without her conscious volition. What he did to her with the sensuous pressure and probing of his caressing fingers was diabolical!

Somehow, at some point it had become no longer necessary for him to keep her wrists imprisoned, and her hands clung to his shoulders instead of beating furiously at them. He touched her where she wanted to be touched, reaching nerve endings and creating sensations she had never known existed. Giving in, she felt herself tossed and whirled about in a vortex of emotion that made her arch herself up against him fiercely and almost welcome the sharp stab of pain that made her cry out and gave way in seconds to another kind of pain that was not really pain at all, although it too made her give a choked, almost animal sound that she herself didn't even hear for the pounding drumbeat of her pulses.

More . . . and more . . . and, incredibly, even more. Like nothing she could have imagined, nothing she had dreamed of, nothing she could describe to herself or even explain. All she was aware of was the motion of his body over hers and the feel of him inside her, filling emptiness and taking her to the furthest reaches of pleasure.

From there, free-falling to reality was like waking from a kind of trance in which she had not been herself at all but a passionate, sensual creature who could give herself up unreservedly to desire and its slaking. She became suddenly conscious of everything. The rumpled, disordered bed and the dampness beneath her. Marco's body still possessively straddling hers, still a part of her. Was he asleep? If he said something cruel and sarcastic to her *now,* she'd . . .

He moved to free her partially of his weight, his mouth lazily nuzzling at the soft, sensitive spot between her neck and shoulder. *"Dio mio,* but you are a temptress! So tight and so warm . . . incredibly, you make me want you again!" The growl of his voice against her sensitive flesh sent vibrations through her that were partly fearful and partly . . . something else that his words excited in her, bringing out some ancient, primeval instinct that made her want to *touch* him. Hold him with herself, inside herself. Learn the texture of his night-black hair. Discover if he could make her feel the same fierce rise of passion again and the same fulfillment.

Sara's hands slipped down his back and back up again to his shoulders and the back of his neck. From there one hand moved down again, exploring the length of his hard body as far as she could reach, and finding, almost by instinct the place where their bodies were joined.

"*Strega!* Witch!" She heard him whisper harshly against the spring of hair at her temple as he began to move and swell inside her again while his hands caught in the thickness of her hair to pull her face up to his for his savage kisses and moved from there under her, to thrust her hips up against his.

She had been told by all the books she had read and all the girlfriends she had talked to that this kind of thing could never happen in real life. *Again?* Triumphantly, joyfully, she was finding out that they were all wrong!

She was still floating down gently, feeling light as a feather, when she heard him say something to her that didn't really register and didn't matter either, not *then*. Drowsily, Sara turned her face against his shoulder, murmuring sleepily against it as she snuggled herself closer to him; arms tightening about him as she did.

Whatever he said had been in Italian and it might have been "good night" or even *"domani"* which was a word Italian men were very fond of using, especially to their mistresses. Without being aware of it, she had started to smile in her sleep. Mistress. Who would have thought it, she was actually someone's mistress! Marco's, to be exact, and that was really very funny because she had begun by hating him.

The next thing Sara became aware of was the sun; pushing at her eyelids with hot, bright fingers. And then a feeling of loss.

Had she actually been dreaming? Sara reached out a tentative, exploring hand to encounter only a pillow and she frowned. Dream? But when her body moved, an unaccustomed soreness made her wince — her eyes blinking open to squint against the sun that streamed in inquisitively through the gap she had left in the curtains. With a muffled groan she turned over to face the other way and the empty side of the bed.

Oh, damn! She didn't really want to think about it just yet, but neither could she stop the sudden flood of recollection. Reaching for the pillow almost automatically, Sara hugged it against her as if for reassurance while her eyes stared unseeingly at the wall. So she'd finally gone and done it; but how strange that it had been Marco of all people whom she had been determined to detest even before she had met him! Marco, who had been the only man she'd known who could seduce her with a kiss — turn her into what he wanted her to be, what he *expected* her to be. And he still believed her to be someone else. Delight, her sister, whose name he muttered in her ear and against her mouth while he made love to Sara. Just plain Sara who had always been rather straitlaced and wasn't at all the kind of woman who men found exciting unless she was acting a part.

What on earth was she going to do now?

There was one side of her nature that was her father's and had been trained to be practical and pragmatic. *Careful.* But then there was also her mother in her; all the passion and the recklessness that she had tried and *they* had tried to subdue. *Why?* And for what?

Sara stretched her arms above her head, a feeling of delicious languor creeping over her as she remembered. Perhaps she, and not her sister, deserved all those things he had said about her earlier. Certainly she felt no regrets and no guilt at this moment. It had been *Sara* he had wanted and made love to, whether he had known it or not! But *she* had known it — with every tingling inch of her body, and without any lingering vestiges of shame.

What's done is done. And there's only going forward from now on. She thought of Marco's body and the way muscles moved smoothly under sun-browned flesh . . . under her hands. Flushing, she remembered the way his hands had explored her so intimately, discovering things about her that she hadn't known herself. Knowing now, Sara found herself moving restlessly against the disordered sheets. Of course he'd left her because of the servants. But when would he come back?

Chapter 27

It wasn't until later that the doubts began creeping in to nag at her mind, and with them returned some traces of the sanity she had lost last night along with her embarrassing virginity. And it *had* been quite an embarrassment to face Serafina and know that the austere housekeeper would realize at once what had taken place last night. Sara could not help grimacing. She'd thought about washing her stained sheets herself in the bathtub and hanging them out on the terrace to dry. But unfortunately Serafina had come in while the bath was still filling and had taken everything in — including a discarded night-gown with a torn strap lying on the other side of the room where it had been hurled.

In spite of herself, Sara had not been able to prevent herself from blushing, just as if she'd been a naughty little teenager.

The usually stone-faced housekeeper was actually human enough to show some slight change of expression when her eyes encountered the sheets that Sara had been in the process of tearing from the bed. But by the time her eyes had come back to Sara's flushed face, they showed nothing; even when Serafina said in a disapproving voice: "There is no need for the signorina to concern herself with such things. I will see to changing your bed linens myself." Hearing the sound of water running into the marble bath, Serafina shook her head. "And if you had rung for me, signorina, I would have come to run your bath for you. In the future, please ring for me when you are ready in the mornings and I will come myself."

It was not so much the words that the housekeeper had used but their *significance,* Sara thought now as she tried to make herself relax in the pampered, perfumed luxury of her own sunken marble tub. While she had kept her own personal thoughts hidden, Serafina had been offering her tacit acceptance of Sara's changed position. From now on Serafina herself would see to Sara's room and her clothes as well as the bath in the mornings. . . . Sara smiled ruefully at her wavering reflection in a steamy mirror. What had he called her once during the night? *Cortigiana!* In a voice that was like a snarl. Well, she should certainly feel like a courtesan now, she supposed. And wondered the next moment how many other women he had kept here in these same apartments, to wait on his whim and his pleasure. And then dismissed when he had tired of them — no doubt with an expensive little gift of jewelry or a new car.

Well . . . Sara thought flippantly, I'd settle for the car! And then wondered why she didn't *feel* as flippant.

After all — where *was* he? He'd intruded on her bath before, when she'd just *detested* him, and now . . . oh, damn! She must *stop* this. Look at everything in a coldly logical way, which was probably how *he* would look at it. She had put up a pretty good resistance, which had intrigued him; but now that he'd won, it was quite possible that he might not want her again. Or if he did . . . Sara let herself slip a little farther under the water, wishing she could train herself not to blush. He had certainly wanted her last night!

Newly familiar feelings returned suddenly to tug at her nerve endings as the thought reminded her of everything that had happened last night . . . and tentatively, almost wonderingly, Sara touched herself. *There* — where he had been. Still a little soreness, a tenderness, but . . . oh, God, how could the clinical "How To" books that everyone read these days really prepare one for the reality and the *feelings?* Like losing control, and losing restraint, and wanting anything and everything that was being done to you . . .?

Without her realizing it, her eyes had half-closed with the sensuousness of her memories. Only to be jerked open by the voice that addressed her sarcastically from some distance above her. "I had hoped that I was able to keep you sated for a while! But here I find you lying immersed to the neck in warm water with that dreamy expression on your face and nothing more than your own hand to bring you satisfaction! Which one of your lovers were you fantasizing about this time?"

"Oh!" Sara's hand went up to her face as if she'd like to shut the sight of him out, as he stood over her still dressed for riding — his dusty boots planted squarely apart and his dark Sardinian face mocking. "I was certainly *not* —" Sara had begun indignantly, when he cut her off.

"Oh — but please don't stop! I was enjoying watching you, with that languid, secret look on your face and your lips slightly parted." He gave his harsh growl of a laugh at the expression on her face, with heightened color staining her moist cheekbones. "Ah, come! You are surely not going to pretend that you're not well aware that to watch a woman doing to herself what you were doing is supposed to be a — you have an expression for it — yes, to be a 'turn on' for most men?"

Oh — but she must have been *mad!* Both to let him get his way with her and to think that she had stopped hating him. While she tried to pick a suitably scathing retort, he hunkered down on his booted heels, continuing to watch her through taunting, heavy-lidded eyes that gave none of his feelings away. "I hope I haven't put you off? Whoever your fantasy lover was, you certainly wore the look of a woman who is having a good time!"

She had had *enough!* And if he thought he was going to have everything his way now, he was going to find he was mistaken!

Sara curved her lips in a false smile before she said as ingenuously as she could manage: "Oh, but I always imagine a kind of composite man when I fantasize, if you know what I mean. I just take the best things about all of my lovers and . . . sort of put them together!" Her smile became brilliant in the face of his lowering look. "But what on earth are *you* doing here? I thought you might have . . . have gone out, as you usually do during the day."

Deciding to ignore her riposte, Marco gave a curt shrug, his narrowed, frowning eyes still studying her disturbingly. "I wonder how you managed to find out so much about my movements!" he drawled. "I hope those giggling little maids haven't been *too* talkative!" Her lips tightened at the implications of *that* while he continued in the same lazy voice that had always intrigued her as well as infuriated her, "And as for my being here just now . . . well, what do *you* think?"

Oh, but he was being a *beast!* And this time he wasn't going to get around her, damn him, with his insults and his love-words all mixed up together and wicked long-fingered hands that knew far too well how exactly to arouse a woman's body to the pitch of not caring what happened to her.

Very coldly Sara said: "I have *not* finished with my bath yet — if you don't mind! I intend to soak in here for *ages,* in fact. So if you'd please . . ."

In her angry thoughts she consigned him to his master the devil, while in *his,* Marco found the devilish prompting that urged him on impossible to resist.

"I think that's an excellent idea!" he said calmly as he sat down to begin taking off his boots. "You're an imaginative little devil aren't you? And thank God you don't pretend to have certain inhibitions like some women. You're honest about the way you live your life, at least!"

Sara lost her temper at that. It was too much — first the strain and tension of last night and all the strangely mixed-up emotions in her since; and now . . . *now,* after everything he'd done to her and made *her* do, he actually dared to come back to face her and to torment her.

"And you are a . . . a patronizing *bastard!*" she shouted at him, surprising herself.

"Am I?" His boots and shirt already discarded, he had one hand on the belt of his pants when he paused to reply to her. "It's a moot point, I suppose, to any person who has heard the story of my mother's promiscuity and its results. But I assure you that as far as I know, I was born of the short but legal union between my father and my . . . mother."

His voice was dry and without expression but Sara winced from the barely suppressed fury with which he yanked his belt free of its loops and flung it behind him. She wished he wouldn't keep his eyes on her so intently, as if he was weighing what he might do with her next.

In spite of her determination not to be intimidated, Sara found herself licking suddenly dry lips and actually stuttering.

"I . . . didn't . . . I don't . . . ."

She averted her eyes instinctively when he dropped his pants.

"There's no need to pretend. The servants love gossip, and I'm sure you soon learned whose rooms these used to be." She felt the caressing movement of the water against her skin and knew he had joined her — suddenly filled with a panic and wanting to escape.

"I . . . I really think I've been in here too long. I'm starting to feel a little dizzy . . . ." Quickly she raised herself out of the water and turned to run, but his hand shot out and grasped her just above the ankle, staying her on her hands and knees.

"A very provocative position." His voice

complimented her tauntingly. "And sometime I mean to explore all the possibilities it
suggests. But for now — I want you back in
the water. It reminds me of all the things
I wanted to do with you in the pool last
night. . . ." His voice had taken on a pecul-
iarly husky timbre that sent strange little
shivers of almost fearful anticipation up her
spine, and to combat the feeling, Sara tried
to kick free of his hand.

"Stop it! I said . . . I just told you I feel
dizzy . . . ."

"You don't feel dizzy. Why don't you stop
playing these silly little games with me?" His
voice deepened, becoming almost savage. "I
want you — and you have already made sure
of that with your teasing and your tricks!
I've had you — and still I continue to want
you. So you can come back here to join me,
unless the way you remain poised up there
means . . . ."

"It simply means that I am trying to get
away from you! What makes you think you
can just march in here any time you damn
well please and expect me to be ready to . . .
to *serve* you? I'm not your property like those
unfortunate females your plundering ancestors used to purchase at the slave market!"

His fingers tightened to tug at her ankle
implacably, making Sara realize with an
inward groan that he refused to offer her any
alternatives to *his* desires.

"Come on! Aren't you getting cold out there? Or are you sulking because I haven't paid *your* price yet? I can just picture you on the block in some busy marketplace in Morocco or Algiers — shown naked to all your prospective buyers! Do you think that you would have cringed away from their greedy eyes, or stood tall and proud of your delightful little body?"

"Will you stop talking that way! Oh, all right — stop pulling — I can get back in by myself." Her voice was sulky and her green eyes as cloudy as pieces of jade now as they looked at him with dislike.

What a stubborn little bitch she was, Marco thought; and then surprised himself by wondering exactly what was going on in her head. Annoyed, he shrugged the fleeting thought away. Why in hell should he be concerned with her *mind,* when what he really wanted from her lay between those long, shapely legs of hers that could cut through water like a knife and carry her from one end of a tennis court to another to retrieve his most impossible serves? Damn her, she had no reason for acting as skittishly as a reluctant maiden!

"Well? And now what? I suppose there must be some slavish task you want to set me — should I scrub your back for you, perhaps?"

He studied her through narrowed eyes, outwardly resisting her angry barbs while he thought, *Dio* — she might be all warm, moist yielding in bed, but she certainly was a spitfire out of it!

He grinned at her wickedly. "That's certainly a great idea, *cara*, but . . . since you've been thoughtful enough to offer — why don't you continue with that massage you started to give me last night? You never did get to the front of my body, and now that we know each other better . . . surely you wouldn't mind?"

She wanted to retreat from him — from his suggestive words that made unwanted thought-pictures in her mind and from the way his eyes seemed to grow even darker when they looked at her, as if he was possessing her already in his mind. And at the same time Sara knew, with a sense of fatality, that she would do nothing of the kind. She had a feeling, in that instant, of being somehow caught in a time warp. As if her being brought here to this centuries-old ducal palace in Sardinia that had seen so many different invaders come and go had somehow placed her in another time, as another person quite outside of modern, practical Sara who had existed in a safe, secure, *placid* world where nothing like this could ever happen outside of books.

Her eyes seemed to dilate, looking into his. He took her hand, impatiently, and put it on himself, wondering why she seemed to hold back. *Cristo!* What did she want — courtship? Foreplay to get *her* ready?

''Delight . . .'' There was an almost caressing note in his voice that she already seemed to know so well.

Delight, he had called her! Sara reacted with sudden anger, snatching her hand away. Why did he have to remind her all too often that she was supposed to be not herself but her lively, lusty sister who had boasted of having tried almost everything at least once? Get things back in perspective, Sara!

Smiling at him teasingly she placed both her hands on his shoulders. ''Oh — you want to move far too fast. *I* prefer, when I'm giving a massage, to start at the top.''

She thought she glimpsed a suspicious look in those lazily hooded black eyes before he leaned his back against the side of the tub and placed one arm around her waist, with all its unpleasant implications of ownership. ''So — why don't you begin then? But please remember that this water will not stay warm forever!''

Chapter 28

Afterward — ah yes, afterward she might regret her own weakness and the way she gave in to his arrogant demands without too many protests. But the circular marble bath was still warm at the time and scented headily with the perfumed bath oil that Serafina had poured in so lavishly; and his hand had moved slowly up from her waist to the back of her neck where strands of hair clung wet and dripping. And from there — still not removing his eyes from hers — to her shoulder, caressing lightly there before his fingers found and traced the shape and contour of her breasts, then concentrating on a nipple that had become, without her willing it, achingly erect.

Sara's own hands seemed fastened to his shoulders. Involuntarily she looked down to see the contrast of his brown fingers against her paler skin — fingers invoking mounting sensations that she could not control.

"Oh . . ." She felt as if she was swaying

and clutched at him harder.

"Touch me. Touch me just as I am touching you . . . ."

She almost fell against him when his other hand found her under the water, his thumb brushing teasingly back and forth, making her shudder, making her mindless, spineless, all over again.

"Touch me, *carissima*. Please." His voice was rough and urgent, but the thought that he had actually said "please" to her brushed against the edges of awareness before she reached out almost blindly and did as he asked her to — encountering — touching — holding — *feeling*. This was Marco, showing his need for her. *This* was what had given her such intense pleasure last night. . . . It was as if there was a point when the thought of everything she *didn't* know dropped away and she acted purely by instinct. Her hand held him and moved on him until she heard his indrawn breath and the whispered blasphemy as he pulled her against him almost savagely, holding her with her breasts pressed tinglingly against his chest while with impatient fingers that had already brushed hers away he readied her and positioned her over himself.

Animal — animal — animal! There was a jeering voice in her brain that screamed at her accusingly, but she was too far gone to stop either herself or him; and after a while there was nothing that mattered except this and him as she clung to him like a drowning woman, with her nails digging into the flesh of his shoulders as she rose and fell and rose and fell with the fierce and sweeping tide of desire and finally collapsed gasping and moaning against his neck and tasting the salt taste of him while inside she contined to vibrate — spasm after spasm like aftershocks following an earthquake.

"You hellcat! *Megera!*" He swore at her both in English and Italian as he propped himself up on one elbow to frown down at her. "I thought I warned you to watch those sharp claws of yours! How am I going to explain these little crescent-shaped scars to my other women?"

Sara had been resting with her eyes closed and her body filled with all kinds of delightfully *satiated* feelings. But as usual his words, if not his voice, seemed always designed to rub her up the wrong way. Other women! He dared to talk of other women *now?* And especially after the passionate, unbelievably sensual things he had whispered to her in the bath and after he had carried (*carried,* her mind repeated blissfully) her back to bed to make slow love to her all over again?

Without moving she resisted the temptation to open her eyes and *glare* at him. "You mean that none of them are as passionate as *I* am? All of *my* other lovers act flattered that they can make me get so . . . carried away."

"And so I too should be proud to carry on my back the trophies of this unbridled passion that is so easily aroused in you? Poor Carlo!"

Poor Carlo, indeed. That he *dared* . . . and especially since Delight and Carlo were supposed to be engaged and in love.

Opening her eyes, she met a dangerous look in his as they squinted down at her and said lightly in spite of it: "Oh, but Carlo just *loves* it! And of course *he* can arouse much more unbridled passion in me than anyone else — and that's why I decided that Carlo could be the only man I'd give up all the others for!"

With what limpid candor her false green eyes looked up at him as she uttered her outrageous statement! It took a decided effort for him to fight the temptation to strangle her and silence her right then, although he could not resist tightening his fingers over her and shaking her with such violence that he saw a look of fear spring into her eyes.

He spoke through gritted teeth with each harsh word almost flung at her. "Carlo! I'm afraid you had better give up the idea of marrying Carlo, or having anything more to do with him — or anyone else, for that matter! I know what a promiscuous bitch you've been and still are in your conniving little mind, but let me warn you that I intend to keep you here as my new little toy — my whore and my plaything until the day comes when I've tired of you. But until that day, be sure that you'll lie with no other man but me, and that you will *be* here for my use as and when I please! Do you understand that?"

Sara felt as if her head was about to be jolted off her neck and she clawed at his face in sheer self-defense, drawing blood.

"No . . . stop . . . *no,* damn you!"

The next instant she felt a startling, blinding instant of pain and blackness and dancing lights — realizing only some moments after that he had slapped her open-handed across her face, snapping her head sideways.

"I have heard you say too often that I am a throwback to my Moorish ancestors," his voice grated at her through the sudden welling of tears she couldn't hold back. "And you are probably right. You should never have whistled for the devil, *mi amante,* if you weren't prepared for the consequences."

Snatches of what he'd just said to her kept resurfacing in her mind, even while she made him an angry, sobbing denial.

"I *won't!* You can't make me — I'm not going to be your . . . your captive slave girl!"

"You will, assuredly, be anything I choose!" his voice warned her grimly. "And if you force me to it I will not hesitate, like my forebears, to tie you spread-eagled on this bed while I do whatever I will with your pale, writhing body. But perhaps that *is* what you want?" His voice had dropped to a low, huskily insid-

ious whisper that made her shiver. Oh, God
— he really *would!*

She tried to reject the terrifying thought
with her sobbed-out protests.

"No! They'd know — the servants . . .
everyone! That you have to . . . have to keep
a mistress by *force.* Carlo will know — I'll tell
him and he'll always hate you. I'll tell
everyone — all the newspapers . . . Interpol
. . .! And I'll . . . I'll . . ."

"You'll do nothing of the sort and you know
it too, don't you? Passionate little hypocrite
that you are!" Still sobbing she twisted against
his grasp uselessly. "You're going to enjoy
every minute and every hour of your . . .
enforced captivity here, and you'll probably
end up begging me to let you stay — after I've
had my fill of you."

His toy . . . plaything . . . kept here for
his *use* . . . ! And if she didn't submit he'd
have her tied and helpless, in any fashion he
chose. . . .

"I hate you, I hate you! Even if you . . .
you force me to . . . I could never stop hating
you!"

"Yes? Then prove it, my little liar! Prove
it both to yourself and to me."

She gave one last despairing, inarticulate
cry of rage and frustration before, inexplicably, he went from cruelty to pretended
gentleness, coaxing her with the variety of
his kisses that stopped up her mouth and the

teasingly intimate touch of his hands that had now begun to roam possessively over her shrinking flesh.

"Ah, *cara!* Why do you taunt me to such rage? I'm sorry that I struck you hard enough to make you cry. . . . Shall I do something to make up for it? Shall I?"

His mouth hovered over hers so closely that Sara could almost feel the brush of his lips. How had he changed so fast, from wild animal to tender lover? She didn't *want* his caresses, his kisses, his touch, and yet he had already shown her contemptuously how little her objections meant to him. Even if she fought him now, he would soon render her helpless.

"*Cara* . . . *carissima* . . . that's right . . . let me show you how much I want you . . . don't be so stiff!"

No . . . no! But her despairing protests were in her mind only as he began to explore her body everywhere with his lips and his tongue — an agonizingly slow voyage of discovery during which his wandering mouth would pause to suck and nibble at her most sensitive, secret places until she was driven mindless and rudderless and twisting and turning under him with conscience and inhibition and rationality deserting her so that she responded to him fiercely, letting him put his mouth wherever he wanted, do whatever he wanted, until — with her fingers caught in his hair — she felt the stabbing of his tongue inside her and the slight roughness of beard stubble rasping against the most sensitive point of all, holding her there while her body arched and convulsed in spasms that didn't seem to stop and she screamed without knowing she did with agony and ecstasy and primitive fulfillment.

She lay afterward as still and as limp as if she had been in a swoon, coming spinning back, spinning back . . . slowly and reluctantly to where she was and what he had made of her. And even when realization came, she was too tired and too drained for it to matter.

Not even when he moved his body upward over hers and he guided himself into her, and she tasted herself against his mouth for a moment before he moved it to whisper harsh, mumbled words against her ear, some she understood and some she didn't — and not even when he plunged into her and moved faster and harder against her until he suddenly buried his face in her tangled hair and she heard the short, harshly uttered *"Dio!"* and felt the shudder of his body as she felt him enlarge and throb almost painfully inside her.

She didn't know, in her floating state of lethargy, when he left her, drawing a sheet up over her body to replace the heat and the hard length of his.

"I'll see you soon, my little slave girl!" he whispered with an almost caressing note in his rough voice; and his fingers smoothed the sweat-damp hair away from her face. "Be good, until then!"

He had gone from her again as he at least was free to do; and now the waiting began. . . .

There was not enough spirit left in her for her mind to be able to formulate protests. Her tingling cheek felt hot and swollen as she turned her head on the pillow. Don't think — don't try to think yet! her brain urged her, and she let herself fall easily and almost eagerly into the oblivion of sleep.

Why couldn't she have slept forever? There were far too many things that she would have preferred *not* to think about to be faced along with the sun. The *sun?* The room was full of light, pouring in from widely opened shutters, and there was the delicious fragrance of coffee to sting her nostrils.

"I am sorry to wake you up, signorina. But Il Duca thought you would like to have breakfast before he takes you out riding with him." Serafina looked significantly toward the sunlit terrace as Sara, who had jerked upright, now snatched up a corner of the sheet to hold over her nudity. "If you will sit up straighter, signorina, I will adjust the pillows behind you, bring the tray . . . ."

"I must have slept right through the evening and the night!" Sara mused aloud. Her body felt stiff and sore — in certain places. Damn him, damn him!

Serafina's bustling efficiency tactfully ignored the dark bruise on Sara's cheekbone, and the sudden rush of color that threw it into prominence in the bright morning sunlight.

"You slept a long time," the housekeeper said as she busied herself with the bed tray. "You have not eaten since yesterday morning, but orders were given that you should not be disturbed — not even for dinner. You must be hungry now, so please eat while I run your bath. Is there anything you would like to have pressed? Bianca irons carefully and very fast."

Did the usually taciturn Serafina keep talking just to put *her* at ease? Sara wondered. What did Serafina *really* think?

Probably that it was none of her business, Sara answered herself bitterly. It was clear that Il Duca's autocratic word was law here in his domain, and when he spoke everyone was expected to jump to attention; when he gave an order . . .

"I don't have any riding clothes," Sara said sullenly over the rim of her cup of steaming coffee while she darkly considered what he'd do if he were faced with open rebellion. Taking her riding with him indeed! Couched as a statement instead of a request.

"Il Duca asked me to say that formal riding clothes are not necessary here. He said any kind of *pantaloni* would do. If I may, signorina?"

345

Well, none of this was really poor Serafina's fault, Sara had to admit. She should have her arguments with *him* — and she would! Here and now in the bright light of day, all those ridiculous threats of his just seemed . . . ridiculous! He wasn't a Barbary Coast pirate, and this sunnily cheerful suite didn't really resemble a seraglio at all! Which showed what imagination — *fantasy,* rather — could do. Fantasy — that's all it had been. And they had both got carried away — *he* even more so than she. . . .

Rather gingerly, Sara's fingers touched the painful bruise he'd left on her face. The brute! She was a woman. How dare he strike her so viciously just because she'd paid him back in kind? Slave girl indeed! Ha! Let him find another, more gullible female to play his fantasy games with. She had read enough to be quite well informed about . . . about — casting balefully in her mind for a suitable word Sara came up with it. *Perversions.* All those words he'd whispered to her while he . . . words telling her exactly what he'd like to do to her — what he'd make her do for him. Disgusting, *lewd* things she didn't want to think of in the clear and rational light of day.

Chapter 29

She had hurried over her bath — no sensuous soaking today — insisting that Serafina stay close at hand in case she needed anything. And now Sara took the pair of freshly ironed jeans that Serafina handed her and tugged them on, hoping she was still the same size — this had to be the tightest pair of pants she possessed and she had only bought them because Delight had insisted she must go to Giorgio's and buy herself some of the latest designer jeans.

"Wish I could come with you, kid, but . . . anyhow go get yourself a real tight, sexy pair for a change, huh? Just for me — and my image around this town! God, am I glad baggies went out fast!" Delight, on the phone. Playing cloak-and-dagger, Sara had thought then; never guessing, never realizing that her sister's apprehensions were perfectly well founded.

God — if Delight knew what he'd actually

done?

She would probably think it the funniest thing ever! Sara had to admit to herself. Delight would think it was just fantastic that her rather prudish sister was having a real Adventure — being carried off by a *Duke,* no less, was at least traveling first-class. All she'd lost was her virginity — which she'd been tired of anyway. And it hadn't been *all* bad — he'd really been rather tender and nice the first time, when he'd been drunk. . . .

Angry at herself, Sara whirled about to face the mirror while she fastened her belt. Damn him! She was *still* going to get even with him, one way or another. What did they call it here in Italy? Vendetta. . . .

She didn't look *too* bad. . . . The faded blue jeans *were* tight, but they still left her lots of room. And the red silk blouse clung nicely at all the right places too. Rather daringly, Sara undid another button. There! She might as well play Delight to the last. A Delight with Sara's practical, clinically logical mind. She was sure that when she talked to him in a calmly rational manner, pointing out to him without seeming to accuse (what a *nasty* temper he had!) that now that he'd achieved his object and had — ugh — *laid* her a few times, he might as well let her go. If he felt he *must* pay her, then he could make it a Lamborghini sports car. Top-of-the-line, of course, just as *she* was. Oh, yes — he should really appreciate that subtle little touch!

But he would let her go, of course. When she told him who she really was he'd be only too glad to avoid a scandal. Why, in the old days, he would have been forced to marry her, and poor Daddy would probably have had to fight a duel! That particular flight of fancy brought an unwilling smile to Sara's determinedly tight lips as she finished pinning up her hair, sliding in a tortoiseshell comb to keep it up. Poor Daddy would probably have a heart attack if he ever found out. His carefully nurtured little Sara would *never* do anything crazy and reckless and downright *wicked!* She wasn't at all like that wild half sister of hers! Or was she?

Maybe there was more devil than angel in her after all! Here she was, actually daring enough to go looking for the big bad wolf himself. And why not? What was there left to be afraid of? Sara marched down a flight of marble stairs with the usually impassive Serafina all but clucking in her wake.

"But, signorina . . . Il Duca assured me that he would send for you when he was ready. There is no need —"

"Send for me when *he's* ready, indeed! Well, I'm sorry, Serafina, but he's *your* Il Duca and not mine, even if he has made me his *amante* — without my asking for the position, I might add! And when *I'm* ready I detest having to wait for some lazy man who has *me* waked up early while he spends a few extra hours in bed!''

Sara hadn't meant to say quite so much to the housekeeper, but it had just seemed to slip out — and, in spite of the fact that Serafina had actually been startled into a gasp, wouldn't retract any of it. Enough with hypocrisy, let *all* of the ducal retainers discover what their feudal lord was *really* like. Her mind dwelt vengefully on words that would describe him. Reprobate! Philanderer! Sadist! Degenerate! Come back to twentieth-century American frankness, Sara! What he was . . . was an asshole! And he'd better not tempt her to tell him so!

''Signorina . . . please reconsider. Il Duca . . .''

Sara stopped in mid-stride when they reached a landing and sighed. ''Serafina, I'm sorry! But would you *please* stop referring to Marco as 'Il Duca'? In America we don't use titles. (Ha! Daddy would really love that one!) And in any case, what is wrong with my wanting to know where *his* rooms are? After all he comes and goes in mine quite freely!''

She could tell that Serafina had finally given up from the way the poor woman had started to finger her rosary.

''The door is in that direction, signorina. To the right, you can't miss it, with the seal of the family on the door handle. But I hope that the signorina will change her mind. Il —

the signor would not like —"

"Why wouldn't he be flattered to discover that I'm so impatient to see him?" Sara gave one of her sweetest smiles. "Thank you, Serafina — I promise I won't let him blame you in any way. *Grazie*."

"*Prego*. . . ." Serafina muttered under her breath as she watched that straight young back and long slim legs move purposefully in the direction of Il Duca's private apartments. *Povera!* Did she really know what she was letting herself in for, poor little ex-virgin who already bore the mark of the Duke's cynical view of women? Ah, that mother of his — to leave such scars on her son! He appeared to hate women and mistrust all of them, and yet . . . Serafina could feel that there was not something quite right here. Why exactly had Il Duca brought her here — a virgin, supposedly affianced to Carlo his brother? And why had he violated her and made her one of his mistresses? *That* part of it hardly seemed possible! No matter what faults he possessed, the Duca di Cavalieri had hitherto shown himself to be a proud man who took care to protect his family's honor. Mistresses he had — several, if his personal chauffeur Bruno was to be believed. But always discreetly kept, never flaunted in the public eye. And certainly not flaunted *here!* What had got into him?

With her mouth pursed, Serafina gave a sudden shrug. Who really understood the ways and whims of the nobility, anyway? What was in the blood came out. . . . She watched the young woman she had grudgingly learned to like pause before the frowning, iron-banded door for a few moments before she reached up to knock on it sharply. Poor thing! And she was a real lady too, always polite, always considerate. A pity.

At just about the same time that the house-keeper turned away to go back to her duties, the door was opened roughly with an even rougher oath. Just when she had *almost* lost her courage. Now, facing an angry face that was half-lathered with shaving soap, it became a matter of self-defense.

"Buon giorno! I thought you wouldn't like me to be late, and I would *hate* to miss my first riding lesson!"

He was looking at her as if he would gladly have consigned her to his master the devil at this moment — his black brows drawn together in his usual glowering frown.

"And how in the name of hell did you —"

"I persuaded Serafina — but you mustn't blame her! It was only when . . . when I explained how things were between us that she relented. Can't I come in?"

He gave her the definite impression that he would have enjoyed slamming that heavy wooden door in her face, especially if she had been standing close enough. Sara decided to push her luck. "You didn't say *buon giorno* back," she pouted. "Talk about a lack of manners . . . !"

"Please!" Obviously regaining control of himself he stepped back with an overdone show of gallantry. *"Buon giorno.* And as soon as I have this door closed again you must tell me too *exactly* 'how things are between us.' "

With only a *slight* quailing of her nerves, Sara walked in with her bright morning smile still pasted doggedly on her face. And she *didn't* jump when he slammed the door again — this time behind her.

"You'll pardon the fact that I was in the middle of shaving?" His black eyes had mocking glints in their depths as he seemed to study her thoughtfully; lingering over her breasts where the flame-red shirt outlined rather than concealed — on the defiantly slim-fitting jeans that made her look *almost* as slim as a boy. But she wasn't, and he knew that all too well. Why was he standing around only half-shaved and with nothing more than an exceptionally brief towel carelessly knotted around his hips when he had expected *her* to be ready an hour ago?

The smile was proving to be too much of an effort, *especially* when he kept staring at her in that very peculiar way he had some-times, as if he wished he could pick her brains apart and open up her every thought and feeling to his inspection. Nervously, Sara turned away, fiddling with an ornately carved

353

paper knife with a gold-chased jade handle. Another ugly wolf's head, of course! What else?

"Please, don't let me hold you up any longer," she said in what she hoped was a casual-enough tone of voice. "Do go ahead and . . . and do whatever, and I'll just . . ."

Evidently he had decided not to play any longer. His voice came to her in what was almost a snarl.

"I don't like your coming here to look for me! And I'd like to know exactly what you told Serafina! *Per amor di Dio* — haven't you learned any discretion?"

"Discretion? What's that? And don't you agree that it's a strange word coming from you?"

Unable to keep her temper, she swung around to face him with green fire in her eyes.

For a long, considering moment he seemed to weigh what he should do next. What was there left? *Beating* her? And surely even he would not go that far!

She couldn't have known that it was the almost shocking sight of the ugly bruise staining her cheekbone that held him back from another explosion of primitive rage. Yes — primitive, unfortunately! And, just as unfortunately, there was something about *her* that seemed to get under his civilized armor and turn him into the brute beast she'd accused him of being.

What a *bisbetica* — a spitfire she was to be sure — his brother Carlo's little Delight of the wanton, teasing body who was now *his* delight for as long as he wanted her, in spite of the fact that her tongue could sting like a viper. He really shouldn't allow her to undermine his usual self-control.

"We will discuss this matter later!" Marco said curtly, with a look that warned her to try his patience no longer. "That is — unless you had in mind some sport *other* than riding?"

Sara opened and then closed her mouth as he seemed to wait an instant for her reply. She really *did* want to ride, and he *did* have beautiful horses.

"*Bene,*" he announced when she didn't reply but stood there with her lips tightly pursed together. "Then I will finish shaving and get dressed — if you don't mind." His hand gestured briefly at an uncomfortable-looking chair in heavy dark wood, with a high back. "Please sit down."

How formal he could be when it suited *him,* Sara thought resentfully as she watched his retreating back and heard the decisive slam of his bedroom door as he closed it behind him.

And there was yet another example of his unfairness! *He* had doors with locks on them and was openly displeased at her intrusion on his privacy, whereas he allowed her no privacy at all, with his casual comings and goings in *her* rooms that were permitted no locks. How very convenient for him that his mistresses were never given the opportunity to refuse him!

The fact that he appeared to be in a much better mood when he finally emerged from his room freshly showered and shaved and dressed for riding didn't make her any less angry, although she managed to conceal it creditably enough.

"There now, *mia diletta!* I didn't take too long, did I?"

Sara put her clenched fists behind her as she made a pretense of matching his mood. *His* Delight, indeed! Conceited, arrogant bastard! But she was going to hang on to her temper this time, even if it choked her. He *had* to let her go! How else could she ever exact her revenge.

To cover her real feelings she made a casual gesture that encompassed this rather austere room with its ugly dark furniture where he had kept her waiting as if she'd been a petitioner for his ducal bounty. "I have been studying your room and it surprises me, you know. I had rather expected . . . well, something a little more magnificent, I suppose. But this room reminds me of an office, with its stark furnishings."

He raised a slightly mocking eyebrow before he indulged her by replying.

"So it's not opulent enough for you? Well,

you were right — I do use this room as an office, and as such, it suffices. I don't need any distractions when I have business to attend to." His voice carried a sardonic undertone, especially when he emphasized the word "distractions" for her benefit. "Actually, so as not to disappoint you too much, *tesoro mio,* this is *not* the official bedchamber of the Dukes di Cavalieri, which is overpoweringly magnificent enough to suit even *your* expensive tastes." His eyes dwelt significantly on her tiny diamond ear studs before he shrugged the subject away. "However, it's really too much for one man with its enormous four-poster bed and echoing corners! This little suite suits me perfectly until the time when I must share the other with my wife. And now, come — I thought you were impatient for a ride?"

For his *wife,* he had said in that indifferent voice — and for the life of her, Sara couldn't resist her sharp question. "Your wife? You're *married?*" While he was speaking, Sara had not been able to resist shooting an inquisitive glance through the bedroom door he'd left open — her eyes going straight to the portrait that hung above his bed. "Your poor wife! I suppose that's *her* portrait over your bed?"

For the first time since she had known him his burst of laughter sounded genuine, and not merely a harshly ironic sound.

"*Married!* Why, *cara* — does the thought

357

really upset you? You don't need to worry, though — I've no intentions of getting married until I must think seriously about producing an heir, and that won't be for several years longer. And as for the portrait — the lovely lady *does* happen to be the present Duchessa, but she was my father's second wife and not mine. She is certainly as beautiful and a truly loving person on the inside as she appears to be in her portrait. My stepmother is truly a woman to worship and respect!"

Sara had opened her eyes wide in disbelief when she heard the strangely softened tone of his voice; but it was more in order to cover her own warring emotions that she made the flippant comment.

"Oh, well! I guess it's true that all Italian men are in love with their mothers — and I suppose that stepmothers are no exception to the rule!"

She really hadn't expected the angry force of his reaction as he snarled at her: "And what, precisely, did you mean by *that* nasty little innuendo?"

"Oh, for heaven's sake!" Sara despised herself for stepping back. "Honestly, I didn't *mean* anything by it! I'm sorry if I've unwittingly rattled any family skeletons!"

For a moment he looked as if he might enjoy breaking her neck — and then his darkly dangerous face became as wooden as a mask that hid everything from her.

"Please don't concern yourself any longer with my family or its history." He gestured her coldly to precede him out of the room. "And I would also appreciate your not exchanging tidbits of gossip with the servants. And now let's go before I change my mind and send you back upstairs again to meditate in your room!"

There was a grimly threatening note in his voice that warned her into silence even while all her instincts clamored for biting retaliation against his contemptuous relegation of her to the position *he* had forced on her. Chattel. His *amante,* his *puttana* — and anything else he chose to call her.

Sara had to clamp her jaws together until they ached, and concentrate very hard on her final victory — *and* her vindication! All the way out to the stables as she tried to keep up with his long-legged strides that only pointed up his lack of consideration for *her,* she tried to visualize the look that would surely come to his face when he discovered the truth. That the real Delight Adams was safely married to his precious brother in spite of all his efforts, and he had made a public villain as well as a fool of himself by carrying off Delight's older sister. Let him just try and talk himself out of *that* one, especially when her father learned the whole story!

Chapter 30

There was such strained tension between them that even the disgustingly obsequious stable hands must have sensed it. Several times Sara would feel darting black eyes upon her while she waited for her horse to be saddled while *his* big brute of a stallion that matched its master stamped and snorted restively. How she would have loved to have ridden Il Malvagio — probably aptly deserving of being named the Evil One! But at any rate, she had been allowed to pick out her own horse; *that* privilege accorded her because he probably hoped she would fall off ignominiously. Well — what a lot of surprises Il Duca had in store for him!

"Do you think you can mount without taking a fall?" Hooded dark eyes flicked over her with obviously angry impatience as he held his own mount back with one sinewy hand. He wasn't bothering to hide the fact that he very much regretted his invitation now.

"Ruggiero will help you up — please pay attention and try to hold firmly on to the reins as you see me do." His voice became a drawl with a hidden sting that was meant for her alone. "You will find, if you still persist in wanting riding lessons, that a horse is very much like a woman and needs to be made to understand who is the master! You might be sorry that you did not take the safely placid animal I offered you in the first place. Fiametta is a frisky little filly who needs discipline."

"You don't have to be concerned," Sara said as if she'd really believed that he was. "Playing tennis and racquet ball has given me strong wrists. And," she added brightly, "Fiametta is such a pretty little thing, with her shiny chestnut coat and the white star on her forehead! I'm glad you haven't yet disciplined all the spirit out of her. Can you actually *enjoy* docile females around you?"

Ruggiero boosted Sara up into the saddle at that moment, saving her from his undoubtedly caustic rejoinder. Sitting astride on horseback again gave Sara a lift of her spirits, and for a moment she forgot all about *him* as she lightly tested the sensitivity of her filly's mouth; remembering just in time that she was supposed to be a novice.

Sitting just a bit too awkwardly, she managed to send him a false smile.

"Well, let's go? And I've watched a lot of

Westerns, honestly. If you'll just start off slowly enough so I can watch how *you* do it, then I'm sure I'll be able to manage perfectly well. I pick up things really fast, you know!"

"And how should I know? I am sure there is still a great deal I could learn about you!"

"Oh, but why bother? How boring for you if you knew *everything* and I was *quite* tame! I suppose you'd soon turn me in for a newer model."

"It would be advisable for you to stop babbling inanities and pay attention to that *cute* little filly you are riding — *and* to me. That is, if you wish to remain in that saddle you are perched upon so gingerly. It might prove embarrassing for you if you were thrown before you have gone any farther than this courtyard. We can continue our interesting conversation later."

The big stallion was as impatient as its rider as it reared and pranced, rolling dangerous red eyes at Fiametta who immediately began to behave in a ridiculously skittish fashion; forcing Sara to take stern measures.

"Please!" she gasped with pretended apprehension as she let one hand clutch at the horse's mane. "Can't you keep *your* nasty brute under control? If you'll just start off . . ."

His look consigned her to damnation before he snapped: "Very well, then, at your own risk! *Andiamo.*"

Il Malvagio took off like his namesake, throwing a few temper tantrums along the way that demanded all of Marco's attention. Sara, her rapport with Fiametta established, shot by him with a beatific smile. This was freedom — and sheer heaven! And she no longer cared what he thought, why should she? Sooner or later he would have to find out that she had been playing a game of charades with him, keeping up a clever deception that had taken him in almost too easily.

The courtyard with its constricting walls gave way to a riding path that actually led to a polo field. Fiametta, obviously used to limitations, began to canter and then to gallop around the perimeters of the field with Sara leaning forward against her neck, whispering soft encouragement.

And then, destroying her mood of contentment, she heard the pounding of other hoofs behind her — pursuing relentlessly and catching up too soon; ruthlessly strong fingers snatching the reins from her and sawing back on them to bring everything to a halt.

Fiametta reared with displeasure, almost unseating her rider. Furiously, Sara shook escaping strands of hair out of her eyes. "Why did you have to do *that?*" she cried out at him without thinking. "She's got such a soft mouth and now you've probably *hurt* her, you devil!"

"*Davvero?*" The deceptively growling softness of his voice was belied by the dangerously speculative look that seemed to linger on *her* mouth for far too many seconds. "You will have to explain to me later how you contrived to learn so much about horses in such a short time — and you'll come up with a plausible explanation, I'm sure! You've watched many, many Westerns, am I not right? And of course — I had almost forgotten — you 'pick things up' with amazing facility!" He released Fiametta's reins with a sardonic inclination of his dark head. "And now that I am reassured that your mount was not running away with you, shall we continue with our pleasant ride? You will then have a chance to demonstrate more of your newly acquired skills, won't you?"

Glinting devil-lights in the depths of his black eyes warned her not to answer his gibes. Not now — she might as well use the unexpected respite he offered her for pure unthinking enjoyment before he decided it was time to go for the jugular.

Sara kept expecting — half dreading — the inevitable moment when he would drop all pretense of politeness and restraint. And *then,* of course, she would have her chance to . . . to *demolish* him. And especially his much-vaunted family *honor!* How would his idolized stepmother who was such a *good* woman, react? And above all, how would he ever find a *suitable* wife for himself who would be willing to accept his tarnished name?

Ahh — sweet revenge! She really ought to feel more elated than she did; but just let him start in first and then she'd have her righteous anger to support her. And in the meantime — there was the sun pouring down as warm and gold as honey and the hot wind in her face that smelled of crushed herbs and aromatic mountain shrubs and the feel of motion and freedom. Why should she think of unpleasant things? Why, just for these few moments, think at all?

Sara was constantly aware of him, his fierce stallion sometimes riding flank to flank with her mount and sometimes racing ahead with a fluid length of stride and speed that poor Fiametta could never hope to match. She knew he watched her but refused to meet his eyes. Not now — not yet. There was no need for the inevitable conflict between them to spoil a day like this and a time like this. Was it possible that *he* might feel the same way?

From racing back and forth across the grassy expanse of the field, they had both slowed their mounts to a canter. Her hair was falling down, its smooth chignon ravished by the wind, her tortoiseshell comb hanging down at her neck. Automatically, Sara put one hand up to hold it before it fell, but her fingers were brushed away and, with a feeling of stark, unreasoning terror that made her gasp, she felt the pressure of his thigh against hers as he leaned over to take the comb from her hair.

"Hold still! There's no need to jump like a scared cat!" His touch was warm and far too lingering against the back of her neck as he deliberately made long work of disentangling the comb from thick strands of hair that had become wrapped around it.

"It's . . . you don't have to —"

"It's a pretty comb, and you would have lost it. But I like your hair better *this* way. . . ." He raked his fingers through it to send it tumbling down to her shoulders with pins flying in all directions — quite ignoring Sara's indignant outcry. "It's quite beautiful now that you've let that ugly permanent grow out."

Fiametta was becoming difficult to hold, taking all of her attention for a few seconds so that all she gave him was a coldly sarcastic *"Grazie!* I'm flattered that you noticed!"

"Prego!" She looked up at last to see him regarding her with that slightly twisted smile she had come to know so well. And instead of giving her comb back to her he had put it in his pocket, the wretch!

He appeared to be studying her quite intently, from her slim, jeans-clad legs to the clinging red shirt that now clung even more closely to her sweat-dampened body, and his look suddenly made her feel self-conscious and awkward — and suddenly prey to all kinds of confused emotions. *Damn* him — blast his black devil's soul to hell! Why did he have

366

the power to keep her staring back at him as if she were mesmerized, when just one cutting word would put a safe distance between them again?

It was *he* who spoke abruptly to break the sudden, strangely tense silence: "Since you seem to be quite capable of handling Fiametta without my help, I thought you might like to ride farther afield — that is . . ." His dark eyes lingered on her bare head of richly colored hair with all its subtle shading of color brought out by the hot sun and he frowned, stone-dark eyes flicking back to her face with a look of disapproval. His voice was dry. "You are not wearing a hat, I notice, and our Sardinian sun is far hotter than most foreigners expect — or know of. Perhaps —"

"Oh, *please!*" Thankful that her breathing no longer felt constricted Sara leaned forward eagerly, forgetting her pride. "Please, I . . . I'm really quite used to going bareheaded under hot tropical sun, and I just *love* riding! And the horses are still quite fresh, too — *can't* we?"

With a gesture that was strangely foreign to him, Marco ran his fingers through his wind-ruffled black hair, still frowning with irritation. Why in hell had he yielded to the sudden impulse to take her with him to the mountains? After everything she'd done to irritate him, the little cheat! And now here she was with those wide green eyes wiped clear of hate or fury and shining with anticipation for a change, while she pleaded with him like a little child might do, begging for a treat. What he *should* do with her was . . .

It was the need to change the direction of his thoughts that made him give her a curt nod as he reined his horse around.

"Very well, then. But if you get sunstroke remember that the responsibility was yours! And since you seem to know so much about horses, try to stay close behind me. Some of the trails are very narrow and wander in all directions — it would be too easy to get lost."

Following him meekly (at the prescribed ten paces! she thought, furiously) Sara fought the impulse to utter a sarcastic retort and settled for sticking out her tongue at his back. *Very* undignified, but nevertheless satisfying. What an utterly infuriating man! How would any unsuspecting woman stand to be married to him with his lordly airs and his caustic, biting tongue and his pompous arrogance . . . ! Running out of adjectives Sara shook herself mentally as she watched those wide shoulders ahead of her. Why should she care who he married? He wasn't going to be *her* problem once she'd left here!

In the meantime, she might as well enjoy the scenery about her, Sara thought as they followed a path through a wooded area and emerged abruptly into a clearing with a stone hut. Two men lounged on wooden chairs outside it, but they were not asleep as Sara had thought at first — leaping up with their hands on guns.

Cops and robbers! Sara thought incredulously. It's the famous Mafia! Should she scream, or would that make them shoot her? She must have made some muffled sound that he, with his animal hearing, had caught, for his body twisted in the saddle as he turned to frown at her again. "What did you say?"

"I . . . I really didn't say anything!" Sara stuttered. She *couldn't* have said it aloud! At his skeptical look she added quickly, "I was just . . . coughing! The dust, I suppose — but that's all right, I'm just fine *now!*" Her voice had brightened when she'd been able to see that those men *knew* Marco. In fact, they too kept calling him "Il Duca." Perhaps *he* was the head of the local chapter, like the Godfather.

Sara hoped that none of her thoughts showed too obviously on her face as he studied her loweringly for a few seconds longer before turning back to the men. "You can stay mounted," he flung back at her over his shoulder as he dismounted with lithe-bodied ease and whispered a word of command in his stallion's pricked ear that held the big horse in place as if he'd been tethered there.

More orders, Sara thought resentfully, although she as well as his horse both obeyed. At least he accorded her a grudging, "I won't be long" before he disappeared into the hut with one of the men; leaving the other to keep an eye on *her* no doubt! Resentment deepened and she bit her lip. What did he think she might do — try to run away with his horse? Hah! She wasn't *that* much of a fool as to imagine she'd get anywhere except lost. And it was beginning to get slightly unnerving for her to have a swarthy, dangerous-looking man who wore a gun in a black leather holster standing a very few feet away from her and — and watching her! As if she'd been a dangerous prisoner. . . .

And then even her thinking froze as Marco emerged from the hut with a very efficient-looking gun that he also wore in a holster. Standing there with a gunbelt strapped around his waist and his white shirt open more than halfway down his chest, his night-black hair slightly rumpled so that it fell partially over his forehead, he looked . . . he looked as if he belonged in another century of brigands and mercenary armies and robber barons. Just as dangerous, just as ruthless, just as unscrupulous and cruel. She gave a slight shiver of mingled fear and fascination. The same feelings she might have if she was ever confronted by a real wolf — wanting to run like the wind, without daring to look back; and frozen in place all the same, not able to stop staring at the primitive, snarling beast that looked back at her.

"Well — what is the matter with you now?" His voice was distinctly abrasive as he paused to cock an eyebrow at her before he mounted. "Does the gun scare you?"

"Of course not!" Sara snapped back, irritated with herself for continuing to indulge in wild flights of fancy. "It's just that . . . that wearing that gun makes you look like a bandit!"

"Unfortunately, that is the reason why I have to wear a gun when I ride the mountain trails. In these days, one never knows. And that is why I employ so many guards. I have them stationed everywhere."

That last significant reminder was meant for *her*, Sara supposed and was not able to restrain herself from asking with a falsely candid look of *interest*, "Oh, really? And are they supposed to keep people out or *in*?"

The narrow-eyed look he turned to give her over his shoulder was warning.

"Both — if necessary. And now, if you will follow me without wasting time in pointless questions . . ."

Chapter 31

If she hadn't been actually enjoying her ride Sara would have ended up screaming at him or throwing something at him — preferably one of those boulders that were lying around everywhere like carelessly scattered pebbles. He was insufferable! Once they had gone some distance from the clearing and had started up a narrow path he pointed out, he made her change places with him, sending her up ahead where he could direct her as to which of the many twisting trails they were to take — *and* criticize her riding skills as well. He'd even had the temerity to inform her that her jeans were too tight — *so* tight, in fact, that they looked vulgar. And *then* he ordered her not to chatter so much.

Sara sucked in a deep breath of the clean, faintly scented air and sighed. At least he hadn't suggested going back.

"Do our mountains with their rough and jagged edges frighten you, Diletta?" He was riding very close to her when he spoke, and the sound of his voice was like those mountains he described. His nearness disturbed her suddenly and made her as jumpy as a cat. Especially when he had used the Italian word for her sister's name.

"*What?* I was thinking, I —"

"I asked if fierce, frowning mountains frighten you."

Her half-laugh came from nerves before she said, almost without thinking, "How well you describe yourself! But since I'm not afraid of *you,* why should I fear your mountains? After all, you're here to protect me, aren't you?"

There was a moment of sheer, frozen horror soon after she'd said it that almost made her heart stop as her dilating eyes watched his hand drop with amazing swiftness to his gun; wrenching it free to raise it in the same fluid movement. He was going to *shoot* her?

But, oh, thank God he was pointing it at someone else! Relief made her sag before she straightened up with a jerk. Someone *else?*

Her eyes swiveled to a smiling face she recognized as well as the voice as he raised one hand in a placating gesture.

"*Olà,* Marco!" Angelo said mildly. "You surely wouldn't shoot your own dear brother?"

Would he? She was holding her breath . . . Sara realized it only after she saw Marco almost slam his gun back into its holster.

"Olà, yourself, Angelo!" Marco's voice was as expressionless as his face had become. "You might have said it earlier, and I would not have come so close to shooting you."

"Well — I guess I can understand!" Angelo said expansively, and his eyes came to rest directly on Sara's flushed, fearful face.

She knew an instant of despairing anticipation before she saw that Angelo was openly looking her over with the admiring air of a man checking out a woman he had just met. Thank God he pretended not to recognize her!

"Well . . . what a happy coincidence that I happened to be riding this way myself. Only on a motorcycle. I left it back there up the trail while I walked down to stretch my legs. But then life's full of chance meetings, isn't it, brother?"

For once, Sara thought as she observed the byplay with curious fascination, for *once* Marco had actually managed to keep both his temper and the evenness of his usually harsh voice.

"I'm sure it is — sometimes."

"You're not going to introduce me to this vision? Central Park, New York, right here in the dangerous wilds of our mountains? But I'm good at guessing. Let's see . . . there's no mistaking that she's one of the incomparable Mona's daughters of course, but which one?" During his slight pause that made her hold her breath Sara could have sworn she caught a glint of pure deviltry in his eyes before he said musingly, "Let's see . . . oh, but it has to be Miss Delight Adams of course — and who else would be daring enough to venture here? I've read that the other daughter is quite a mousy little thing who developed religion or something equally dull . . . maybe it was relief work in Bangladesh — am I right, Miss Adams?"

"Angelo . . . !" Marco's voice might normally have struck terror into her if Sara hadn't become indignant enough to flare up.

"She's *not* a poor dull mouse of a girl by *any* means! Where could you have read something like that?"

"Oh, I'm sorry! And don't think *I* don't know how the newspapers can get things twisted around!" He gave her a grin that was somehow like Marco's, except that Marco never really *did* smile. "But hello there, anyway, and I'll make this short because my brother here looks jealous enough to shoot for real now!"

"Oh!" Sara turned an alarmed look on Marco and saw that his face had hardened into an impenetrable mask, for all that he seemed to have relaxed some of his tension as he stared measuringly at Angelo, and from Angelo to her. And then he shrugged, as if the note of rising fury in his voice had been meaningless.

"*Che importa?* If Delight enjoys your

conversation, please go right ahead. Our horses need resting before we turn back in any case."

"Hey — that's real big of you, brother! Isn't he the greatest, huh, kid? And being a real Duke, no less. I used to boast to everyone back in New York about my older brother being a Duke and all, but nobody'd believe me! Ain't that something? Guess there are advantages to being born on the right side of the blanket! But in case you wondered about me — I'm the local color, you might say. Tourists love it — especially the women who are afraid I'll offer them a ride on my new Honda. But would *you* be afraid? Ah — Marco knows he can trust *me,* don't you, brother?"

This is becoming *unbearable,* Sara thought wildly. Such a lot of hate and resentment and a tension that kept building and building until even *she* felt it; between the two men who were as alike and as different as she and Delight were. It seemed to quiver in the air like the waves of heat from the hot, dry soil of this place that bred hard and harsh men with quickly flaring, volatile tempers that could easily explode, catching *her* in the middle!

In this instance she blamed Angelo, with his friendly smile and his incongruous accent that never failed to shock her when she heard it. *Why* was he doing this? And how had Marco contrived to keep his temper in check for all this time?

"I hadn't noticed any tourists in this area myself. What would they come to see? You're going to make Delight think this is one of the resort areas she's trying to escape, isn't that right, *cara?*"

And now *he* was doing it to her too. Making *her* the drawn battle line. Not on her life! Suppressing a shudder at her grisly choice of words, Sara squared her shoulders and divided her smile equally between them as she prepared to give her best-ever Miz Scarlett performance. Even if Angelo *did* get another dig in first.

"You hadn't *noticed*, brother? Ah — but I guess I keep forgetting that you don't stick around these parts too often. Must seem dull when you could have fun anywhere in the world — meet all kinds of people, like this lovely young lady here . . . ."

"Now, now boys!" Was that *really* her voice, dripping with honey and magnolias? "You know, I get the feeling that you two aren't getting along! And I think that's terrible, for brothers. Why, my sister and I have *never* had a cross word for as long as we've known each other, and *we're* half sisters too. Can't we all cool off? I mean, it's really getting too *hot* for anything else, isn't it?" She shone the full brilliance of her smile on Marco's glowering face for an instant. "Come on, darling, can't we go back now? I'd practically *die* for something long and cool!" And then to Angelo, who was watching her with speculation in his eyes, she said teasingly: "And as for *you,* Mr. Local Color, *no,* neither bikes *or* bikers have ever scared *me* — or aren't you keeping up with the right gossip columns? Sure, I'd love to take a ride with you sometime, if you'll be sure and ask me again! Maybe in a couple of days — or whenever you're too busy to be bothered with entertaining me . . . ." She turned to Marco. "Would that be okay, darling?" Avoiding those glittering black eyes that seemed to try and burn into her flesh Sara turned back again to the ebullient Angelo, who had started to watch *them* narrowly for all of his beamingly genial smile. "You see? Marco doesn't believe in jealousy, he's too sensible. And besides, he's really awfully *sure* of me — aren't you, *caro?*"

Just for a moment her last teasing endearment seemed to hang in the air while Sara's mind kept telling her that if nothing happened right *now* it wouldn't happen at all, please God.

Afterward, Sara remembered hardly anything about their almost recklessly swift journey back, except that her knees had stayed treacherously weak for a long time and the sweat kept pouring off her body until her shirt was soaked right through. Marco had been ominously silent since his last curtly uttered words had finally broken through the tension, cutting them loose.

"And now that you have gained your introduction and your answer, I think it's time for us to go back. You'll excuse us?"

"Sure, sure! Didn't mean to hold you up! Well, as we say around here — *arrivederci!* I'll be seeing you, Miss Adams!"

It was really Angelo's jaunty farewell that kept ringing in Sara's ears as Fiametta carried her down the tortuous path with a swift, sure-footed gait that told of her impatience to regain the comparative coolness of the stables.

They reached the clearing with the stone guardhouse and this time Marco didn't dismount. He had already begun to unbuckle his gunbelt some moments before and now he merely tossed it at one of the impassive guards before he rode on, with Sara following in his wake as usual. They'd been riding for what seemed like a very long time, and he hadn't spoken a word to her, not one! Sara began to think resentfully that at least he might appear grateful. After all, she'd extricated him from what might have turned out to be a really ugly situation. The scandal would have been *terrible* if he'd shot his half brother, with the newspapers and magazines dredging up the whole, old story. And suppose Angelo, who was certainly no angel, in spite of his name, had been carrying a concealed weapon himself? And if he *had* been and had provoked Marco into reaching for *his* gun so that he could claim self-defense, then . . . Sara's logical, practical mind that she had always been proud of gave her a perfectly logical, perfectly obvious answer that she recoiled from.

If it had happened that way, then Angelo would call *her* as his witness. And in spite of his joking comment about being born on the *wrong* side of the blanket, hadn't Serafina said that . . . well, of course! There was no divorce in Italy, especially not *then,* when all this had taken place. And if one looked at it from a purely *legal* standpoint, then Angelo, no matter who had actually fathered him, was still legally the second son of the former Duca di Cavalieri, and *legal* heir to the title and the palazzo with all its spreading acres of land — should something happen to Marco!

Sara bit her lip, wondering why she was letting herself get upset about any of it. Marco had already proved what a strong and utterly ruthless man he was; and she was certain *he* was already aware of everything that had just entered her mind. He was perfectly capable of taking care of himself — in fact, it was poor Angelo she should worry about. In spite of the innate danger she'd sensed in him, and in spite of his smiling, jaunty manner, she had seemed to sense a loneliness in him also that made her feel sorry for him. He *was* alone.

An exile from the country of his adoption and an outlaw of sorts in the country of his birth. A man with no place of his own, born between two worlds and really belonging to neither. Yes, it was Angelo she should sympathize with, Sara reminded herself as Fiametta, who was tiring but still gallantly *trying,* trotted her across the polo field. Clever, agile *helpful* Angelo who had offered her freedom with a flourish, and had, she knew, *definitely* received the message her light, significantly worded little speech had given him. He knew she wanted to see him, and she knew that one night he would come to talk logistics and business. Brushing her hair back from her face, Sara felt the coldness of the tiny diamonds in her ears. For her earrings and an introduction to her mother, she was *sure* Angelo would be obliging — and a great deal safer to travel with than his scowling half brother the Duke!

The great stallion and its rider had obviously reached the stables several minutes before Sara did, and by then she was fuming. How blatantly rude and unfeeling he could become at a moment's notice! Where before he had seemed determined to watch her, *now* he seemed not in the least concerned whether she lost her way or not! He was . . .

He was standing there with that same darkly glowering look she had begun to know too well. Sara lost the thread of her thoughts as she tried to pretend he wasn't there; but then he made it difficult for her by snapping an order at one of the grooms who had run forward to help her dismount and now grabbed at the reins she had dropped instead. It was Il Duca himself who ignored her grudgingly outheld hand and reached up to grasp her around the waist, his hands strong and hurtful as he lifted her roughly out of the saddle, deliberately letting her stiffly held body slide along the length of his as he lowered her to the ground.

"And *you* were the one who preached about discretion!" Sara hissed at him with her eyes shooting angry sparks. "Let go of me! They're all watching!"

"And *you* were the one, *giocattolo mio,* who first threw discretion to the winds when you came to visit Bluebeard's chamber!"

"Don't call me your little toy — I'm *not!*" She tried to wriggle away from the pressure of his hands that continued to hold her with almost contemptuous ease — only stopping to make herself stiffly unyielding when she realized that it would have seemed to any onlookers that she was wantonly rubbing herself up against him.

"Aren't you, Diletta *mia?* Whose little toy would you like to be?"

"Please don't torment me! It certainly wasn't *my* fault that we ran into Angelo!"

She could see nothing beyond the reflection

of the slanting sunlight in his eyes, but she could sigh raggedly when she felt the terrible pressure of his hands relax.

"No — it certainly wasn't your fault, was it?" he said almost equably. And then, "Come, we'll walk together to the house," offering no alternative but to walk with him.

Chapter 32

Shouldn't she have guessed, even before they had reached shade and coolness, where he would take her? Sara caught a glimpse of herself in one of the mirrors he hurried her past, and she looked like another, different woman with her wind-tangled hair and sun-flushed face and her sweat-drenched silk shirt clinging to every contour of her breasts. She looked . . . she looked . . .

She tried to tug her wrist free of his inexorable grip. "Stop dragging me along! Can't you understand that I want to . . . I've got to have a bath and change? I'm just *soaking*."

"Yes — I must confess that I found that almost impossible *not* to notice, especially since you don't believe in undergarments! I am sure that the smiling Angelo noticed too. Your presence certainly seemed to distract his mind, from time to time, from his determination to provoke a serious quarrel between us."

They had arrived at *his* door, not hers, and now she tried to pull back again. "You told me you didn't want me in your rooms! I think *you're* the one who's developed sunstroke!"

With the door open he turned to look at her in a way that made Sara want to run from him. "Do you imagine that your Bluebeard's curious little wife said the same thing to him just before he took her in there himself?" He gave a grating laugh when he saw the expression on her face. *"Dio!* I begin to believe that you have a vivid enough imagination to fantasize anything! Do, by all means, add to the picture that's obviously in your mind the famous 'Sister Anne' who spent her time watching through the window for rescue!" With a strength that was leashed and casual he had already taken her into his ugly office of a room, and kicked the door closed behind them. Bluebeard — who didn't want his family secrets known by an outsider! And oh, for Delight's comfortingly pragmatic presence right now!

It was almost as if he had read her mind — almost. He released her, and casually locked the door, lifting a derisive eyebrow. "And who do you hope will rescue you? Angelo, perhaps, who offers you rides on his motorcycle? You two certainly seemed to get on famously together! Quite as if you had known each other. Is that possible?"

Of *course* he couldn't know! And she was sure she hadn't given herself away. He was guessing. He was . . . jealous. No, stupid! That just wasn't possible. Not Marco! And yet, a heady feeling bubbled suddenly through her veins like a jolt of adrenaline, enabling her to lift her shoulder in an impatient shrug as she deliberately turned away to play with the paper knife on his desk.

"Oh, good heavens! And how on earth and where on earth could I have met that cute brother of yours? He *does* look a lot like you, you know!" She turned back to him, studying his harsh, storm-dark face that seemed to hold thunder back with the clamp of his jaws. And this time she wouldn't flinch. "My saying that oughtn't make you *mad* for heaven's sake! After all you *are* brothers . . . *half* brothers," she amended quickly and faced the smooth growl of his voice.

"Now — I wonder how you could know *that?* I do not recall that your latest admirer called me anything but *brother!*" He almost spat the word out, and waited grimly for her reply.

"Oh, for . . . ! It was an obvious guess, wasn't it? I mean I'm not exactly stupid, even if I hadn't already learned from *you* how damn *feudal* it still is here. So your father had a girlfriend in the village — it must be a common story, I'm sure. Does that answer you?"

Sara met his eyes without wavering,

although the beating of her heart had started to sound like a drumbeat inside her. He *was* jealous! Sheer instinct told her that, even if her mind wanted to shy away from the possibility.

"I've already learned that lies come easily to you! And that you have a quick and agile mind when it suits you to use it. Will I ever know when you're lying and when you're not?" His voice had slowed and deepened and his eyes seemed to darken and fill with shadow, making them opaque, shutting her off from whatever he might be thinking. And the table was at *her* back, holding her trapped before him while his eyes began a slow and deliberate journey over her face and down to her wetly outlined breasts with their pointed nipples that moved too quickly with her agitated breathing.

Please don't! Sara wanted to beg, with all the desperate feeling of a trapped animal rising in her and almost stopping her breath. But her throat, like her motionless body, seemed paralyzed. He stood so close to her that she could feel the heat emanating from his body and yet, since he'd dropped her wrist, he hadn't touched her. Didn't *need* to, she knew with a sinking feeling of despair.

His *eyes* touched her. Everywhere that his hands had touched her before, making her remember too well and start to shake helplessly within herself.

"Diletta — Diletta! *Tentatrice* . . . *maliarda* . . . !"

She knew he had called her a temptress and an enchantress. He had called her Delight. But even *that* didn't matter any longer as she came against him and felt her body fit closely against his. She did what Sara had never done in all her life before and reached up fiercely to pull his dark head down to cover her mouth with his, kissing her again in a savage and almost angry way.

There was no shame and no pride and nothing else that mattered at this moment beyond *this*. He put his hands on her at last and their bodies strained together, reaching blindly for each other through the impediment of the clothes they wore. Until, with a string of explosively muttered oaths, he put his hands under her hips and lifted her onto the table, ignoring her unconvincing murmur of protest. "I want you, Diletta *mia, mi desiderio!* And I want you now! Don't fight me. . . ." He put one hand in the deep vee of her red silk shirt and ripped it viciously downward to bare her breasts, his mouth traveling over them with slow deliberation until he stopped and lingered on her pointed, urgently sensitive nipples, hearing her moan softly at first and then cry out loud when his teeth nibbled lightly on first one and then the other. And then, still standing between her legs, his hands that had been fumbling with

388

angry impatience with her belt and her recalcitrant zipper gave a last furious tug that yanked her too-tight jeans out of the way.

She couldn't remember much more of what happened after that, except that it had been something as wild and as violent as a summer thunderstorm, drowning out everything, except that feeling inside herself that grew and grew and expanded and waited for the jagged silver sword of the lightning strike to cut her in two and pierce her and free her . . . and then leave her shuddering with the aftermath of echoing reverberations like thunder fading and muttering into the distance, like the deep harshness of his voice when he called her "Diletta, Diletta . . . !" Half-curse and half-caress.

Sara felt as if she had been on a journey very far away somewhere; perhaps to the other side of reality, which was something she'd really prefer not to face anyhow. Especially not *now,* with awareness jolting her back to cold rationality far too fast. With the spending, it had seemed, of every tiniest vestige of *feeling* in her body, then at last she became almost dazedly aware of being able to think again. And thinking, almost immediately, that she would much rather *not.*

The woman who had fiercely, wantonly *invited* what had just taken place could not have been her, surely. Not *Sara* the pragmatic, who could always keep things in perspective. Who had already decided to cut her losses and leave behind her what had turned out to be an impossible, almost ridiculous situation. *All she had to do* . . .

All she had to do was to turn her face . . . and doing so, encounter with her lips the harshly rasping texture of his beard-stubbled skin that reminded her of his voice as well. "Mmmmm . . . !" she sighed, with her lips nuzzling against the corner of his hard, unsmiling mouth. Her arms tightened about his neck. Now that she had let go she felt deliciously languorous and *yielding*. No longer tense, no longer quite as angry as she had been earlier.

"What a passionately amoral little slut you are!" His harsh voice had the texture of granite and was meant to rip and tear at her air of contented self-containment. "Even when you are at the heights of abandonment you make me wonder who and what you are fantasizing about with your eyes closed so tightly. Do you ever get enough, I wonder? And how can any one man be enough for a woman like you?"

He had taken her, as she had understood belatedly, without even troubling to take off his clothes; but at least afterward he had lifted her roughly up against himself and carried her into the shuttered darkness of his room, depositing her in bed without much consideration or gentleness while he turned away to undress at last before he joined her. He had rolled his body half over hers and pulled her roughly closer with his arms, letting his hands slide up her back with a possessive, almost savagely savoring slowness, touching and feeling and kneading the softly silken texture of her skin until they reached and were trapped in the heavy thickness of her hair, lingering there almost unwillingly.

"Well?" his voice goaded her. "Where's your usual sharp retort, Diletta *mia?* Or are you too overwhelmed by being in Bluebeard's bed?"

Sara winced slightly at the light tug he gave her hair and felt annoyance pierce her mood of pleasant lassitude. She let her body stiffen before she said with cold pleasantry, "How could I help being overwhelmed? Especially when you've been trying so *hard.* . . . But must I *really* answer all those questions you've been positively *throwing* at me? I mean I *will* honestly, if the answers are supposed to turn you on or something like that — but otherwise . . . why waste time in talk, as my Mama always used to say?"

Of course, there was always the chance that he might *not* kill her . . . and a moment, when his hands freed themselves from the distraction of her hair and touched her neck almost consideringly, when her thinking almost stopped along with her breathing.

Almost contemptuously he brushed with one of his thumbs a pulsing vein in her arched throat. "Why waste time in talk indeed! What do you offer as an alternative — or hope to gain? You make me ask myself questions to which I should already have the answers. Like the reason why you are sometimes like *miele*, like honey and as warm and sweet and smooth to the tongue — and at other times like vinegar, and twice as acid!" Now his fingers encircled her throat, but very lightly, almost not touching her skin. She lay very still, but strangely unafraid, looking up into his shadowed, shuttered face without a word.

She felt as if she was absorbing, by some weird kind of osmosis, the anger and the bitterness and the frustration that he was attacking her with. Absorbing . . . and diminishing in that way.

"Well?" His voice had roughened and harshened, and it seemed to be with an effort that he moved his hand to her shoulders. "Don't you have anything more to say as you lie there watching me with those hard, green-jade eyes of yours that never give anything away? You had better answer me this time, or *per Dio* . . . !"

"What do you want me to say?"

"The truth, for a change. Why do you tell so many lies?"

"Because you *expect* me to lie, of course! If I told you the truth you wouldn't believe me anyway. So . . ." Surprised that her voice sounded so even and almost detached, Sara let her words trail off into the shrug she gave, fighting the heaviness of his hands over her shoulders and upper arms.

"So . . . since we are indulging in this very honest, very intimate conversation — for a change — why don't you try being truthful for once? I can guarantee that you wouldn't shock me." Deceptively, he let his lips brush lightly over hers for an instant before he slid in casually, "For instance, I seemed to sense quite a rapport developing between you and Angelo."

"Angelo?" She repeated it rather vaguely and was rewarded by a snarl.

"Yes. The one with the motorcycle he kept hidden. What make did he say it was?"

"Honda, I think. Oh, yes — he was very cute, and quite kind, I thought. He kept staring at the bruise on my face until I felt quite embarrassed. Didn't you? Do you think Angelo hits his women too? If he does, I certainly don't want to go bike riding with him! And maybe Carlo wouldn't approve either, what do you think?"

"You . . ." The bruisingly whispered obscenity he almost didn't bite off seemed to vibrate between them before he said harshly: "Carlo! If you're wise you will not mention Carlo again — for we've both known for a long time that Carlo is not for you, nor you for Carlo, who hasn't yet gained the experience to handle a sharp, worldly wise young bitch like you! And as for Angelo . . . why waste your time on speculation? You aren't going for any rides on his new Honda, and in fact you're not likely to see him again, unless it's in your dreams, or your sensuous fantasies!"

"What do you mean, I'm not . . . I think you're the one living in a fantasy world of centuries past, surrounded by women who were *slaves* — either bought or taken by force. I'll see Angelo if I please — I didn't hear you objecting at the time, did I? Maybe, in spite of your gun and your rude bluster, you're really scared of him and what he symbolizes! For, in a way Angelo is your alter ego, isn't he? Only, he was begotten through love and feeling and not a sense of *duty,* like —" Just in time she stopped the angry flow of her words that had been meant to flay and cut and . . . hurt.

"Why do you stop?" he said it very quietly, although something was vibratingly threatening in the timbre of his voice that made her catch her breath. "Don't drop the subject that seems to intrigue you so. Angelo the love child, whom you find so 'cute'; and who knew who you are — *knew,* to the extent that he was bold enough to ask you for a ride on the back of his motorcycle . . . where to, I wonder?"

"I think . . ." She tried to keep her voice from shaking with all kinds of emotions that she hadn't had time to sort out yet. "I think we've let this get all out of perspective, you know! Angelo wasn't really interested in *me,* he's one of Mona's fans. Didn't you notice he called her 'the incomparable' in a positively caressing voice? I'm used to it — I can spot Mama-Mona's devoted admirers a mile off!"

"Ah, yes . . . we all have mothers, don't we? And at least yours named her love child rightly. Delight. Diletta *mia . . .* 'O moon of my delight . . .' " He made of the quotation a taunting travesty, rolling his body over hers to lie between her thighs in spite of her belated moves to reject him. Propped up on one elbow above her, he kept that hand in her hair while the other moved up and down her sweat-damp side, lingering over hip and thigh, brushing between their bodies before moving with maddeningly slow deliberation up to the curve of her breasts.

"Stop . . . !" She pushed against his shoulders uselessly. "I . . . I . . . there's no need —"

"For Christ's sake, be quiet!" His voice lashed at her as savagely and abruptly as a blow across the face. "There *is* a need, and you understand it well, hypocrite that you are, Diletta!"

"I . . . wish . . . you wouldn't call me that!"

"Not by your name? But I can think of other names to call you, describing what you are and *how* you are, if you prefer. Perhaps that kind of thing excites you?"

"Even less so than rape!"

"I have never had to rape you yet!" He laughed suddenly and unpleasantly, sliding his hands up the length of her arms until he held her wrists pinioned. "I don't think any man would have too hard a time getting you ready and eager for him. Shall I show you how?"

He didn't have to, Sara thought despairingly, even before he had begun. Already, perverted masochist that she had become, her body wanted his, making her arch up against him.

"*Abbracciami,* Diletta! Kiss me the way you would kiss a lover of your choice . . . a man who didn't know you for what you are and might be entrapped by your soft, sensual lips . . . ."

She *wanted* to kiss him! Why fight a perfectly normal, natural urge? There might be a time later on when she would hate and despise herself for becoming what he expected — what he wanted. For the moment she seemed to be capable only of reaction that was completely instinctive and thoughtless, as she put her arms up to catch against herself the threat and the tautness of his body at the same time that she set her mouth against his in the kiss he had demanded.

396

Chapter 33

Whole days disappeared at a time — and it was a time when Sara deliberately and consciously did not reason with herself, nor attempt to rationalize. She was the complete hedonist — the pampered odalisque to whom the seraglio was not prison but pleasure. *Why not?* Most insidiously corrupting question of all!

Giving in (to what was certainly *pure lust* and nothing else), Sara spent hours naked under the sun on her private terrace, thinking of nothing in particular while she soaked in the heat and the color that the sun lent her skin. None of the servants, not even Serafina, approached to disturb her during these times; but occasionally she would feel, like a physical *thing* the sudden coolness of his shadow fall across her body, just before he joined her to lie over her and in her out there under the sun and the limitless harsh blue of the sky.

Sometimes he would come to her when she

was soaking in her bath and sometimes he would carry her there himself. And now, instead of dining in formal state, he would have meals brought to her rooms and eat with her there — sometimes insisting on conversation and sometimes only *looking* at her without saying more than a few curt words before he lifted her up out of her chair and tumbled her into bed. At those times he seemed to delight in tearing away from her body whatever she had on, leaving on her only his gifts to her — a fine gold chain that encircled her hips with a pendant ruby that barely fitted her navel, and an ankle bracelet of tiny rubies caught in thin gold mesh. Symbols of slavery? She had suggested as much to him with a spurt of anger that made her eyes blaze as she tried to push him away from her. Mesmerized by lust or not, she still retained enought sanity *not* to want to become his little *giocattolo* — his plaything.

"But you *are* exactly that!" he had mocked her, laughing at her sudden fury as he turned her over onto her stomach, holding her down with the weight of his body while he casually went about fastening the catch of her ruby-hung chain. "Why shouldn't I too join the others who have played with you for a while? Do you have an answer for that?" Helplessly she had felt his hand on her ankle, fingers encircling strongly as he pulled her foot up and back.

"Stop that! You're a bloody *brute,* you know. Pulling me about — *forcing* me. I hate you!"

"Do you? Then you don't hate hard enough, *bimba!*"

His "little girl-child" had a contemptuous harshness to it that made Sara wince, in spite of the fact that during her long, sun-drenched hours when she had been *stern* with herself she had mentally sworn to stay *cool.* Accept the fact that her *body* seemed to want this impossible, hateful, arrogant man. There was no emotional involvement of course. How could there be? And she *did* hate him — black-hearted, unscrupulous bastard that he was! Not hate hard enough indeed! Why, she . . . she . . .

It was unfair that he could do this to her, reducing her to *this,* the waiting and the anticipation and the craving for the promise and the wildness and the satiation his body offered her. She could sit outside herself in her thoughts and point out all the risks and the dangers and the illusions and the damn weakness that kept her ensnared in a finely wrought spiderweb of deceit and indecision; and yet none of it counted, not even the thought of Delight and what had happened to her, or Daddy or Uncle Theo. . . . Her mind became like a freshly cleaned slate or a sponge that could absorb only *feeling* and nothing else. If she looked at it pragmatically . . .

But there was nothing pragmatic or even logical about her actions — or lack of action — to date. Why did she continue to stay here under the humiliating conditions he had forced upon her when she could, at any time, have freed herself easily by merely telling the truth? He might blow up at her — he would almost certainly strike her in his rage, as he had done before. But in the end he would surely let her go, and it would all be over; nothing more, when reduced to perspective, than an amusing if rather risqué story to tell to a few close friends or include in her memoirs.

Now, Sara! You know he's going to find out sooner or later, so why not spare yourself the suffering and confess everything *now?* Before he comes again with his animal stride that can bring him across the room far too quickly . . . and before he touches you, and demolishes you and you're defenseless. And by now, how she hated that jeering, scolding voice in her mind, Sara thought with annoyance. Why couldn't she control her thoughts?

The sun had become almost unbearably hot, prodding at her, moving her unwillingly to shade — darkness and coolness. Entering her room again, Sara had to pause there on the threshold until her eyes could *see* again. The first thing she saw was herself, mirrored against a wall and looking . . . looking like some wild Polynesian princess with her hair that had grown into a thick mane and her sun-darkened skin that was almost as dark as his, by now. She saw something that was both knowing and primitive in herself that she had never discovered before; standing here naked in the half-light with the sunlight burning against her back and flowing past her to reflect off the wall with almost dazzling brilliance.

She was here because she *wanted* to be. Because she *wanted* . . . Sara's mind wanted to erase the thought instantly. Forget about wanting. Even if it seemed to merge into *needing*. Temporary aberration — ignore! Frowning back at herself Sara played at taking inventory critically. She probably *could* lose some weight. About the hips, perhaps, but nowhere else, certainly not the breasts. She had a body, thank God, that was firm and limber and *strong*. An athletic body, whereas Delight had always been — well, more volup-tuous. It had been Delight's body and Delight's face on that larger-than-life screen . . . and no one, not even Marco, had noticed or remarked on a difference. But then — a smile that was both secret and sensual and didn't even seem to belong to *her* curved her mouth upward, and she lazily stretched both arms about her head, catlike. But then . . . her mind murmured with deeply female satis-faction as she continued to make a languid survey of her body in the mirror, it's *my* body he wants and can't help wanting. No matter what he calls me or who he thinks I am, I've been mostly myself with him; and it's really *Sara* he's made his *amante, my* mind that keeps him intrigued.

Sara blinked her eyes, running nervously impatient fingers through her hair as she crossed the room quickly to snatch up a silky robe from the foot of her bed, where Serafina had left it. Mirrors! The way she had suddenly started thinking — with her body and her senses rather than her head. Forgetting real thinking, as a matter of fact. Because she wanted not to think for a change, and wanted to let go and feel. Because she was crazy!

There was a refrigerator in her living room now, holding white wine and ice and Evian water — courtesy of Il Duca, who else? For his current mistress — current occupant of his mother's rooms. Had *she* been kept a virtual prisoner too? Sara had often wondered that, as she did now, reaching in the refrigerator for a chilled glass, filling it with ice, pouring over that the cold liquid her dry throat craved at this moment. Cool. Something she wasn't being while she stayed on here. Almost viciously, Sara tied the belt of her thin silk robe about her waist before she began to pace — this time avoiding her reflection in the mirrors. She was aware, in the background, of the sound of softly running water. Her bath . . . of course Serafina knew that it was always at about this time that she came in to escape from the sun and wanted a bath before she slept. And when, and how, had all of this become a routine?

I've got to get away! her mind screamed accusingly, and she had already begun to move toward the door with no locks, walking quickly and instinctively on her bare feet, when it was pushed open.

"You're actually dressed! Well . . . almost. Were you coming to look for me, *desiderio mio?*"

He stood nonchalantly with his back to the massive wooden door, in his riding clothes that made him look almost all animal, with the gold and emerald of his wolf insignia lying against the dark hair of his chest and his booted feet slightly astride as he looked her up and down with a caustic slant to his eyebrows.

Damn him, damn him! Why did just his presence, just looking at him, turn her weak at the knees? Reaching back automatically with one hand, Sara felt her fingers tighten over the back of a chair; the feeling of clutching at something solidly real straightening her back.

"As a matter of fact, I was hoping *not* to run into you, darling. I was thinking . . . of a swim, perhaps. Or riding off somewhere and feeling the wind against my face. Of *freedom,* if you know the meaning of the word . . . ?"

"You have always been free, Diletta!" His

hands that she had come to know so well bent the riding crop impatiently between them while his narrowing eyes studied her face. "Free to make your choices — and to take your chances as well. What kind of *riding* did you have in mind? As long as your desires do not include a powerful new Honda or a ten-carat diamond, perhaps I might be persuaded to indulge them!"

Persuaded . . . *indulged* . . . ! If she hadn't kept some control over herself Sara thought furiously, she might have — have *sputtered!* As it was, she had to draw several deep breaths before she managed to say, with a cold edge to her voice: "Don't you think the party's over by now? I mean . . . I'm sure you've already *proved* whatever it was you wanted to prove in the first place — and you *must* be quite as bored as I am! So can't we call it quits . . . ?"

Of course, while her frigidly detached voice was saying all the right, logical things, she could feel herself tighten inside while she fought to control the erratic jump-beat of her heart. Why did he just keep *looking* at her? Why hadn't he said something or done something that would snap her back to reality and rationality?

Although his voice was quiet enough — rough edges under silk — it was the way the riding whip almost broke under the unconscious pressure of his sun-dark hands that really kept her rooted in place. "So you're bored, *povera piccina?* Bored so soon with just one man? Lost in an unfamiliar setting with no wild disco music and no bright night lights and no sympathetic director or co-star to feed you the correct lines — and the correct reactions!" Although he hadn't yet moved she could almost imagine the bite of the whip he held across her breasts and she must have shrunk from him involuntarily, because his lips curled mockingly in a travesty of a smile. "It's a good thing I know you for the liar you are — or you might have succeeded in annoying me. But the way you're looking at me, standing there clothed in pale-green silk that clings and reveals at the same time . . . what do I see in those lying jade eyes of yours, Diletta *mia?* Are you afraid of this little riding whip that I hold, and of the marks it could leave on your soft, sun-gold skin? Or do you challenge me?"

While she stood frozen, both hands behind her now clutching so fiercely to the arm of the chair that she felt as if her fingers might snap from the strain, Sara found herself watching with horrified fascination the way he ran the braided leather between his fingers before he let it trail with an almost contemptuous gentleness across her shoulders and between her breasts.

"Perhaps you're wise not to answer me, *tesoro!* Because I think you already know all the answers to all those questions, do you not?" He tilted up her chin with the handle of his riding crop, forcing her to look at him, and then moved it down over the tense arch of her throat to part the silk of her carelessly tied robe; going from there, before she could prevent him, to rest threateningly between her thighs.

"You're the liar and the hypocrite, not I!" She had to force the words out between lips that felt suddenly stiff. *"Don't!"*

"No? But since you've made it obvious I haven't yet learned to please you enough so that you wouldn't find yourself bored, I could not help wondering . . . "

"Stop it! You sadistic . . ."

Pressure increased, making her gasp, and then with a harsh, ugly word he flung away the riding crop with such force that it sent a vase smashing against the wall with it. He put a hand in the thickness of her hair pulling her head back, and the other behind her, burning and probing intimately through thin silk as he pulled her body against his, his voice grating at her like the blade of a serrated knife.

"Your kind of woman demands the kind of man you call a 'sadist,' Diletta *mia!* No — hold still and be quiet for a change, or I might be tempted to use that little horsewhip on you! Bitch! *Donnaccia!*" His fingers tightened on her and she cried out protestingly. "You haven't incited me to beat you yet, but I could do so easily, and you know that, don't you? And in case there is something you *don't* know, or pretend not to, let me make it very clear, eh? For as long as it suits me, you'll stay here and you'll be exclusively mine — whether you're bored or not. Do you understand what I said? You're mine, bitch, for as long as I want you — *sei mia, capisce?* No sleek motorcycle, or its reckless owner, between these thighs of yours that have parted so often for so many men. For a change, you're going to be a one-man woman, like it or not."

"I won't! And you're a —"

He stopped up her mouth before she could swear at him, continuing to hold her rigid body against his until gradually, as he continued to kiss her, and his hand continued to caress her even against her will, he could feel the stiffness of her begin to relax until there was no longer any need to hold her by force.

With what treacherous honey-sweetness, she gave in! So easily responding to the almost coldly clinical pressure and exploration of his fingers between her thighs. There was a rug on the floor and he lowered her onto it, enjoying in his present mood her belated struggles to escape.

"If you keep your back turned to me I will take it as an invitation, *mio desir!* Is that how you want to be taken this afternoon?"

"No!" She shot the word at him hotly, and her face was all flushed as she jerked her body around with the silk robe falling apart, caught beneath her hips. "I don't . . . you *know* I don't like . . . kinkiness. You're despicable!"

"And how your moods change!" he said derisively, putting a hand on her taut belly and moving it upward to her breasts. "Sometimes you're ready for anything . . . and sometimes you are full of stupid inhibitions. Does it take a camera and a watching crew to turn you on, as you would put it? Well? I could provide that too, perhaps!"

"You've forgotten the most important ingredient for a *real* turn-on!" Sara felt goaded to retort, even with her breath coming shortly. "You've forgotten the right leading man — would you promise to provide me with just the right guy to make all my fantasies come true?"

"Like Garon Hunt, to whom you made yourself so . . . accommodating? Or is it Angelo who is your latest fantasy lover? And don't tell me Carlo, for I would never believe it, and any more lies from you might tempt me to crush that delicate-looking throat of yours!"

He had straddled her body now, and Sara could feel the taut strength of both of his hands at her shoulders, fingers tightening their pressure as he forced an angry, unwilling answer from her.

"Lies? In other words, you are warning me

to tell you what *you* consider to be the truth! So very well . . . . I think I would pick Garon, of course. He's sexy — and how! But he's sure enough of himself to be gentle too. I find him *very* exciting!''

And now . . . the practical part of Sara's mind cried out despairingly, he's going to strangle you for certain! She could feel herself tense, although she refused to drop her falsely defiant eyes from the black scrutiny of his.

"After just one night? And considering the fact that he left you after just a few hours? As I had thought, you are almost too easily pleased, Diletta. And perhaps not as pleasing in your turn to keep a man's interest for long!''

There was something in the timbre of his voice and the look that he gave her that strangled the words that had started to bubble up in her throat. Words that would have repudiated, would have told him how little he pleased her — that she would prefer any other man over him. But she said nothing, and lay there sprawled out under him, closing her eyes shut tightly while she waited. For anything — for *something*.

"*Per Dio!* I've had enough of this! Look at you — lying here like a martyr with your stone-green eyes closing to shut out the sight of the savage beast who might devour your tender flesh at any moment! Isn't that right?''

Carelessly and with a deliberately taunting slowness he ran one hand over her body as if to prove that he owned it before, with a flick of his fingers that stung her cheek, she felt him leave her. And now, as she continued to lie there like a statue with her eyes still stubbornly closed, she heard his voice come again from somewhere above her.

"You can wrap your silk robe about your body again and have your bath in peace, *bimba!* I won't bother you again, and you can please yourself if you will. . . ."

"Does that mean that I can . . . that you're finally letting me go?" She asked the question keeping her eyes shut against the glowering ugliness she could picture in his face as he looked down at her.

"I'm sorry to disappoint you, *cara mia,* but I intend that you will remain here for a while longer — until I have decided what I will do with you. In the meantime you will have your dream lovers and your own ingenuity to console you, for a while at least. And if you tire of fantasy and want reality for a change, why then . . . you might send me word; and if you ask me very sweetly and I can spare the time . . . then perhaps I might visit you again — that is, if I'm still in the mood for your type."

Her type! And what in *hell* had he meant by that? He was an arrogant, calculating, filthy-minded — oh! Sara sat up with a jerk, staring with hatefully narrowed eyes at the door he'd just closed firmly behind him. *Beg* him to visit her again indeed! The hell this particular wolf-devil presided over would turn cold before *that* ever happened! And she didn't intend to stay here at his command either — he would soon find *that* out!

Chapter 34

"I find that by some unfortunate chance I continue to want you, you jade-eyed sorceress with your wanton gold body and your calculating little mind! And for as long as I want you I shall keep you here in my seraglio just as some infidel ancestor of mine might have done with a trembling Christian captive — for my eyes and my use only! Does that thought terrify you with its implications, *bambina mia*? Until I tire of you, you'll be mine alone; to do anything I want with."

"How exciting! Like what? As long as it's not too kinky . . . ."

Sara found that she remembered too well how her words had been cut off in mid-sentence. With the harsh attack of his mouth over hers at first, until he had forced her into quietness — and from there, as he seemed to map and chart her body with deliberate slowness; first into acquiescence, and then she was overcome by a fierce, almost unthinking response that she had been unable to withhold.

She didn't want to think now of the ways in which he'd made love to her and the ways she had discovered, partly by instinct, to make love to him. And her mind shied away violently from the thought that she might actually miss and even crave what he had forced upon her in the beginning. Ridiculous! She should feel *relieved* instead of disappointed that he had chosen to leave her alone for at least a few hours without the harshly demanding oppression of his presence.

She had heard, not too long after he'd left her, the stridently chattering sound of the helicopter as it took off and had known that he had gone . . . to see which one of his mistresses? Why should *she* care? He probably needed his bruised ego mended, and that wasn't her problem, or her concern. Now she was free to leave, with *him* not around.

But why hadn't she? Why didn't she?

Perhaps her procrastination had something to do with a newly acquired ability to *rationalize,* Sara pondered bitterly; despising herself all the while. Of course he'd be back, she had told herself soon after he'd left her with those cutting words. He couldn't very well deny that he wanted her, after all the times he'd admitted it! He planned on keeping her a prisoner, like some medieval Sardinian Duca who had the power of life and death over his subjects. *"Le droit du seigneur"* . . . hadn't he turned her own sarcastically uttered words against her? But this was the twentieth century, thank God, and he couldn't *really* keep her unless she wanted to stay. What *did* she really want?

He'll come back, of course! Arrogant egomaniac that he is, he won't be able to help it! And maybe for just one more time I'll let him think that he has me . . . just before I leave. In any case, *this* masquerade is almost over!

There was always Angelo, the unfortunate, misplaced, half sibling that Marco seemed to be so resentful of. *Jealous* of! Angelo, eager to help her escape for his own reasons. Knight on a shiny black Honda! Waiting for the signal that she needed rescuing . . . signal that she had inexplicably not yet given; and of course only because she knew and expected that in spite of all his contemptuously light and misleading words *he* would come seeking her again like a wolf scenting and circling his prey . . . giving time for panic before moving in for the kill. Oh, he'd be back all right! Giving her the last laugh before she moved out. And that was why she hadn't moved out yet. Just knowing she could, anytime she wanted to, made all the difference, of course. She'd just wait for him to succumb one more time, that was all. One more time — proving to him that he still wanted her before she disappeared out of his life for good.

It was Serafina, in the end, who reminded Sara of reality. Serafina with her dour comments; and before that the "mysterious" appearance of several of the latest international gossip magazines on her balcony.

The magazines, of course, had to be courtesy of Angelo, who else? Her mother smiled at her enigmatically from the cover of one of them, reminding Sara that by now Mama-Mona was probably only kilometers away in Cagliari. Leafing through them impatiently, Sara was caught (as Angelo had intended her to be, no doubt) by certain suggestive articles about Marco, of all persons. Il Duca di Cavalieri, exposed as an international playboy, for all of his business successes and profits. One article dealt with his so-called "current" mistress, a French fashion designer of some repute. Another dealt with his past mistresses, and the fact that he was notoriously fickle and unfeeling — never keeping a woman for more than six months or so; and leaving them without warning for the next.

Well, of course she had known, had sensed without having to be told what kind of man he really was! Who was the real hypocrite? Why didn't he come back, damn his black soul, so that she could face him with the truth about himself?

Sara had heard the helicopter go — and in forty-eight hours it had not come back.

Bastard! What was he doing? What did he think to accomplish? She just wouldn't be *here,* that was all, when he finally deigned to return. Keep her here for his *use* — never! He'd find out, in the end, how he'd been fooled, and that would be only a part of her revenge. He'd be a laughingstock, if he wasn't sent to jail for abducting her. She would wear a virginal white dress at the trial and cry a lot . . . and he'd never live it down. Daddy would see to that, if no one else would!

As usual, she lay sunbathing on her private terrace with only her thoughts to keep her company until — or unless — *he* came.

Let's be practical, Sara! . . . Oh, yes, it was easy to talk to herself, to shake a warning finger at herself in spite of her basic helplessness in the face of a danger she hadn't known existed and wasn't quite ready to face yet. He might never come back. For all you know, he's forgotten you already. Just another statistic! And yet there had been days and there had been nights when he had *talked* to her; seeming to forget who he was and what he thought she was, and letting the bitterness show. They had had meals together and had argued . . . and jousted. Had *made love,* in spite of all the other cynical, somehow negating phrases he had used sometimes as if he needed to reduce what started to happen and did happen between them to clinical, coarse words that explained nothing and meant nothing.

It was just as well he had taken off when he had — giving her time to breathe, time to think and evaluate.

She was lying in the sun, letting its heat and its light take her through her pores while her mind stayed shaded and detached, when Serafina came — breaking in on her privacy for the first time that Sara could remember since the first time.

"Signorina . . . please to wake up. It is not safe to sleep under our burning sun."

Oh, God — she must have forgotten all modesty since she had come here! Even as she thought that, Sara turned lazily over onto her back, with one arm shading her eyes from the glare.

"What is it . . . ? Is that all? Or has 'Il Duca' deigned to return yet?" She could not keep the caustic note from her voice as she made her small, sarcastic pun. When the woman said nothing, she continued in the same defiantly light way, "If he's back you must be sure to tell him that I am more than ever bored! I don't like being kept a prisoner against my will. Or does he do this with all his women?"

"You, signorina, are the first woman that Il Duca has ever brought here to the palazzo. *Si,* we have all known from an occasional newspaper and a *giornale* of some of his other . . . . interests, but never has he brought one *here*. Never. . . . Forgive me, signorina, for speaking so openly, but sometimes it is better so. I am an old woman, and I have seen much, but . . ."

"I'm sorry, Serafina." Sitting up reluctantly, Sara wished suddenly for something to cover herself with; accepting with gratitude the Indian-patterned cotton wraparound the woman handed her without a word. Her mind felt bemused; as much from the sun as from Serafina's sudden burst of confidence. Whatever was she trying to say? And how should she reply?

Sara found a temporary respite while she knotted the light-textured cotton sarong over her breasts. But her mind burned without her quite knowing why. "His interests . . ." Serafina had said in that totally accepting voice! Damn it, never would *she* accept a man who would casually keep a positive *legion* of mistresses — whoever took his roving eye, in fact. And was still hypocrite enough to deny his younger brother the right to marry the woman he loved, while *he* took and used the same woman — or so he thought — without caring about *her* will, or the consequences of his high-handed actions.

"Serafina . . . what are you trying to say? I am getting very tired of facing evasions or brute force. I think I need to leave here soon, surely you understand that?"

It was as if Serafina deliberately refused to

understand, seizing on unimportant matters instead. "You have had too much sun, what did I say? It could be dangerous, too. . . . Please to come inside with me, signorina."

It took Serafina a long time to come to the point, even though she had obviously come here with the intention of saying *something,* Sara thought impatiently, as she allowed herself to be scolded and clucked over like a child; and even shepherded into her bath, with all its perfumed marble luxury. A sunken bath, indeed! Symbol of decadence, built for pampered odalisques whose only function was to please their arrogant masters. And with *that* thought Sara was able to tear her mind away from an unwanted, unnecessary flash of memory of strong brown fingers soaping her back — soaping her all over. . . .

Why wasn't there a *shower* included in the otherwise luxurious appointments of this enormous bathroom? *He* had one, after all!

"Serafina . . . ?"

The straight-backed old woman with her severely knotted hair and her dark clothing would normally have left Sara to her bath, but this afternoon she had seemed to seek excuses to stay, as she carefully checked the huge heap of fluffy towels that were always kept ready, and the levels of bath oils and bath powders in their crystal jars. Now Serafina looked almost relieved that Sara had chosen to speak to her.

"*Si,* signorina?"

"Serafina, when was this . . . this inordinately large tub put in here? And why isn't there a modern, practical *shower?*"

"It was a former Duca, I think, signorina. The title is very old, and this is a very old part of the palazzo. But when the first Duchessa saw these rooms she wanted them for herself — I remember my *madre* telling me so, and she worked here in my present position at the time. I myself was young, but I had come to work here at the age of fifteen. I remember the Duchessa — both the Duchessas — very well. Long before there was modern heating I used to help carry up the big kettles of heated water. *Ach!* And how many it took!"

Now that she had begun to speak, the usually taciturn housekeeper had become almost garrulous, and it was all Sara could do to stop herself from arching her eyebrows in disbelief. Why, Serafina actually had a very human side to her after all, although it was still hard to imagine her as a young girl of fifteen, toiling up innumerable steps with heavy kettles of hot water. Poor thing, had she ever had a normal, carefree girlhood?

"Perhaps I am boring the signorina . . . these things all happened many years ago, and some of them are better forgotten!"

"Oh — no, no!" Sara said hastily, with curiosity coming to the fore. "Please! There are so many things that I've wondered about, *particularly* the first Duchess, because these were her rooms, and her picture still hangs here, instead of in the portrait gallery. She must have been . . . a very beautiful woman! And she was Spanish, wasn't she?"

"Ah, yes — Spanish she was, *and* very beautiful, very young. Il Duca, her husband, could deny her nothing. Anything she asked for — jewels, fine clothes — she must have. And those were hard times for our country, signorina. Very hard times! There was not as much money in the family as there is now, thanks to the present Duca, and it was sometimes difficult — but indeed the Duchessa had only to wish, that was all. She had everything!"

"Except her freedom, I suppose!" Sara felt herself almost impelled to interject somewhat dryly. What a different story from the one Serafina herself had related to her earlier! A poor, captive young bride kept as a plaything for a tyrannous Duke who belonged, like his elder son, in the Middle Ages! "And what about all the times he left her alone in this vast palazzo while *he* traveled about and, no doubt, visited his favorite mistresses? Perhaps this magnificent palazzo and these magnificent rooms with their marble bath and sun terrace and wide soft bed had begun to feel like a prison to her, poor woman!"

For a moment, as Serafina's face seemed to tighten, Sara thought that she might not say anything more — and wondered why she almost held her breath. But it seemed as if the older woman had said too much and gone too far to stop with what she had already said; even though her next few words sounded like a reproach.

"The signorina doesn't understand at all! It was not like that; although it was true the Duchessa became pregnant soon after marriage. It was then that she asked for these rooms — it was then that her husband the Duca began to travel so often on business, although there was a *dottore* here in residence all the time. Money had to be made, signorina. And in those days there were no noisy flying machines capable of landing here. Travel by road was very, very rough — and dangerous as well, with *banditi* everywhere to prey on travelers. The Duchessa was in no condition —"

"But what about *afterward?*" Sara persisted, even while she wondered why she did. The unfortunate young Duchess had died — one might almost say she had been *murdered* — for want of simple medical care denied to her by her vengeful husband. If he had truly loved her he would have forgiven her!

"If *you* had a young child who needed nursing and a mother's care, would *you* have wanted to travel away from your infant, signorina?"

Touché, Serafina! Almost unwillingly, Sara shook her head. "No, I suppose not! But I'm sure that *she* didn't either, did she? And was he here when the child was born? Couldn't he stay with her after that?"

The child they were talking about was *Marco* — what a strange thought, and how impossible to imagine him as a child, much less a helpless infant!

Serafina too was shaking her head, and her weathered brown face bore an almost brooding expression.

"Il Duca was here, of course, although she — the Duchessa — did not want to see him. She screamed — in spite of the fact that the *dottore* had tried to prepare her, she was not ready for the reality of the pain of childbirth, and how she screamed! I remember covering my ears from the sound of those screams and the words of hate and of anger until my *madre* sent me away. And even afterward . . ."

"Yes?"

"Afterward she did not want to see either her husband or her child, signorina. My mother had quite a time, and so did the *dottore*. It was only because her breasts began to ache so with the milk that she finally permitted her son to be brought to her for feeding. And then she would turn her head away — she would not hold him, she would not touch him — and she would cry and scream and rage until at last a wet nurse was found, a woman from the mountains whose brother . . ." Serafina's lips pursed almost angrily, but before Sara could ask another question she went on quickly in the same wooden voice — "But even if her child was taken care of, she had a husband, signorina. She turned away from him too, in spite of everything he tried to do, everything he continued to give her in spite of the fact that she would not share his bed and did not wish him to share hers. She demanded more and more as the price for having borne a son who would be the heir and the next Duca, and he gave her everything, still hoping, perhaps, that with time she would change. It was in *those* days, signorina, that he would go on journeys that took longer and longer. . . . And once I myself overheard him say to a friend of his who had come to visit that he could no longer put up with the hate that she had begun to feel for him — and that she showed him, whenever he tried to . . . reason with her."

Her bath water was cooling — almost automatically Sara's hand turned the spigot that would send more hot water in. In spite of herself, the story that Serafina had surprisingly revealed to her with all its intimate details had held her attention so completely that she had almost forgotten the present, and the reality of *her* predicament. Forgotten to wonder why Serafina had chosen this time and this moment to disclose family secrets to an outsider like herself.

"So *he* stayed away for longer and longer periods at a time, while *she* . . . " Sara said the words musingly and almost to herself while she tried to adjust her mind to a *different* story. It was quite like the Japanese movie *Rashomon,* she told herself. How many facets were there to *truth,* with everyone seeing it from a different viewpoint? Had anyone really tried to understand the poor little Spanish Duchess before they condemned her as a spoiled and petulant child who cared for nothing but her own comfort?

She looked up at Serafina, who seemed lost in the past, with her thin, work-roughened fingers moving automatically over wooden rosary beads while her eyes stared over Sara's damp head into the distance. It was time for reason and logic, surely!

"Well, he should have taken her away with him, no matter *what!* Perhaps all she needed was to mingle with people again. To have the chance to wear her pretty dresses and her jewels to the opera or the ballet or to cocktail parties. He might even have taken her to a . . . a — well, perhaps they didn't have marriage counselors in those days, but at least to a psychologist who might have been able to help! If she was so young —"

"It was a time of unrest, of too many changes that happened too fast, I tell you, signorina. And soon the war that everyone had been talking about, to set the world on its ears. Ah, but it was unfortunate, so bad! Although there was a time when — Il Duca was away then — when we all thought there might be a change. The child was an infant no longer, and now, perhaps out of boredom, who knows? — the Duchessa would permit him to be brought to her rooms. She even became quite friendly with the nurse and spent much time talking with this illiterate woman from the mountains who had lost her own bastard child. Ah, but it was a bad thing, that strange friendship, bad for everyone . . . ."

"You're not being *fair,* surely!" Sara cried out in protest. "What was wrong with that poor lonely woman searching for a friend, someone to *talk* to, and finding one? And her child — you just *said* she had begun to accept her baby . . . ."

Serafina's voice had harshened, even while her fingers tightened themselves over the rosary she held. "The child she treated as a toy — sometimes caressed and fondled, and sometimes pushed away. And as for the friendship — the woman had a brother, one of the wild, dangerous *banditi* who preyed upon the helpless and the unwary. There was a meeting between them —"

"And he was Angelo's father?"

The words slipped out before Sara could stop them, although she could have bitten her tongue soon after. But Serafina did not seem to be at all surprised, as she turned somber eyes on Sara's flushed face with curling tendrils of hair clinging at her forehead and temples.

"Yes, Angelo, who is his father's son, surely!"

"And his *mother's,* as well!" Sara flashed back, recovering her senses, she thought with a mental shake. "Poor Angelo! If anyone is to be pitied *besides* the foolishly indiscreet Duchessa, I would think *he* is! Banished into exile as an infant, and then . . . and now. . . ."

"Angelo is a troublemaker, signorina! And, begging the signorina's pardon, but he takes advantage of . . . of who he is and what he is! Of Il Duca's generosity, and his sureness that he will not be punished for any of the liberties he takes. He came back here from the United States because he had got himself into trouble there — did anyone, I ask you, force him to choose the bad life he led? He did not even go to prison like so many others — no, it was arranged that he should come back here, still a free man. And since then . . . signorina, I beg you to be careful! Do not trust this Angelo who comes and goes in the night as he pleases because he takes *advantage.* . . . I have said too much, and I know it, but only because — there was *another* child, signorina. Another innocent child who grew up with the knowledge that his mother

427

had never wanted him and in the end deserted him without a thought. These are scars that children grow up with and carry, even when they are no longer children but grown men, who have learned early to hide their feelings away . . . ."

Chapter 35

Sara had been brought up to think clearly and — of course — rationally. Taught that *feelings* were something one had to bring out in the open and examine carefully and detachedly like little squirming dots and lines under a microscope. Above all things, everything must be seen in perspective! And she had actually succeeded quite well until recently, hadn't she? She should give herself that much credit, in all fairness; just as she had tried explaining to Serafina. What a strange afternoon it had been! She must try to remind herself that at least she had matched frankness with frankness. Even if she could not *possibly,* by any stretch of imagination, imagine *Marco* as a little boy!

"Serafina . . . but please, try to imagine things as they are *now!*" Out of the heated water with its perfume that suddenly seemed oppressive, Sara found herself almost shivering as she wrapped herself in the depths of the huge towel that the woman had handed her. She saw herself reflected again in all those mirrors and turned away from them with decision.

"I . . . I really *do* appreciate your telling me everything, but you see . . ." Forcing her voice not to falter and to go on more strongly she said, "You *have* to see how different *these* circumstances are! I mean — well, I'm not his . . . his *wife,* for one thing; you know as well as I do what I am, and what he's made me, and . . . and even that it's my own fault for letting it happen. I'm not — oh, I'm really not *blaming* anyone for this but myself, you know. I should have . . ." Catching her lower lip between her teeth before she made any more damaging admissions, Sara began to towel her hair vigorously, so that her voice sounded muffled when she spoke again.

"You really *do* have to understand that I . . . I just have to go away! Things have become . . . quite impossible. I won't let myself be kept here as a *plaything* and he says he won't let me go until *he* pleases! Don't you see? It's certainly not at all to be compared to the way his *mother* deserted him, for heaven's sake; and has nothing to do with my having any kind of . . . of strong feelings for poor Angelo, nothing at all, but if he's the only one who would help me escape then I . . . that's the way it will have to be, I'm afraid!"

Serafina's voice sounded as if she was wringing her hands.

"But, signorina, *please!* You must believe what I tell you now, and the reasons for my telling you of all the things that took place in the past. Il Duca . . . ah, he has many faults, and what man or woman has not? He seems so hard, and he has had to be hard and a man with a man's responsibilities before he had time to be a boy. But I tell you, and this I swear by the Blessed Virgin Herself, that never have I, or any of the other servants, known him to be *this* way before!" With an agitation that was totally foreign to her usually austere manner and formal politeness, Serafina seemed to brush aside the protest that Sara had barely begun to utter as she continued in the same urgent manner. "He has never brought another woman here, to his palazzo — yes, this I have already said. And he has never . . . Il Duca has never been one to show *emotion,* signorina! Neither laughter nor rage — nothing to be read on his face. And he has never liked this home of his well enough to stay here very long; especially of late. But since the day when he brought *you* here — *si,* there has been a change! No one can keep up with his moods any longer. He has been angry, in such a black humor that even his own valet, who has been with him for over fifteen years now, shakes his head and finds it hard to believe. And he — Il Duca

— has also put aside his *business* that has always meant so much to him and taken most of his time on previous visits, to spend this time with you. Yes, with you, signorina! You must not go away, not even if . . . if there has been a quarrel between you. Quarrels only arise from *feelings* of some kind, is that not so?"

Oh, God! How to face *this* unexpected flow of words and thoughts she wasn't quite ready for? And yet she could not hide her face away in the protection of her towel forever, either.

Sara relinquished it with a sigh and found that Serafina already had her silk robe ready for her to slip on.

"Grazie." Her murmured word of thanks was purely mechanical. A cover-up for a jumble of emotions she didn't want to try sorting out just now under Serafina's watchful eyes.

"May I get the signorina a cool drink? *Acqua minerale,* or some chilled wine, perhaps? And afterward a rest might be good — I will see to it that you are not disturbed and bring the signorina's dinner upstairs myself. Anything you desire . . ."

Sheer perversity and the need to shy away from her own strangely mixed-up feelings made Sara say almost *testingly:* "And what if all I want is freedom? Even a certain amount of it — a horseback ride perhaps, since it is still light outside. Or to take my dinner in the dining room for a change — anywhere but here in these rooms that have been made my prison. What about that? What orders did *he* give before he left in his noisy helicopter that can take him anywhere he pleases to go while I . . . *I* am left here to rot, for all he cares?"

It was as if she *needed* to fan her righteous anger in order to keep herself immune — her viewpoint objective. The man they were speaking of was a dangerously unscrupulous tyrant, after all — deprived childhood or not! No — there was no excuse that she could accept for the way he had treated her, no matter who he had thought her to be. She should cling to that thought, and that thought only.

"I will pour out a glass of wine for you, signorina. And a short rest, perhaps, while the sun is still high? Il Duca will soon be back, I am sure of this, and then . . . then perhaps everything will be different!"

Still frowning mutinously, Sara watched Serafina's hastily retreating back. The sly old woman! She'd said her piece and planted her seeds, and now she was obviously going to shut up and avoid any further questioning.

Well, we'll see about that! Odalisque . . . Seraglio — what did he think he was, a . . . a *sultan?* Cruel, decadent, arrogant, *monster!* He wasn't capable of any of the feelings that Serafina in her blind devotion to "Il Duca" attributed to him. He wanted nothing more than his way, and willing women who would throw themselves at his feet, begging for whatever crumbs he chose to throw at them along with his discreetly expensive presents of bikini chains and ankle bracelets! *Forcibly* put on — in her case at least. Damn him! The first thing she'd do when she was free again was to have both removed — *sawed* through if necessary — and returned to him with an appropriately curt and cutting note.

While her mind alternately planned and discarded the right words to use, Sara allowed herself to accept the moisture-beaded glass of wine that Serafina had already poured. Why waste perfectly good wine? And it *was* good — Puligny-Montrachet, her favorite, one of the best years ever. And Serafina had set out sesame crackers and cheeses as well, while she muttered disapprovingly that the signorina had *not* had breakfast and was getting far too thin. Please to eat — and here was another glass of cold wine — *vino* was good for the constitution and the health, there was no harm in drinking more.

Afterward Sara couldn't *really* remember falling asleep, still wearing her robe although she had meant to get dressed and had had Serafina lay out a pair of jeans and a blouse for her. In any case, she had slept, and there had been dreams — of the unsettling kind she didn't *want* to recall.

"Marco . . . ?" Had that been part of a

dream too or had she actually said his name aloud, waking herself up?

"No, no! It's only Angelo — and please don't scream, I think the old woman has put one of those silly, giggling young maids to keep watch outside your door — in case you sleepwalk, I guess — or for some other reason . . . ? Hey, are you awake? Sorry about dropping in like this without a formal invitation, but like I'm sure you've guessed by now, I'm not the formal type! Are you awake?"

And suddenly she was. Quite wide awake and sitting bolt upright in bed with her eyes blinking to adjust themselves to the gloom and only a slight, nagging headache to remind her of all the wine she must have consumed by herself.

"Angelo! What —"

"Yeah, you've got it right this time! Angelo, not Marco. Hey — you haven't been dumb enough to *fall* for him, have you? The only reason I'm here — not meaning to intrude — is because your last message to me sounded loud and clear in spite of my scowling brother being right there; and I thought I might have heard from you by now. Especially since I left them magazines for you. You get them?"

He was sitting on her bed, and belatedly, Sara snatched the covers up over her far-too-scantily-clad shoulders, hearing Angelo's soft chuckle come to her out of the darkness.

"Still the shy type, huh? But no nun either,

435

I begin to get the impression. Not that you have to feel nervous about me being here sitting on your bed and all, *or* about my letting on to anyone at all which sister you *really* are, because like I said before I'm the kind of guy who keeps his word, see? And also the kind of guy who does his homework, if you get what I mean? And I *keep* every little thing I've read about Mona — *and* all her kids, including *pictures*. . . . But you can trust me to keep my mouth shut — *and* in other ways, if you get my meaning? I never have messed around with any broad — pardon the expression, it slipped out — who wasn't ready, willing and *anxious,* and you happen to be Mona Charles' little girl, even if you ain't so little any longer. So — to cut this all short before I let you go back to beddy-bye — what's up? You still want to get away or not? Because if you do, now's the time, and I'm the only one who can help you. And if you don't —"

"Of *course* I want to . . . to escape!" Sara shifted uncomfortably, wishing that her dreams hadn't been *quite* as vivid as they had been; actually making her say *his* hated name out loud. Her fault for drinking so much wine and Serafina's for telling her so much that would have been much better left unsaid.

"Yeah?" Angelo's laconic question made her unaccountably annoyed.

"Well — of course! I suppose the reason I — that I've seemed to procrastinate for so

436

long was that *he* isn't here, and that, and the sun, made all this suddenly seem like a vacation — you know?"

He didn't sound convinced, and now that her eyes had become used to the dark Sara could catch the slight shrugging motion of his shoulders.

"Well — I'll tell you what! I'm a pretty good judge of character, I think, and one of the reasons I jumped the gun, so to speak, was because I had it figured you were the sensible, independent type, know what I mean? And what with brother Marco's loving step-mom deciding to pay him a surprise visit to check up on why he's been so unavailable recently; *plus* bringing with her this very rich young lady who's supposed to become his fiancée, if they haven't already got it settled between them . . . well, correct me if I'm wrong, kid, but I thought maybe this was exactly the right time to step in and offer you my services — *free,* if I might add! — again. It's up to you, of course."

"His . . . !" All the treacherously languorous feelings left over from her dreams had vanished in a flash, leaving Sara filled with nothing but cold rage — as much at herself for her weakness as toward *him.* Marco — who adored and *respected* his stepmother and actually had a fiancée in spite of his so-called mistrust of all females. Damn and blast his hide!

"Now, now — *please* keep your voice down, won't you? They won't get here until tomorrow afternoon at least — they've had to drive on account of the chopper not being available. And that gives us time to make *our* plans. You don't have to worry — although I sure am glad you're the athletic type. All you have to do is follow me closely and do everything I say and there'll be no sweat. You and I will be off and away and my brother the Duke won't know a goddam thing about it until you're safe and sound. And by the way — not to sound prying, but I'm a curious guy, whatever *did* happen to Delight? I remember reading something . . ."

Fired by her fury *and* remembering to keep her voice down for the much-maligned Angelo's sake, Sara managed to give a creditably brief account of what had led her to this particular piece of foolishness — leaving a lot out; although she had the feeling that Angelo had already read between the lines.

"You *sure* you don't want to go right now?" he said thoughtfully, after she had finished. "After all, why be embarrassed? There's liable to be quite a scene if they find out *you're* here, and the Duchessa — for all her sweet ways — can be quite a Tartar, I've heard! Not that that old witch Serafina won't manage to keep your presence here unknown, if she can help it. It might be better if —"

"Oh, no!" Sara almost hissed the words,

with her fingers clenched over the edge of her sheet; wishing she had something near at hand to throw. Vendetta! How well she had begun to understand the true meaning of that word!

"No? But surely . . ."

She sucked in a deep breath of cool night air before saying in a more controlled tone of voice: "Not tonight, but *tomorrow* night instead, if you're still willing to take the risk. Tomorrow afternoon — or whenever they get here, I *think* that Il Duca's stepmother *and* his fiancée might have their pure and worshiping eyes opened wide as to his *real* nature! He . . . he's really been quite nasty and overbearing, and I think I owe myself the satisfaction of getting even. Not just for myself but for Delight as well. Oh, Mama-Mona would just *love* it! She'd be so proud of me — and of *you* for rescuing me, of course!"

"You really think so, huh? And so at last I'll get to meet your lovely Mama in person! Well — they do say revenge is sweet, and what's a few hours?" Sara knew she ought to be ashamed of herself for manipulating poor Angelo so, but he actually sounded pleased, and almost swaggeringly sure of himself. "Don't worry about a thing, kid! Just wait up here for me — and be sure to get rid of anyone else. And you can bet on the fact that I'll *be* here right about this time. Only thing I'm sorry about is I won't be here to see their faces when you lay it on them!"

439

Well, Angelo would be proud of her too, Sara vowed to herself after he had left as quietly as he had arrived. She was going to savor every tiny detail of her revenge, which would be partly *his* revenge too. Revenge — and the last laugh.

She tossed and turned in that wide bed and felt her skin burn and sleep elude her now. Perhaps she *had* slept too long in the sun. Hot, primitive sun in a still-primitive land — making her feel, for a while, as if she had been cut off both from civilization and from reality; truly a prisoner of a darkly dangerous Moorish corsair who used women as chattels. Thank God Angelo had opened her eyes! And oh, how she could not help despising herself for almost . . . for almost allowing herself to fall in love with him in *spite* of the cold-blooded way in which he'd used her!

Sara almost sprang out of bed to go to the refrigerator with long, pacing strides. What a thought to flash across her mind! What a foolish, ridiculous thought! In love indeed . . . and with *him* of all people? It was hate — dislike and disgust she felt for him, not love! How could she have confused the two?

Still angry at herself and wanting to change the strange direction of her thoughts, Sara switched on a light and helped herself, defiantly, to more wine. She caught a glimpse of a tousled reflection of herself in one of the mirrors she couldn't seem to avoid — her hair already tumbling down below her shoulders and long enough to brush against her nipples.

Stop it! she warned herself. Enough of *that!* Perhaps she should have gone with Angelo tonight, instead of taking the risk of waiting. Tomorrow would tell!

Chapter 36

The tomorrow she had alternately dreaded and anticipated came late for Sara, who had found the sleep she sought far too elusive for far too long a time. And she was even later waking up because Serafina, with a cunning Sara did not want to believe of her, had not opened the heavy wooden shutters that would let the sunshine in to wake her. But at least *this* time there had been no dreams that she could recall!

There was, when Sara woke up and forced her eyes open, another pair of eyes staring apprehensively into hers before they looked away, and the young maid who had been stationed beside her bed jumped up to begin walking toward the door.

"Buon giorno, signorina! I am supposed to fetch Serafina the very moment . . ."

Between the stammering near-incoherency of Caterina and Serafina's urgent insistence that this day should follow the pattern of every other — the signorina had circles under her eyes and surely needed more sleep? — Sara managed to order a breakfast she couldn't eat. And in the meantime, mustering all her resources, she managed to pretend acquiescence; murmuring off-handedly that she was going to lie in the sun for as long as she could today.

"It's a good idea, signorina. I will be busy for a while, but Caterina will wait outside your door in case the signorina should need something. I will come again . . . ."

"Thank you, Serafina. I feel quite *lazy* today. You might make it a point to wake me again today as you did yesterday, though. I'm more than liable to fall asleep."

Easy words. Casually uttered words. Words designed to lull them all into satisfied relaxation, deliberately meant to distract and throw off. To deceive — as *she* had been deceived! Poor little Caterina, innocent though she might be, was the easiest to trick.

Sara had first forced herself to lie in the sun as she usually did each day, while she tried to calculate what time it was. Three — perhaps four? And were they here yet? Oh — they must be, she could almost sense it from the feeling of bustle and activity and the sound of servants' voices that were accidentally raised at first and then as quickly lowered.

An hour — had she really been able to contain

herself that long? Perhaps an hour, but she had waited long enough and needed to *act* now, before her courage deserted her. On her feet now, Sara padded to the closed door.

"Caterina? Are you still there?"

The girl almost burst into the room. "*Si*, signorina. I am to be here for as long as you might need me. If there is anything —"

"Yes, please. My bath . . . and some more wine? I daresay Serafina would know where it is kept, if you don't."

In the end, it had all been almost too easy! Serafina was nowhere to be seen and Caterina too well trained, in spite of her age, to argue with an order. After all, the signorina hadn't acted as if she planned to go anywhere, how could she have known? She'd started the bathwater running and had scuttled back down all those flights of stairs to fetch the wine of a very particular kind that she would have to look for. In her eagerness to please, Caterina had quite forgotten the lack of locks on the door she was supposed to guard. Who could have known that the pretty signorina with the sun-gold lights in her hair would take it into her head to actually venture downstairs? *Or* that she would choose not to wear anything more than a towel, and that only too carelessly wrapped about her body?

It had to have been Divinely decreed, Sara was to think later. For all the guesswork involved, she really couldn't have timed it better, not even if she had known beforehand that the Duchessa enjoyed *al fresco* meals beside the pool.

Perhaps there was more of her mother and of Delight in her than she had ever suspected before, and perhaps it was only the cold feeling of rage that kept her from ignominious flight before she had descended, with impudent nonchalance, the last of those interminable marble steps. Afterward, her only *real* recollection was the stunned looks on the two faces that had turned toward her, watching her jaunty progress. Everything she did and said seemed to happen without volition; as if she'd transformed role into reality.

It was something that not even the servants, transformed suddenly into frozen statues, would easily forget. Both Serafina and Caterina, searching impatiently for the very particular kind of wine that had been ordered, missed the greatest, and most successful performance of Sara's short-lived career.

Even her "surprised" hesitation was perfect as she widened her eyes at the two women — noting almost annoyedly that *one* of them was quite young and rather pretty — in a blonde, insipid way, of course!

"Ohh! I'm sorry . . . didn't know there was anyone else here! Are you friends of Marco's? How nice to have company for a change! And what a neat idea to have lunch *here,* instead of up in my room or in that stuffy big dining room — such a *bore,* isn't it?" She smiled at them both in turn, noting with vindictive satisfaction that *neither* of the two women, older or younger, seemed capable of speech yet. "D'you mind if I go ahead and have my swim, as I planned? I haven't been in since Marco's been away, and just soaking in a dumb old bathtub tends to get old after a time, if you know what I mean?"

Another bright smile and Sara dropped the towel, diving in cleanly and with hardly any splash at all. It relieved some of the tension inside her to swim two lengths of the pool before she put her elbows on the edge, pushing dripping wet hair out of her eyes.

"Hi!" The first thing she noticed was the ugly patches of red that had mottled the pale complexion of the blonde, at whom she now directed her sweetest smile and her most confiding tone. "I guess I should have introduced myself before, huh? I'm Delight, and I'm Marco's girlfriend — current, that is. Who're you?"

Oh — there had been more, *much* more — both Daddy and Nanny Staggs, who had tried to bring her up *properly,* would have been appalled if they could have seen and heard her. She had been an absolute *bitch,* borrowing one of Marco's favorite terms of endearment — and she didn't care! Not even the slightest pang of guilt had altered her guileless look when the younger woman had *surged* to her feet, knocking over her chair clumsily. She had a screechy, fishwife kind of voice too, Sara decided critically.

"Oh . . . oohh! *Madonna mia,* but I will *not* put up with such humiliation, not even for a title! I have enough money of my own and men who would *respect* me enough not to . . . to install a cheap little slut under the same roof!" A red-nailed finger pointed with almost ludicrous drama at Sara, who had to fight to keep her expression confused. "*Look* at that! Look at her, the shameless American hussy who *boasts* of what she is to your son and swims *naked* in front of everyone . . . ! What an escape I've had, to be sure! I . . . I . . . ."

As the words seemed to sputter into raging incoherence and the Duchessa attempted to soothe and calm, Sara's clearly and deliberately enunciated words seemed to cut across the confusion, drawing everyone's attention to herself again.

"Jee-sus! What's eating *her?* I mean, what have I done, to rate all the name-calling? It's not *my* fault I'm here . . . I was engaged to marry *Carlo,* when big brother *dragged* me out here — and in the middle of a Garon Hunt movie, no less! And listen, I'm not the possessive type at all, *I'm* not jealous! I know Marco digs some really kinky scenes with other gals for variety, and I've never objected yet!"

The stridently shrill voice that she already

hated rose by several octaves as the blonde forgot she was a lady. "Bitch! *Puttana! Sciamannona!* I hope you drown in there!"

The Duchessa, who seemed to be a *real* lady in spite of all Sara's resentment, now sent her a *quelling* look that reminded her of the headmistress of the extremely exclusive private school she'd been forced to attend — a woman that Sara had been positively terrified and overwhelmed by.

"That is more than enough, young woman! Go back upstairs this instant, and please do not forget your towel! I will deal with you later. And now, Lucia — you really should *not* let yourself get so angry; you don't have the right complexion for it, my dear! Come, why don't we find some privacy away from the servants?"

Without another backward glance to see if her imperiously uttered command had been obeyed or not, the Duchessa swept herself and the still-sputtering Lucia out of sight and earshot with a regal kind of splendor that Sara was forced to admire in spite of herself and the prejudices she had already formed in her mind. Had she gained a victory and her carefully planned revenge or lost a battle?

All the hovering servants had vanished as if by magic — all the *male* servants, that was. Sara had just hoisted herself up out of the pool when her towel was handed to her by a wooden-faced Serafina who looked at her in much the same way as the Duchessa had.

"What a bad, wicked thing to do! You make me ashamed, as I am sure your own *madre* would be if she could have seen and heard you! Speaking that way, like . . . like all those things that . . . the Signorina Lucia called you! An insult to the Duchessa in her own home — I cannot answer for the consequences when Il Duca hears about *this!* But I think that he will be more angry than any of us have ever seen him before, and you *ought* to tremble with fear!"

Sara was immediately angry with herself for the slight shudder that had gone through her body, even though it was only caused by the chill of the air after the warm pool.

Hah! She didn't really care how angry he might be — in fact she *wanted* him to be angry. Angry, and frustrated, when he returned and found her gone with Angelo.

She preceded the still-scolding Serafina back up the marble stairs in tight-lipped silence; consoling herself with the thought that in a very few more hours she would be free at last. And in the meantime she was *not* sorry for anything she had said — not even the icy-eyed Duchessa with her autocratic manner could force a retraction from her.

Back in her room — in her *prison,* Serafina barely stayed long enough to utter a curt "request" that made Sara seethe all over again.

If the Signorina would kindly remain in her rooms and put some clothes on before the Duchessa sent for her? And if the signorina was hungry, food would be sent up. . . .

Bread and water? Sara wanted to ask caustically, but instead she bit her lip and refused to let herself be *baited*. A few more hours — that was all! And in the meantime, what did she have to be afraid of? The Duchessa couldn't really *do* anything to her, after all, and she'd be long gone before Marco deigned to return — to find his precious, *suitable* fiancée no longer his. And that would only be the *first* of the unpleasant shocks he would soon encounter!

Still in a seething mood of rebellion, Sara occupied herself in dressing — stretch denim jeans (great for wall climbing!) that fit her like a second skin and a brief white cotton shirt knotted right under her breasts and leaving very little to the imagination. Then . . . she looked at herself critically in the mirror, trying to decide on her image. Lots and lots of makeup, vulgarly overdone, or none at all? Sara frowned consideringly before she decided with some reluctance that the makeup wouldn't do because of Angelo, who might think she was giving him a come-on. In the end, she compromised by using just the faintest smudge of brown eye shadow that blended with her newly acquired tan, and eye liner. A touch of almost transparent gold lip gloss . . . not bad!

With her hair braided into two beribboned pigtails, Sara was able to smile rather smugly at herself. She *could* pass as a precocious sixteen-year-old if she tried hard enough; and maybe the Duchessa would believe it? And maybe, after all, the Duchessa would decide to ignore her presence here.

Never mind the Duchessa *or* her black-browed, hatefully arrogant stepson who had grown up thinking that all women were whores and deceivers! By tomorrow all this will be *nothing* to me, Sara thought fiercely. By tomorrow she would be returned to a safe and civilized world where she could be her *ordinary,* practical self again; escaping from this strange Arabian Nights fantasy that had somehow enmeshed her. Everything that had happened to her, everything she had let herself do with an almost mesmerized abandon had been part of a fantasy — all make-believe. And it was something she had to remember!

Almost by habit, Sara found her eyes traveling to the portrait of the Duchessa di Cavalieri who had been mother to both Marco and Angelo. Poor, smiling Duchessa who wore the wolf's-head insignia with all the casual assurance of a woman who thought the wolf had been tamed. *The wolf had had her in the end!*

"She was a shallow, selfish and completely

immoral woman — and not particularly intelligent either, even if she *did* keep my poor Giancarlo quite infatuated by her. But that's beside the point. It was to talk about *you* that I climbed all those miserable steps!"

Spinning around on her sneakered feet Sara met the steel-blue eyes of the *present* Duchessa, that seemed to bore through that particular part of her midriff that was exposed by the short white shirt, before they moved upward; lingering on her rather carelessly done-up braids.

"Oh — *I* would have come down if I'd known! I *did* want to explain that I didn't mean to upset your friend by anything I said. . . . I mean I do realize that lots of *older* women get crushes on Marco . . . ."

Quite unexpectedly, shocking Sara, the Duchess laughed.

"As you intended her to, poor Lucia insisted on leaving! And were you hoping to fool me with your Little Miss Teenage look *after* your carefully contrived *contretemps* this afternoon? Luckily, I never *did* particularly care for Lucia. . . . Yes, please do sit down, and so will I." Sara hadn't been able to help sitting down, and now she eyed her formidable adversary warily as the Duchess in her turn sat down opposite her, crossing slender, elegantly shod feet at the ankles.

"Where were we? Oh, yes. What on earth is all this about? And what are you doing here?

452

You're not Marco's usual type . . . but you *do* appreciate frankness, I take it? There was also something you said about Carlo, who happens to be *my* son . . . ."

By the end of about five minutes, Sara had begun to feel as if she and the Duchessa had reached a somewhat cautious *rapport;* or at least an understanding. Beginning with a surprising statement by the Duchess, as she repeated: "Yes, *Carlo* — who, when I last heard from him, was happily married to a woman he called 'Delight' and expecting to be a father any day. It was one of the things I came here to talk to Marco about. He tends to take his role of head of the family rather seriously, and he and my poor Carlo are always bumping heads! But what *is* this about Carlo? And Marco *taking* you from him? I must tell you, my girl, that I happen to know both my son and my stepson very well, and you don't fit. If Carlo was serious about you he would have told me — and it is *not* like my cynical, serious Marco to bring a young woman here, to his home. So . . . shall we talk about it?"

Sara hadn't really felt like talking about *anything* — all she wanted was to escape from the interrogation she was being put through.

"Well . . . Carlo and I *used* to have a thing going —"

"Really? When? He's been seeing his present wife for at least a year, as far as he's told me — and I also happen to know that Marco did *not* approve. . . . Heavens, I've felt as if I was nothing more than a *buffer* between the two of them for *ages* now! What does Carlo look like?"

That was the question that had undone her. Sara's mind went blank, even while it groped for the memory of the portrait Delight had showed her once. All she could see in her mind was the image of the one man she detested most of all — black hair, black eyes, black nature!

"Well . . . he's got dark hair, of course . . . ."

"I *thought* as much!" the Duchess retorted, giving Sara another look that reminded her too vividly of Miss Illingsworth — school — and being caught raiding the orchard with cherry stains all over her fingers and mouth. "And that eliminates Carlo, of course; so you can either think up another improbable lie or tell me the truth, which might really be much simpler, you know, unless you happen to be one of those unfortunate people who *cannot,* for psychological reasons."

"I am *not* a pathological liar!" Sara hated to find herself on the defensive.

"Thank you, that was exactly the phrase I was looking for. And I'm glad to hear you're not, my dear. Please *do* feel free to tell *me* the truth, and I just *might* be able to prevent Marco from . . . becoming violent. He has a *very* nasty temper when it's aroused, or have you already found that out?"

Looking into the Duchessa's implacable face, Sara decided that she might as well give in; especially since she was expecting Angelo in just a few hours. She wasn't a very good liar anyway — not unless she was really angry! And somehow, she didn't care to dwell on the thought-picture of Marco *angry*. Furious, in fact, as he would be when he finally found everything out, including the fact that he'd been duped. She'd rather tell the Duchessa than Marco. . . .

"Well . . . the *real* truth is that I'm Delight's sister, and she . . . I agreed to pass myself off as her to put Marco off while she and Carlo . . ."

The Duchessa nodded approvingly. "Now *that* story makes more sense! Shall we have some wine while you tell me the rest of it? I should tell you that I was quite angry with you until Serafina came to your defense . . . quite surprisingly, because she's a very straitlaced old woman who usually disapproves of everyone! But in your case . . . *do* go on, please. Even if it isn't all true, I'm sure you'll make it a most interesting story!"

Chapter 37

It could have been worse, Sara was to think later; and the Duchessa might have turned out to be *really* nasty instead of just politely questioning, and leaving her with the impression that final judgment had been withheld. Sara hadn't told her everything, of course — only as much (or as little) as she felt she had to — but it had been with a feeling of utter relief that she had seen her elegant tormentor rise to leave.

"Well, I suppose the *final* outcome of all this will depend on Marco and upon you, won't it? But I should warn you, my dear, he is *not* the kind of man who easily accepts being fooled! And you had better get yourself prepared for the worst if he's been reading any newspapers recently. The wedding of Carlo and your sister — even if he didn't tell *me* until afterward — by an Indian cardinal was much publicized!"

Marco . . . Marco! Why should she care,

or fear, what Marco's reactions might be? He must know already. . . . Pretending, for Serafina's benefit, that she had decided to go to bed early, Sara turned out all the lights and lay under the covers fully clothed with her body as tense as a bow. She had to keep calm, and she had to stay single-minded. She had to escape before *he* came back and walked into her room without announcement to seize her and to *use* her and make her forget pride and dignity and hate and revenge — everything but the way he could make her feel in spite of herself. She had to go — she *had* to go! She had to be free, and belong wholly to herself again.

"Hey! Let's go!" Angelo's voice — and somewhere in the background, softly at first before it assaulted the still air with its machine-gun rattle, Sara heard the sound of the helicopter returning.

She must have moved quite mechanically, like an automaton driven by the survival instinct. And following Angelo hadn't been easy, although she was thankful at the time that it took all of her concentration and her balance. Afterward — and it had seemed like *hours* — Angelo congratulated her.

"You know what, you're really great! 'Something else,' as they'd say back in the U.S. You ridden a motorcycle before?"

The sound of the chopper was still in her ears; the thought of Marco's anger was like a goad at her back. To escape this particular dark avenger she'd dare anything!

"No, never. But I learn fast. Just tell me what I must do."

Hurry, hurry, hurry! her mind kept repeating urgently as she mounted behind Angelo and wrapped her arms around his waist as he instructed her.

"Remember to watch where you put your feet, kid! Those pipes can burn and leave scars. Keep tight hold of me, and let your body kind of lean easy the way mine does — you'll get the knack of it pretty soon. And remember, you don't have to worry about a thing! I know every road and every dirt trail and every bump — light or dark. There's no way he's going to catch up with us, not even with that goddam helicopter of his!"

The motorcycle went downhill, coasting for a while before Angelo started it up. After that, even if the helicopter had swooped down upon them, Sara thought she would not have heard it over the roar of the powerful motorcycle and the rush of the wind in her ears. In any case, she found that all her concentration was centered upon *not* being thrown off, and she clung to Angelo with her face against his broad shoulders and her eyes tightly closed.

Time seemed to rush by as quickly as the miles they must have covered, and not thinking remained easy as long as she concentrated upon the *feeling* of this mad ride through the darkness of a Sardinian night, that seemed to go on forever, with a rhythm that repeated "forget — forget — forget" like a metronome beat in her head.

"Listen — you don't have to worry; there's no way he's going to find us now! How could he know where we'd be heading for, anyway? He probably thinks . . ." Angelo gave a laugh that sounded harsh enough to be Marco's — "Yeah, knowing the way his mind works, he probably has us all snuggled up in bed together by now! Not that it wouldn't be a fun idea — begging your pardon, Miss Sara, except it would be difficult right now — only my uptight brother doesn't know that, does he?"

Her words in reply would only get carried away by the wind. Sara remained silent and was glad of Angelo's tireless chatter that carried them out of darkness into the gradually spreading pinkish light of dawn. Slowly they moved down from the mountains toward the sea. Soon the roads they traveled became wider and more congested with traffic that he cut in and out of with a careless ease and swiftness that made Sara close her eyes and keep them closed.

If she survived, she would never accept a ride on the back of a motorcycle again! If she could only live through this mad, crazy ride she would be happy to go back to a sedate and better-planned and organized way of life. She had had her adventure and Mama would laugh as she hugged her with that rich life-loving chuckle of hers — glad to see her and glad that her solemn little Sara had finally broken out of the mold she had been positively *encased* in for all this time. Encased — stifled. It had taken Delight to help her emerge. And then she had discovered all on her own what *fun* it was not to bother with restrictions and conventions. Some of the things she'd *done!* It was just as if she'd stepped out of one world and into another where the memory of her other self, her other dimension, could make her face grow hot with embarrassment.

"You were doing fine all this time," Angelo commented mildly, even while he continued to drive like a maniac. "You don't have to clutch so tightly again, kid, even though I could take it as being kind of flattering, you know? But we're almost there, so just hang loose and stay relaxed because you know you're in safe hands for a change. And if I've got my timing right like I usually do, we should get to the place where they're supposed to be filming — it's called the Castello — at just about the time they'll be ready for a coffee break."

The number of kilometers on the road signs that said Cagliari seemed to diminish within minutes, together with her heady feeling of excitement at having escaped in the nick of time. Escaped — or run away? Sara didn't want to think about it. Each kilometer that brought them close to Cagliari also took her farther from the palazzo and her silken prison. Farther from the wrath of her erstwhile captor who ought, by now, to have realized that tennis wasn't the only game he could be beaten at. He hadn't tried to follow her — thankfully, of course! By now he must positively *hate* her. The Duchessa would be annoyed, and Serafina would purse her lips and shake her head — comparing her to the late Duchess, no doubt. She'd had to leave all of her clothes — would they send them back to her or would *he* personally destroy them, one by one? Not that the clothes mattered — no doubt there would soon be another occupant of the suite she had dubbed the Seraglio who might be able to wear them — another *victim* he would enjoy playing with and tormenting.

"Well, here we are at last, and all safe and sound like I promised you!" Angelo's voice sounded cheerful in spite of all the miles they had traveled. "They have a bunch of barricades up, and watchful *carabinieri* who obviously don't like the looks of *me,* so it's up to your powers of persuasion now, kid!"

The policemen didn't quite approve of the looks of her either, as Sara discovered; and it was only her fluent Italian and her positive insistence, coupled with Angelo's suggestion that she unbraid her hair, that finally got them past the suspicious guards — two of whom actually accompanied them to the makeshift dressing room that had Mona Charles' name emblazoned across the door.

Mona was never surprised — not by *anything;* not even the sight of the daughter she hadn't set eyes on for over two years or her male companion.

"Sara *darling!* How nice of you to drop in — and your friend too, of course. You look so *healthy,* baby, that tan is just fantastic. And so is . . . ?"

Mona, being Mona, had already zoomed in on Angelo, whose eyes hadn't left her since they'd walked in. Sara felt as if she'd made her belated introduction to thin air.

"Mama, this is Angelo, who was nice enough to bring me here. Angelo, this is —"

"You brought her here! Wasn't that sweet of you? I haven't seen Sara in *ages* . . . hasn't it been ages, sweetie? Your father's just been so *stuffy* lately that we haven't been able to communicate at all. Have you heard what Delight's been up to? Angelo . . . mmm, what a lovely name! Do you like white wine, Angelo? There's some in the cooler over there, if you'd like to pour us some. It feels like a celebration!"

They all needed to celebrate something, Sara guessed. Two glasses of wine, swallowed far too fast, while she watched with fascination how Mama-Mona really put a *hex* on a man, were enough to put her to sleep. From the depths of her hazy half-world she *thought* they'd begun to talk about her, just as if she weren't there . . . but was she? She kept trying to listen — and drifting deeper and deeper until everything vanished, except for dreams in which she was tossed about on an ocean with waves as steep as mountains — watching one higher than any of the others start to curl and curve over her until suddenly she realized that she was actually being carried like a sack of potatoes over the shoulder of a dark-faced pirate with gold rings in his ears who dropped her roughly on the deck the next moment and began to cut away all her clothes with his wickedly curved scimitar. Of course — she should have known him for a Moorish corsair who would rape her first before he auctioned her off at the slave market . . . unless she pleased him.

Never . . . never! Her mind screamed defiance, but her limbs seemed weighted and lifeless — incapable of even token resistance as he lowered his naked body over hers, smiling familiarly and scornfully at her shameful surrender. She *knew* him, and she hated him, and she wanted to shut his face out of her mind and her thoughts, but even when she closed her eyes she kept *seeing* him through eyelids suddenly gone transparent. Dark, scowling, threatening. Rough texture of his voice; harshness of his lips set against hers. Sometimes laughter, sounding gratingly unfamiliar, like the smile-wrinkles that could suddenly appear at the corners of his night-black eyes and his mouth.

"Diletta *mia* . . . *sei mia* . . . you're *mine,* for as long as I continue to want you, do you understand? And I continue to want you, witch!"

Diletta — Delight. Not Sara. Who could want a *Sara?* Such a plain, uncompromising, *puritanical* name! No promises of excitement or enchantment. Just a feet-on-the-ground name pinned to a girl who lived up to it — or had, until now.

"Baby . . . come on, wake up, baby! You've slept for at least six hours and we have to go now." Mama-Mona's voice, coming fuzzily through a tunnel. "Angelo *mio!* Are you sure you didn't *give* her something? All she had was two glasses of wine!"

"I swear I did not — and how could I lie to *you?* No, she's just plain tuckered out, I guess — all the excitement she hasn't been used to . . . she'll be just fine, I promise you. Hey, kid, it's me, Angelo. Time to wake up, you hear? Your beautiful mama's ready to go home, and you should be too."

"Baby, are you really okay?"

"Of *course,* I am!" Sara found herself responding automatically as she sat up and tried to rub the sleep out of her eyes. "Just tired, that's all." She stretched, trying to avoid Mona's eyes that were suddenly far too

464

knowing as they searched her face. "Hey —
I really needed that sleep! Where do we go
from here?"

"Anywhere you want to, baby — but for
now maybe the Hotel Mediterraneo where
we're all staying? Angelo's going to be my
bodyguard, and with a free weekend coming
up I thought we might visit the Costa Smeralda — I have some friends there, and it's
usually a lot of fun. You're going to stay for
a while, aren't you, now that you're here?"

"Do they have a disco at that hotel? And
lots of cute guys?" Now that she was standing
on her feet again, Sara thought she might be
able to stay that way, in spite of all the aching
muscles that suddenly made themselves felt.

"Hmm!" Her mother's voice sounded skeptical, even when Sara met her eyes with a
determinedly bright grin that was meant to
deceive. But one of the nice things about
Mama-Mona was that she never *prodded.*
"Well, now that you're awake, darling, *do*
comb your hair at least — in case the *paparazzi* are lurking outside — as they usually
are! Perhaps you should borrow my spare
sunglasses as well . . . what do you think,
Angelo?"

"Of course! Then you will look even more
like two sisters!"

"Aren't you a sweetheart!" Mona chuckled
richly as she perched an enormous pair of
sunglasses on Sara's nose — stepping back to

study her for a few seconds. "Isn't he *adorable?* We should have met before. . . . But honestly, sweetie, you look fantastic. *Love* that tan, and the way you're wearing your hair now. We've got to have a straight girl-to-girl talk when we get back to the hotel — Delight's kept me up-to-date on everything but *you* haven't, you know!"

Well, of course Mona would understand everything — and *explain* everything without condemning. Sara gave her a mock-salute that surprised them both.

"If you really want to catch up, Mama *mia,* it might take quite some time. Little Sara's finally grown up."

"Fantastic, darling! What fun we're going to have!"

Sara hugged her mother and avoided Angelo's cynically upturned eyes, *wishing* he didn't remind her so much of his half brother. Why couldn't she be more like Mona, who knew just how to make the bastards of the world come crawling to her feet? But then, she had always known and always accepted the fact that both Mama-Mona and her half sister, who had been aptly named Delight, had that certain something that was known as sex appeal. A sure and certain knowledge of being all female, all woman — Lilith and Eve combined. A feeling and a sureness that she too had felt while she soaked like Cleopatra in a sunken marble bath and felt the perfumed oil that scented it penetrate her skin to leave it shiny and moist, even after she had dried herself. And had known even more strongly when she looked into coal-dark eyes that traveled over her and *wanted* her before his hands began their slow exploration of her body. Wanted — it was something every woman understood and sensed, wasn't it? Something she had learned and admitted too late, maybe.

"Let's go, darlings! I've got this enormous suite with *two* bedrooms — one just for my extra luggage — which just happens to include a few things that you might be able to wear, baby. Those jeans are cute and quite sexy on you, but you can't wear them all the time, you know!"

Relieved to have her mind distracted, Sara let herself be swept along by Angelo, who had a casual arm around her waist and a less than casual arm about her mother. "Such a lucky man they're going to think I am! Twin beauties . . . who wouldn't envy me?"

Angelo's compliments were as extravagant as ever, but his eyes and his attention seemed glued on Mona, who laughed teasingly up into his face. Well, of course Mona could still have any man she wanted, young or old. And so could her half sister.

"Hey, Mona baby! How come you didn't let on you had a double? And *some* double! Want to ride back with *me,* sweetheart? It'll be less crowded."

Matt Baker was one of the best-known directors in the industry — good-looking enough and wild enough to have his picture taken as often as the stars he directed.

"Hel-lo!" he murmured, catching up and detaching Sara neatly from Angelo's casual arm while he planted an expertly passionate kiss on her surprised, half-open mouth.

"And where have you been hiding out, beautiful *bambina?* Sexy wench . . . !"

He kissed very well, Sara thought with surprising detachment. His kisses didn't make her tingle from the soles of her feet to the crown of her head, but of course *that* had been a purely physical reaction and nothing more. Matt Baker had a reputation that even *she* had heard of; as a super-stud. Maybe that was what she needed.

"You're not too bad yourself, *caro.*" Her voice was a sexy Mona-drawl that made Mona herself lift arched eyebrows in delighted appreciation and Angelo clear his throat to cover his surprise. Matt Baker grinned his famous grin that made his gray eyes squint at the corners. "Well, now —"

"Only, you *do* tend to move in far too fast, and I just love a man who takes his *time,* if you know what I mean? You American men . . ."

How easy it was, and what a good actress she had turned out to be! Even her accent was Italian, making Angelo hide a grin that Matt

Baker didn't see as he *really* paid attention to her now, taking her in from her Adidases to her rather damp and rumpled cotton shirt that served to emphasize her tan and her bare midriff.

"Maybe I can show you something different about American men if we spent some time together, sweetheart. *Lots* of time!"

She pulled back from his possessively encircling arm, pretending she hadn't caught Mona's admiring wink. "You have a really terrible reputation, you know! And I'm rather old-fashioned in my way. All these people taking photographs . . ."

As they walked from the safety of the barriers and the fierce-looking *carabinieri,* the electronic flashes were almost blinding and Sara didn't have to fake the way she instinctively covered her face with one arm.

Matt Baker's arm tightened around her protectively. "Listen, sweet baby, a girl like you could change my reputation for good, if you just gave me a chance. Jesus — what a doll! I know you're one of Mona's kids — but how come I never heard about you before? Or saw your picture?"

"Well — it's because I was one of mama's indiscretions, I suppose. And I was brought up by an old-fashioned father." Well, that much was true, at least! "As a matter of fact," Sara went on brightly as she allowed Matt to lead her through the curious crowd that clustered around, "I was actually a *virgin* until just a few weeks ago — can you imagine that?"

"I don't know if I can or not, baby — considering the way you *look*. . . ." Matt Baker's eyes went over her, studying every detail of her appearance before he bent his head to murmur in her ear, "But I sure would like to find out. . . ."

Well, maybe she *would* let him find out! Maybe that was the best way — the only way to stop the strange, uncalled-for feeling that was almost like *yearning* for everything that she had just escaped from.

She allowed Matt to pull her close as he hustled her through the autograph-hungry crowd to his car — a Maserati that he drove with the same kind of careless confidence with which Angelo had handled his motorcycle. Like Angelo, he drove with concentration, thank goodness, which was just as well, considering the crowded streets that slowed them down.

"You're going to the hotel, aren't you?" His eyes seemed to brush over her before he turned them ahead of him again and Sara made an effort to unclench her hands.

"Yes, please. I'm going to have to borrow something to wear from Mona, you see, because I left almost *everything* I owned behind when I ran away."

"This is getting more interesting all the time, honey-child! Ran away, huh? Dare I ask why or from whom?"

"From a . . . tyrant!" Well, he had been, hadn't he? And perhaps if she kept talking she wouldn't have to notice how recklessly Matt Baker drove. "He kept me locked up in his palazzo as if I'd been a *slave* or something! If not for Angelo I might never have escaped. And I *know* it sounds impossibly melodramatic," Sara added rather stiffly when she caught Matt's quizzical look, "but it's true, all the same. My father probably has Interpol looking for me by now!" Which was probably quite true also, she reflected with related uneasiness. It was exactly the kind of thing Daddy would do, and she should send him a telegram from the hotel.

"Looking at you, you lovely little wench, I think I can understand why a man might be tempted to keep you all to himself," Matt drawled. He put one hand on Sara's thigh and she stiffened instinctively, which intrigued as well as challenged him. What a sexy little number, with that mane of hair and that dark-gold skin that made the green of her eyes more vivid! She talked sexy and had certainly acted that way, but he knew women with a kind of sixth sense that always told him exactly how each one of them needed to be seduced; and in *this* one he could feel a kind of prudishness that might be quite exciting to break through.

Just as casually as he had put his hand on

her, Matt removed it — much to Sara's relief. The car swerved sharply to barely avoid a motor scooter, and at that moment, with a triumphant roar, a familiar-looking motor-cycle shot past them with inches to spare.

"And that, I take it, was Angelo!" Matt said grimly. "Mona must be crazy!"

It *had* been her mother riding behind Angelo with her hair flying, her eyes concealed by enormous sunglasses. She had given them a nonchalant wave as they passed, and was obviously much more at ease on the back of a motorcycle than Sara had been!

"What kind of a bike was that? Honda? On a straight stretch of decent road *this* baby could take it with no problem!" Matt said in a tone of voice that made Sara want to close her eyes with terrified apprehension. He *wasn't* going to try to . . . the Maserati took the next bend on what *felt* like two wheels, and she *did* close her eyes, with even thought stopping as she heard her own heart pounding like a drumbeat.

She didn't open them again until she heard Matt swear disgustedly. "Shit! The tricky bastard must've taken a shortcut through one of those alleys!"

If she could hear him talking then she must still be alive, at least. And there wasn't a rush of wind in her face and the purring growl of the powerful motor in her ears so they *must* have stopped.

"You okay, baby? I didn't scare you, did I?" Matt remembered her with belated concern that made Sara furious. If her legs hadn't felt so weak she would just have gotten out of his damn car that he drove like a lethal weapon and stalked away from him without a word!

As her eyes came back into focus Sara took a deep breath, prepared to tell him exactly what she thought about his driving, but he wasn't even *looking* at her any longer.

"Oh, *Christ,* not another big public scene, with the movie not in the can yet! Mona seems to collect more jealous lovers than . . ."

Sara's eyes had followed the direction of his gaze, and she didn't even hear what else he said. There was quite an interested crowd gathered at the front of the hotel, all watching avidly while Mona, dressed like a female biker in black leather pants and boots, clung protectively to Angelo's arm. Protectively — because the tall man who stood facing them both seemed *definitely* the more dangerous looking of the two men. In fact — and Sara's heart had started to pound madly all over again — in fact he looked positively *menacing,* with those scowling dark brows drawn together and his narrowed eyes negating the coldly polite smile that twisted his lips.

Mona was being magnificently regal in spite of her unsuitable attire, and Angelo, who still had his bike to contend with, looked thunderstruck.

"Of course I'm not going anywhere with you — I don't even *know* you! I happen to be with Angelo, who adores me, don't you, darling?" (What had Matt said? "Mona seems to collect more jealous lovers . . .")

Acting almost by sheer primitive instinct Sara reached over Matt and pressed down on the horn that had sent so many pedestrians jumping for safety. This time even Matt jumped, before he turned to look at her. "Hey! What . . ." Again, Sara didn't really hear him. They were *all* looking at her now. Angelo, beginning to grin; her mother, *not* used to being upstaged; the bystanders; and . . .

Now that her knees seemed no longer rubbery, Sara yanked the door open and got out of the car with commendable poise. "That's not one of *Mona's* jealous lovers, you know. He's *mine.*" Very deliberately, she leaned down to kiss Matt's nicely shaped, sensual, *sexy* mouth that could and probably did, drive most women wild. Most *other* women, that was! He was quick witted enough to kiss her back rather thoroughly in *spite* of the jealous lover; and experienced enough to tell that the chemistry was missing — for *her* at least.

There was a speculative look in his gray eyes as Sara pulled away rather too abruptly. "Thanks for the ride! It was *such* fun!"

474

He lifted a careless hand. *"Prego!"* But she'd already turned and started to walk away from him. Purposefully.

Chapter 38

It was definitely Sara's scene, with every eye fixed on her as she walked away from the white Maserati and Matt Baker with a conscious, almost insolent air of insouciance, and Mona Charles was enough of a professional to recognize it.

Beside her, she heard Angelo say softly, "Ah! So *that's* how it really is! I had a feeling from the very beginning . . . ." But Mona, like the rest of them, was watching the young woman who was her daughter — wearing the oversized sunglasses that effectively masked her expression.

Sara had never been quite as close to her or seemed quite as like her as Delight, her love child. Until right now, at this very moment when Mona stood watching her walk with a long naturally easy stride that reminded her of a young pantheress stalking her prey. Who looked far too capable of reversing those roles, actually! Poor Sara! Mona almost shuddered with an unfamiliar feeling of protectiveness. The man looked perfectly capable of *violence*, even of murder, for all that he stood there waiting for her with a deceptively negligent air.

He was *waiting* for her, and it was all Sara could do, now that she had come *this* far, not to let her steps falter — or take her running back to safety! Even the familiar glower had disappeared from his dark face now, leaving it as expressionless as a harshly carved mask with black holes for eyes. But even if she couldn't see it she could *feel*, with the quickened rush of her blood and the nervous hammering of her heart, the cold *fury* in him — only barely held in check.

Find something to say *quickly*, Sara my girl, or they'll boo you off the stage! her mind warned her grimly, and she managed to smile — a little too brightly.

"Oh, *hi*, Marco! *I* hadn't really expected to run into you again, you know! Were you looking for me or for —"

"*Hadn't* you?" His voice sounded almost too smooth, but she, with her quickened senses could hear the wild-beast growl that underlay it.

She tried for careless insouciance again, trying to ignore the way his eyes had fixed on the telltale pulse that fluttered at her throat.

"Well — *no,* actually, but since you're here you might as well meet Mona *formally,* I suppose! Especially as the *oddest* coincidence seems to have brought you here! And did you happen to bring my clothes with you? I just didn't have time —"

Reaching him where he stood as implacably as Nemesis, she tried to turn aside to Mona, but he stopped her words and stopped her half-formed movement with the hand that encircled her wrist to make a prisoner of her again. Looking into his eyes, Sara had the frightening feeling that he would crush every bone without compunction if she tried to tug herself away.

"Not exactly coincidence, I'm afraid. I also happen to read the newspapers. And sometimes I guess correctly. Luckily — wouldn't you say? Especially since I do happen to have your clothes — and you must be tired of wearing those decidedly grimy garments by now, I'm sure, knowing how fastidious you always appeared to be about bathing and changing clothes. . . ."

She looked back at him and into those dark-coaled eyes and was suddenly unaware of everything and everyone around them both as a strange feeling of fatalism overcame her, holding her trapped and immobile and incapable of any of the brave speeches she had prepared.

With that damnable, detestable arrogance of his that would probably infuriate her always, he chose to ignore everything but his object — his victim!

"Shall we have our discussion in public, my little actress — or in private? And I'm sure that even *you* must agree we have a great deal to talk about?" The pause he allowed her for a reply was barely perceptible before he said in the same deadly calm voice, "Good, since you seem to be in a reasonable mood for a change, I suggest we go inside." He could actually manage a polite *smile!* But it was not directed at her but at Mama-Mona instead. "Miss Charles, I must offer my apologies for mistaking you for your daughter — it *is* Sara I have here, is it not? I hadn't realized there was such a strong family resemblance, I am afraid, although now that I have met *you* it's easy to see who the real beauty is."

The merest tightening of his fingers was enough to stifle Sara's indignant gasp and allow Mona to move center stage again.

"So you *can* be charming, darling! How sweet! And shouldn't we *all* go inside together so that this crowd that keeps getting larger and larger can go away? And *then* you can take Sara off for your little talk . . . ."

How *could* Mona desert her that way? *Abandon* her seemed even more appropriate, Sara thought rebelliously, although she let him take her along without protest, her lips tight and her head high. She might, in fact, have been on her way to the guillotine — which actually seemed quicker and more merciful than what faced *her!*

Being marched through the lobby and trying to avoid more staring eyes felt like being in the eye of a hurricane, Sara thought despairingly; and made her one last tried and true attempt at escape. "If you don't mind I really *do* have to use the loo! Mama, if I can borrow yours? I'm sure I must look an absolute *mess!*"

"It won't be necessary for you to go all the way up to the second floor, *cara mia.* I have taken a suite here myself, and it is right — here. Miss Charles, I look forward to meeting you again. Angelo? Ah — it is certain that you and I will meet each other again *soon,* is it not?"

Sara had barely time to wonder whether poor Angelo was quailing too before she found herself ushered with overdone politeness into the room he had threatened her with; hearing with a sinking heart the ominously sharp click with which he locked the door.

There was a kind of inevitability to this, she thought almost dazedly before she turned to face him again, with a last, desperate attempt at defiance.

"Well? Now that you've *dragged* me here, why don't you *say* something?"

He was standing with his back to the door, his booted legs astride and his arms crossed over his chest. He was dressed for *riding,* she thought belatedly and irrelevantly, and was immediately relieved to notice that he hadn't brought his leather-thonged riding whip with him. Or *had* he?

Diabolically, he seemed to sense some of her thoughts, for he gave her a sardonic inclination of his head before he drawled in an unpleasantly sarcastic voice that seemed to flick across every nerve of her: "If you're looking around like a little scared rabbit faced by a wolf for some means of help or escape, I'm afraid that there *is* none. And now — since you have no alternative but to face the wolf himself — is there anything you wish to say first?"

"Damn you!" Sara flung the words at him with all the last-ditch fury he had goaded her into. "How *dare* you stand there like a . . . a *prosecutor?* And treat *me* as if I were a *criminal,* or a . . . a runaway slave? Especially when everything that happened was *your* fault, the way you tried to interfere and manipulate and — how could you have the colossal nerve to think my sister wasn't *good* enough to marry your brother? Well — you deserved to be fooled! You — with your high-and-mighty arrogance and your hypocrisy . . . your string of mistresses that you keep along with your *suitable* fiancée, who has a terrible complexion and not too much to say unless she positively screeches . . . ."

Sara had stopped to draw in a long, gasping breath when he said caustically: "Indeed! Poor Lucia! And I suppose *you* gave her no provocation whatsoever to make her decide she did *not* want to be my fiancée? You had better be careful with your lies *this* time, Signorina Sara, no matter how fond you are of deceit and *acting* . . . !"

She backed away from his look, fending him off with more angry words. "And *you* had better remember, hadn't you, what *you* are guilty of? I do believe that *kidnapping* is still considered a serious crime, even in the wilds of Sardinia — and I should warn you that by now my father has probably —"

"I have already been in communication with Sir Eric." The casual way he dealt her that particular shock made her gasp again.

"You . . . !"

He went on inexorably in the same expressionless voice as if she hadn't tried to speak. "I informed your father, with whom I happen to be acquainted, that you and I had met in Los Angeles, had developed a mad passion for each other and — decided to elope. And that is *almost* the way it happened, is it not, *tesoro?*" She kept searching his face incredulously, not quite able to believe the words she was hearing.

"*What* . . . ?"

"Please let me finish, so that we can get on with what we have to do. And we have . . ." He glanced casually at the gold watch on his wrist before looking back at her. "We have about seven hours, I should think, before it's time to go back. Time enough for shopping for something suitable to wear, unless you'd rather fly to Paris?"

"Would you mind telling me exactly what you are *talking* about, for God's sake?" Sara realized that her voice had risen to become almost shrill, but she couldn't help it. He was . . . he was . . . And then his reply hit her like a bombshell.

"I'm talking about our wedding, of course. What *else* did you think I had in mind? And it's only fair, I suppose! Lose one fiancée and gain another — there's some poetic justice in that, don't you agree with me?"

The room seemed to be revolving around her in a most peculiar fashion. Surely she wasn't going to *faint,* for the first time in her life, before she could tell him exactly what she thought of him, his high-handed actions, his ducal palazzo, and everything else she hated so about him?

"I don't . . . I won't . . . ." To her chagrin, Sara found that she had actually begun to weep — the angry, embarrassingly noisy sobs she couldn't stop almost choking her. "I . . . I won't be married in such a . . . calculated, cold-blooded way! I won't be . . . be *used* and manipulated any longer . . . do you hear me? I won't put up with your . . . your harem of other women and your — I don't *want* to be married just because you . . . know Daddy and you . . . you know very well what you *thought* about me and what you *called* me . . . and . . .''

When she had stopped trying to gasp out her almost incoherent protests Sara realized that she was crying against his chest, and his arms were holding her against him as if he — as if he actually *wanted* her there. And of course she still had enough sense left in her to realize how ridiculous *that* thought was! He was only pretending to calm her down so that she would do exactly as *he* pleased.

Sara tried to protest this further indignity; to pull away, but his arms held her like the prison she had tried to run away from just hours earlier.

"Oh, stop! I'm not — Italian men *always* marry virgins, you . . . you said so yourself! And I'm not a —"

His voice, coming from somewhere above her, sounded almost unbearably harsh. "Ah, yes — Serafina enlightened me on that score, I'm afraid. And my stepmother as well — on whom, by the way, you have left a decided impression!"

Sara almost flinched at the note in his voice before he smoothed it into a threatening, growling purr. "And have you any more excuses left, *diletta mia?*"

"*Don't* call me that! Oh! how dare you, especially *now?* When you — I won't be married to a man who . . . who doesn't l-*love* me even if that *is* a hopelessly old-fashioned way of thinking! And you've never . . . you're so damn *high*-handed you wouldn't think of . . . of *asking* me if I —"

"Per Dio!" The words sounded like an explosion, making her try to wriggle free in sudden panic; only to find his arms tighten around her until she thought he meant to crush every bone in her body. "Do you realize what an impossible, stubborn spitfire you are? *Ask* you — hah! First you nag and taunt me into leaving you and that sharp tongue of yours — and by some lucky coincidence I *then* find out what my stepmother later confirmed. *After* I had returned, meaning to — *look* at me, do you hear?" With her head pulled back by rough fingers entangled in her hair, Sara had no choice but to obey; only to find that he had lowered his head so that his mouth hovered far too closely over hers as he grated between clenched jaws: "I wonder if you knew, and perhaps enjoyed in your female, fickle, calculating mind, what my reactions might be? For you must have known . . . *maliarda,* triple-damned enchantress . . . *mi diletta, mi tormento* . . . how could you not have known?"

"Marco —!"

"No, damn you, will you listen for once without interruption? I have been driven half mad! And all because of you — I was ready to kill you when I came looking for you, and when I found you gone and everything so empty and so silent . . . I think I went a little crazy then, and perhaps I am more than a little crazy now, to be saying all this into those wet green eyes of yours that stare at me like green stones and your mouth that makes me want to — why in hell do you think I want to marry you? Must you know? It is because I want you and I will have you, and because no matter who I thought you were and *what* I thought you were, and all of my efforts and my cruelties and my words I had begun to love you, my delight, my torment, my heart — *mio cuore* . . . is *that* enough for you? Eh?" He almost snarled the last words at her before his storm-black glance caught the almost beatific smile that had suddenly curved her lips, parting them in a ragged sigh.

"Oh, Marco! Why . . . you didn't really have to *shout* at me, you know! I mean . . . I didn't want to fall in love with you either — and especially under the circumstances — and anyway unrequited love is such a silly, stupid . . . and I didn't feel I could *stand* it anymore! So I . . ."

He never *did* give her a chance to finish saying what she had begun, Sara reflected dreamily some moments later, but it didn't matter at all, and especially when he kept kissing her in that deliciously, fiercely posses-sive manner that made her go weak at the knees. So weak that he had had to lift her, quite naturally . . . and carry her just as naturally and as inevitably to the big, canopied bed.

And once they had arrived there, it seemed so much easier to put off questions and answers and explanations and . . . even thinking itself, for a while. After all, they were going to spend lots more time together. Time enough for her to think of all kinds of ways to keep him so busily occupied that he wouldn't have time for any other woman. Just *his*.

A note on the text
Large print edition designed by
Fred Welden.
Composed in 16 pt Times Roman
on a Mergenthaler Linotron 202
by Modern Graphics, Inc.